Meadow Lane

MAUREEN REYNOLDS

MEADOW LANE

BLACK & WHITE PUBLISHING

First published 2016
by Black & White Publishing Ltd
29 Ocean Drive, Edinburgh EH6 6JL

1 3 5 7 9 10 8 6 4 2 16 17 18 19

ISBN: 978 1 78530 015 8

A CIP catalogue record for this book is available from the British Library.

Typeset by Iolaire, Newtonmore
Printed and bound by CPI Group (UK) Ltd, Croydon, CR0 4YY

In memory of Alick and George

PROLOGUE

Evie couldn't find her bearings. Everything had changed and there was no sign of Meadow Lane. It was as if it had never been or maybe it lay hidden behind the row of new housing that was so different from what had been there originally. Gone were the seven houses of her childhood while the occupants were now just a poignant memory...

Instead there were bright new flats with shiny double glazed windows and blue painted security doors at the entrances. There was no sign of the lane's nameplates that had been attached to each end of the lane, oblong metal sheets with white letters printed on a black background that she had passed hundreds of times without giving them another glance. However she felt a small knot of disappointment that they were gone forever.

Suddenly one of the doors opened and a young woman appeared. She was pushing a small child in a pram. A pram with three wheels, so small that it hardly seemed big enough to hold the occupant, so different from the Silver Cross prams of Evie's childhood.

Yes, all memories of Meadow Lane had been erased except from her mind and she wondered if the ghosts of the dramatic happenings of 1955 still lingered behind these new facades.

Somehow she doubted it and she slowly made her way back to the car that was parked a few hundred yards away.

1

Meadow Lane!

Evie often sat on the old wall by the side of the house and wondered why it got its name. It conjured up visions of a rural idyll instead of a tiny narrow lane that stretched between the busy Hilltown and Caldrum Street, a straggling row of seven houses with scrubby grass at the back and a large patch of derelict ground to the front with not one flower blooming in the muddy earth.

Today was no exception. It was a cold, damp Sunday in January with the mist settling on the roofs and mingling with the smoke from six chimneys. The seventh house was empty on this winter day. Evie pulled her scarf tighter around her neck as she waited for her next-door neighbour and friend Thomasina to come out of her house.

Evie sighed loudly. Thomasina was late as usual and at this rate it would be dark before they set off to visit Evie's granny. This was a weekly visit which never varied and it served two purposes: to check on her granny's health and to have her tea. Suddenly the noise of a door being banged shut made her look up. Thomasina appeared looking like a refugee from Greenland, her winter coat tightly belted, wide eyes in a small white face peering out from between a woollen hat and a thick scarf covering her mouth.

Evie rolled her eyes as she stood up. 'Tommy, I've been

waiting half an hour for you and now you look like Scott of the Antarctic.'

Tommy merely pulled her scarf closer but she made no apology for her lateness, which was nothing new. She gazed at her friend. 'Well, we better get going or it'll be bedtime before we see your granny.'

This annoyed Evie as it was Thomasina's fault for being late. They walked quickly to the end of the lane and onto the Hilltown which was quite busy in spite of the weather and it being a Sunday. Evie's granny, Mrs Evelyn Williams, was a widow and her house was a small one-bedroomed flat two flights up at number nineteen Ann Street. The close was in darkness when they arrived and their footsteps echoed loudly as they climbed the stairs.

'The tea will be stewed, Tommy, because you're always late, and I hate strong stewed tea,' said Evie, already anticipating the tongue-curling taste.

However, when they went inside, a warm fire was burning in the grate and the table was set for the meal. Mrs Williams was bustling around with a pan in her hand. 'Take your coats off and sit down. The tea is ready.' She began to spoon out large mounds of scrambled eggs onto slices of boiled ham lying pink and curled on the plates. Evie was dismayed to see the teapot with its knitted cosy already on the table.

'I've made scrambled eggs and boiled ham, I hope you like it.'

Tommy made a face at Evie as if to say the explanation wasn't needed as the food was laid out for all to see but she said, 'That's smashing as I'm starving.'

Mrs Williams beamed at her. 'That's what I like to hear, Thomasina. You're a girl with a good appetite. Not like Evie who eats like a sparrow.'

Tommy smirked at her friend and Evie gave her a quick dig with her elbow. The tea was as strong as she had feared it would be but with sugar and lots of milk she managed to drink it. After they had eaten they sat around the fire.

'How's your dad, Evie? Your mum was telling me he's been very busy. I was hoping he could come and fix my dripping water tap. It's driving me crazy.' She pointed to the small sink by the window and the girls could hear the steady sound as the water dripped into the enamel basin.

'Yes, he is very busy. In fact he was called out today and he wasn't home when I left.'

'That's the problem with being a plumber. It's all these burst pipes.' She turned to Tommy. 'And how are your parents, Thomasina?'

'Dad always has a lazy day on a Sunday as the pub is closed, and Mum is fine.' She didn't add that her father had been snoring in a chair when she left and her mother had been moaning that all the work was left to her and not that lazy so-and-so sleeping in the chair. Tommy's dad was a barman in the Windmill Bar and her mum had a part-time job in Burnett's bakery shop.

'Did you have a good tenth birthday, Evie?' asked Granny. 'I hope you liked the new pyjamas and the birthday cake.'

Evie, who was very fond of her granny, got up and gave her a hug. 'Thank you. I loved my presents.'

Not to be outdone, Tommy said, 'I'll be ten in March, Mrs Williams.'

Evelyn Williams smiled. 'In that case we'll have a cake for you as well, Thomasina.'

The clock on the sideboard chimed six and it was time to leave. The girls put on their coats as Mrs Williams fussed around them. 'Now, mind and go straight home. No lingering about in the dark.'

They promised her they wouldn't. For one thing it was too cold, and it was also now pouring with rain, so they hurried up towards Meadow Lane, anxious to get back into the warmth.

Tommy linked her arm with Evie as they hurried up the wet pavement. 'I like your granny, Evie. I don't have any grandparents although I've got some aunties and uncles in Ireland but I've never met any of them.' She sounded so sad that Evie suddenly felt sorry for her.

When they reached the lane, the one gas lamp that was situated outside Eliza and Martha Potter's house at number five barely lit the path but Evie was pleased to see her father's van parked on the spare ground in front of her house. Tommy followed her into the small living room. Bill Gow was sitting in front of the fire reading the *Sunday Post* while her mum Grace was listening to the wireless. They both looked up as the two girls plonked themselves down on the settee.

'I hope you enjoyed your tea,' said Grace. 'What did you have?'

'Yes, Mum, we did. We had scrambled egg and boiled ham.'

Bill muttered behind his paper, 'I see it was the same as always.'

Grace was annoyed. 'My mother does her best, Bill.'

Bill, who didn't want to ruffle his wife's feathers, said, 'Sorry, I know she does.'

Tommy said, 'It was a smashing tea. I really enjoyed it. She said I had a great appetite but Evie eats like a sparrow.'

Evie, annoyed by her friend's remark, glared at her. 'Granny has a dripping water tap, Dad, and she's hoping you can fix it this week.'

Bill looked at Evie over the edge of his paper and said he would try and go tomorrow to sort it out.

Tommy, unaware of the previous glare, said, 'She'll be pleased about that as she kept saying the dripping sound was like a Chinese water torture, didn't she, Evie?'

Grace's mother was still the drama queen, thought Bill, but he sensibly stayed silent and turned the pages of his paper to read about the antics of the Broons and Oor Wullie.

Tommy stood up. 'I suppose I better get off home. It's school tomorrow and Mum likes me to be in bed by nine o'clock.'

Evie walked with her to the lane. 'Now remember and not be late tomorrow because if you are then I'm leaving without you, Tommy.'

Tommy laughed. 'Oh you're a right nark for being early, Evie. My mum always says there's no hurry in Ireland.'

'Well you don't live in Ireland now, do you?'

'I know we don't. We live in this place where nothing exciting ever happens.'

Tommy waved a final goodbye as she opened her door. Anna Cassidy's voice called out, 'Close the door, Thomasina, you're letting the cold draught in.'

Later, as Evie got ready for bed, she glanced in her mirror. She didn't think she looked like a sparrow. Her fair hair was cut short and although her face was thin and pale, her arms and legs weren't that skinny. But she knew she wasn't as pretty as Tommy who had dark curly hair and hazel eyes that always seemed full of mischief.

She propped herself up in her bed with her favourite book and surveyed her room. It was very small but she loved it. Her parents had the bigger bedroom that was off the kitchen, but it wasn't as nice as this one which faced the front of the house and Evie liked being able to hear people walk along the lane.

At nine-thirty, Grace popped her head around the door but Evie was sound asleep.

2

Anna Cassidy wasn't a happy woman. She had just had a row with her daughter Thomasina who had slept in for school and then rushed out of the house with her coat unbuttoned and a slice of toast and jam in her hand.

'I didn't see Evie waiting for her so she'll be in a strop all day but it's her own fault.' Anna pulled the bright pink quilted housecoat around her slim waist and joined her husband at the table.

'If Thomasina stopped reading in her bed and went to sleep then she wouldn't keep sleeping in,' she said, reaching for the teapot to refill her cup.

Thomas Cassidy sat reading the *Courier* newspaper and didn't look up. 'That lass will be late for her own funeral,' he said, lighting up a cigarette and blowing smoke across the table.

Anna's face twisted in a fury when she saw that the teapot was empty. 'Do you never think to make more tea when you know you've had the last cup?' she shouted across at her errant husband who merely blew more smoke in her face. She reached for the cigarette packet and, finding it empty, her fury erupted.

'You've pinched the last fag. You're just so selfish.' Picking up the cups, she placed them in the basin with such a resounding clatter that Thomas put his paper down.

'For God's sake, Anna, you can go out to the shop for more. It's not as if we live at the back of beyond.'

Anna flounced around the kitchen, her annoyance unabated. Thomas could be such a selfish man. She thought about Bill next door who had built the outside toilet at the back door into a small extension with a large white sink and hot water geyser. They didn't have to run out in the cold and rain every time they needed a pee, but she held her tongue because she and Thomas had rowed about this quite often and he had merely shrugged his thin shoulders. 'Well, he is a plumber after all,' he had said.

Rising from the table, he came over to the sink and put his arm around his wife's waist. 'Sorry about the ciggie, love, I'll bring some more home this afternoon after the pub closes.'

Appeased by this show of caring, she nodded. 'Okay then but make sure you don't smoke them all when you come in.' The kettle was boiling so she made more tea. 'Do you want another cup?'

He said, 'No, I need a clean white shirt ironed, can you do it now, love?'

For one brief moment Anna almost threw the cup at him before common sense took over. Thomas would never change, never in a hundred years, she thought with a sigh.

At ten-thirty, with his white shirt newly ironed, Thomas left for work while Anna got dressed. She didn't start work until twelve o'clock but there were dishes to wash and some housework to tackle. As she gazed at her reflection in the dressing table mirror, she saw a woman with dark curly hair framing a pretty face. She puckered her lips as she spread scarlet lipstick over her mouth while thinking that life hadn't quite gone to plan. As a young girl in Belfast she had dreamed of becoming a teacher but now those dreams lay dead. Meeting Thomas and getting married at seventeen then becoming a mother nine months later had scuppered her chances. She frowned at the mirror in annoyance until she saw tiny wrinkles forming around her eyes and tried to smooth them out with her fingers. She looked around to see if there was a spare cigarette lurking somewhere but she was out of luck. Muttering to herself, she said angrily, 'Trust that selfish son of a bitch to make sure he smoked the last one.'

She put on her coat and headscarf. It had started to rain again but she needed her shot of nicotine before starting the chores which meant she had no choice but to go to the newsagent's at the end of the lane to buy some more.

Hurrying out into the lane with her head down she almost collided with her next-door neighbour, Maryanne Roberts. 'Lord I'm sorry, Maryanne, I didn't see you. I'm rushing out to the paper shop.'

Maryanne was well wrapped up in a brown raincoat with a hood pulled low down over her face. Anna walked along beside her but the woman stopped. 'I can't hurry, Anna, so just you go ahead.'

Anna gave her neighbour a quick glance and was dismayed to see that she didn't look well. 'Are you feeling all right, Maryanne?'

Maryanne nodded. 'Aye, I'm fine.'

Although not really reassured, Anna hurried along the lane. If Maryanne didn't want to chat, then that was all right with her. The paper shop was empty when she entered so she got her packet of ten Woodbines and made her way home again. She decided to make another cup of tea to go with her cigarette as there was plenty of time to do the housework. Because Thomasina stayed at school for her midday dinner, unlike Evie who came home, Anna knew she didn't have to cook a meal before setting off for her job. She sometimes wished she was a good housewife like Grace who didn't work but spent most days cooking, baking and keeping her house immaculate. Feeling guilty with this thought she got to her feet and cleared the table then noticed the dust on the sideboard and mantelpiece. She made a note to polish the furniture after tea when no doubt Thomasina would be next door and Thomas would be back at work for his evening shift in the bar.

She gazed out of the window at the rain which was now heavy and turning the spare patch of ground into a sea of mud. God, how I hate the winter here and January in particular, she thought. Back in Belfast the weather wasn't better but she would have the company of her three sisters and two brothers and their children. She stopped washing the dishes and sighed as she remembered the rows that had led her to come here to Dundee. She made a conscious effort not to think about that time as she put on her coat and headed out to work.

Thomas had been glad to escape from the house. He was busy changing the barrel of beer when his neighbour Albert Scott appeared at the bar counter.

'My usual please, Hopalong,' he said, fishing his money from a small leather purse. Thomas smiled at the old man. Sometimes it annoyed him when people called him by his nickname but he didn't mind it from Albert. He put the pint of beer on the bar and rang up the money on the till.

'And how are you today, Albert?' he asked.

Albert frowned. 'Fed up with all this awful rain. I didn't feel like coming out in it but I hate being cooped up in the house. I'll get my messages afterwards so I'll be paying a visit to your good wife in Burnett's.'

'Well I hope she's in a better mood than she was this morning,' said Thomas.

Albert laughed. 'Oh I think she's a lovely woman. You're a lucky man to have such a good-looking wife like her.'

Thomas muttered, 'I suppose I am.' He didn't feel lucky at that moment as his leg was giving him gyp. It was this wet rainy weather that made his limp worse and sometimes he felt quite bitter about the accident that had shattered his leg and gave him his nickname, as in Hopalong Cassidy, the cowboy star of the movies. He muttered again under his breath, 'I wouldn't mind having his fame and fortune.'

Albert looked at him. 'Whose fame and fortune are you talking about?'

'Hopalong Cassidy's, Albert.'

Albert laughed again. 'I wouldn't mind some of that myself.' By now he had finished his beer so he pulled his scarf tightly around his neck.

'I'll be off then,' he said, as he moved slowly towards the door. 'Lord, I think I'm getting arthritis but I suppose it's this awful damp and cold weather.'

Thomas looked up from washing some glasses and he nodded sympathetically. 'I'm just the same, Albert.'

Albert stood outside on the pavement for a brief moment before making his way up the hill towards Burnett's bakery. Once inside the shop, a blast of warm air and a tantalising aroma of freshly baked bread cheered him, especially as Anna gave him a wide smile as she reached for the small loaf and a sausage roll which was his usual purchase.

'How are you today, Albert?' she asked as she handed over the two brown paper bags.

'I was just saying to your good husband that I think I'm getting arthritis and he was saying it's the same with his leg.'

Anna suddenly felt contrite about her treatment of her husband before he left the house. She should have known his damaged leg was sore but then she remembered how selfish he was sometimes and she pushed the guilty thought from her mind.

'Are you going straight home, Albert?'

He nodded.

'Well make sure you don't get too wet. Did you light the fire before you came out?'

'Yes I did and I've done my housework. I don't sleep very well so I get up early and get on with the chores.' He didn't add that he had hardly ever done any housework when his late wife, Jean, was alive. Like a bolt from the blue, the sudden remembrance of Jean made him feel depressed but he smiled when Anna said she would pop in to see him after teatime.

After his departure Anna turned to serve another customer but she couldn't get rid of the thought that old age wasn't a laughing matter.

3

Maryanne Roberts made her way home from the grocer's shop with her net bag feeling quite heavy with the couple of pounds of potatoes and the bag of sugar. Going to the shops was more of a pleasure now that the rationing had ended and not before time, she thought sourly. The war had ended in 1945 but it had taken the government until the early fifties to lift the restrictions.

At the end of the lane she had to stop briefly as the pain began again. She thought it was time to go to the doctor but she still delayed the decision due to the fear of what might be wrong with her.

Inside the house she hung up her wet coat and headscarf and warmed her hands in front of the fire. Putting the potatoes and sugar into the cupboard was a delaying tactic as she kept her face turned away from the blue airmail letter that lay unopened on the table.

It was her usual weekly letter from her daughter Sadie who lived in America and no doubt it would tell the same old story of how unhappy she was. Maryanne suddenly felt so weary and she felt as if she couldn't take much more of these continual tales of woe. She decided to make her midday snack before reading it, and she cracked an egg into the frying pan and put a slice of bread under the toaster. She had read somewhere that bad news was easier to take on a full stomach.

Half an hour later she was sitting with a cup of tea and the open letter in her hand. As predicted, Sadie's large writing that swirled over the page described how desperately unhappy she was with her life as a former GI bride and the mother of nine-year-old Edwayne.

Suddenly a sharp spasm of pain made her gasp and she dropped the letter as she bent over in agony. When the pain subsided slightly she made her way to the cupboard just as the front door opened and Grace Gow called out, 'It's just me, Maryanne.' When she saw that her neighbour was in pain, she said, 'What's the matter?'

'I think it's indigestion, Grace, and I'm looking for the Rennies.'

Grace took her by the arm. 'Sit down, Maryanne. I'll get the tablets.' She had to rummage in the cupboard before she found the box. Maryanne put two in her mouth and lay back on the chair. 'I'll feel better when they begin to work.'

Grace didn't look convinced. 'You are getting these pains a lot and I think you should see the doctor.'

Maryanne shook her head. 'No. I'll be fine in a minute.'

Grace saw the letter lying on the fireside rug and she picked it up and handed it over. 'How is Sadie?'

Maryanne was mortified as tears rolled down her cheeks and her chest felt so choked with emotion that she couldn't speak. By now Grace was alarmed and she pulled up a stool and took her hand in hers. 'Maryanne, what is it?'

'Sadie, Ed and Edwayne are fine.' She wiped her eyes with the back of her hand. 'It's just that I'm worried about being off work again. I'm frightened I'll lose my job,' she said, putting the letter on the small table beside her chair.

'If you're not well then surely they'll understand at the factory.'

'No, I don't think so. There are rumours that there may be layoffs due to a lack of orders. At least that's the gossip that's going around.' She stood up. 'I'll make a cup of tea.'

Grace was already on her feet. 'No, you sit still and I'll make it. I've brought some pancakes I made this morning. Do you want butter and jam on them?'

'No, just butter.'

Maryanne wasn't hungry but she ate a small piece of the pancake. She liked Grace popping in regularly and bringing some home baking but at this moment she just wanted to lie down and forget all about Sadie and her problems, and her own work troubles in the packing department of Keiller's sweetie factory. She had worked there for ten years but if there were layoffs then no one was safe.

Grace's voice cut over her thoughts. 'I'll be off then but I'll send Evie in later to help you with any jobs you need done.' She carried the empty cups to the sink and rinsed them out. 'And please go and see the doctor, Maryanne.'

Maryanne promised she would think about it if the pain came back again. After Grace's departure she picked up the letter. She hadn't wanted to let Grace know about Sadie's unhappiness as everyone thought she was living a film star life in America. If only they knew. Sadie hated the farm she lived on with her husband and son. It is so isolated, she wrote, and she could go days and days without seeing another soul once Ed went to work and Edwayne went off to school.

She went and lay down on the bed. What did Sadie think her mother could do? Living on the other side of the world was hardly the same as living just down the road like her workmate Dorothy whose daughter Donna lived next door to her mother.

She placed the letter under the pillow. 'I'll write back tomorrow,' she muttered. She was dropping off to sleep when another sharp pain made her gasp. For a moment she thought she was going to be sick but the feeling passed.

'What am I going to do?' she thought, and she started crying again.

4

Granny Duff had never been a granny. In fact she had never even been a wife. How she acquired the title was a mystery and the reason for it was lost in the mists of time.

Her usual dress was a long black, or sometimes brown, skirt of thick wool, a chunky jumper and during the cold winter months she sometimes wore a soft checked shawl around her thin shoulders.

She knew she had never been pretty but old age hadn't been kind to her. Her thin, colourless features were emphasised by pale grey eyes and a wrinkled neck that she tried to camouflage with a black sequin scarf which looked exotic and out of place with the rest of her appearance.

She was very houseproud and spent most of her mornings dusting the myriad selections of photographs and ornaments that jostled for space on her sideboard and mantelpiece but on this particular wet, dreary morning she was feeling quite lethargic. It's this rotten weather, she thought as she settled down in front of the fire with the morning paper. She had checked her cupboard earlier and noticed that she was almost out of tea and sugar and she hoped Grace would pop in so she could ask if Evie could run out to the shop after school.

She relied on Evie and Tommy to help with the shopping and she was grateful that they were so reliable and cheerful, especially Tommy. Evie was quieter and more introspective but she liked them both very much.

The rain continued to batter against the window which depressed her even more but at least it wasn't snow. Christmas and the start of a new year, 1955, were just a few weeks ago and life seemed flat.

Not like the excitement of Queen Elizabeth's coronation which now was a fading memory. She glanced at the coronation calendar that hung on a hook beside the fireplace and decided it was maybe time to take it down and keep it in a drawer. She certainly wasn't going to throw it away.

There was a knock at the door and she turned round, fully expecting to see Grace but it was Eliza from next door. Before she could speak, Eliza swept in on a cold draught of air with her hair wet from the rain.

'I'm sorry to be a nuisance, Bella, but I wondered if you could lend me some sugar. I've run out and my mother is a pest, being her usual drama queen and saying she can't possibly drink her tea without sugar. She had to drink her tea often enough without sugar during the rationing but she now says because everything is back to normal she can't live without her Tate and Lyle.'

Bella took a cup out of the cupboard and spooned some sugar from the cut-crystal bowl that she was so proud of. 'I haven't got much to spare, Eliza, as I'm hoping Evie and Tommy will come in after school and go to the shops.'

Eliza pounced on this statement. 'Can you tell them to come in and see me as I need messages as well.' Clutching the cup of sugar, she sat down by the fire. 'I would go myself but I'm waiting on the district nurse who is coming to see Mum.'

'How is Martha keeping?' Bella asked.

Eliza groaned. 'She's playing up today. Everything is wrong with her. If it's not her arthritis it's her eyesight. She has her new specs she got from the National Health but they're seemingly no good. She says she can't read the paper but she was able to tell me all the folk who have died. Their death notices are in the paper and she reads it with a great deal of enjoyment.'

On that cheery note, she stood up just as there was another knock at the door and Grace appeared, carrying a plate covered with a tea towel.

'I've made some cakes, Bella, and I thought you might like some.'

Bella said, 'I'll put the kettle on.' She turned to Eliza. 'Do you want to stay and have a cup of tea?'

Eliza shook her head reluctantly. 'I'd love to but I better get back as Mum will be wondering where I've got to. I'll bring the sugar back when the girls go to the shop for me.'

Bella explained that she hoped the girls could do shopping for them both. Grace sat by the fire as Bella took the best china cups from the dresser. She loved this old-fashioned house with its long forgotten custom of having tea from the best china cups and all served on the well-polished table with its lace tablecloth.

'I've been to see Maryanne and I feel so worried about her,' said Grace.

Bella sat down. 'What's wrong with her?'

Grace hesitated. 'I'm not sure but she should go and see the doctor. She's got terrible stomach pains and she keeps swallowing indigestion tablets.'

Bella looked thoughtful as she popped one of the small cakes on a dainty plate. 'Try and persuade her to see the doctor, Grace.'

Grace promised she would as she looked around. 'You've got some lovely things in this room.'

'I inherited most of it from my mother. It was to be our home when Davie and I were married but when he was killed at the Battle of Loos, well…' She stopped and gave a big sigh. 'Well it never happened and I've never met another man who mattered as much to me as he did.'

Grace was sorry she had mentioned the subject and she said so.

'It was all so long ago so don't apologise. Anyway I'm just grateful that the girls help me so much.'

Later, Evie and Tommy arrived back from school. Tommy was pleased to see that Evie's mum had been baking but even though she enjoyed the cakes, they were a bit on the small side and nothing like the cakes that her mum often brought back from Burnett's bakery.

'Before you have your tea, can you run along and do Granny Duff and Eliza's shopping for them?'

They put their wet coats back on and ran along the lane. When they reached Granny Duff's house they found her sitting in her chair with a photo frame on her lap. It showed a tall, handsome man in the kilted uniform of the Black Watch. She had been polishing it with a duster and her eyes were red as if she had been crying. She quickly wiped them with a lace-edged handkerchief. 'I've got a bit of the cold,' she said. Evie and Tommy said nothing and she suddenly realised that no explanation or excuse was needed. The girls were too young to understand how something so small as a photo had brought back painful memories from forty years ago. Far from viewing Davie's death in the way she had explained to Grace, this photo was from another lifetime and the hurt and anguish had barely subsided over the years. The life she had visualised when Davie was alive now lay in tatters as it had done for decades.

5

Martha Potter was sitting in her favourite chair which was pulled up right beside the fire. It was blocking her daughter's chair but Martha was unapologetic about this. This was her house and she thought it was her right to rule the roost.

She was annoyed when Eliza hurried in. 'Where have you been? I'm dying of thirst and waiting for my tea.'

Eliza sighed. When her mother was in this mood there was no arguing with her. 'Grace came in and brought some home baking for Bella.'

'Home baking,' said Martha in a loud petulant voice. 'Did she give some to you?'

'No she didn't, but she asked me to stay for tea.'

Martha was indignant. 'I hope you told her that I needed you here, especially as she didn't give you any cakes for me. I could be dying of starvation for all my neighbours think of me.'

Eliza sighed again. 'Grace brought you some pancakes yesterday.' Then under her breath she muttered, 'And you ate all of them.' Eliza looked at her mother slumped back in her chair. She was putting on more weight and she now looked like a small barrel. She made a mental note to cut down on the purchase of sugar and all the fattening foods her mother enjoyed. It was as if she was making up for all the years of rationing but even then she had been plump.

'Grace was saying that Maryanne isn't well and she is trying to get her to go to the doctor.'

Martha groaned. 'She isn't as ill as I am. That girl of hers, that Sadie, hasn't made things easier for her. Running off and getting married to an American if you please. She was quite a flirt was Sadie and she thought she could have any man she wanted and when she broke up with that young man she was going out with, well, he was quite devastated when she went away to America.'

Eliza listened in silence as this was old news. If the truth be told, Eliza liked Sadie and wished she had had the chance to meet a handsome American and go off to the other side of the world with him. She pictured her mother's face if that had happened, and this gave her a bit of pleasure.

Martha noticed the smile. 'What are you grinning for?'

Eliza wanted to say that she wished she had run off with a GI but she remained silent. However, she added just one spoon of sugar to her mother's cup instead of the usual three.

Martha suddenly spotted Albert Scott passing the window. 'Eliza, run outside and ask Albert to come in.'

Eliza gave a loud dramatic sigh. Honestly, she thought, Albert was probably wanting to get home instead of visiting Martha, but she did as she was told.

'Mum wants to know if you can come in and see her.'

Albert hesitated but he turned and retraced his steps. Eliza saw that he was carrying a couple of paper bags from Burnett's bakery and she suddenly realised her mother had spotted them. However Martha was all smiles when her neighbour came in, his overcoat and woollen hat wet with raindrops.

'Eliza's just put the kettle on, Albert. Sit down and take off your wet coat and hat and sit down by the fire.'

Albert was slightly bemused by his bossy neighbour. She put him in mind of his late wife who liked to rule the roost, just like Martha.

Eliza carried the old wooden tray to the small table by the

side of her mother's chair. Martha frowned when she saw the plate of Rich Tea biscuits.

'Have we nothing else to eat?' she said, eyeing the bags in Albert's hand. 'I see you've been to Burnett's.'

Albert nodded. 'Aye I have. It's something for my tea. I like to be served by Anna as she always picks out the biggest cakes and sausage rolls for me.'

Martha picked up a biscuit with a sour look on her face. 'Oh I see,' she said, biting a bit of the biscuit like some martyr eating week-old bread.

Albert said, 'Did you hear we're getting new neighbours in the empty house next door to me?'

The two women looked surprised. 'No, we haven't heard. Who is it?'

Albert said he didn't know too much but it was a young couple and she was expecting a baby. 'I met them briefly yesterday. They come from Skye and he's a joiner going to be working with his brother who has his own business. I think they are moving in next week. I hope the weather is better for them.' He glanced out of the window at the rain which was still falling heavily. 'Well, I'd better be on my way.' He put his wet coat and hat back on and said he would keep them informed with the news of the new people coming into their little community.

After he left, Martha put the half-eaten biscuit back on the plate. 'I thought he might have offered me one of his cakes.' She was most disgruntled.

As she took the cups over to the sink, Eliza said, 'For heaven's sake, you've got cakes on the brain.' Putting the dishes away she wondered about the new neighbours, this young couple from the Western Isles plus a new baby. That should make the lane a bit more lively.

Meanwhile Martha was trying to read the *Radio Times* without her spectacles. 'I can't find my specs, Eliza, have you put them somewhere?'

Martha's specs were a bone of contention as she was forever breaking them by sitting on them or dropping them on the tiled hearth. She certainly got her money's worth with the National Health optician on the Hilltown.

'Well, that's what the National Health is for,' she would say when Eliza got annoyed with her. 'It was established for people like me who have to be treated nicely in their old age and I'm just glad someone is thinking about my health and wellbeing.'

6

When Albert got home he hung his wet coat and hat over the kitchen chair. The fire needed some more coal which he took from the brass box by the side of the fire, picking up each lump with the brass tongs.

Although Jean had been dead since coronation week in 1953, he still carried on with her housework routine. Monday was laundry day, on Tuesday he polished the furniture and the rest of the week he did the daily chores that had never changed in the forty years they had been married.

Later, he placed his sausage roll in the oven. One thing he did miss was her cooking which she tackled with the same precision as her household cleaning. Monday was mince, Tuesday macaroni, Wednesday sausages, Thursday egg and chips, Friday was fish and the weekend was steak pie which was served over two days.

He couldn't lie to himself that the marriage had been deliriously happy but there had been contentment, at least on his part. Jean was always too stressed to be able to relax, especially if she couldn't finish the ironing or polishing the brasses. Albert sincerely hoped she was resting in peace in whatever heaven she had entered.

The noise of the letterbox broke his reverie. It was the *Evening Telegraph* delivered by the skinny wee lad who lived on the Hilltown. He passed the window and Albert saw that he was wrapped up against the rain, his balaclava pulled so low over his eyes it was hard to imagine he could see ahead, but he hurried on so Albert thought he must be all right.

Earlier in the day he had been chatting to Anna in the bakery and she told him that she was worried about her husband. The weather was playing havoc with his sore leg and he wasn't sleeping very well with the pain. He liked Anna and Thomas and their lassie Thomasina and he wondered if he would feel the same about his new neighbours when they arrived next door. That empty house had been the main topic of conversation in the lane for the past month, ever since old Mrs Prior died in the infirmary with pneumonia and her son had arrived from Glasgow to clear out her belongings.

Folk in the lane had been outraged that he hadn't visited his mother in years. Martha had said what they all felt when she stated, 'When he hopes to make a bob or two with the furniture he's no long in hot footing it up to Meadow Lane.'

After eating his tea, he opened the newspaper. He loved reading all the news, especially the local stories and the death column. Sometimes he recognised a name and he was grateful that he was still hale and hearty. He tried to skip over any troublesome news as his motto was there was nothing new under the sun, and unfortunately the world would always be a terrible place for so many people and reading about it wouldn't help them. There would always be wars and earthquakes, volcanic eruptions and starving people. He thought about all the carnage this country had suffered with the two world wars and the recent conflict in Korea.

Albert tried not to dwell on his own horrors in the so-called Great War, the war to end all wars. Well, that was a lie for a start. Although he didn't want to recall it, the thoughts came unbidden to his mind and he was back in the mud and stench of the trenches in Loos.

He remembered Davie Bell, Bella's fiancé. They had joined up together, both of them full of patriotic fervour and eager to do their bit for King and Country. He tried to recall how long it had taken them to realise the terrible reality of war. He remembered the fear when the officer had blown his whistle and the futility of going over the top. The lads had charged over the muddy ground, straight into the German machine guns. They never stood a chance.

Suddenly he stood up to switch on the wireless. He loved the Light Programme unlike Jean who liked listening to the Home Service. A blast of music filled the room and was soon followed by the cheery banter of a comedian. Sitting back in his chair he began to laugh at some of the funny jokes. This was how life should be lived, he thought, a comfy chair, listening to a comedian telling outrageous tales about his mother-in-law.

Albert smiled. He could tell some tales about his late mother-in-law and they would be funny all right but not funny ha ha.

7

Grace, Evie and Tommy liked to go to the pictures on a Friday night but on this particular night Bill had been called out to a frozen pipes job and by five-thirty he still hadn't returned.

'Does that mean we can't go?' Evie asked.

Grace looked uncertain. She always liked to have Bill's evening meal over by the time they set off but there was no certainty when he would be home. She saw the look of dismay on the two girls' faces and made up her mind.

'I'll put your dad's tea in the oven and I'll leave him a note,' she said, placing the steak pie and potatoes in the oven before going to the lobby to put on her coat. 'Put on your scarves and gloves as it's gotten much colder.'

As they stepped out into the lane they noticed that ice had formed on the ground and the air was so frigid it made their faces sting with the cold.

'You had better watch your step, I don't want you to fall,' said Grace, taking their hands as they walked either side of her.

'Maybe we'll meet Dad on our way there,' said Evie, but there was no sign of him as they slowly made their way down the Hilltown towards the Plaza cinema.

Grace, with her mind still on the meal she had left behind, said, 'I hope we don't have to stand in a queue as we'll be frozen by the time we get in.'

However by the time they reached the cinema they were able to make their way to the admission kiosk right away. Tommy was excited that they were going to an Abbott and Costello film as she was a fan of the comic duo's antics but then she noticed that the other film on the programme was a cowboy film starring Hopalong Cassidy.

When they were seated, she said, 'My dad's nickname is Hopalong so that also makes him Hopalong Cassidy. It was when he worked on one of the Hydro Electric dams and a rock fell on his leg and broke it in two places. That was before he married Mum and that's why he walks with a limp.'

Grace said it was such a shame but then the lights dimmed and the first film began. She had bought her favourite bar of Dairy Milk chocolate while the girls had their bags of sweeties. With the warmth of the auditorium and the entertaining and funny film she soon relaxed and forgot about leaving Bill's tea slowly drying up in the oven.

Later, as they left the cinema, Grace was dismayed to see that it had been snowing and the pavement was covered with an inch of snow. She debated giving the chip shop a miss but she knew the girls always enjoyed their bags of chips so they walked as fast as they could to Dellanzo's fish and chip shop before hurrying home with their hot parcels.

Bill was sitting in front of a blazing fire and was fast asleep. He woke up when Grace moved around making cups of cocoa. Leaning forward he helped himself to some of the chips, much to Evie's annoyance as she was nearest to him.

'Mum, give Dad some of your chips as he's eating all mine.'

Bill pretended to look hurt. 'Sorry but I'm still hungry after my dried-up meal. The tatties were shrivelled up and the steak pie was almost cremated.'

Grace looked mortified. 'I'm sorry, Bill. When did you get home?'

He laughed. 'I'm just joking. I finished work on Mrs Cotton's pipes and I was home by six o'clock.'

Evie rolled her eyes. 'Honestly, Dad, you had us all feeling sorry for you.'

'Well obviously you didn't feel sorry enough for your poor old father as you begrudged me a couple of chips.' But he was laughing as he spoke. 'Oh by the way, Grace, Tommy's mum came in an hour ago to say that Maryanne was ill again and Anna wondered if you could maybe look in and see her.'

'I'd better go in now and see her.' She turned to the girls. 'Do you want to play a game of Monopoly or do you want to come home with me, Tommy?'

'I'd like to stay a bit longer if that's all right as Mum usually lets me stay up late on a Friday night.'

Grace put on her coat and scarf and headed out of the door. The snow was still falling and the wind was freezing cold. When she reached Maryanne's house she opened the door and called out, 'It's just me, Maryanne.' Anna was sitting by a meagre fire, wearing her coat and hat as the room was very cold. She stood up and put a finger to her lips and pointed to the settee which was placed against the wall. 'She's fallen asleep at last but she been having a lot of pain. She had to come home early from her work today but she still hasn't seen the doctor.' Maryanne was covered with a pink quilt but her face looked thin and drawn.

'Heaven's above, this room's freezing. I'll put some more coal on the fire.'

Anna shook her head. 'There isn't any coal in the bunker, I've checked.'

Grace opened the door and headed back home, saying, 'I'll just be a minute, Anna.' When she entered the kitchen, Bill and the girls looked up. Before anyone spoke, she said, 'Bill, can you fill up a couple of buckets of coal and take them to Maryanne's house? She must have missed the coal-man this afternoon.'

Bill did as he was told and as they carried the buckets along to Maryanne's house, Grace said, 'I don't think she's had the money to buy coal because Anna said she came home early from work and she would have been in when he called.'

Bill shivered when he went inside. 'God, this room is like an icebox.' He began to shovel coal on the barely burning fire. 'Still, we'll soon have the place warmed up.'

Anna stood up. 'I'll have to go home as Thomas will soon be home from the pub and he'll need his supper.'

Grace said she would stay. 'Tommy's playing Monopoly with Evie unless you want her to go home.' Anna said she could stay but to send her home by ten o'clock.

Bill asked Grace, 'What are you going to do about Maryanne?'

Grace had no idea but she decided to stay with her until Maryanne was awake and maybe when she was in her bed she would feel better.

'You can go home, Bill, and get Evie to bed by ten and send Tommy home. I'll wait here for a wee while longer to see if she's able to stay on her own.'

Bill nodded and went out. 'I'll bring more coal later on.'

By now the room was warmer and Grace went over to the settee. Maryanne opened her eyes and a spasm of pain crossed her face. Grace helped her up and placed a cushion behind her head. 'How are you feeling now?'

Maryanne tried to stand up and the quilt fell at her feet. 'If I go to bed I'll be all right,' she said but she no sooner spoke when another spasm made her sit back down and Grace saw the film of sweat on her face.

'I'll call the doctor out to see you as it's clear you're not well.'

Maryanne was mortified. 'Oh don't do that. I just need some more Rennies and to get a good night's sleep.'

Grace went through to the small bedroom and was worried as she realised it was even colder than the kitchen. 'I think you should sleep on the settee tonight and I'll stoke up the fire to keep you warm. Anna said you came home early from work.'

Maryanne's eyes filled with tears. 'I'm worried I'll lose my job, Grace, as the factory is paying off workers.'

Grace didn't know what to say but she tried to reassure her that as she had worked at Keiller's for many years surely her job was safe. 'Do you want me to make you something to eat or a hot drink?'

Maryanne shook her head. 'No, I just want to sleep.'

Grace went and stoked up the fire and placed the quilt back on the settee. 'I'll be off then but I'll look in later to see how you are.' Maryanne immediately closed her eyes and Grace tiptoed to the door. No one in the lane ever locked their front door until bedtime so it would be easy for her to pop back in again before she went to bed.

Back in her own house, Bill was reading the paper and Evie was in bed. 'What do you think is wrong with her?' he asked.

Grace shook her head. 'I'm making sure she goes to see the doctor tomorrow morning as she can't go on suffering these pains any longer, and another thing I noticed is that her cupboard is almost bare so she's either not eating or she hasn't any money to go to the shop.'

Bill said he would see the coalman on his way to work in the morning and order a couple of bags of coal which meant her house would be warm at least.

But as it turned out, things were to take a dramatic turn for the worse when Grace popped in at eleven o'clock to find Maryanne collapsed on the floor and in terrible pain. Hurrying home she got Bill to phone for an ambulance which he did from the telephone box in Ann Street.

The ambulance arrived within half an hour and Maryanne was taken out on a stretcher. The snow was wet and slushy as she was taken along the lane and the curtains from the Potter house were pulled aside. Eliza opened her door and saw Grace walking alongside the patient. 'What's the matter with Maryanne?'

Grace started to explain when Martha's voice called out, 'What's going on, Eliza?' Grace said she would see them after seeing Maryanne safely into the ambulance.

'I'm worried about leaving the house,' said Maryanne as she was being placed in the vehicle. 'I also need to let my work know.'

Grace promised she would see to everything. 'Now you're not to worry about anything but just concentrate on getting better.'

Maryanne tried to smile but another spasm of pain made her gasp out loud. The driver shut the door and slowly drove off, sending a stream of wet snow onto the pavement and almost covering Grace's shoes. Eliza was still at her door and Martha was still calling out.

'I can only wait a minute, Eliza,' she said as she sat on the fireside chair. Martha was dressed in her nightgown, a full-length blue flannel garment, and she had her hair covered by dinky curlers. Her eyes were gleaming with the thought of some juicy gossip.

'Maryanne's been taken to hospital as she's not been well for some time. I don't know what's wrong with her but we'll probably hear soon.'

Martha looked disappointed by this meagre bit of news and she yawned loudly. Eliza went over and helped her to her feet and for a moment Grace thought Martha looked like a stranded whale. Eliza walked her mother to the comfy looking bed in the corner of the room.

As she walked home, Grace passed Anna's house but since there was no light shining in the window she hurried into her own house and warmed her hands at the fire. Bill went and made some hot tea and Grace sat back in the chair and thanked her lucky stars that she had her husband by her side. Not like poor Maryanne who, for as long as she had been her neighbour, had lived on her own. Her daughter Sadie had been married and living in America when the Gows moved into Meadow Lane but she had seen a photograph of her and she was a lovely looking woman.

However there was no photograph of any husband.

8

Maryanne was frightened as she was wheeled into the ward. Everything was quiet as most of the patients were asleep. The nurse pulled the screen around her bed and a young, serious looking doctor appeared at her side.

'You're suffering from severe pain I believe, Mrs Roberts?' he said, leaning over her and pressing a cold hand over the painful area. She called out as the pain radiated over her abdomen and the doctor looked thoughtful. 'How long have you had this pain?' he asked and she told him a few weeks. 'It's your gall-bladder and I suspect a stone has got lodged in the tube.' Maryanne was almost frightened to ask what that meant but he continued to speak to the ward sister who had now also appeared. 'Mrs Roberts will need tests and surgery as soon as possible so I'll put her down for tomorrow.'

The sister nodded and the doctor gave Maryanne a quick smile before leaving. As she was already in her nightdress the young nurse got her settled into bed. The ward sister said she would bring her something to make her sleep before she disappeared around the screen. Maryanne lay in this strange bed with the cold white sheets and closed her eyes against the bright light that shone above her head.

Soft footsteps and the rustling of a starched uniform made her open her eyes again. The young nurse was standing with a glass of water and a pill in a small plastic container. She helped

Maryanne to sit up and after she swallowed the pill, the nurse busied herself with the blanket and pillows, making sure her patient was comfortable before slipping away silently.

Maryanne was left to ponder and worry about the future. The thought of maybe losing her job and God knew how could she cope with no income plus how would she manage in the house after this operation? Then there was the worry over Sadie and her unhappiness with her marriage in America. Where was it all going to end?

She listened to all the strange noises in the ward. Someone was snoring but thankfully not too loudly and another patient was mumbling some incoherent words. Someone further up the ward had a coughing fit and she heard soothing words as the nurse attended to the unknown woman. It was certainly an alien world for Maryanne as she had never been in a hospital before. Thankfully the pain had eased to a dull ache before she slowly relaxed as the sleeping pill took effect and she was soon asleep.

Back at Meadow Lane, Grace was unable to sleep so she got up and went to sit by the fire. She didn't want to waken Bill as he had work to go to in the morning but she was worried about Maryanne. It was clear that she hadn't been eating and the fact that the house was cold and the cupboard empty was obviously because of the lack of money. It looked like she didn't get paid when she was off work which had been quite often over the past few weeks.

Grace prided herself that she knew everything about her neighbours' lives as it was impossible to live in this small community and not know everyone's business – but although Maryanne was friendly, it was clear that she was a very private person and kept a lot of her life to herself. Not like Martha and Eliza whose lives were an open book.

Bill had said he would catch the coalman and put in two bags of coal but now Grace wasn't so sure. Perhaps Maryanne might feel it was charity and Grace didn't want to embarrass her. Standing up, she went back to bed. In the morning she would ask Bill what he thought and she would go to the infirmary to see what the diagnosis was.

Bill was snoring when she slipped under the covers and she snuggled up against his back to keep warm. One good thing about her husband was the fact that he was always warm in bed whereas she never warmed up at all. I'm a proper old cold potato, she thought.

It was still dark when Maryanne wakened up but she was surprised that the lights soon went on and two nurses began to take hot drinks to each of the beds. The nurse passed her bed. 'Nothing for you, Mrs Roberts, as you're due for surgery this morning.'

For some reason this statement depressed her. She would have appreciated a hot drink as her mouth was dry and the pain was still rumbling away, although she was relieved it was bearable. She couldn't remember when she had last eaten but she had a vague notion it had been on Thursday morning.

She lay back on her pillow as the morning routine of the ward went on around her and she must have fallen asleep again because she awoke to see the doctor and ward sister at her bed. Now the pain was back with a vengeance. She tried not to think too much about what lay ahead and very soon she was being wheeled along to the theatre to have her gallbladder removed, as explained by the surgeon. Actually she was glad that something was happening; if it meant freedom from the pain she had been suffering for ages then it would be worth it.

She was apprehensive as she was wheeled through the theatre door but she was given an injection and told to count to ten. Later she remembered that she only reached three.

More snow had fallen through the night and the streets were white. Evie and Tommy left after breakfast to do Granny Duff and Martha and Eliza's shopping. Bill also left to travel to the plumber's workshop in Ann Street. His boss Charlie

Baxter would no doubt be in the office and working out all the jobs that had to be done.

Before Evie left, Grace told her to go and see her granny in case she also needed her shopping done. Later, Anna called in on her way to work and she was surprised to hear that Maryanne was in the infirmary. 'It was very late when I found her lying on the floor,' Grace said. 'I didn't want to waken you as your light was out. I was going to come and tell you but it's been a very busy morning.'

Anna was upset that she hadn't been there but Grace said she had been a great help to Maryanne during the day and the early evening. 'I thought I would go up to the infirmary in the afternoon to see what's happening,' said Grace. 'Do you want to come with me after you finish work?'

Anna was practically sitting on top of the fire as she was so cold. 'I can't because Thomas will be home in the afternoon and he needs his tea before he goes back to work. Tell her if you see her that I'll visit on Sunday.' She stood up and gave a last lingering glance at the fire. 'Well I'd better be off although the thought of trudging through the snow makes me feel ill. God I hate the winter.' She belted her tweed coat and tied a woollen headsquare around her head and opened the door, letting a blast of cold air into the room.

Grace decided to finish her breakfast but Eliza opened the door and hurried in. Like Anna, she was wearing her thick winter coat and her ankle boots. She sounded out of breath as if she had travelled miles instead of the few yards along the lane.

'What's the news on Maryanne? Mum's annoyed we haven't heard any more.'

Grace tried to keep her patience as she knew the Potters liked to know everything. 'I'm hoping to go up to see her this afternoon so I'll give you more news later.'

Eliza said this would be fine. 'I've told Albert about the ambulance so he'll probably be in to see you as well but I don't think Bella Duff has heard.'

Grace said she would go in to see her later and if Albert didn't manage to get out then she would also go in to see him. Although, she thought, Albert usually liked his pint of beer at the Windmill Bar so he would maybe drop in on his way back.

Eliza left. As Grace finally started to eat her toast, which had grown cold and soggy, she was amused. Her neighbours made her sound like an oracle or town crier, the bringer of all the news to the lane.

At eleven o'clock the girls rushed in along with another blast of frigid air. Their cheeks were red and they were laughing. Grace suddenly felt old and thought it was great to be young and carefree. Evie hung her coat on the hook at the back of the kitchen door while Tommy sat down and placed her wet coat over the back of the chair. Evie said, 'Granny wants to see you this afternoon.'

Grace was in the process of ladling out two bowls of soup for them. She turned round. 'Did she say what she wanted, Evie?'

Evie shrugged as she joined Tommy at the table. 'No, she didn't.'

That meant Grace wouldn't be able to go and see Maryanne but she always felt a wee bit guilty about her mother. Although she saw her regularly, a couple of times a week, she often thought she should maybe spend more time with her but then she remembered how independent her mother could be when it suited her.

The girls were supping their soup and Grace was amused by the thick slice of bread that Tommy was dipping into her bowl. Evie, as usual, was eating hers so slowly that it would be cold by the time she finished it.

Grace pulled on her new leather ankle boots with the fur trim that had been a Christmas gift from Bill, although she had chosen them and even bought them, and she was so proud of them. Seemingly Tommy also liked them. 'I love your new boots,' she said, in between spoonfuls of soup and helping herself to another slice of bread.

'I'll nip down and see your granny, Evie. When Dad comes in tell him there's soup for his dinner.'

Grace decided she could maybe phone the infirmary from the call box which was on her way to her mother's house so she made sure she had some pennies in her purse to make the call. She had mentioned getting in touch with the infirmary to the ambulance driver and he had given her the phone number. Hurrying down the Hilltown, she was careful not to step into slushy puddles. The street was quite busy in spite of the cold, snowy weather and as she passed Burnett's bakery she saw Anna at the counter and she gave her a wave.

The telephone box was musty smelling and wet when she opened the door and the black phone was damp and uninviting but she stepped inside and placed her handbag on the shelf which was also damp. She followed the instructions that were printed on the wall and when she was connected she pressed button A.

A cool, professional sounding voice answered and Grace explained that she was a close neighbour who had called the ambulance last night. After a few minutes, the voice announced that Maryanne was in surgery and wouldn't be allowed any visitors until tomorrow. Grace thanked the nurse, if that was who the cool voice belonged to, and said she would visit on Sunday.

Evelyn Williams lived at nineteen Ann Street so Grace hurried through the close and up the stairs to the flat. Her mother always polished her brass doorknob and nameplate every day and when she answered the door she was wearing her apron and had a duster in her hand. Grace followed her through the lobby to the tidy kitchen and she saw the table was covered with old newspapers and all the brass ornaments that were her mother's pride and joy.

'Evie said you wanted to see me, Mum.'

Evelyn picked up an ornate looking bell and began to savagely polish it with her duster. 'Yes, Grace, it's just to say that

I can't have the girls for their tea tomorrow as I'm going out with my next-door neighbour, Elsie Conners.'

Grace said, 'You should just have told Evie and Tommy about not coming tomorrow.'

Evelyn looked hurt. 'I thought you would like to hear my plans.'

Grace felt ashamed. 'So, Mum, what are you and Elsie Conners doing on a Sunday?' She tried to sound bright and concerned, the old feeling of guilt making its insidious intrusion inside her head.

Evelyn was now attacking a large brass plaque but she looked excited. 'Do you remember me telling you that Elsie Conners' son has a good job in Edinburgh?'

Grace nodded. 'Yes, he's with the Civil Service and works in the tax office.'

'That's right and now he's bought a car and tomorrow he's coming to take us both for a run and we're having a high tea somewhere. Isn't that exciting?'

Grace said that it was and she was pleased for her mother. Ever since her father died ten years ago, her mum's life had centred round Evie and herself and now she was due some pleasure. Grace did what she could for her but with her own family to look after she realised her mother was lonely.

'Why don't you come to us for your tea tonight, Mum?'

'Oh I don't think I can manage tonight, love, as I've got the rest of my housework to finish.'

Grace wanted to burst out laughing but she said, 'Have a lovely time tomorrow and I'll see you on Monday and you can tell me all about it.' She gave her mum a hug as she left to go home.

Evie and Tommy liked to go down the town on a Saturday afternoon. They had a shilling each that Granny Duff gave them for helping with the shopping while Eliza and Martha gave them a Rich Tea biscuit as a thank you. Tommy would scoff hers immediately but Evie kept hers in her pocket until

Tommy asked for it later in the day. They liked to go to Woolworths with their shilling plus the shilling they both got from their parents. Evie always saved some of her pocket money every week but Tommy gaily spent it all.

'Why do you save your money?' she asked as they walked down the Wellgate.

'Mum says it will help me when I leave school, as a little nest egg is good to have.'

Tommy thought this was a weak excuse. 'I hope when I grow up I'll marry a rich man because I'm so pretty, so I don't need a nest egg as he'll have pots and pots of money.' Evie knew she wasn't as pretty as Tommy so she would no doubt need her savings as she couldn't count on marrying a rich man. Evie didn't have this faith in herself. She often wished she had Tommy's confidence and cheerful outlook on life but she didn't, so she decided to keep saving but not to say too much to her friend.

Once inside Woolworths they soon forgot about their views on growing up as they wandered around the store where they spent ages choosing what to buy. Evie bought another colouring book but Tommy liked to look at the lovely hair slides and the sweet counter. An hour later they made their way home, linking arms and laughing at Eliza choosing the two Rich Teas from the biscuit barrel with all the seriousness of picking some expensive trinket from a treasure chest.

9

The day after her operation Maryanne felt as if she had gone ten rounds with some heavyweight boxer, she was so sore. Even breathing made the pain worse so she was glad when the surgeon appeared at her bedside with a clutch of students – five serious-looking, white-coated young men and two women plus the ward sister. The surgeon, whose name was Dr Norman, explained to this small group that his patient had just had her gallbladder removed as it was full of gallstones. He asked Maryanne how she was feeling.

'I'm still very sore,' she said. She wasn't sure what else to say as she felt a little overawed by the faces that stared at her wound when the surgeon pulled the bedcover down a bit to show off his handiwork. Turning to the ward sister, he said, 'Mrs Roberts can have painkilling tablets, Sister.' The woman nodded and said she would do that.

After the group moved off to the next patient, a nurse appeared with a jug of water and two tablets which Maryanne swallowed with a bit of difficulty as her mouth was still dry. The cold water was bliss as it slipped down her throat, and she prayed that the painkillers would work soon.

Later, lying back on her pillows, she felt a peace she hadn't had in a long time. There was something therapeutic about lying in her comfy bed watching all the comings and goings in the ward. Her bed was right beside the door which meant she only had one person on her left, an elderly woman who was sound asleep and hadn't even wakened up when the doctor did his rounds.

I could be happy, she thought, if it wasn't for the worry over my job and the continuing tension from Sadie's letters. She felt she could lie there for ever as the ward was lovely and warm, so unlike her house over the past few weeks where the kitchen was freezing due to the lack of coal. She owed the coalman for two bags he had put in one day while she was at work and she had been dodging him ever since as she didn't have the money to pay for them.

With all these thoughts churning around in her mind she drifted off to sleep and woke up in surprise when the nurse was pulling her table over the bed. 'It's time for some lunch,' she said, as she placed a bowl of soup with a slice of bread in front of her. Maryanne had slipped down the bed while asleep and the nurse helping her up caused a sharp pain which made her cry out, but once she was sitting up the pain wasn't as bad. Maryanne wondered how many painkillers she was allowed in a day and hoped there were more to come.

The soup was tasty and she managed it all, realising this was the biggest meal she had eaten in a couple of days. In the next bed she noticed the old lady had also been helped up and a nurse was feeding her. Glancing away, she thought the patient looked really ill.

Grace was getting ready to go to see Maryanne and she was waiting for Anna who wanted to go as well. As it was a Sunday, Anna had had a lie in and now she was making a meal for Thomas and Tommy. It was a combination of breakfast and dinner and afterwards she slipped on her thick coat and boots. They weren't as fashionable as Grace's boots and she had owned them for a few years but they were still serviceable although a bit scuffed. She glanced at the marks and went to the drawer where she kept the shoe cleaning box. She rubbed black shoe polish into the leather and buffed them up.

Thomas was reading the Sunday paper by the fire with a cup of tea at his elbow. Tommy was planning to go to Evie's house so he would have the house to himself to enjoy his one day off in the week. For some reason Anna disliked a Sunday even although she also had the day off. She was finding her work was getting heavier as the bakery had asked her to work extra hours when needed, which meant she sometimes went in to work in the morning as well as the afternoon. However, the extra money helped.

The two women were pleased when they stepped out onto the lane as the snow had stopped and the pavements were clear of the slush that had been difficult to walk on. The wind was also not so cold and a weak sun tried to penetrate the cloudy sky.

Anna said, 'I wonder how Maryanne is today after her operation.'

'We'll soon find out but I hope she'll be free of all that pain she's been suffering from.'

They were passing the Potters' house when Eliza opened the door. 'Are you going to visit Maryanne?' She turned round when Martha's voice called out loudly, 'Are they going to the infirmary, Eliza?'

Eliza sounded fed up. 'I'm just asking them.'

Anna answered that they were. 'We'll let you know how she is after we've seen her.'

Eliza said she wished she could come with them but she couldn't leave her mother. 'I don't suppose I could ask some-one to come in and look after her?' she said, hopefully. Grace said she didn't think anyone would be available.

'I wondered about Evie and Tommy, if they could come in for a couple of hours.'

Grace said she wasn't keen on them looking after an elderly

woman. 'What if your mother fell or took a bad turn, Eliza? The girls wouldn't know what to do.'

Eliza looked disappointed. 'Oh, it was just a thought.' She turned on her heel and closed the door.

Anna was laughing as they emerged into the Hilltown. 'Honestly, that pair are like Old Mother Riley and her daughter. I enjoyed the last film they made and Old Mother Riley screeches like Martha.'

Grace felt more sympathetic. 'I feel sorry for Eliza as she doesn't have much of a life. It can't be much fun looking after her mother every day. I think I'll offer to sit with Martha one night this week and let Eliza out to visit Maryanne although I'll be furious if your Thomas tells me she's been in the Windmill Bar.'

Both women started laughing as they made their way along Constitution Road. There was a queue waiting at the main door of the infirmary as visitors gathered to see their families and friends but the queue moved quite quickly and Grace and Anna were soon sitting at the side of Maryanne's bed. When she saw her visitors, she tried to sit up straighter but she winced in pain at the stitched wound. Grace said not to sit up and she placed next to Maryanne the bottle of orange squash and the packet of biscuits she had brought with her.

'How are you feeling, Maryanne?' asked Anna, who brought out a bar of chocolate and another bottle of squash from her message bag.

Maryanne said she was fine but still a bit sore. 'I've had my gallbladder taken out as it was so full of gallstones. One of the stones got stuck in the tube and that was the cause of my feeling ill.'

'Well you should be much better now after that,' said Grace. 'The main thing is to rest and recover and hopefully you'll be home soon.'

Maryanne closed her eyes and Grace took her hand. 'Is

there anything you want Anna and me to do? Maybe write to Sadie to tell her about your operation.'

'I'm really worried about my job, could you go down to see Dorothy who lives in James Street. She works with me and she can tell the supervisor that I'm in here.' She stopped and reached for a drink of water which Anna handed to her. 'I'm also worried about paying the rent and the coalman.'

Grace said, 'Anna and I will sort things out for you so don't worry, and we'll lock up your house. It's one thing keeping an open door when you're in the house but not if it's to be empty.'

The sound of a bell marked the end of visiting time and the two women stood up. 'We'll be back next week so try not to worry and concentrate on getting better.' Anna gave her a small wave as she left the bedside. 'Cheerio Maryanne, see you soon.'

Grace was about to do the same when Maryanne caught hold of her hand. 'If you want to drop a line to Sadie, her address is on the calendar by the side of the fire and I'm grateful that you'll speak to the rent- and coalmen.' This speech seemed to tire her out and she lay back against the pillows.

'If you're worried about money, Maryanne, you should see the hospital almoner as she can help you with your worries. Please ask to see her, will you?' Maryanne promised she would.

Anna was waiting for her in the corridor. 'Does she want us to write to Sadie?'

Grace nodded. 'I'm also worried about her financial situation and I told her to see the almoner as she deals with patients' money problems and their wellbeing.'

'It's such a shame she lives on her own with no husband to support her, and the fact her daughter lives in America doesn't help,' Anna said. She was desperate for a cigarette but she didn't like smoking in the street. She sincerely hoped Thomas hadn't smoked them all. At least Maryanne didn't have that problem in her house.

The wind had grown stronger and colder. Grace thought it was coming from the east which she always thought was a wind that could cut right through you.

They weren't surprised when Eliza rushed out as they passed her window. 'How is Maryanne?' She sounded out of breath as if she had been running but seemingly it was her mother's fault. 'She lost a book she was reading and I've been searching for it since I spoke to you. I've just found it and where was it?'

Grace and Anna shook their heads, not quite in unison but not far from it.

'It was under her seat. She's been sitting on it all the time.' Poor Eliza was exasperated. 'Still, it could have been her new specs which would have been a disaster as the optician has given her a warning to look after them.'

When Anna went inside her house, the room was warm with a blazing fire. Thomas looked up from his paper. 'We're out of cigarettes, love, do you want to run out to the paper shop for more?'

If Anna had had a rolling pin she would have thrown it at him. As she made her way towards the small paper shop she was fuming. A short time ago she was telling Grace what a shame it was that Maryanne had no husband to support her and now she realised the woman was lucky. As she trudged up the Hilltown she muttered under her breath that Maryanne was welcome to her Thomas and jolly good luck to her if she accepted.

10

As it turned out, Eliza didn't get to visit Maryanne even though Grace turned up to look after her mother. Eliza was so upset and annoyed that she was almost crying. 'It's that old besom, she says she wants to come with me but how can she do that when she can hardly walk?'

Grace was bemused, as it was well known that Martha hadn't been able to walk for a few years. Then Martha called out, her voice sounding querulous like a spoiled child, 'Is that you, Grace? I've just told Eliza that I want to come with her.'

Grace went inside the kitchen. 'How will you manage to walk to the infirmary? There's lots of braes and it's quite a long walk.'

Martha was annoyed. 'Don't tell me about the braes and roads in Dundee, I was walking on them long before you were born. I don't mean to walk there.'

Eliza was slowly losing her temper. 'If you don't plan to walk, how are you going to go and see Maryanne? Do you think I'm giving you a piggyback?'

'No I don't, I thought your husband Bill could take us in his van, Grace.' She sat back on her chair with a satisfied look.

It was now Grace's turn to be annoyed by this selfish woman but she had the answer. 'Bill doesn't own the van, Martha, it is the work's van and he doesn't have it tonight as his boss needs it tomorrow.'

'Tomorrow,' said Martha. 'So why can't he have it tonight?'

Grace said he couldn't but this answer wasn't what Martha wanted to hear.

'Well all I can say is that there are some selfish people in this world.'

The pot calling the kettle black, the two women thought, but Eliza said that was the matter settled and now after all this argy-bargy she wouldn't go, so Grace went home. When she got in the house she was fizzing with anger. Bill looked up, surprised to see her back so soon but before he could utter a word, Grace snapped out, 'That awful woman, I don't know how Eliza puts up with her.'

When she told him the story he said, 'I suppose Eliza doesn't have a choice as there's no one else to look after her mother.'

Grace conceded that was the truth. 'All I'm saying is I'm glad it's not me.' Then she remembered her own mother and that perhaps she would have this problem at some time. 'I think I'll go and visit Mum and see how her day out went.' She set off, pleased that it was a pleasant evening. The days would soon be lengthening and spring wasn't that far off. When she got to Ann Street, her mother was sitting listening to the wireless. Like Bill, she looked surprised, then a worried frown crossed her face.

'Is everything all right, Grace?'

'Yes, Mum, it is, I just thought I would pop in and see how your day out went.' For the second time that night she was annoyed. Why did her mum think the only reason she would visit her was if something was wrong?

Evelyn turned the wireless off. 'Oh it was a great day. Elsie's son arrived about ten o'clock and we went to Broughty Ferry where we had tea and scones in a café by the beach then we went on to Arbroath and had a lovely high tea in a posh hotel called the Marine. Then we came home at six o'clock and her son went back to Edinburgh. He's asked us both to come and stay with him in the summer for a few days and we can see the shops and do sightseeing in Edinburgh, isn't that wonderful?'

It certainly was, thought Grace and immediately felt guilty that she hadn't giving her mother a treat like that, but Bill worked really long hours. However, she promised herself she would take her out for the day when the weather was better. Perhaps they could go on a coach trip as there were notices in the local paper that advertised day trips to various places.

She had been twenty-seven when she married Bill and he was eight years older which meant he was often tired after his day's work. Still, she knew Evie was a big help to her granny and that made her feel better.

'I'd better be getting home, Mum, but I'll pop in and see you later.' As she was walking away from the close she saw her mother pulling the curtains and she gave her a wave but Evelyn didn't notice it. It's been quite a day, she thought as she walked quickly up the hill. She hated being piggy in the middle with Martha and Eliza but the fault had been Martha's as she never stopped to consider that people could have other plans that didn't include her, and it was time that Eliza put her foot down with her.

Evie and Tommy were in the house when she got back and they were both laughing at something.

'We don't know what is wrong with Eliza,' said Evie. 'She was standing in the lane muttering to herself when we passed.'

Tommy butted in. 'We asked what the matter was and she just snarled at us and stomped back in the house.'

'Martha was shouting at her,' Evie added.

Grace didn't want to gossip about her neighbours so she just laughed as well, giving Bill a warning look not to say a word.

Later in the week she went to the post office to get an airmail letter to take up to Maryanne so she could write to Sadie and give her the news of her operation. Anna was working during the afternoon so Grace had to go by herself. Maryanne still didn't look too well and she confided that she wasn't eating. 'I really can't face any food, Grace, and the nurses are saying I have to try and eat something.'

'What's the food like?'

'Oh there's nothing wrong with it but I feel sick and eating is the last thing on my mind.' Maryanne looked upset. 'But I know I have to get my strength back as I want to get home soon.'

Grace thought she was better where she was as the weather was still cold and being in the house on her own would be a problem, especially as she was such an independent and private woman who didn't like to broadcast her life to anyone. Grace took the airmail letter from her handbag. 'I've got this for you to write to Sadie but if you want you can tell me what you want to say and I'll write it down and get it posted.'

Maryanne lay back on her pillow. She had a defeated expression which alarmed Grace.

'If you would rather leave it today we can do it some other time.'

'No, better get it over and done with, Grace. Just write and tell her I've had this operation for gallstones but I'm fine and will be home in no time.'

Grace thought she looked anything but fine, but she took the biro pen from her bag and wrote down what Maryanne said. 'Do you want to sign it?' Maryanne took the pen and scribbled her name at the bottom of the letter then laid the pen down on her table with a weary expression. Grace then thought she would cheer the patient up and mentioned the row between Eliza and Martha but, although she smiled, she didn't seem interested. However, as Grace was getting ready to leave, Maryanne took hold of her hand and thanked her. 'You're a good friend to me and I appreciate it. I talked to the almoner as you suggested and she tells me that I will get insurance money every week in the shape of a giro cheque and even though it's not as much as my wage, it will be a big help.'

Grace said she was pleased that this worrying subject had been broached, and with this helpful outcome. This was one thing Maryanne didn't have to fret over and maybe she would recuperate more quickly. As she made her way home, the sun came out and although the wind was cold there was a promise of spring and the days were getting longer. Maryanne forgot to give her Sadie's address but fortunately she saw it on the calendar and she would copy it down later and get the letter posted.

She was passing Bella Duff's house when she came to the door and called her in. 'How is Maryanne?'

Grace said, 'I don't think she's doing as well as I hoped but maybe the next few days will see an improvement.'

Bella went to the sideboard and took out a box of lace-trimmed handkerchiefs and a bottle of 4711 cologne in a blue package. 'I want to give her these small presents as I've never used them.' She then went to the cupboard and brought out a box of Black Magic chocolates. 'Albert handed this in today for her so I said I would give them to you.'

'Oh, what a shame, Bella, I've just come back from seeing her but I'll be going back at the weekend.' She took the presents and added, 'She'll be so pleased by these, Bella, especially the cologne as it's so warm in the ward. She can dab it on and smell nice.'

Bella was wearing a brown skirt today and a brown jumper that looked like cashmere but it was bobbled as if it had been washed too many times. However, Grace thought she looked quite elegant and wondered once more how she had come by the title of 'Granny', especially as she wasn't one. She knew Evie and Tommy always referred to her by this title so maybe it was children from the previous people in the houses in the lane as she knew Bella and Albert were the oldest tenants with Martha and Eliza coming third in the hierarchy of the place.

When she reached her own house she put the chocolates on the highest shelf in the cupboard because if Bill or Evie spotted them they might get eaten. Picking up Maryanne's key from the hook by the door, she went in to look for Sadie's address. The house still felt cold but she had been in and tidied the kitchen up and had made up the fire in the grate. All it needed was a match to light it when the patient got home. Bill had spoken to the coalman and he had put in a couple of bags of coal. If Maryanne wasn't pleased by this show of charity then Grace was going to say it wasn't and that she could pay Grace back at any time.

Sadie's address was also on an envelope that had once held a letter and Grace copied it out, noticing that she lived on a farm with a box number in Nebraska. How Sadie would take the news was anybody's guess, but she had to be told that her mother was ill as she would be worried if she didn't hear from her for some time. Maryanne didn't mention her daughter very much except to say she was doing well in America. Grace had overheard Martha saying she was a selfish girl with no thought for anyone but herself, but Grace didn't believe it. Martha never stopped to consider how hurtful her gossiping could be.

11

Saturday dawned bright and sunny and the cold wind had gone. Tommy skipped into Evie's house and announced, 'It's my birthday tomorrow and I'll be ten.'

Grace and her daughter already knew this as Tommy was in the habit of announcing her forthcoming birthday days in advance. Evie was putting on her coat, ready to go for Granny Duff and the Potters' messages. She rolled her eyes. 'Yes, we know that, Tommy. You've mentioned it every day this week. I think the entire school knows about it.'

Tommy was too excited to notice the sarcasm and she said, 'Yes I know, I hope I get loads of cards from everyone.'

Grace gave her a fond look. 'You must come in tomorrow and we'll celebrate it. I know Evie's granny has made you a cake.'

Tommy's eyes were bright with excitement. 'Oh, that's super.'

When the two girls left, Bill said, 'It must be great to be ten again and full of life.' Grace agreed as she cleared the breakfast table. She thought about getting older and how the joy somehow went out of one's life. She had never been one for make up or fancy creams but she had noticed recently the tiny wrinkles around her eyes and mouth. Maybe I'll treat myself to some face cream, she thought. Tommy's mother had some Pond's cream on her shelf and she looked good for her age. As Grace put the dishes in the hot water she also noticed her hands looked weather-beaten and rough and she sighed. There was no use trying to fight age, so she put the thought out of her head.

When Evie and Tommy knocked on Granny Duff's door, it was barely opened before Tommy mentioned her birthday again.

Bella said, 'That's wonderful, Tommy. When you come back with my groceries I must give you something to celebrate becoming ten.'

Evie gave her friend a nudge. 'Stop it, Tommy. You're practically asking for something for your birthday from everyone.'

Tommy gave her a vague look. 'No I'm not. I'm just telling everybody.'

She gave the same news to the Potters but they didn't mention any gift. Eliza just handed over the list and the money. 'Now make sure you get whole biscuits. Last week some of them were broken.'

The two girls laughed as they set off for the shops. 'Now mind and don't get broken biscuits,' said Tommy, imitating Eliza's voice.

True to her word, when they delivered the groceries, Granny Duff had a small parcel wrapped up in pretty paper. 'Don't open it until tomorrow, Tommy,' she said.

However, Evie got a laugh when they went into the Potters' house. Eliza opened the paper bag and checked all the biscuits to make sure there were none broken. Satisfied that they were all intact, she opened the biscuit barrel and took out three biscuits. 'As it's your birthday, Tommy, I'm giving you an extra Rich Tea.'

Tommy gave her a smile. 'Thank you, Eliza.'

Once outside, Evie thought her friend was going to choke as she was almost doubled up with laughter. 'I'll not eat it today but keep it for tomorrow.'

Grace had made a pot of stovies and the girls sat down. As

usual Evie ate little but Tommy had a second helping along with two oatcakes. If they didn't know the Cassidys they would assume they starved their child, Grace had said to Bill after the girls left for their trip into town to spend their money.

A few days earlier, Evie had decided on her present for Tommy. In a little gift shop in the Murraygate she had noticed a lovely hair slide shaped like a glittering bow. It cost more than her usual shilling, in fact it was half a crown, but Evie decided she would forgo her savings this week. The problem was to get to the gift shop without her friend, but when they were in Woolworths the problem was solved when they met Ann who was in their class at school. Tommy went up to speak to her and Evie said she would meet her at the front door later. Tommy gave her a puzzled glance but when Ann mentioned her birthday she soon forgot about Evie leaving so mysteriously.

The assistant in the gift shop took the slide from the window and put it in a small box. 'Is it a gift?' she asked and when Evie nodded she added, 'Would you like me to wrap it?'

'Yes please, my friend will love it.'

The woman wrapped it in pink crepe paper and tied a silver ribbon around it. Evie had planned to give it to Tommy in a paper bag but now it looked really wonderful and expensive and she was pleased. Later when they met up, Tommy asked her where she had been. Evie said she had to get something for her mother so Tommy took this as a fact and said no more.

They were entering the lane when a large removal van drew up and the driver rolled down his window. 'I'm looking for number seven Meadow Lane. Is this it?'

Evie said it was and they stood to one side as he jumped down from the driving seat along with another young lad. They went to the back and opened the doors, revealing a load of furniture. A small plump woman appeared and spoke to them and the men began to unload the van.

The woman smiled at the two girls and said, 'Hullo, I'm

Morag and this is Rory,' and she turned to a tall slim man who appeared at her side. 'We're moving into number seven and it's nice to meet you.
Do you live here?'

Tommy said they did. 'I'm Thomasina but get called Tommy and this is my pal Evelyn who gets called Evie. We live at the other end of the lane. My mum and dad are called Anna and Thomas Cassidy and Evie's mum and dad are called Grace and Bill Gow.'

Evie waited with bated breath in case she also mentioned her birthday but thankfully she didn't, mainly because, at that moment, Eliza appeared as if she was going out to the shops. Tommy opened her mouth to do the introductions but Eliza was too quick for her.

'Hello, are you our new neighbours? Albert next door to us told us you were moving in soon. I'm Eliza and I live with my mother Martha who will be pleased to meet you soon. She's housebound so she can't come out to say hello.' All the time Eliza was chattering she was watching all the furniture being carried into the empty house. Although she had pretended to be out to do her shopping, the truth was she had been sweeping her front doorstep when she spotted the van and had overheard Tommy. Hurrying inside she had told her mother about the new arrivals.

'Go outside, Eliza, and tell me all about their furniture and belongings. Mind and ask them to call on me when they've got settled.'

Morag and Rory excused themselves as they said they had to help the removal men. 'I want to make sure they put everything where I want it to be,' said Morag with a smile. 'It's lovely meeting you all and we hope to see more of you soon.'

They disappeared into the house and Eliza retreated back to her front door, forgetting in her hurry to mention that she was supposed to be going out. As she passed the window, she glanced inside and the young couple waved. Eliza made some hand motions to convey she had forgotten something but the couple began to talk to the young removal lad and Eliza had the grace to blush.

While all this was going on, Evie and Tommy stood watching Eliza's charade and they started to laugh as they made their way along the lane.

Meanwhile Martha was eagerly awaiting her daughter to come and tell her all the news. 'Your face is all red, Eliza, what's the matter?'

'I pretended to be going to the shops but they saw me heading back here. They'll be thinking I'm some nosey parker.'

Martha wasn't interested in what they thought. 'Well, what kind of furniture do they have, is it all new or old fashioned like ours?'

'No, it all looks brand new and it's that new contemporary style like we saw in that advert in the paper. It's all light wood and not heavy looking like ours.'

Martha lay back on her chair. 'Our furniture isn't heavy looking, it's just well made to last a lifetime.'

Quite so, thought Eliza, although I quite fancy that new style instead of the dark wooden chairs, table and sideboard which took an age to polish, especially the fancy scrolls on the chair legs and sideboard doors.

Martha said, 'I like it when there's a bit of excitement in the lane because nothing ever happens here.'

12

On Sunday morning, Tommy rushed in to see Evie wearing a new dress and shoes.

'A happy birthday, Tommy,' said Grace as she cleared the breakfast table.

Tommy did a twirl in her new frock. 'This is my present from Mum and Dad, isn't it lovely?' Evie said the dress was indeed lovely. It was a cotton floral frock with a full skirt and a white net underskirt, more appropriate for summer than March but it suited Tommy with her dark hair. Evie handed over her card and crepe paper wrapped present and Tommy's eyes widened in surprise at the package with its silver ribbon. 'Oh, Evie, what a super present.'

Evie said she hoped she liked it but Tommy seemed engrossed in the wrapping. 'Do you mind if I don't open it as I want Mum and Dad to see it.' She rushed out again.

'That girl is like a whirlwind,' said Bill, laughing.

Grace wanted to know, 'Is she having a party, Evie?'

'No, Mum, but Anna said we were to go in later in the afternoon.'

'I'm going to see Maryanne this afternoon but I'll pop in afterwards and give her my present and card. I got her a box of chocolates so I hope she likes them,' said Grace, stacking the dishes by the kitchen sink. 'I thought with the appetite she always has she would like sweets.' Evie said she would.

The door opened and Tommy reappeared, wearing her everyday clothes of a skirt and jumper. 'Mum said I've got to keep my dress for this afternoon.'

Grace said she wanted to see Anna so she left the girls playing a game while Bill settled down by the fire. He loved Sundays as it was good to have a day off work, especially in the winter and spring with all the frozen pipes.

Anna and Thomas were finishing their breakfast and Grace sat down with a cup of tea. 'I'm going to see Maryanne this afternoon, Anna, as I got a couple of presents from Bella and Albert. Also a letter came from Sadie yesterday so I'll take it up as well.'

'I can't manage, Grace, as I've said I would put on a wee party for Tommy. It's just you, Bill and Evie plus your mother as she came in the shop yesterday and said she had promised to make a cake for Tommy and she'll bring it with her.'

After Grace left, Anna tidied up the kitchen, made some cheese and Branston pickle bridge rolls and placed beside them a selection of cakes she had bought from the bakery. Thomas watched all this. 'Can we afford all this, Anna?'

Anna gave him an exasperated look. 'I got the rolls and cakes at a cut price because they weren't sold as we were closing for the day and I bought the dress and shoes from McGills store and the agent will call every Friday night to collect a weekly payment.'

Thomas nodded. 'It's just that you are always saying we're hard up.'

'I've been working extra hours, Thomas, but I don't expect you've noticed. I'm thinking of asking for a full-time job as Tommy always goes in with Evie after school and I don't think Grace will mind.'

'Well, maybe you should ask her first,' he said.

Later, Grace made her way to the infirmary for the afternoon visiting hour. Maryanne's ward lay up a couple of flights of stairs and along a corridor. She was slightly out of breath when she reached the bed and once again her heart sank when she saw the patient who didn't look much better than the last time she had seen her. However, she put on a bright smile.

'Hullo, Maryanne, how are feeling today?'

Maryanne turned her weary looking face and said she didn't feel any better.

'Are you managing to eat?'

Maryanne shook her head. 'No, not much. It's just that I still feel so sore and I'm even frightened to cough in case I burst my stitches.'

Grace was sympathetic. 'Just give it time, Maryanne.' She held out the box of chocolates and the two presents from Bella. 'Here's something to cheer you up.' She thought Maryanne was about to cry as she opened the gifts.

'Everyone is so kind. I'm really lucky to have such good friends.'

Grace took the bottle of cologne and opened it. 'I'll dab some on your forehead and that'll make you feel better.' Maryanne lay back on her pillows and let Grace sprinkle some on her handkerchief. The aroma did seem to perk her up until Grace handed over the letter from Sadie. 'This came yesterday and I posted your letter to her but I don't expect she got it before this arrived.'

Maryanne took the letter and put it on her locker. 'I'll read it later, Grace.'

Grace stood up. 'I better get off as it's Tommy's tenth birthday today and we've been invited to her party this afternoon.'

Maryanne struggled to sit up. 'Thanks for coming and give Tommy my good wishes.'

By the time Grace arrived home, Bill, Evie and her granny were all in the Cassidys' house. The table had a white cloth on it and in the centre was an iced sponge cake with ten candles which Evelyn had baked. Tommy was wearing her new dress and shoes and everyone clapped when she blew out all the candles with one blow. She was as high as a kite as she opened all her cards and gifts. When it came to Evie's present she carefully removed the paper and ribbon, saying she was going to keep them in her drawer. When she took out the sparkly hair slide she gave a whoop of delight. 'I've been looking at this in the window every week, oh thank you so much, Evie.' She clipped it onto her hair and it did look lovely. She went to the mirror above the fireplace and twisted her head back and forth to catch the gleam from the slide. She went back to Evie and hugged her. 'Thank you so much, I just love it and I'm going to wear it for ever. It must have been dear and I hope you didn't spend all your money on it.'

Evie was pleased by her reaction to the present but she merely shrugged. 'No, it was worth it as I knew you would like it.'

'Oh I do, I do.'

Everyone laughed. Then the bridge rolls were handed round and Anna cut the birthday cake and they all said how tasty it was, much to Evelyn's delight. 'I did say away back in January that I would make a cake for you, do you remember, Tommy?'

'Yes I do but I thought you would forget.'

Evelyn said nothing but her expression said it all: *as if I would go back on a promise.*

Anna put two slices of cake on a plate. 'Take this along to Granny Duff and Albert, Tommy. Mind and thank them for the lovely scarf and the card that Albert sent.'

Tommy had put on her scarf. It was a soft shade of blue and made of chiffon that floated behind her.

Evie stood up as well and they went along the lane carrying the cake like it was the crown jewels.

After they left, the conversation turned to the new neighbours. Anna asked if Grace had met them but she shook her head. 'Evie and Tommy were speaking to them at the removal van yesterday and Tommy was saying Eliza appeared just to nosey around.'

Thomas said he believed they came from the Western Isles

to work in Dundee. Anna, who had been chatting to Albert who seemed to know more about them than anyone in the lane, said, 'They come from Skye and the husband Rory is joining his brother who has a joiner's business. Morag, his wife, is expecting a baby in a few weeks so it'll be nice to have a young family in old Mrs Prior's house.' She turned to Grace. 'How is Maryanne, is she getting better?'

Grace shook her head. 'I wish I could say she is but I don't think so. She isn't eating and she says her stitches are still sore. Still, I delivered a letter from Sadie so that should cheer her up.'

After Tommy and Evie took the cake to Granny Duff and Albert, they met Rory and Morag standing at their doorstep. They were speaking in a foreign language and the girls couldn't wait to get back home to impart this new knowledge. Tommy was first to blurt out, 'Mum, the new couple are foreign and Evie says they are Germans.'

Bill, who hadn't said much during the tea party, laughed. 'They're not from Germany,' he said. 'They will be speaking Gaelic.'

The two girls looked puzzled. 'Gaelic?' said Evie. 'I thought it sounded German.'

Anna said, 'No it isn't, they come from Skye where they talk like that. It's an old Scottish language.'

On that note, the party broke up and the Gows and Evelyn Williams went back home. It had been a great afternoon but now it was time to finish the chores that Grace did in preparation for school the next day while Bill settled back as usual with his Sunday paper until his wife reminded him to walk her mother home as it was getting dark. He stood up but didn't look happy while Evelyn put on her coat and fussed around with her handbag, scarf and hat.

Grace said to him, 'I hope Sadie's letter cheers her mother up.' Bill muttered something which she didn't catch but Evie smiled. She had heard him mutter that her mother didn't cheer him up. Poor Granny, she thought.

It was coming up to bedtime in the ward and Maryanne finally opened the letter. As usual it was full of woe as Sadie wrote of how unhappy she was. Far from cheering her mother up, it made her even more depressed as she lay back on her pillow and tried to sleep. At least when she was sleeping she didn't worry so much as she did when she was awake.

13

Albert left the house with his waterproof raincoat. The sun was shining but the weather forecast on the wireless had said blustery showers were on the horizon and he didn't want to get soaked.

He made his way to the shops then on to the Windmill Bar for his daily pint of beer. Thomas was cleaning the counter and there were only a couple of customers sitting at a table: two elderly men like himself who had time on their hands and were probably lonely sitting in their houses. He nodded in their direction before heading to the stool by the bar. Thomas had his pint all poured and Albert fished about in his leather purse for the money.

'How did Tommy's party go, Hopalong?' he said, taking a large swallow of beer.

Thomas shrugged. 'It was fine, Albert. Mind you it's more of a woman's thing with all the planning and food, but Tommy loved it.'

Albert was taken aback by this lacklustre view of the party as he was usually more chatty about his family. 'Is everything all right?'

Thomas glanced at the other two customers. They were engrossed in playing dominoes but he lowered his voice. 'As a matter of fact I'm not, Albert. I'm getting tired of working here every morning and night and I would like a better paid job. The problem is getting one, as some days my leg is so sore it's hard to stand on it. Mind now and don't mention this to Anna.'

Albert was a bit annoyed by this as he wasn't one for gossiping and there was no way he would mention anything to Anna in the bakery. Still, maybe Hopalong didn't realise this so he said, 'Certainly not, I wouldn't dream of it. But I do hope you manage to get something else as I remember you told me you used to earn good money when you were on the roads and the hydro schemes.'

Thomas said, 'Yes, those were the days and I wish I still worked there. There was always great banter on the schemes as there were loads of Irish workmen there.'

'Do you miss Ireland?' asked Albert.

Thomas laughed. 'Lord, no I don't. I left when I was fifteen and came here to work. It was when I went back for my mother's funeral that I met Anna and the rest is history.'

By now, Albert's glass was empty so he stood up to go. 'Well I wish you all the best then.' Albert walked slowly home under a sunny sky that didn't have a hint of blustery showers but he thought it was better to be safe than sorry. He decided to give the bakery a miss as he felt sorry for the Cassidys and he didn't want to face Anna, not that he would have said anything about her husband's confession but his face sometimes gave his thoughts away.

Anyway, it was his day for going in to see Bella and he didn't want to be late. She was waiting for him and he was glad to take off his coat. Bella gave him a quizzical glance as he hung it on the hook. He noticed this and explained about the weather forecast but she laughed and said, 'You don't want to take notice of weather forecasts as they're never right.'

She brought over the tray with the two glasses and the bottle of sherry, handing one to Albert who felt that another drink, especially sherry, was a drink too many. If it had been another beer then he would have enjoyed it but Bella wouldn't think of keeping beer in her cupboard. However he dutifully sipped it as he didn't want to hurt her.

Bella and her late fiancé were old friends of Albert's and he remembered when she moved to this house. It had been intended that she would live here with Davie when they got married but afterwards, after the tragic news of his death, her mother had moved in with her. Like him, she now lived alone.

Albert didn't like to think about the war but he knew Bella liked to reminisce and she sometimes brought out the old photo album which showed a world far removed from the present day.

'I've always liked this one of Davie and me, it was taken at the beach at Carnoustie.' She handed over a faded snap of a young couple sitting on a bench and holding hands. 'We asked an old man to take it.'

Albert hadn't seen this particular photo which showed Bella looking carefree and happy in a summer frock and Davie, tall and good looking in a short sleeved shirt and cotton trousers. Little did they know then that their world was going to collapse the following year at the Battle of Loos.

'If it hadn't been for that dreadful war then Davie and I would have been together,' she said softly.

Albert agreed with her. 'I never like to think too much about that time, Bella. Jean used to chastise me for not talking about it but I couldn't. When I think of the futile deaths of young men like us I could cry. I was one of the lucky ones who came home but thousands didn't.'

Bella closed the album and put it back in the sideboard. Albert said, 'Try to put it all behind you, Bella, as it's almost forty years ago. I often wish you had some sort of social life instead of being cooped up in here with your memories. I've had an idea: why don't we go out on a day trip on a coach when the weather gets better? It'll do us both the world of good.'

Bella smiled. 'I'll look forward to that, Albert, and thank you for asking.' She lifted the decanter of sherry. 'Let's celebrate our forthcoming day out with another glass.'

'Actually, Bella, I'd rather have a cup of tea.'

She rose from her chair and filled the kettle at the sink. 'Right then, tea it is.'

Before he left she asked him, 'How are your new neighbours settling in?'

'They're a lovely couple, Morag and Rory, then of course a new baby will be living next door in a few weeks. I don't know what they are doing to the house but his brother was there yesterday and there was lots of hammering and banging going on. The brother has his own joiner's business and Rory will be going to work for him.'

'Well I must say it's nice to have young people in the lane again,' Bella admitted.

Albert chuckled and she asked him what was so funny.

'It's Eliza, she walks past the house on numerous occasions as if she's keeping her eye on them. The poor fool thinks no one notices her but I'm sure they do and they must wonder what kind of people live near them.'

Bella laughed. 'I bet Martha is almost bursting to know all about them and poor Eliza has to do her dirty work and go out spying. Grace was telling me that Evie and Tommy met them on Saturday when they were flitting and Eliza had this funny charade of poking her nose in but pretending she was merely a passerby.'

Later, when Albert stood up to leave, a sudden squally burst of rain rattled against the window. 'I knew the forecast was right, Bella, the rain has come on like they said.'

Bella was putting more coal on the fire and she smiled. 'So it seems the forecast was right.'

At bedtime, Albert hoped all this talk of the war wouldn't bring on his horrific nightmare. For years he had tried to put that episode in his life to the back of his mind; sometimes it worked and sometimes it didn't. His subconscious mind had the nasty habit of reliving the past and now and again after the nightmare he had a bad feeling for most of the next day. Before going to sleep, he decided to concentrate on the new folk next door who had their whole life in front of them with their baby. He remembered Jean's anguish at not having a child and the slow realisation as the years passed that there would be no children in the marriage. Then, without warning, the thought came unbidden to his mind about the scene with her mother. After five years of no babies, she had marched in one day and accused him of being at fault. 'You must have been injured in the war, Albert, that's why my daughter can't have any children.' He had looked at Jean but she said nothing which meant she thought the same. He almost said it could also be Jean's fault but he didn't want to hurt his wife. He told himself it wasn't the lack of courage that held his tongue. After all, he had been brave enough during the war.

14

Eliza saw the sun the moment she pulled back the curtains and she decided she would go to the shop for fresh bread. Her mother was still sleeping and she hesitated, wondering whether she should nip out or wait till the old woman wakened up. She was slipping on her coat when the decision was taken out of her hands as Martha opened her eyes and tried to sit up in bed. 'Where are you going?' She sounded disgruntled and Eliza saw her trip to the shop being stopped.

'I thought I'd go and get some fresh bread as this loaf is a bit stale.'

To her surprise her mother said this was a great idea. 'I'll stay in bed until you get back, just pass me my specs and my library book. You can go to the paper shop and get my *People's Friend* and the *Weekly News*.'

After Martha was settled, Eliza escaped out the door. It was a lovely morning, sunny and mild, the kind of day that sometimes comes at the end of March, and she enjoyed the warmth on her head. She hated the bad weather as it meant she was cooped up in the house with her mother and some days she felt she would scream with boredom and frustration, but on a day like this she felt the stresses of her life ebbing away.

She wanted to go past Morag and Rory's house as she would love a chat with them but it meant passing Albert's door and she knew he thought she was a nosey busybody so she went towards the Hilltown end of the lane and down to the bakery.

There was no sign of Anna but Mrs Bell was serving a small queue at the counter. When it was her turn to be served, the woman said, 'How nice to see you, Eliza, I haven't seen you for a while.'

Eliza said she had been getting her messages from Tommy and Evie due to the cold, wet and snowy weather.

Mrs Bell said it was great to see the end of winter but said, 'I hope today isn't a flash in the pan as I often think March and April can be changeable.' She put the loaf into a paper bag. 'How is Martha, is she keeping well?'

Eliza said she was fine. 'Mind you, it doesn't stop her complaining.'

Mrs Bell laughed. 'I see she hasn't changed then. I've known her for years and she's always been like that.'

Eliza smiled and said nothing as she left the shop, but her mood felt heavy and the earlier feeling of wellbeing was gone. She was passing the Gows' house when Grace opened the door.

'Hullo Eliza, you're out early today.'

Eliza stopped and held up the bag. 'I thought I would go to the bakery as it's such a lovely morning.'

Grace said, 'Come in for a moment and I'll give you some scones as well for your mother.'

For the second time that morning, Eliza hesitated. She wasn't sure about leaving her mum alone for much longer but she then made up her mind and went inside. Bill had already left for work and Evie was getting ready to go to school with Tommy.

Grace put four scones on a plate and covered them with a cloth. 'I'm having another cup of tea, Eliza, do you want one?'

Eliza heard herself say she would and she sat down at the table which still held the breakfast dishes.

'How is Martha?'

'I've left her in bed with her library book so I can't stay too long, Grace. I just felt I wanted a bit of space to myself but I expect I'll get an earful when I get in.'

Grace made a sympathetic noise. Eliza looked flustered. 'Oh, don't get me wrong, I love my mum but sometimes it gets a bit much for me and I feel like running away.' She stopped and gave Grace a stricken glance. 'Not that I would do that. I mean, who would look after her if she didn't have me?'

Grace listened but said nothing. Eliza stood up. 'I better get back but thanks for the scones, Mum will love them.'

'I hope you have a couple of them for yourself and don't let her eat them all.'

Eliza said she would. 'I've been trying to cut down on her eating as she is putting on more weight. I only put one spoon of sugar in her tea instead of her usual three and I've tried to make her portions of food smaller.' She gave a big sigh. 'Not that it works because she always asks for seconds.' She turned round when she reached the door and said, 'How is Maryanne?'

'She's out of hospital but has been sent to a convalescent home at Auchterhouse. I think it used to be a cottage hospital but now it's used to let patients who have had surgery recover before being sent home. I'm going to see her this week, I get the bus at Courthouse Square, so I'll give you any news after I see her.'

Eliza said to tell her that they were both thinking of her and hoped to see her soon.

After Eliza had left, Martha got up with some difficulty and made herself a cup of tea, adding four spoons of sugar. She knew Eliza had cut down on her sugar but unknown to her, she had ways of sabotaging this. It was the same with the chocolate biscuits which they sometimes bought. Eliza kept them in a tin on the top shelf of the cupboard but Martha reached up and pulled three chocolate wafers from the tin. After she finished her snack she hurried back to bed and propped the library book up. She had no intention of reading it as it was a totally boring book. She would have a word with her daughter about the books she brought back from the library. Glancing at the clock she wondered where Eliza had got to as it had been almost an hour. That would be another thing to bring up. This thought gave her some satisfaction. After all, what pleasures were left to her now? She had to make some mischief to brighten up her day.

Eliza hurried in and put the bread and scones down. 'I met Grace and she gave me a couple of scones for you,' she said as she put the kettle on to make breakfast.

'I thought you were taking a long time to get one little loaf of bread and a couple of papers.'

Eliza gave a gasp. 'I'm sorry, Mum, but I forgot to go to the paper shop.'

Martha's mouth was agape with astonishment. 'How can you forget to get my papers when I mentioned them before you left?'

Suddenly Eliza felt emboldened. 'Well I did.' Martha's eyes opened wide but Eliza went on, 'I'll go for them later or if I don't manage I'll ask Evie when she comes back from school.'

Martha's annoyance was growing. 'After school, that's ages away and I've nothing to read.'

'You've got your library book.' Eliza placed a plate of scrambled eggs and toast and a buttered scone in front of her mother.

Martha wanted to carry on this argument but the sight of food made her think again. There would be time later to continue this row.

Later that morning, the opportunity arose to resume her grievances. 'I don't understand how you could forget my papers.'

Eliza, who was trying to do some housework, groaned. 'I said I'd get them later.'

Martha, however, was like a fractious toddler. 'I'd like them now as I don't like this library book. You always get boring books for me from the library.'

This was news to Eliza, who brought back the crime club

thrillers that her mother asked for, but as she knew from past rows, there was no arguing with her when she was in this frame of mind. Grabbing her coat from the hook, she said, 'All right, I'll go and get them now but then I want some peace and quiet to get on with the housework.' She marched out of the door and hesitated. She didn't want to go past Grace's house again as she couldn't stand the sympathy from her. She made for the Caldrum Street end of the lane and decided to get the papers from the newsagent's in Ann Street. As she was passing the MacCallum's house, she almost collided with Morag who was coming out her door backwards with a sweeping brush. She turned and smiled when she saw Eliza.

'Hullo, I'm sorry I almost knocked you over.' She was dressed in a blue cotton smock that covered her bump. 'I'm trying to get the house in order before the baby comes and Rory and his brother are bringing round the new curtains,' she said, smoothing a strand of hair that escaped from the rest which was tied back in a ponytail.

Eliza thought this was a very fashionable hairstyle but she asked, 'How is the work coming along in the house?'

'Oh, we were lucky. Murdo, Rory's brother, did a lot of work over the weekend and we're almost finished.'

Eliza said that was good, especially as the baby would soon be born.

Morag placed a hand over her stomach. 'To be truthful I'll be glad when it's over as I feel so huge. It'll be great when I can see my feet again.'

Eliza laughed, and thought how great it would be if her mother could ever see her feet again. She was ready to pass on when a small white van came along the lane. It was emblazoned with the owner's name, MacCallum Joinery. Morag gave the occupants a wave. 'That'll be the new curtains. Rory and Murdo were picking them up from Smith and Horner's shop on the Hilltown.'

The two men got out of the van and Eliza gave a gasp when

she noticed Morag's brother-in-law. He didn't resemble his brother as he looked older and had a stockier build. Fortunately Morag didn't hear her intake of breath and she greeted the two men with a smile. They were carrying a large brown paper parcel and they greeted Eliza as they passed by.

She was flustered. 'I must be off but it's nice meeting you.' She was at the paper shop before she calmed down. Mrs Jennings asked after Martha, and Eliza answered without thinking, 'She's fine but waiting to read her magazine and paper.' As she made her way home she couldn't get over the sight of Murdo MacCallum as he looked so like Michael. Of course Michael would be much older now, the same age as herself, but the last time she saw him he had resembled Murdo. She remembered that last meeting and how wrong everything had gone. How she wished she could relive that moment and how different her life might have been. Passing Morag's house she was dismayed to see that the van had gone but the new curtains were in the window and they were lovely. Pale cream with a small blue pattern and a cream lining, they looked expensive and bright. Not like their own curtains which were a deep wine velvet that made the room look like a cave.

Martha started to complain the minute she opened the door but Eliza merely put the papers in her hands and went to finish the housework. Her mother looked at her in amazement. 'What's wrong with you?'

Eliza had no intention of mentioning anything but to her surprise she heard herself saying, 'I met Morag MacCallum and her husband and his brother.'

'So that's why you're so grumpy.'

Eliza was angry. 'Grumpy, am I? Well, I'll tell you why. Murdo MacCallum looks so like Michael that I'm shocked.'

Martha snorted. 'Oh, him. Well, all I can say is you were well rid of him.'

Eliza turned away. Her eyes had filled with tears, but she was determined not to let her mother see them.

15

Maryanne was sitting in the patients' lounge at Auchterhouse in a chair by the window. The sun was shining and the grounds outside looked inviting but she didn't want to go outside as she thought the breeze still held a trace of winter.

She noticed Ina and Betty from her ward, who were sitting on a bench. Both women were smoking but as she had never been a smoker she didn't have the urge to join them. Her pain had settled down and she was feeling much stronger now and she hoped she wouldn't have to stay here much longer. Not that she disliked the place as everyone was so kind and helpful, but she longed to get back to her own house.

The surgeon had said she wouldn't be able to go back to work for a few more weeks so she reckoned she would be just as comfortable at home. Strangely enough there had been no more letters from Sadie, for which she was grateful, but on the other hand she was worried something was maybe wrong.

The nurse came in to say that dinner was ready. Maryanne met Ina and Betty as they came through the door and they all went into the dining room. Maryanne could smell the smoke from the two women and she was glad she had never developed the habit.

They sat together and the assistant brought in bowls of lentil soup. These meals were the one thing Maryanne enjoyed about the home, as the food was all cooked in the kitchen and not carried in from a distance.

Ina asked her if she was expecting any visitors that afternoon and she replied that her neighbour, Grace, was coming. Betty and Ina weren't expecting visitors so they said they would go and sit out in the sun after the meal.

In the afternoon, Grace appeared with her message bag from which she pulled several magazines and a couple of packets of Ginger Nuts. 'I thought you might like something to read and Bella sends the biscuits for your afternoon cup of tea.'

Maryanne asked her, 'Thanks for the papers and thank Bella for thinking of me, everyone has been so good to me.' She placed the magazines and biscuits on a table. 'Are there any letters, Grace?'

Grace leaned forward and took her hand. 'You deserve it, Maryanne, but no, there's no letters yet. Now tell me, is there any word of getting home?'

Maryanne shook her head. 'I hope it won't be long and I'm hoping it'll be before next week.'

Grace was undecided if she should bring up the subject of Sadie's silence, but before she could make up her mind whether to speak or not, Maryanne said, 'I don't know why Sadie hasn't written. After all I did write and tell her about my operation so you would think she could answer.'

'I did post your letter and I copied the address from the one in your house.'

'I know you did, Grace. Maybe she's busy on the farm as I know there are periods when everyone has to muck in.'

Grace said that was obviously the answer but later, as she travelled back in the small bus, she did wonder about it and hoped it wasn't bad news or that Sadie was also ill.

Because she was worried, she popped into Maryanne's house to see if the postman had delivered a letter but there was nothing lying on the mat. She had tidied up the house after Maryanne was taken away but now she noticed how grubby the window looked with the sunlight shining through it.

Fetching a bucket of hot soapy water from her own kitchen she tackled the grubby panes and was pleased when the glass was gleaming and the entire room looked better with the clean window. She looked at the clock on the mantelpiece and saw that it was almost four o'clock. Evie and Tommy would soon be home so she emptied the dirty water down the sink and locked the door on her way out.

Anna had asked her if it was all right if Tommy stayed with them till she got home, as she had asked for extra hours and was now working full-time in the shop, which Grace didn't mind. After all, she thought, Tommy spent lots of time with Evie after school so it was no hardship. She suspected that money was tight in the Cassidy household so the extra hours would help with the bills.

At four-fifteen, the two girls rushed in and Evie made straight for the cake tin, taking one for herself and one for Tommy. Grace didn't mind but she still chastised her daughter. 'You won't be able to eat your tea if you stuff yourself with cake, Evie.'

Evie, with her mouth full of crumbs, said that she and Tommy were hungry, but Grace thought it was more likely that it was Tommy who needed this snack.

Anna arrived at five-thirty and Grace told her the news from the afternoon at Auchterhouse. 'Maryanne is looking much better and is hoping to get home next week.' She lowered her voice so the girls wouldn't hear. 'There's still no letter from Sadie and I know she's worried, Anna. I think I'll drop her a letter myself and see what's going on.'

Anna looked doubtful. 'Do you think you should? You know how Maryanne likes to keep her life private.' Grace said she would think about it while Anna left to wash up after Thomas's evening meal. 'I leave something for him to eat before he goes off to work but he doesn't think about doing the dishes,' she moaned as she set off next door.

Grace was laying the table for their meal when Bill arrived. She looked at the clock. 'You're a bit early, Bill,' she said. 'The tea isn't ready yet.'

Bill had a strange expression on his face, like he had a secret and was bursting to tell her. He handed over a small paper brochure while she had a questioning look.

'I've bought a television set,' he said. 'It's in the leaflet.'

She sat down with the brochure in her hand and flicked it open. It showed various models of televisions and radios. One set was marked with a cross. Grace was speechless as Bill never did anything without discussing it with her. In fact he had no idea about the running of the house or the paying of the bills as she had always dealt with everything. He handed over his wage packet every Saturday morning and if he needed money for anything he just asked for it.

'How are we going to pay for it, Bill?'

He smiled. 'That's no problem, Grace. I got a bonus at work and I've been thinking about having a television to watch at night. Evie will love it.'

'Let's just think about it,' she said but he beamed at her.

'It's being delivered this week and the television aerial is being installed tomorrow morning.'

Grace was in two minds about this expense as she would have liked to have saved it in the post office savings account but now that it was a *fait accompli* she had to accept this newfangled machine. Of course when Evie heard the news she was delighted and she ran in to tell Tommy the good news.

'We can watch the children's programmes after school,' said Tommy who was as delighted as her friend.

The next morning, the electrician appeared with a ladder and was soon on the roof installing the aeriel that had a black cable running down the front of the house and through the kitchen window. 'That's it all set up for the television set, Mrs

Gow,' he said, getting her signature on a sheet of paper. 'I think your set is coming tomorrow.'

Grace went outside and what looked like a giant 'H' was fixed to her chimney. Albert happened to be passing and he gazed upwards as well.

'Bill's bought a television, Albert,' she said.

Albert was impressed. 'It'll be such a change from the wireless. I saw some of the Queen's coronation on one in 1953 and it's like going to the pictures.'

Grace wasn't impressed. She enjoyed her night at the pictures as she liked to pick and choose which films to see in one of Dundee's many picture houses whereas with this box in her kitchen she would have to view whatever was beamed to the aerial. However it looked like she had no choice and if it pleased Bill and Evie then she was happy to sit and gaze at the television screen.

The next morning a van arrived with the television and the electrician who delivered it put it on the table that Bill had placed by the fireplace and began to attach the cable to the set. 'I hope you get a good signal here,' he said as he fiddled with the back which had a socket to take the cable. Suddenly a black and white image appeared and Grace sat down to watch it. The man then said it was all sorted out. 'Happy viewing,' he said with a smile as he departed to his van.

Someone knocked on the door. It was Eliza. She was all flustered as if she had run along the lane twenty times. 'We've heard you've got a television, Grace.' She was mesmerised by the picture. 'How does that picture manage to come from that thing on your roof and into that box?'

Grace sighed. 'I've no idea, Eliza, you had better ask Bill as he was the one who bought it.'

'Mum was just saying she would like to see some of the programmes,' said Eliza hopefully.

'I thought Martha wasn't able to walk any further than the front door.' Grace suddenly visualised the future with Martha,

Eliza and Uncle Tom Cobley and all squeezing into the kitchen to watch it.

Eliza said that was true. 'We only manage to sit out on the doorstep in the summer in our Lloyd Loom chairs so I can't see her toddling along. It would be nice if we lived next door to you but we don't.'

Thank the Lord for that, Grace said silently.

By the time Bill came home in the evening, the residents of the lane had all heard about the new acquisition in the Gow household. In fact Anna had said to her husband that she would also like one but Thomas said he thought they were very expensive. 'I was talking to Mrs Bell in the shop and she said you can buy one for a deposit and pay it up weekly. There are a few shops that sell them and quite a lot of people own one,' Anna said but Thomas wasn't listening. This was something he did all the time when he didn't want to get into a row about smoking the last cigarette or buying a television.

While this conversation was going on, Eliza was in Bella Duff's house telling her all about it. 'Mum was just saying how she's always wanted one as well but I've told her we can't afford one.'

Bella was amused by all this chatter which had certainly set the lane alight. It was just a pity that Maryanne wasn't here to join in with all the gossip. Nonetheless she was relieved when Eliza said she had to go.

Eliza was almost at her house when she spotted Morag walking along the lane with a small bag of messages. 'Have you heard that the Gows have bought a television?'

Morag said she hadn't but added, 'We don't have one but Murdo does. He says there's not much entertainment on it although he likes *What's My Line?* on a Sunday night. He thinks Gilbert Harding who is on the panel is very rude but he gets away with it.'

This was all news to Eliza who didn't know one programme

from another but she nodded wisely. 'Mum and I much prefer the wireless.'

Morag said, 'Would you like to come and see what we've done to the house?'

Eliza could hardly contain her excitement and she followed Morag into the house. Inside was all pale walls and light coloured furniture and the curtains that she had glimpsed were even lovelier when viewed from inside. There was a strange looking chair by the fireside that looked like it was made from wicker and was a strange shape. Morag saw her looking at it. 'We got that chair from Rory's grandparents who live on Orkney. That is a common chair there.'

'It looks really comfortable,' said Eliza diplomatically.

Morag laughed. 'Yes, it will be when I get my figure back after the baby is born. I don't think I would like to sit in it just now in case I get stuck.'

Eliza debated about telling her about Murdo's resemblance to Michael. Plucking up her courage she said, 'Your brother-in-law looks so much like someone I used to know, his name was Michael.'

Morag looked interested. 'That's a coincidence, isn't it? Is he someone you were fond of?'

Eliza said she was once engaged to be married to him but it hadn't worked out and now she didn't know where he was. Morag thought this was so sad and she said so. 'Maybe one day you'll meet up with him again.' Eliza thought it unlikely but said nothing.

Back in her own house she told her mother about the television and the super interior of Morag's house. 'That's what we need to do here. Get those dark curtains down and get light coloured wallpaper to brighten up the room,' she said.

Martha looked at her with alarm. 'Where is all the money coming from for all this?' Eliza said she could use some of the money her mother kept under the bed. 'Use my money for doing up a room when it's perfectly good? No, I'm saving up for a television to keep me amused.'

Never mind making me amused, thought Eliza.

'What other news is going around?' Martha asked. Eliza thought of how she spoke about Michael to Morag but she had no intention of telling her mother that. She looked at Martha with wide eyed innocence. 'No, nothing else.'

16

Grace arrived home from the shops on Saturday afternoon in a bad mood. Bill was sitting watching the television. Evie and Tommy had hesitated about staying in with him but the lure of Woolworths proved too strong and they had set off to spend their pocket money. Evie was pleased to see that Tommy was wearing her new hair slide and she thought it suited her as she had a strong head of curly hair that gripped the slide firmly. In her case, with her fine silky hair, the slide would have lived up to its name and slid downwards.

Grace put her bag down on the table with a thump. 'Honestly, Bill, I'm fed up to here.' She pointed to a space under her chin.

Bill, who liked to have a life free from tantrums and most of life's cares, said, 'What's the matter?'

Grace was unpacking her groceries and putting them away in the cupboard. 'What's the matter? I'll tell you, shall I? About twenty people in the shops all commented on the fact we've got a television. In fact old Mrs Burton said it was easy to see where we got the money for it because of the plumber's bill she got last month.'

Bill annoyed his wife by bursting out laughing. 'Tell the old besom to mind her own business. I didn't do any work on her house so I had nothing to do with her bill.'

Grace wasn't going to be appeased. 'Even Anna keeps on

and on about it. She says she wished Thomas was earning enough to buy one for her and Tommy. She said the last letter she had from her sister in Ireland was boasting of how well her husband was doing in his job and that she might manage a holiday this year.'

Bill, who was normally good-natured and easy-going, was beginning to get annoyed. 'We can't help it if Hopalong doesn't have a big wage. What difference would it make if we didn't have a television, will that make them any better off?'

Grace could see the logic of this argument but she wasn't going to give up that easily. 'Don't call him Hopalong. Anna hates that nickname.'

Bill held up his hands in supplication. 'All right then, what difference will it make if Thomas doesn't have a big wage?'

Grace gave a big sigh and proceeded with her chores. She liked a tidy cupboard and everything in its place. She poured the bag of flour into the blue and white tin, the cornflour into the white tin and the baking powder into the red tin. The tea then went into the caddy and the sugar into a large jar. After all this she stood back and admired her handiwork She now knew she could put her hands on anything she needed. She wasn't one to criticise her next-door neighbour but she had once spotted Anna's cupboard and it was a right mixter maxter of opened and unopened bags. She must have spilled a bag at some time and there was a small layer of crystallised sugar on the shelf.

Bill started to chuckle at the programme that was on the television and Grace thought now was the time to drop her bombshell. 'Oh, by the way, I dropped in to see Mum and she had also heard about our new acquisition. Seemingly her pal Elsie Conners' son is planning to buy a set for his mother and she said it was great that we had one and that she would get the *Radio Times* and mark off which programmes she would like to see.'

Bill said that was a good idea. 'It'll take her out of the house and do her the world of good.'

'Well I'm glad you said that, Bill, because she plans to come here to do her viewing.'

Bill almost fell off his chair. 'WHAT? I hope you said it might not be possible, Grace.'

Grace went through to the bedroom to put a tin of talcum powder on the dressing table so she didn't answer but she smiled to herself. That puts his gas at a peep, she thought. Although she had seen her mother, Evelyn hadn't said anything about being in the house every night but she had said she would do her viewing when Elsie got her television. When she came back into the kitchen, Bill had switched off the set and was now sitting reading the paper. 'I must say that getting this television seems to be the most exciting thing that's happened in the lane,' she said. The words were no sooner uttered when the two girls rushed in. They looked at the blank screen in dismay.

'I hope it isn't broken, Dad,' Evie said while Tommy nodded.

'No it isn't, Evie, let me put it on for you both,' he said, glancing at his wife as if to say he had made the right decision in purchasing it.

Grace left the three of them to sit in a huddle while she put the tea on. Suddenly there was a knock at the door. 'I hope it isn't someone wanting to see something,' she muttered as she opened the door. To her surprise, a telegram boy was standing on the doorstep.

'I've got a telegram for Mrs Roberts,' he said, 'but there's nobody in. Can you tell me when she will be at home?'

Grace was flustered. Why would Maryanne get a telegram? 'Mrs Roberts is in the hospital,' she said. 'I'm hoping to go and see her tomorrow if you want me to take the telegram to her.'

The boy hesitated and said that she could take it but it had to be delivered right away. Grace called out to Bill who came to the door. 'This is a telegram for Maryanne and it has to be delivered right away.'

Bill was good at thinking on his feet. 'I've got the van outside, I'll drive you to Auchterhouse.'

The boy handed over the telegram and Grace went to put on her coat, calling out to the girls that they wouldn't be long. All the way on the journey she fussed about the contents. 'It must be bad news, Bill. No one ever gets a good news telegram. I don't know how Maryanne will take it.'

'Don't worry, Grace, there's no use getting in a tizzy over it. We'll deliver it and then go from there. If it is bad news then we can be there for her.'

Grace agreed that was the best idea but it didn't stop her worrying. Although Maryanne was getting stronger she was still recuperating and something like this could easily make her ill again.

Bill drove quite quickly and soon they were at the hospital, where he waited in the vehicle. At the reception, the nurse pointed out that visiting times were over so Grace explained her mission. 'The patients are due to get their evening meal,' the nurse said, but as it was a telegram she led Grace into the small lounge.

'I'll send Mrs Roberts in to see you,' she said, walking away quickly, her shoes making squeaking noises on the polished floor.

After a few minutes Maryanne appeared with a worried frown. 'What's the matter, Grace?'

Grace held out the telegram. 'This came for you this afternoon.'

Maryanne sat down on the edge of a chair and held the thin letter in her hand which Grace noticed was shaking.

'Do you want me to open it?'

Maryanne said no, she would do it. She quickly lifted the flap and read the message. Her face went white as she looked at Grace. 'Oh, no.'

Grace was almost frightened to ask what was wrong but she said, 'Is it bad news?'

Maryanne nodded. 'It's from Sadie. She sent it from Liverpool and she's on her way here with her son Eddie.'

Grace hadn't realised she had been holding her breath but now she gave a deep breath of relief. 'That's good news, Maryanne. She must have decided to come and see you when she knew you were ill. It'll do you the world of good to see her again.' Maryanne said it was but she didn't sound very convincing, as Grace confided to Bill on the homeward journey.

17

Morag started to have twinges that began half an hour after Rory left to go to work that morning. To make matters worse, he said he would be working late because Murdo wanted to finish the work they were doing in a shop in the Wellgate. They didn't normally work a full day on Saturday, usually finishing by twelve, but the shop owner had asked for the work to be finished that weekend.

He had been reluctant to work late because of the baby but she had assured him, 'Don't worry about me because the baby's not due for another ten days.'

Comforted by this, he had set off and Morag had begun to tidy the house when she felt the pains. They weren't too bad but by afternoon had increased and she was now starting to panic. Her suitcase was already packed in preparation for the birth and she went into the bedroom for it. Carrying it through to the kitchen, a sudden flood of fluid brought her to a halt. She knew her waters had broken but she was at a loss what to do. The clock struck six and she still didn't know which way to turn.

She was frightened to go out into the lane but as she was fretting about this emergency, she saw Evie pass the window. Hurrying as quickly as she could, she reached the door and called out to her. By now Evie was almost at her house but thankfully she turned around.

Morag shouted out, 'Can you get your mum to come here, Evie?'

Evie hurried into the house. Her dad was watching the television and Mum was setting the table for the tea which was later than normal because of the trip to deliver the telegram. Her dad looked up. 'Did you get the evening paper, Evie?'

She nodded and handed it over. 'Mum, Mrs MacCallum wants you to go and see her.'

Grace stopped putting out the plates. 'Did she say want she wants?'

Evie said no. 'But she shouted out quite loudly.'

Grace said, 'Oh heavens, I hope it isn't the baby coming. I better go and see her.'

Evie went with her as they walked quickly along the lane. By now, Morag's pains were coming every ten minutes. She had managed to change her clothes and a pile of wet washing was piled up beside the sink. 'I think the baby is coming, Grace, and Rory is working late today. I have to get to the DRI as I'm booked to go there for the birth.'

Grace turned to Evie. 'Run along and get Dad to bring the van here, tell him it's urgent.'

After Evie left she reassured Morag. 'First time babies rarely come quickly but we'll get you to the infirmary as soon as Bill brings the van. It's lucky he has it home with him today as sometimes he doesn't. We've just come back from seeing Maryanne.' She picked up the suitcase and helped Morag to her feet which she was reluctant to do.

'I think the baby will come if I stand up, Grace, I can feel it.'

Grace went to the door to see if Bill was coming but as she opened it she found Eliza standing on the doorstep. 'Is every thing all right? I saw you and Evie hurrying in.' She stepped inside the kitchen.

Grace said that the baby was ready to be born. 'Bill will take us to the infirmary, Eliza.' The words were barely out of her mouth when she heard the sound of an engine and Bill appeared.

'The van's not very comfortable, Grace,' he whispered at the door. 'I'm not sure if it's the best transport for a mother-to-be. Maybe I should go and phone for a taxi.'

'There's no time, Bill, she has to get in immediately. It may be a false alarm but I'd be happy if she was having the proper care.'

Grace and Bill helped Morag to walk to the van and it took some time to get her settled on the passenger seat while Eliza carried the suitcase and placed it in the back amongst the plumbing equipment.

'I'll sit in the back,' Grace said, as she pushed aside pipes and wrenches and squeezed in beside the case.

Bill was driving out the lane when Morag gave a sudden shout as the pains became intense. Bill was torn between driving as fast as he could to get her to the infirmary or taking his time when he saw a rough part of the road. He didn't want to jolt her and the baby.

Thankfully the infirmary wasn't that far away and they reached it within five minutes. Grace clambered out and opened the passenger door. Morag's face was covered with sweat and they were happy when she was quickly taken away to the maternity ward by a nurse. Before she was wheeled away, Morag said, 'Tell Rory I'm fine and he's not to worry.'

Grace said she would pass the message on but she knew Rory would be a mass of nerves, especially as he had been absent when his wife went into labour.

Because the clocks had gone forward for British summer time, it was still light by the time they got back. Eliza was hovering in her doorway and Grace told her that Morag was now in good hands. 'I'll probably not see her husband when he comes home from work but can you give him the news and tell him to come to the house, Eliza?'

Eliza felt important to be included in this dramatic

happening and said she would look out for him. She went back inside to give all this news to Martha who was fidgeting on her chair and wondering what was going on.

Back in the Gow house, Grace finally got the meal on the table and she said, 'I hope everything goes well and that the baby is born today. What a day it's been.'

After tea, Tommy arrived and Evie gave her all the news as they settled down to watch television. At six o'clock the television usually closed down and the interval appeared. It was sometimes a potter who was making a bowl on a turntable which was strangely soothing but by now the evening viewing had started. Tommy had asked why there was an interval and Bill said it was to allow young children to go to bed and not sit up until late at night watching the black and white picture.

It was eight o'clock when Rory appeared and he was distraught. 'Morag said she was fine this morning and I told her I didn't want to work but she insisted. I'm so sorry you've been put to all this extra work but thank you. I'll go right up to the infirmary now and try to see her.'

Grace said to Bill, 'Morag might not have the baby for hours but the nursing staff will tell Rory to go home if that's the case. Do you remember when I had Evie you sat in the waiting room for five hours until she decided to make her appearance?'

Bill said he remembered it as if it was yesterday and not ten years ago.

Morag was in the alien world of the delivery room and it was almost midnight. The smell of disinfectant and the strange sounds made her feel sick and the pain was unbearable. She wished Rory could be with her to hold her hand but that wasn't possible, although the midwife had told her he was in the waiting room which made her feel a bit happier. He might not be in the same room as her but he was in the same building.

The midwife was a quietly spoken older woman and she kept reassuring her that all was going well but Morag thought she was going to die. With every spasm of pain she thought she would pass out, but the woman told her with every spasm the baby was coming closer to being born.

The clock was on the wall opposite and she saw it had moved to two o'clock. She wanted to tell the midwife to give Rory the message to go home but she couldn't get the energy and she hoped he had the sense to leave. Then at two-thirty the midwife said, 'When the next pain comes I want you to give a big push.'

Morag did as she was told and she felt as if she was going to burst a blood vessel with the effort. Suddenly the baby was born and it gave a wail as it faced the world for the first time. Morag thought this was as much an alien world for the tiny mite as it was to her.

The midwife looked at her. 'Congratulations, you've got a wee girl.'

Morag felt the tears forming in her eyes at this momentous statement and later, when the baby who was wrapped in a warm blanket was placed in her arms, she became so emotional that she did cry.

The midwife smiled. 'Enjoy your new baby lass while I go and get you a cup of tea and some toast.'

'Will someone tell my husband the good news?'

'We'll send a message to him and he'll be able to visit in the afternoon,' she said as Morag was wheeled away back to the ward where the baby was put in a cot at the foot of the bed.

Rory was still in the waiting room when he heard the news and he was almost delirious with joy as he walked away into the darkness. A baby girl, he thought, what a blessing for them both. He would see them both later and he would send the news to Morag's parents, his brother Murdo and his parents afterwards. They would be as delighted as he was.

When he reached the lane, all the houses were in darkness

and to be honest he felt exhausted but he planned to rise early and let his neighbours know the good news. He also planned to thank Grace and Bill for all their help. He was grateful they were able to get Morag to the infirmary as she must have been worried by his absence at this crucial time.

As it turned out, Grace was still awake so she decided to get up and make a cup of tea. She didn't want to wake Bill up but he heard her and joined her in the kitchen. The fire was still glowing and the room was warm.

'What a day it's turned out to be,' she said as she stirred her tea. 'I hope all the drama is over. I wonder if Morag has given birth yet.'

Bill nodded. 'Thank goodness it's Sunday so we'll have a restful day later.'

'I would like to visit Morag in the afternoon but I'll see what Rory has to say. I don't know if they have any other relatives in Dundee apart from his brother. I wouldn't like to visit if there is family as it's only two visitors for each patient and I wouldn't like to impose.'

Bill said that was the best thing to do. He rose and put his cup on the table. 'I think we better get back to bed now and try to get some sleep.'

He managed to fall over almost right away but Grace's mind was still turning over all the drama of the past few hours. Maryanne was due to come home in a few days but Grace wondered how she would manage. On her last visit Maryanne had confided to her that although she felt stronger she was still a bit sore after her operation.

'I have to take it easy for about six weeks,' she had said, which was easy if there was someone at home to look after her and do the chores but this was something she didn't have.

An hour later, in spite of her worries, Grace managed to get some sleep but by eight o'clock when she woke up she still felt tired. However, as Bill said, as it was a Sunday they would have a restful day. Perhaps after a cooked breakfast they would read the Sunday papers and later watch the television or maybe go for a walk to the park for some fresh air with Evie and Tommy if they wanted to come.

However, as it turned out, the best laid plans were due to go astray. They had just finished breakfast when Rory appeared. He was carrying two bunches of flowers wrapped in newspaper. 'I just want to say a huge thank you to both of you for all your help,' he said, handing over one of the bunches to Grace. 'Morag had a girl early this morning and I've got these for when I go up to see them.' He held up the remaining bunch. 'I got these from a friend who has an allotment on the Law.'

Grace was so pleased she almost burst with pleasure. 'That's wonderful, Rory, we're so pleased for you all.'

Bill stood up and shook his hand. 'Congratulations, Daddy. It'll be midnight feeds from now on.'

Rory laughed. 'I won't mind doing that.'

Grace looked at her husband in amusement. 'Will you listen to him, Rory, he never got up for one night feed in his life.'

Bill looked sheepish. 'Well I had work to go to in the morning. There was always someone's plumbing work needing done.'

Evie was listening to all this banter and when they all laughed she joined in. She would go next door and tell Tommy the good news later.

After Rory departed, the door opened and Eliza appeared. 'What's the news, Grace? I saw Rory walking away along the lane early this morning but by the time I got dressed he was gone.' She sounded aggrieved at not catching him.

'Morag's had a baby girl early this morning,' Grace told her.

Eliza was amazed. 'Early this morning, I thought she was about to give birth when she got in the van.'

'First time babies have a habit of not coming quickly. Although I had the same notion as you did, Eliza.'

Eliza said she better get back to tell her mother the good

news. 'I'll also pass on the news to Albert and Bella.' She departed looking very important which made Bill laugh when the door closed.

'She thinks she's the town crier. Oyez, Oyez, all you townspeople, Meadow Lane has a new resident.'

Grace didn't answer but she sat down with the newspaper and put her feet up on a footstool. 'I'll wash up later after my second cup of tea.'

Evie had gone next door and Bill sat in the opposite chair with another paper. 'It's great to be back to normal and have a mundane Sunday with no more drama.' Suddenly there was a knock on the door and he grunted, 'For goodness sake, who's this now?'

Grace went to the door and was met by a woman, a young boy and four large suitcases. The woman was very good-looking while the boy looked shy. 'I'm sorry to bother you but my mother isn't in and I wondered if you have a key.'

Grace must have stood open mouthed because the woman added, 'I'm Sadie, Maryanne's daughter, and this is my son Eddie. We've come from America.'

It took Grace a moment to take all this in but she said, 'Come in for a moment while I get the key.' Sadie said she would leave the cases on the doorstep and they both entered the kitchen while Bill looked astonished.

Grace told him this was Maryanne's daughter and her son. 'I'm afraid your mother is still recovering from her operation, Sadie. She's in a convalescent home in Auchterhouse but she is due out in a few days.' She got the key from the hook and handed it over. 'If I'd known you were coming so soon I would have put a fire on and got some groceries in.'

Sadie seemed put out by this news. 'I thought she would be home by now as her operation was ages ago.'

'She has been really unwell, Sadie, and it's taken her some time to recover, especially as she was suffering from gallstones for ages before she saw a doctor.'

Sadie's lips thinned. 'How like Mum to be like that.'

Grace was taken aback. 'Well, it all boiled down to her being frightened to give up her work.'

While all this was going on, the young lad sat and said nothing and when Evie and Tommy hurried in, he looked down at his hands.

Grace decided introductions were called for. 'Evie, Tommy, please say hello to Sadie and Eddie, they are Maryanne's daughter and grandson from America.'

Eddie looked at them briefly and returned his gaze to his hands. Tommy said, 'You're from America? That's super.' Evie stayed silent but she felt the same way as Tommy. Grace walked to the door. 'I'll help you with your cases,' she said and mother and son followed her to the empty house.

18

When Grace opened the door they entered the house, which had a musty, unlived-in smell and that empty look that comes from being unoccupied for a while. Although Grace had tidied it up, she hadn't wanted to poke about too much so it had only been a case of setting the fire and going around with the sweeping brush and a duster. Sadie gazed around the room as if remembering it from her youth. 'I see it hasn't changed a bit and is still as frumpy as I recall it.'

Grace was annoyed but she remained silent. This was the first time she had seen Sadie as she was already married by the time the Gows had moved to the lane but she didn't really approve of her overbearing manner. Maryanne had worked hard to keep a roof over her head and now Sadie was being critical of her old home.

While this scrutiny was going on, Eddie stood at the door along with the suitcases. Sadie called out to him, 'Bring the luggage in, Eddie, and put it in the back bedroom.' She looked at the settee then turned to Grace. 'I'll have to work out the sleeping arrangements. I expect one of us will have to sleep on that.'

Grace almost said it better not be her mother, but as it was none of her business she said nothing. As Eddie was pulling one of the suitcases into the kitchen, the door suddenly opened and Anna appeared. She stared at Sadie and Eddie but addressed Grace. 'I saw you passing the window. Is everything all right?'

Grace did the introductions. 'Anna is your mother's next-door neighbor, Sadie, and Anna, this is Maryanne's daughter and grandson from America.'

Anna scrutinised the newcomer and she was bemused by the beautiful woman with long blonde hair tied back in a ponytail. She noticed the black pencil skirt that fitted snugly around her slender hips, the blue short jacket and the black high-heeled shoes.

'Hello Sadie, I'm pleased to meet you.' Anna felt guilty as she wasn't the least bit pleased to see her as she had once noticed Maryanne in tears after reading one of her letters.

Sadie gazed at her. 'You're from Ireland, aren't you?'

Anna said she was, as was her husband Thomas.

Grace was worried about Eddie as he hadn't spoken one word and he now sat down on a chair and looked out of the window at the patch of mud that now had some scrubby patches of grass. She went and sat beside him. 'Did you have a good journey, Eddie?' He nodded but still remained silent.

Sadie then said she had better get sorted out with her arrangements, which sounded like a dismissal, but Grace wanted to give her the latest news of her mother. 'When you go to visit your mother, Sadie, I'll come with you and show you where to get the bus to the convalescent home.'

Sadie looked displeased by this. 'I thought you said she was due to come home in a few days so I'll see her then. I have to get Eddie enrolled in a school and look for a job for myself so that will take a few days.'

Grace and Anna looked at one another wordlessly but Sadie had turned her back on them to open one of the cases before carrying a pile of clothing towards the bedroom. 'I hope my mother has enough drawers and wardrobe space for all this,' she said as she disappeared into the room.

When they were outside, Anna was furious. 'What kind of daughter is she that she'll wait a few days to see her mother?'

Grace agreed but she was puzzled. If Sadie and Eddie were here on a holiday why was she enrolling the boy in a school and looking for a job. How long was she expecting to stay? 'I wasn't going to see Maryanne today, Anna, but I had better go and tell her that Sadie has arrived. She is expecting her as she got a telegram from her yesterday.'

Anna nodded. 'I've only just met her and I don't like her but I feel sorry for that boy. Have you noticed he's never said one word? I hope Tommy and Evie will bring him out of his shell.'

When Grace entered her own house, Evie and Tommy were full of meeting the Americans, as Tommy put it. Bill raised an eyebrow when she told him of her plans to go and see Maryanne and he resumed reading his paper. When she was leaving, he remarked, 'That Sadie is quite a good looker, isn't she?' For some reason Grace was annoyed by this and she was quite curt as she said her goodbyes. Walking down to Courthouse Square, she soon felt better as the sun appeared from under a dark cloud but she knew Maryanne was going to be upset by not being at home when her family arrived.

As it turned out, Maryanne burst into tears, much to Grace's amazement. After a few minutes she dried her eyes and apologised. 'I'm sorry, Grace, but I wish she had stayed in America. I'm looking forward to seeing Eddie of course but Sadie has always had the knack of upsetting everybody and I think she won't have changed.'

Grace was going to ask her how long Sadie was planning to stay but she didn't as she suspected Maryanne would be as mystified as she was. Instead they spoke about Maryanne's release which was within the next few days.

'Sadie was sorting out the sleeping arrangements when I left.'

Maryanne suddenly looked fierce. 'She'll be taking over

my bedroom but she'll bloody well sleep on the settee when I come back.'

As she waited for the bus to take her back, Grace was pleased by Maryanne's reaction and hoped she would keep to her decision not to give up her own bed but she didn't think this would suit Sadie.

Meanwhile, back at the house, Sadie had sorted out the clothes and the sleeping arrangements. 'You can have the wee box room, Eddie, and I'll sleep in the back room.'

Eddie went into the room without a word and sat down on the single bed with its yellow candlewick cover that looked a bit grubby. He pulled it aside and saw a couple of grey blankets and a striped flannelette sheet with a matching pillow. He began to cry silently, large tears dropping down his cheeks as he looked around him.

This room looked identical to his bedroom back in America but whereas that room was warm, this one was freezing. The view from the small window overlooked the lane and the patch of scrubby land. Back in Nebraska he could gaze over miles of cornfields with the sun shining in an endless sky. Even in winter when it was very cold, the fields could sparkle with frost or snow, the view was great, not like this poky, dark house in this narrow lane surrounded by buildings. He had never met his grandmother, although there was a photograph of her in the living room back home, and he had no idea of what she liked or disliked.

His mother popped her head around the door. 'Do you like your room, Eddie?' When he shook his head, she muttered, 'Oh you'll soon get used to it. I'm making a cup of coffee, do you want one?'

He stood up and went back into the kitchen and sat down at the wooden table with its oilcloth cover that had a garish pattern on it. Sadie noticed this as well. 'This is a horrible cover, I'll have to get rid of it. If a plate of food is put down on it you won't be able to see it against that background.' She picked up a small jug. 'I need to borrow some milk. I won't be a minute as I'll ask next door if they can spare some.'

She hurried out of the house and knocked loudly on Anna's door. Tommy answered it and Sadie explained what she was after while striding into the small hall.

A male voice called out, 'Who is it, Tommy?'

Before Tommy could answer, Sadie went into the kitchen. 'I hate to bother you but can I borrow some milk please?' She held out the jug. 'I brought a load of groceries with me but stupidly forgot the milk.'

Anna walked over and took the jug from her hand while glaring at Thomas who sat with his mouth open. Sadie walked over to him. 'We haven't met although I've met your lovely wife. I'm Sadie and I hope my boy Eddie will become friends with your daughter and the girl next door.'

Thomas stood up. 'I'm pleased to meet you, Sadie. If you need any help to get settled in please let me know.'

Sadie said she would as Anna almost thrust the milk jug into her hand. 'Thank you, Anna, you've saved my life as I'm gasping for a cup of coffee.'

After she left, Thomas sat back down again and lit a cigarette. Anna was furious. 'You can close your mouth now, Thomas, as the blonde bombshell has gone.'

Thomas was unrepentant. 'I was only being friendly as she's had a long journey.'

Anna said that was so but added, 'Let's hope she doesn't need any help as it'll mean getting up off your backside.'

Thomas laughed. 'I think you're jealous of her.'

Anna glared at him and turned to the sink to finish washing the dishes, a job she had been doing when her visitor had rudely entered her house.

Thomas stood up and walked over to her. 'I'll tell you one thing, love, she's not as good-looking as you.'

This compliment seemed to calm her and after the dishes were done she sat down beside him, although she was still annoyed at him. Sadie had only been in the lane for a few hours and already she had caused a row between them. Tommy had stayed silent during this spat but now she said, 'Mum, why don't we have coffee instead of always having tea or milk?'

Thomas looked up. 'It's because we're not Yankees, Tommy.'

19

Sadie was pleased by the reaction she had caused in the lane. It was just like old times and it gave her a feeling of being at the centre of things and not just a nobody in the wilderness of Ed's farm back in America. She was confident that Eddie would soon settle in his new home, it was just a matter of time.

She was sipping her cup of coffee when Grace knocked at the door and came into the kitchen. Sadie was annoyed over this casual coming and going and this was something she was going to sort out soon. Maybe this was the way her mother liked to live but she wasn't going to have people popping in and out, even though this was something she herself was guilty of as she had already popped into Anna's house as if she owned it.

Sadie put her cup down with a dramatic sigh and gazed at her neighbour with a glare. Grace was aware of this slight but she wasn't going to be cowed by Maryanne's daughter.

'I hope you're remembering your mother comes home tomorrow, Sadie.' When Sadie nodded, Grace continued, 'I'm going to Auchterhouse in the morning and we can go together on the bus.'

Sadie smiled but the smile didn't reach her eyes and it vanished in an instant. 'Oh I can't come with you, Grace, as I've got an appointment at the school with Eddie. I want him to be enrolled as soon as possible.'

Eddie heard all this conversation through the open door and he was unhappy. It looked like his mother had made up her mind that this was to be their home, and he rushed through to the kitchen.

'I'm not going to this school. I want to go back home to Dad and Grandad.'

Sadie was infuriated by this outburst but she didn't want this nosy woman to witness her son's unhappiness. 'Of course you want to go with Evie and Tommy.' She gave a brittle laugh and rolled her eyes at Grace. 'Kids, eh. What can you do with them?'

Grace almost retorted that she could go back home to her husband in America where Eddie would be happy but she didn't. It wasn't any of her business and this was something that Maryanne would have to sort out.

Eddie rushed back into his room and Grace said she had to get her shopping done. After she left, Sadie went into Eddie's room and sat down on the bed with the yellow candlewick cover. She began to pull at the tiny tufts of material, trying to compose her words that would placate her son but he stood up and hurried out of the house. Sadie went after him but he was striding along the lane where he met Albert. Eddie stopped when the old man spoke. 'I hope you're settling in, Eddie.'

Eddie nodded but stayed silent. He had been brought up to respect his elders and he didn't want to snub the man but Albert went on. 'You must come and visit me and Bella Duff some time. We knew your mum when she was a small girl.'

Eddie said he would and hurried away while Albert gave him a quizzical look. He's not a happy lad, he thought.

Eddie reached the Hilltown and as he passed Burnett's bakery he was seen by Mrs Bell who was lifting a sponge cake from the window display. The customer also looked out. 'Is that the American lad?'

Mrs Bell said it probably was. News of Sadie and Eddie's

arrival wasn't restricted to the lane but was a topic of gossip around the surrounding streets. Most people thought that Maryanne's family was over for a holiday and to look after her mother during her illness. However Mrs Bell was shrewd and she wasn't as sure of this as others were and she was sure the young lad didn't look happy.

This was verified when Albert came in for his loaf of bread. 'I think I saw Eddie passing the window. He didn't look pleased to be living here,' said Mrs Bell.

Albert wasn't a man to gossip but he knew Mrs Bell was the great-niece of Bella's late fiancé Davie so he didn't want to snub her.

'I think he's finding it hard at the moment to settle in, but his granny comes home today so maybe that will help.'

Mrs Bell wasn't pleased by this terse statement. 'I've heard that Sadie and her son are back here to stay for good. Is that right?'

Albert said he didn't know as he hadn't seen Sadie except for a few brief moments. Thankfully two customers came in and he was glad to escape. He had a terrible feeling that things in the lane would never be the same again, then he dismissed that stupid notion. Once Maryanne was back home perhaps Sadie would get tired of living here and she would go back home.

20

It was the middle of April and the weather had been cold and wet. Grace saw the heavy rain when she pulled the curtain aside in the morning. She gave a huge sigh and hoped the rain would go off before she set out to pick up Maryanne. She was so annoyed at Sadie for not accompanying her but she was fast believing she was a selfish woman and she felt sorry for her mother and son.

She trudged off down the hill towards the bus stop and when the bus reached Auchterhouse, Maryanne was sitting waiting for her with her small suitcase at her feet. She had said her goodbyes to her friends and the staff and the two women went towards the homeward bound bus. The rain was streaming down the windows and although Maryanne's coat was a waterproof one, Grace hoped she wouldn't get soaked on the way to the house. She had brought her umbrella so that would help a wee bit.

To break the silence, Grace said, 'You'll be glad to get back to your own bed.'

Maryanne didn't seem too happy about the prospect. 'I would be more happy if I knew I didn't have Sadie at home.' When Grace looked shocked, she added, 'Oh don't get me wrong, I love my daughter and grandson but I wish they were back in America with her husband and Eddie's dad.'

Grace nodded but didn't say anything as this was a feeling

she shared. When the bus arrived in the city the two women were pleased to see the rain had stopped and a bright sun shone on the wet pavements so the umbrella wasn't needed although the wind was still cold.

As they walked towards the lane, Grace hoped that Sadie had lit the fire as Maryanne was used to being in a warm and comfortable home but when they opened the door she was dismayed to see a pile of cold ashes in the grate and a basin full of dirty dishes in the sink.

Maryanne looked around at the unwelcoming room with annoyance. There was a small pile of discarded clothes on the fireside chair which Grace picked up and placed on Eddie's bed before filling the kettle and putting it on the stove. While she waited for it to boil she cleaned out the fire, putting the ashes into the bucket from the cupboard under the coal bunker.

Once the fire was lit and Maryanne was settled in her chair, Grace nipped out to her house and brought back a tin of home baking. 'I'll get the tin back when you've finished with it.' She then tackled the dirty dishes and hung the wet tea towel up to dry.

At that moment, although they didn't know it, Sadie and Eddie were sitting in the headmaster's room at the school. Sadie had spent ages getting ready for this visit and had wanted to wear her blue shirtwaister dress with her white gloves but because of the rain she had to settle for a woollen jumper, plain pencil skirt and her blue swagger coat. Eddie was dressed in his long cream trousers and cream coloured windcheater.

Mr Bellamy, the headmaster, was quite bemused by the sight of the lovely young woman and the quiet, blond haired boy as he wrote down the answers to his questions.

Sadie was quite at home as this was her former school which she had pointed out to the man. 'My son's name is Edwayne Joel Boyd but he likes to be called Eddie. We've come here from Nebraska and will be living with my mother who has been ill.'

Mr Bellamy wrote this all down before asking, 'Will Eddie be at school for a short time?'Sadie looked at him as if she didn't understand the question. 'I mean, will you be going back to America when your mother gets better?'

Sadie laughed. 'Oh no, we are here for good. We won't be staying with my mother for long as I hope to get my own house shortly and I'm looking for a job.'

Mr Bellamy looked at Eddie but the boy was gazing out of the window. It was a strange set-up, he thought, but it wasn't his job to pry into his pupils' domestic lives. As he stood up, he said briskly, 'Well as Eddie will be ten years old in November he will be in Miss Malcolm's primary five class.'

Sadie and Eddie followed him along a corridor to a classroom with high windows that rattled against the rain and wind. When they entered, the teacher walked away from the blackboard and twenty-five pairs of eyes watched intently from their desks.

Evie and Tommy gave a little wave but no one noticed except Sadie who gave them a wide smile. Most of the girls smiled back and nudged one another while the boys were either uninterested or jealous of Eddie's clothes.

After giving the teacher all the information, he left and Miss Malcolm turned to her class. 'Boys and girls, this is our new pupil Edwayne Joel Boyd who will be joining us tomorrow.'

Sadie butted in. 'He likes to be called Eddie, Miss Malcolm.'

The teacher nodded. 'Please say a big hello to Eddie.'

There was a loud chorus and Eddie wanted to run out of the room and keep on running to anywhere rather than this place. Sadie poked him in the back. 'Say hello to your new classmates.'

Eddie looked at the floor and almost whispered a greeting and then it was time to head off back home. When they were out on the street he erupted with fury. 'I'm not going to that school. I want to go back to see Dad and Grandad and stay at my old school where I've got loads of friends.'

Sadie was dismissive. 'Oh I know your friends, those farmyard kids with no ambition to be anything else but corn farmers. You'll do a lot better here, believe me.'

Eddie ran off up the hill while his mother hurried after him. Thankfully the squally shower had passed and the sun was out. She caught up with him at the entrance to the lane. 'You'll see your granny when we go in.'

Grace and Maryanne were sitting by the fire when they entered. Maryanne stood up and held out her arms to her grandson. 'Eddie, I've waited a long time to see you,' she said as she gave him a hug. Not wanting to upset his granny, he smiled at her and said he was pleased to see her as well. Meanwhile Sadie glared at Grace who took the hint and stood up.

'I must be going, Maryanne, but I'll see you later.' She touched Eddie on his shoulder. 'Cheerio young Eddie.'

After she left, Maryanne asked him where they had been. Before he had time to answer, Sadie said, 'We've been to Rosebank School and Eddie is going there tomorrow.'

Maryanne looked at Eddie. 'Is that what you want?'

Eddie burst out, 'No, I don't want to go, Granny. I want to go back home to my old school and see my dad.'

Maryanne said gently, 'Eddie, Grace has made a super jam sponge and she has bought some lemonade. Do you want to go and see her as she has made the cake especially for you?'

He left the room without looking at his mother and after he had gone Maryanne looked furiously at her daughter. 'I've always known you were selfish, Sadie, but to make your son's life a misery is the final straw. I think you better plan to go back to your husband right away. After all, you couldn't wait to marry him if I remember rightly.'

Sadie gave her mother a withering glance. 'Yes I did and now I don't want to stay with him. He's boring and I'm sick of my life out there so no matter what you think or want it's not going to happen. I'm looking for a job and when I've got enough money saved up I'll be looking for my own house and we'll be happy.'

Maryanne stayed silent throughout this statement and she made her way out of the house to go and see Grace and Eddie. Her homecoming had been spoiled by Sadie and she didn't want to be in the same house as her. She was still sitting drinking tea with Grace when Evie and Tommy came in from school. Eddie had just left and the girls were full of the scene that morning. 'Eddie is going to be in our class,' said Evie while Tommy added, 'All the girls are jealous of us because we know him.'

Grace smiled at their eager faces. 'Well tomorrow you can all go to school together and your pals will be more envious.' Maryanne nodded but said nothing.

21

There was an argument going on the next morning between Sadie and Eddie. He was adamant that he wasn't going to school. This argument was witnessed by Grace, Evie and Tommy but fortunately Maryanne had gone back to work so she missed the drama.

Sadie tried to placate her son but he wasn't in the mood for her pleading words. 'You'll enjoy your new school, Eddie.' She turned towards the girls. 'That's true, isn't it?'

Tommy opened her mouth but Evie gave her a nudge so she stayed silent.

Eddie was dressed in his cream trousers and windcheater but his face was red and angry. 'I'm not going because I'm going back to live with Dad soon so I'll be back in my old school. Dad and Esther will look after me if you don't want to go back.'

Sadie lost her temper. 'Well you're not back in America, Eddie, so you'll just have to make the best of it. I'll be looking for a job and we'll be happy here.'

Grace sat down beside him. 'Just go today, Eddie, and see if you like it.'

Evie smiled at him and Tommy gave him her wide- eyed gaze and by now his anger had begun to subside so he picked up his bag and walked out of the room. 'If I don't want to go back tomorrow then I'm not going.'

With that threat hanging in the air, the two girls followed him onto the lane and walked on each side of Eddie as if he was a prisoner on his way to the gallows.

As usual, Tommy was chattering on while Evie stayed quiet. 'I hear your name is Edwayne Joel. That's a funny name.'

Eddie glared at her. 'Well, you are a girl and you've got a boy's name so that's funny also.'

Tommy didn't take offence. 'My real name is Thomasina but I'm the same as you. I like to be called Tommy while you like Eddie.'

'I'm called after my dad Ed and also after my grandad, Joel.'

With these explanations taken care of they made their way to school. It was a mild spring morning and when they reached the playground it was full of children running around without their coats. Eddie made to follow the girls into the playground but Evie explained, 'I'll take you round to the boy's entrance as it is on Rose Street. We have different playgrounds but there is just the small wall dividing us and we'll see you in the class.'

Eddie looked apprehensive when faced by a new gate but Evie said he better hurry up as the school bell was due to ring and she had to hurry back to wait with Tommy in the girls' queue.

Once inside the playground, Eddie was faced by a noisy group of boys who seemed intent on pushing and shoving each other. He surveyed the large grey walls of the school and the concreted playground with dismay. It was all so different from his school back in Nebraska. Lutton School was a modern building with a large green playing field surrounded by trees, and nothing like this hemmed-in dismal building which was surrounded by tenement houses.

He felt so unhappy that he could cry but he knew boys didn't shed tears so he made his way to the main door just as the school bell sounded. A score of young faces turned in his direction but it was a thin-faced boy who wore wire-framed glasses who told him which queue to stand in.

'You're in my class so if you want you can stand beside me and we can go in together.'

Eddie gave the lad a grateful look and stood quietly as the pupils all filed in slowly through the main door. They made their way to a large classroom and as the children all took their seats he once again was overcome with insecurity. Evie and Tommy were sitting together and he was aware that most of the girls were gazing at him with undisguised attention. A few even twisted their heads to get a better view.

Then the teacher came in. 'Good morning, Eddie, it's lovely to see you.' She pointed to an empty seat beside the boy who had befriended him. 'Please sit down beside David.'

As he made his way to the empty seat he said, 'Thank you, ma'am.'

The teacher blushed slightly and a couple of the girls covered their mouths as they tried to stifle giggles.

'You can call me Miss Malcolm, Eddie.'

The first lesson was arithmetic which pleased him as it was one of his best subjects.

'We'll begin with ten questions on mental arithmetic. Write down your answers.' There were groans from some of the boys at the back of the class.

Eddie made short work of his answers and when the papers were all gathered in they were asked to take out their reading books. As Eddie had no book, David kindly shared his and the pupils all bent their heads to read while the teacher marked the mental arithmetic answers. Eddie was aware of her looking at him before speaking.

'There are two pupils with full marks, Evie and Eddie, while Bruce only got one answer right.' Bruce was a stocky boy with a scowling face which was made worse by some of the girls gazing at him. He had no interest in doing sums which three of his uncles, who were all amateur boxers, said were unnecessary if boxing was going to be his job after leaving school.

At playtime, back in the dreary playground, Eddie once again stood by the door. Bruce wandered over and spoke in a sarcastic manner. 'Edwayne. Are you related to John Wayne, the cowboy?'

Some of his pals sniggered but Eddie ignored him which seemed to infuriate the boy. 'I asked you if you got that funny name because you're related to a cowboy?'

Eddie walked away but Bruce rushed after him and grabbed his windcheater, tearing the pocket as he did so. When he saw the damage he had caused, Bruce strode away with a swagger as if he had won a boxing match while Eddie tried hard to contain his anger.

David came up to him and looked at the torn jacket. 'Will your mum be angry at that?'

Eddie said she would probably be furious and as he joined the queue when the bell went he knew once again he would never fit in this environment, even if he lived to be a hundred. A feeling of desolation washed over him and he longed to be back with his father, Grandad and Esther with her lovely pecan pies and maple syrup pancakes. He had known for ages that his mother had been unhappy at home but he couldn't understand why she preferred this life to her old one and why, oh why did it have to include him?

Meanwhile back in Meadow Lane, Grace asked Sadie round to her house for a cup of tea. By now, Sadie was upset after the argument with her son and Grace tried to calm her down but as she was busy with the teapot and cups, Sadie seemed to get angrier.

'I can't believe he wants to go back to America to live on a corn farm. When he comes home from school he has hardly any friends who live near us. It's just Ed and his grandad Joel and I'm angry he mentioned Esther.'

Grace didn't want to pry but she had been surprised by this new name being tossed into the conversation this morning.

However, Sadie, in her anger, was past being discreet. 'Esther was Ed's sweetheart. They were at school together and he was engaged to be married to her when he left to come to Britain with his navy unit. Then he met me and we fell in love and were married within months of meeting one another. She's the daughter from the farm a mile or two from us. She's such a pudding faced young woman and no wonder Ed ditched her to marry me. She's Joel's housekeeper and all her time is spent making jam and baking pies and she's forever in an apron with flour on her hands.'

Grace, who was in the process of opening two of her home baking tins and bringing out the homemade jam, suddenly stopped and looked at Sadie who was now sitting by the window. The sun was shining and it made her look golden as it glinted off her long blonde ponytail. She was a beautiful woman and it seemed a shame that she could be so scornful of another woman who didn't have her good looks but who seemed to be a genuinely lovely person.

She thought ruefully that Esther was someone who resembled herself with her baking and jam making and ordinary domestic pleasures. Grace placed the jam and baking tins back in the cupboard and gave Sadie her cup of tea with a small plate of custard cream biscuits.

'I hope your mum doesn't get too tired on her first day back at work, Sadie,' said Grace who was keen to get the subject changed from Esther.

Sadie was dunking a biscuit in her tea and when she looked up, a small piece fell into the cup. As she fished it out she sounded bored. 'Oh I expect she will be. She never seemed to have much energy, even when I was growing up. I've always said she doesn't eat enough and she's far too thin but she won't change now. That's why I'm hoping to get a job and look for another house for Eddie and me.'

Grace just nodded. She thought Sadie sounded hard-hearted but maybe it was because she was young and healthy and had no experience of being middle aged and ill. She said, 'I hear Morag is coming home with her new baby today. Bill was speaking to Rory yesterday and he's getting time off to pick her up this afternoon.'

Sadie didn't seem interested in this piece of news and she finished her tea then stood up abruptly and said she had shopping to do and as she departed through the door Grace felt she had been hit by a whirlwind. She wondered how Eddie had got on at school today. Sadie hadn't mentioned him once but Grace hoped he was all right.

As it turned out, she was quite right to be worried about him as she found out when the three of them returned after four o'clock. Eddie had gone into his own house but Evie and Tommy were upset about the torn jacket.

'I asked him if his ma would be angry and he said she would be furious and more than likely to rush off to the school tomorrow and he doesn't want that to happen,' Tommy said.

Grace told Evie to go and bring him here and bring the jacket. When Eddie appeared he looked upset but Grace took the jacket and inspected the torn pocket.

'I think I can stitch this so it'll look just like new, Eddie.' His face brightened. 'Sit down and have some tea or milk and pancakes while I get the needle and thread.' She turned to the girls. 'Morag has come home with her baby. Do you want to go and ask if there is anything she needs?' The two girls didn't need another telling and they both hurried to the far end of the lane and knocked on the door.

Morag didn't need anything done but she invited the girls in to see the baby. She was about to change her nappy and they sat in amazement at the tiny pink bundle who was crying as her mother did her best to cope with the terry towelling square and the big nappy pin.

'I suppose I'll get better at this in time,' Morag said as she held the baby in her hands before placing her in the large Silver Cross pram which stood in the corner of the kitchen.

Tommy's eyes were like saucers while Evie asked, 'What are you going to call her?'

'Catriona. It's my mother's name and Rory likes it as well.'

Evie liked it also and said so. Morag said it would soon be time for her feed and she would tell the girls if she needed any help with shopping. On that note they made for the door with Tommy going on and on about how she once had a doll that was bigger than Morag's baby.

'If I were Morag, I would be scared in case I dropped her as she's so small. I once dropped my doll and it had a huge crack in its head,' she added.

Back in the house they couldn't stop chattering about Catriona but they were as pleased that Eddie's jacket was now repaired as he was.

'Who tore the pocket, Eddie?' Grace asked as she handed it over.

He didn't want to answer but Tommy piped up. 'It was that horrible Bruce Davidson. He's jealous of Eddie because he's American and good looking. Not like him who has a face like a scowling pig.' Evie said Tommy shouldn't say things like that about someone but Tommy was unrepentant. 'Well, Evie, it's true and he hates it when all the girls say they like Eddie.'

Eddie thanked Grace for the pancakes. 'I love the ones that Esther makes but your ones taste better. Esther puts maple syrup on hers.'

Grace said he could have had golden syrup on his if he had said so. Before he could reply Sadie swept into the house with a string shopping bag slung from her slender wrist.

'I didn't know what to have for our tea, Eddie, but I've got two tins of tomato soup, a tin of beans and three sausage rolls.'

Eddie stood up and he followed his mother out of the door. Tommy called after him, 'We'll see you tomorrow morning.'

He looked back but said nothing and as they passed Tommy's house, Thomas, who was standing at the window, suddenly felt so sorry for the lad with the beautiful mother.

22

Sadie had a splitting headache because of the argument that morning with Eddie, who had again been adamant he wasn't going to school. What had made it worse was the fact that it had all been in front of Grace, Anna and the two girls.

She wished they would stay out of her private life but on the other hand she would need Grace's help with Eddie when she finally found a job. It would be handy if he could stay with her after school until she got home.

After an age, with Grace cajoling Eddie, he had finally gone off to school in a temper with the two girls. After a glass of lemonade and an Askit headache powder, Sadie made her way to Mrs Jennings' paper shop to buy a *Courier* newspaper. The front page was filled with job vacancies and as she was getting short of money, finding a job was a priority. She was busy scrutinising the paper when she met Albert.

'Anything interesting in the paper, Sadie?' he asked with a smile.

She was annoyed at this intrusion but she tried hard to be pleasant. 'Oh I'm just looking for a job, Albert, and I'm hoping there is something suitable today.'

Albert nodded. 'Come along with me and see Bella. She's been asking about you and I know she will be pleased to see you.'

This was the last thing she wanted but to her astonishment

she found herself saying that would be fine. Albert said he would just pop into Burnett's bakery for his loaf and they could walk back together.

Anna was behind the counter. 'I see you're chatting to Sadie. Has she recovered from the fight this morning?'

Albert said he didn't know about that but they were both going back to Bella's house. As he walked out of the door, Anna called after him, 'Good luck then.' Thankfully Sadie had walked a few steps away from the shop so she didn't hear this remark and they walked back along the lane.

'I haven't seen your mother since she went back to work, Sadie. How is she keeping?'

Sadie, who was too full of thinking about getting a job, was quite offhand. 'She's fine, Albert. Glad to be back I think.'

When they reached Bella's house, Albert went inside first. 'I've brought a visitor to see you,' he called out.

Sadie, who had always known her as Granny, said, 'I've been meaning to come and see you, Granny, but I've been busy.'

Bella and Albert had both heard about the rows with Eddie but they both smiled. Bella brought out the best cups, saucers and plates plus the milk jug and sugar bowl and placed them on a large tray.

'Do you want tea, Sadie?' Sadie said she preferred coffee but Bella frowned. 'I don't have any coffee.'

Albert said he had some Camp Coffee in his cupboards but Sadie gave a small shiver. 'That's all right, Arthur, I'll give that a miss if you don't mind and I'll have tea. I've gotten used to drinking real coffee in America and not the watered down stuff they sell here.'

Bella, who was standing behind her, gave a small shrug. 'Well then, we'll all have tea.'

Sadie sat down in one of Bella's comfy wing backed chairs which she had loved as a child. The room looked exactly like she remembered it with the lovely old-fashioned furniture,

Persian carpet and nice pictures on the walls. She also remembered this tea set and she made up her mind that when she got her own place she would have nice things like this.

'Mum told me your wife Jean died a couple of years ago, Albert. I mind she was always cleaning the house when you were at work. Do you still work for the Prudential Insurance?'

Albert shook his head. 'No, I retired a couple of years ago and I only had a few months with Jean before she passed away. Her death was sudden but peaceful, but I was glad we had that wee while together after I retired.'

Sadie glanced at both of them and raised her eyebrows. 'Are you and Granny...' She stopped. 'I better start calling you Bella as Granny was a child's title. Are you going to get married?'

Bella almost choked on her tea and seemed flustered. 'Oh for heaven's sake, where did you get that idea from, Sadie? Of course we're not going to be married as we are just old friends.'

Sadie didn't seem to be embarrassed by her statement and she glanced at the photograph of Davie Bell in his Black Watch kilt and with a huge smile on his handsome face. 'I always thought Davie was a good- looking man. What a pity he didn't survive the war.'

Bella said it was, but time was a great healer and it had been forty years ago. 'When are you going back to America, Sadie, now that your mother is well and back at work?'

It was Sadie's turn to look flustered. 'I thought I had made it clear that Eddie and I are back here to stay. In fact I'm looking for a job and that's why I've bought this paper.' She held out the *Courier*.

Albert looked unhappy. 'What does your husband say to this? Won't he want his wife and son back home with him?'

Sadie was unabashed. 'Well he can't have us. Honestly, Albert, we live miles away from the nearest small town, Ed and his father have a farm which grows corn and all I can see from my living room window is miles and miles of fields.'

Albert threw a glance at Bella who also looked shocked. 'But surely it's better there than living in these small rundown houses with no views. What does Eddie think about this?'

Sadie recalled the angry scene this morning but said with a smile, 'Oh, he loves it, he really does.' She stood up. 'Well I better be off as I want to look at the job vacancies and see if there's anything that suits me. You'll remember I used to work in an office before getting married but I'm willing to try anything.'

Before she left, Albert said, 'Martha and Eliza are hoping you'll pop in and see them.'

Sadie sighed. 'Is Martha still as domineering and nosy as I remember her? I always felt sorry for her poor daughter.' On that note she swept out of the door, leaving the two occupants bemused by this latest news. As Bella collected the cups to put them in the basin, she said, 'The people I feel sorry for are Maryanne and Eddie.'

Albert took down the tea towel from its hook as he usually helped Bella with the washing up. He looked really unhappy. 'I feel the same and I can't see a happy outcome from this news.'

Sadie was glad to escape. She liked Albert and Bella but she hated them asking all those questions. Her headache had gone so she scrutinised the paper. There seemed to be loads of jobs for tractor drivers and orramen, whatever they were. There was one job that stood out: an office assistant with some sales experience for an electrical business. Sadie wrote down the address and noticed it said applicants could visit the shop which was situated in King Street.

She put on her best dress and white gloves and headed off. The sun was shining which made her feel optimistic and when she reached the street she had to walk up the hill past lots of small shops until she reached the address in the paper.

The shop, which was called D. Fleming and Son, was quite

big with double fronted windows that showed a couple of television sets and a selection of radios. The inside of the shop was roomy with one large counter, which held a cash register, and some glass fronted shelves with various electric lamps and assorted goods. A tall, skinny man was behind the counter and when he looked up from his notebook he seemed surprised by this beautiful woman who approached him with a big smile. She launched into the reason why she was here.

'Hullo, my name is Sadie Boyd and I've come about your advertisement in the paper for an office assistant and saleswoman.'

The man seemed to be tongue-tied and muttered something about getting the boss of the shop and he disappeared through a small door at the back of the counter. Sadie could hear speaking but the words weren't clear so she put her handbag down and stood looking around her. The job didn't seem to be to her liking but if she got it she could get some money together while she looked for something more suitable.

Suddenly the door opened and a plump elderly man with a shock of white hair appeared. Sadie noticed his shirt buttons were straining at the seam and his jacket had an old-fashioned look.

'Bert says you've come about the job. Have you any experience of office work and selling our stock?'

Sadie said she had worked in an office before her marriage and moving as a GI bride to America. The man, who said his name was David, looked puzzled. 'Why are you looking for a job if you're on holiday, Mrs Boyd?'

'I've come back home to be with my mother who has been ill and I won't be going back to America so I'm looking for employment.'

'I don't suppose you'll have an insurance number or a P45,' he said dryly. 'Still, you can go to the insurance office in the Overgate and explain your situation. If you get all the paperwork then I'll consider hiring you.'

Sadie picked up her bag. 'Thank you, I'll go there now and I'll let you know how I get on.'

After she left, Bert appeared at the counter. 'She'll certainly bring in the male customers if you give her the job.'

Sadie spent half an hour looking for the insurance office and finally found it on the corner of the Overgate and Tay Street. The office was quiet at this time of day and there was a small scattering of men sitting on chairs. They were smoking and talking amongst themselves and paid no attention to her. She made her way to the desk and a young woman asked if she could help her. Sadie explained her situation while the woman wrote down all the particulars. Sadie did emphasise that she was home for good with her son and she needed to get a job.

The woman left her sitting while she went through a door at the back and when she returned she said she would have to look up her previous work before her marriage and they would write to her.

Sadie wasn't pleased by this, but she had no choice but to smile and say she needed to have an insurance number soon, and then she left. Full of disappointment she made her way back to the shop with the feeling that the job would be taken by now but David the owner said he would take her on, starting on Monday of the following week, and they would sort out all the preliminaries later. 'The shop opens from eight-thirty to five-thirty with a half day on Wednesday. We also have a workshop so I'll need you to do all the invoices and other office duties.'

Sadie said she would be back on Monday and she went home feeling pleased with herself. It would mean leaving the house before Eddie in the morning and also coming back after school had finished but she was going to ask Grace if he could stay with Evie and Tommy.

However, her elation was deflated when she got back to the lane. Eddie was at the Gows' watching television with the girls but he seemed downcast. The reason was soon apparent when she saw his windcheater. It was smeared with mud and the pocket was torn. Before she could ask what the hell was going on, Tommy burst out, 'It was Bruce Davidson's fault. He's a big bully.'

23

Maryanne was as furious as her daughter when she arrived home from work and was told about the torn jacket. Grace had given it a good brush which had removed some of the mud and she had once again stitched up the pocket.

Evie and Tommy stood with Eddie when Sadie questioned them. She looked at Evie. 'Why is this Bruce Davidson doing this to my son?'

Evie hesitated and Tommy butted in. 'It's because he's jealous of him. All the girls in the class are always speaking about Eddie and Bruce doesn't like it.'

Sadie picked up the jacket. 'Right then, I'm going to go to the school tomorrow to tackle this bully.'

Eddie burst out, 'No, I don't want you to do that as you'll just make it worse.'

Maryanne, who was still annoyed, said, 'But he has to be stopped, Eddie, as he can't go around ruining your clothes and getting off with it.'

'If I had the same kind of school uniform as the rest of the boys then he wouldn't do this.' Eddie looked at the girls as if to get them to agree which they both did.

Sadie made up her mind. 'We'll go down the town tomorrow afternoon and get some new things. Now run off and play while I make the tea.'

Eddie trudged out the door as if running out to play was

the last thing he wanted to do. Sadie turned to her mother. 'I can't afford to buy new clothes at the moment. Do you still have that account at McGills store that you used to have when I was at school?'

'No I don't, Sadie, as I can't afford new things either, but if you go to the store I'm sure they will let you open a credit account.'

That seemed to please Sadie and she set about making scrambled eggs and toast for the tea. Maryanne, who ate a meal at dinner time in the canteen in the sweet factory where the prices were cheap, didn't want anything and she said she was going to visit her pal, Dorothy. She was really annoyed that Sadie was planning to stay and not go back to her husband but she knew it would be useless going on about it.

Sadie was also feeling fed up as the elation of finding a job had been overshadowed by all this nonsense at school and now she had the added expense of a new outfit and probably new shoes as well. Eddie seemed to be growing taller by the day and she wondered if her wages would be enough to keep them both.

The next morning, she said she would meet Eddie from school and they would both go down to McGills. What she didn't tell him was the fact that she had written a strongly worded letter and had asked Evie to give it to the teacher but not to say a word about it. Evie was unhappy about this but she put the letter into her schoolbag and duly handed it over when they were in the classroom. Miss Malcolm opened it and after she read it, she went out of the room and appeared a few minutes later with the headmaster.

All heads turned when he called Bruce from his desk and took him outside. Evie was aware that Eddie and Tommy were looking at her but she picked up her arithmetic book and began to read it like it was some fabulous adventure story. Some of the girls were nudging each other and whispering but the teacher told them to get on with their lessons. Half an hour later Bruce appeared. His face was red and furious looking and he glared at Eddie as he passed his desk.

At playtime, he sauntered up to Eddie and snarled, 'My uncles are world famous boxers and I'm going to get them to come and knock your head off.'

As Eddie walked away he was joined by David. 'I wouldn't worry about his uncles, Eddie. My dad says they're not good boxers as they are too fat.'

For the first time in ages, Eddie laughed out loud. 'Thanks for that, David, you're a good chum to me.'

David's face lit up. Like Eddie he was also a bit of an outsider due to his small physique. The bell sounded and they went in together with Eddie still smiling.

Sadie was at a loose end now she was alone in the house so she made up her mind to go down the town. She went into McGills to look at the boys' department and ask about opening an account. The first person she met was Alex Little who she remembered from her teenage days when he regularly came to the house for the weekly payments from her mother. He recognised her straight away and said he would arrange a credit account. 'Heavens, Sadie, you don't look a day older from the last time I saw you. You were getting married I believe, so how's married life?'

Sadie wasn't going to tell her life story so she smiled and said it was great. 'I'm bringing my son here this afternoon, Mr Little, as he needs new school clothes, so will the account be open by then?'

The man was all jovial. 'I'll see to that, Sadie, so don't you worry your pretty head about anything. Tell your mother I was asking for her as I haven't seen her for some time.'

Sadie promised she would and she wandered out into the sunshine. The weather was great, she thought, and it promised to be a good summer. With that happy thought in mind she wandered down the Wellgate and walked as far as Castle Street where she knew Braithwaite's coffee shop was situated. It was hard to get a decent cup of coffee in the town so she bought a small bag of roasted ground coffee beans and planned to make a cup as soon as she got home.

However the plan was put to one side when she noticed the airmail letter lying on the floor behind the front door. Her heart sank as she read the few lines from Ed. He hoped her mother was now feeling better and was hoping she would be coming back soon with Eddie as everyone was missing them. She frowned as she read the last few words. Maybe everyone was missing Eddie but she knew they wouldn't be missing her.

Taking the letter over to the empty fireplace, she lit a match and put the flame to the corner of the flimsy paper. It soon burnt to a minute pile of ashes which she prodded with the poker until the letter was no more. Then she brewed her coffee, dreaming of her new life. She decided to ignore the letter and if she did then Ed would want to be with her, which meant he could come to Dundee to live and give up the farm. After all he had spent quite a long time in Britain during the war and he always said he loved this country. He could easily get a job and they would find a house and everything would be rosy. There was just one problem and that was the fact that she no longer loved him, but that small fact wouldn't matter as he had their son Eddie to look after and he was the biggest joy in his life.

After making her coffee she sat down at the wooden kitchen table and looked around the room. All the furniture dated from her childhood and everything was either faded or old. The chair she was sitting in was uncomfortable and the bed wasn't much better. She hoped to move from here as soon as she got some money together and the fact she had got that job was a lucky bonus.

The sun shone through the small window and Sadie noticed Morag pushing her pram along the lane. It was too lovely a day to be inside so she joined her neighbour. Morag looked pleased when she walked alongside and peered into the pram. Catriona was sleeping and the cream coloured canopy shielded the baby from the sun.

'She's a lovely baby, Morag. I mind when Eddie was born and I loved pushing him around our farm. It's a pity they grow up so quickly. I've got to take him to get new clothes for school this afternoon and it only seems like yesterday when he was in romper suits.'

By now they had reached the Hilltown and Morag said, 'Is Eddie settling in at his new school?'

'Yes he is.' There was no way she was going to mention all the problems. 'I've been for a job interview today and I start work next week. It's an electrical shop on King Street.'

Morag seemed genuinely pleased by this news. 'Well, good luck with that. I know the shop as we bought a couple of table lamps from there. It's quite a busy place so you'll enjoy working there.' She stopped at the small grocery and put the brake on the pram. 'I'm going in here to get something for the tea and also for Rory's pieces that he takes to work for his dinner break. Oh before I forget, we are having Catriona christened this Sunday in Bonnethill Church. I hope the weather stays sunny like this.'

Sadie said she hoped so as well and she made her way to the school. There was still half an hour before the children got out but she thought she would find somewhere to sit while she waited. On reaching Rose Street she saw a small wall across from the gate so she sat on the warm stones and watched as an elderly woman made her way up the steep road. As she passed, Sadie saw how frail she was with her deeply wrinkled face and thin hands that clutched a small bag.

She gave a small shudder and hoped she wouldn't look like her when she got old. It was a great feeling to be young and healthy and beautiful and she knew she was lucky to have good looks because it opened lots of door for her. Especially this afternoon with the job and meeting Alex Little after all these years which had produced an account without lots of questions asked.

She was brought out of her reverie when the school bell sounded. One minute the street was quiet and the next it was a mass of noisy boys pouring through the gate. She would like to have met Bruce Davidson but in the crowd it was hard to pick anyone out.

Eddie appeared with a small, serious looking boy and when he saw his mother he crossed over while his friend made his way down the road.

'Who is that, Eddie? Is he a chum of yours?'

Eddie said his name was David and yes, he was a chum. This pleased her because it looked like he was settling in after a bad start. They then made their way down to the Wellgate steps and McGills store.

Eddie was adamant. 'I want school clothes like all the rest of the boys, Mum, and not something fancy.'

Sadie made a soothing noise. 'Of course we'll get you what you want.' Anything for a peaceful life, she thought.

Eddie gave her a suspicious glance as he was so used to her having her own way in everything, even his clothes. However he had nothing to worry about as the assistant produced grey trousers and shirts, a dark navy jumper and a navy blue anorak for when the weather was cold and wet. It was all dull and serviceable but just what he was looking for. He didn't want to stand out in his American outfits and get ridiculed by Bruce and his pals.

Sadie decided he also needed new shoes as he was finding it hard to put on his old ones which were getting too small for him. Within an hour they were carrying all the parcels up the hill and she was getting over the shock of how expensive everything was and these were items she would have to replace often as her son got bigger. She hoped her wages in the shop would cover it all and she suddenly realised it was a hard job being without a husband to foot the bills. Back home in America she usually bought clothes from a catalogue or sometimes from the general outfitter in the main street in Lutton and when the bills came in, Ed would pay them either with cash or a cheque.

When they reached the lane, Evie and Tommy were pushing the large Silver Cross pram with its fringed canopy backwards and forwards with Catriona sleeping soundly inside. At five o'clock Morag called from her doorway, 'It's time for the baby's feed, girls.'

Tommy pushed the pram right up to the door where Morag lifted her child out. 'After her feed it's time for her bath and then bedtime. I like to get this all done before her daddy comes in from work,' she said, placing kisses on Catriona's head.

They walked back to their own houses, passing Martha and Eliza who were sitting on basket chairs, enjoying the evening sunshine. Sadie also noticed the Potters but gave them a wide berth as she headed indoors to deposit her parcels on Eddie's bed. She knew they wanted to see her and get all the gossip about her life and she would go some day but not now. Spending all that money had made her a bit depressed and she still hadn't bought anything for the tea.

Popping her head outside she saw Evie. 'Can you run down to Lipton's and get me a half pound of bacon, six eggs and a white loaf?'

Evie took the money and she was back in a quarter of an hour with Eddie in tow. He opened the parcels and hung up the trousers and anorak before putting the shirts and jumper in the drawer of the ancient looking cupboard.

'Now mind and look after your new clothes, Eddie, as they cost a lot of money. If that Bruce guy tears anything else then I'm sending the bill to his mother.'

Eddie sat down on the bed and closed his eyes. Life wasn't

getting any easier and he was worried that his father hadn't sent any letters to see how they were getting on or, even better, insisting that they came back home.

Feeling exhausted, Sadie sat down on the chair and decided to wait till her mother came home in case she wanted something to eat as well. Maybe, she thought with a sigh, Maryanne would also cook it.

24

Saturday was another hot sunny day. Evie and Tommy got ready to go into town. 'Do you think Eddie will want to come with us?' asked Evie.

Tommy said she would ask him and she knocked on Mary-anne's door. Sadie answered and she sounded delighted by this request. 'Eddie, Tommy wants to know if you want to go into town with them,' she called.

Eddie came out of his bedroom dressed in his cream coloured trousers and a white short-sleeved cotton T-shirt. He didn't seem pleased by this request but on the other hand he didn't want to stay in on this lovely day so he gave a halfhearted shrug and went outside.

Tommy was ecstatic that he was joining them but Evie also looked happy. As they set off down the hill, Tommy asked him if he had any money to spend. 'Evie and I like going into Woolworths and spending our pocket money there.'

Eddie said he had two shillings but he wanted to save it instead of spending it.

Tommy rolled her eyes. 'You sound like Evie. She likes to save some of her money as well but I like to spend it all.'

When they reached Woolworths, Tommy said, 'I don't suppose you have a shop like this in America.'

Eddie looked surprised. 'Don't be daft, Tommy, of course we have Woolworths stores in America, although not one in our small town. This business was started by Frank Winfield Woolworth who was an American millionaire.' Tommy didn't believe this but Evie backed him up although she wasn't a hundred per cent sure if this was the truth.

Once inside, Tommy made straight for the sweet counter, while the other two didn't spend any of their money. One thing about Tommy was that she was a generous soul and offered them a sweet from the bag. Eddie, who had lovely white teeth, didn't have one but Evie pulled a toffee from the bag.

Tommy still couldn't believe about the shop being started by an American. 'Why does he have shops in this country when he doesn't live here?'

'He has stores all over the world, that's why he became a millionaire, and although he's dead now his family still own them.'

They were making their way along the Murraygate when they spotted two of their classmates, Jean Reid and Amy Hutton. When they saw Eddie they came running over the road with squeals of delight. Amy was a very pretty girl and she knew it. The fact that Eddie dressed differently from the other boys she knew and that he was American were so appealing to her. She put her arm through his and tried to pull him away while Jean stood by with a bemused smile.

'We're just going to meet my mother, Eddie. Do you want to come with us as she's treating us to our dinner in Franchi's restaurant?' Much to Amy's disappointment, Eddie said a polite thank you but said he had to be somewhere else and they said a quick cheerio to him while ignoring Evie and Tommy.

Tommy was furious. She mimicked Amy. 'We're going to a restaurant, Eddie, do you want to come?'

He laughed. 'As a matter of fact I would have gone but I want to find a post office as I need to buy an airmail letter to write to my dad.' He winked at Evie while Tommy stood open mouthed.

Evie said there was a post office on the Hilltown beside the Plaza picture house so they made their way there.

Sadie sat in the house after Eddie left. His departure was followed by Maryanne's, who was going to meet up with her friend Dorothy who wanted to buy a new frock for a family wedding and wanted someone with her to give their opinion.

Sadie hated sitting in the dismal house with its old and well-worn furniture so she wandered along the lane to see the Potters. She gave a rueful laugh at this move. What had her life turned out to be when she traded one dismal house for a conversation with two dreary people?

Eliza was making a cup of tea for her mother when Sadie skirted around the two basket chairs outside the door. They hadn't moved out in the sunshine because it didn't shine on the front of the houses until early afternoon.

Martha looked delighted with her visitor. 'I was wondering when you would pay us a visit, Sadie. I thought we had offended you.'

Eliza gave her mother a warning glance but Sadie wasn't in the mood for sarcasm. 'No, Martha, I've been really busy with going for new clothes for my son and also looking for a job.' She refused the cup of tea when Eliza offered her one. 'No thanks, I've just had a cup of coffee.' She looked at Martha. 'I bought the coffee from Braithwaite's shop.'

Martha, who was in the middle of eating a Rich Tea biscuit, said, 'My, you are Mrs Moneybags, aren't you?'

'In America, coffee isn't a luxury but an everyday drink.'

Eliza wanted to defuse this conversation. 'When are you going back, Sadie?'

Sadie gave her a look. 'I'm not going back, Eliza. I've just said I went for a job interview and I've got the job.' Martha spluttered on her tea while Sadie seemed delighted by this reaction. 'Yes, I've got a job as an office assistant and saleswoman at D. Fleming and Son on King Street. I start on Monday.'

'I know that shop, that's where we bought our wireless from a few years ago. It's a busy place if I mind right,' said Eliza.

Martha wanted to know why she was home for good. 'Is there a reason you're not going back to your husband, Sadie? Has he divorced you?'

Sadie was outraged. 'No he hasn't. I'm hoping he'll come over here to stay.' She turned to Eliza. 'We have a farm which is miles from anywhere. The nearest small town is twenty miles away and although it's a pleasant place there's nothing happening there. My one pleasure is going to the movie house on a Saturday but it's closing down so there's nowhere else to go.'

Eliza sympathised with her but she said there wasn't too much to do anywhere. 'One place is much like any other.'

Martha butted in. 'What nonsense, Eliza. You've had a fulfilling life here with me. What else do you need?'

Sadie could have gladly strangled this selfish woman. 'I remember when I was a girl, you were engaged to be married to Michael, Eliza.'

Martha snorted. 'She had a lucky escape from that.'

Eliza looked sad. 'No, we didn't get married. My dad died suddenly and Mum couldn't cope on her own so I postponed the wedding. Michael got a job abroad and we just lost touch.'

Martha said, 'If he had wanted to get in touch with her he would have.'

Eliza was tired of all this talk of Michael so she changed the subject. 'Morag and Rory are having the baby christened tomorrow and I'm hoping to go to the church with Grace and Anna. Would you like to come as well, Sadie?'

Sadie said no, she wanted to get ready for her work on Monday. Martha was surprised. 'Do you need a whole twenty-four hours to get ready?'

Sadie was annoyed but she nodded. 'Well it's a big step for me and I want everything to go fine.'

She stood up and Eliza said she wanted to go to the baker's shop so she would walk along with her.

'Get some cream cakes and chocolate biscuits when you're out,' said Martha.

When they were outside she apologised for her mother's rudeness.

'I haven't thought of Michael in years but when Morag and Rory moved in next door I saw his brother Murdo and he resembled Michael so much when he was that age, so now he's on my mind all the time.'

Sadie sympathised. 'I know how you feel but marriage isn't all honeymoons and roses so maybe you did have a lucky escape.'

Eliza didn't look convinced but she headed towards the shop while Sadie went inside.

Evie, Tommy and Eddie had arrived back from the town and Eddie had gravitated towards the Gow household while Tommy went inside her own house. Thomas had been making the tea and had placed three plates with boiled ham and sliced tomatoes on the table and was busy slicing a loaf. 'Put the kettle on, Tommy, your mum won't be long now as she gets away early on a Saturday.'

Tommy did as she was told. 'Dad, did you know Woolworths store was owned by an American millionaire? Eddie told us that.'

Thomas said no, he didn't know that. 'I always thought it was owned by someone in Dundee.'

Anna came in at that moment and Tommy repeated the story to her but her mum was tired as she flopped down on a chair. 'What a busy day I've had. The shop has been packed all day and it's been so hot.'

Thomas said the tea was ready 'After your tea you can put your feet up for a rest. No doubt the bar will also be busy tonight with people wanting to quench their thirst with pints of beer.'

The next morning was also sunny and hot. Eddie was up early and when he went outside he met Evie and Tommy. 'We're going to the church to see the baby christened, do you want to come with us?' asked Tommy.

Eddie didn't really want to go but as there didn't seem to be any alternative, he agreed.

Grace and Eliza appeared, dressed in their best dresses and jackets and wearing hats. Tommy said her mother had decided not to go as she was having a lie-in. Then coming along the lane was Morag, Rory and Murdo pushing the pram with the baby asleep inside. When they came abreast of Eddie, Morag handed him a small decorated bag. 'This is Catriona's christening piece, Eddie,' she said.

The two girls waited but the party passed on. 'Why did we not get a bag,' asked Tommy who looked deeply disappointed.

Grace explained that thc tradition was to give this gift to the first man or boy they met if the baby was a girl but if it had been a boy then one of thc girls would get it.

Eddie decided to put this bag in the house. His mother was still fast asleep but his granny was sitting at the table with her breakfast of tea and toast. Eddie told her about the gift.

'You better put it in your room,' she said.

Before putting it on the dressing table, he opened it. There was a piece of iced cake and a two shilling coin wrapped in tissue paper and he was deeply touched by this so-called tradition. He joined the rest and they made their way to Bonnethill Church where they found seats at the back as it was full of worshippers.

Morag wore a green dress and jacket while the two men were looking handsome in dark suits. There was a young man and woman standing beside them at the font and the baby looked lovely in a long white robe with a frilly hat.

The girls were transfixed by this service but Eliza couldn't take her eyes away from Murdo and the sight of him brought back painful memories.

After the service they made their way back to the lane where Grace had put on a feast of lemonade, tea, sandwiches and cakes. The MacCallums had made their own arrangements for their christening meal but everyone else enjoyed Grace's hospitality. Tommy wanted to know who the two strangers at the church had been and Eliza explained they were the baby's godparents and that every christening had these people who promised to look after the child's spiritual life.

'The other people in the front pew were the parents of Morag and Rory,' she said. 'I saw them when they came to look at the house with the young couple.'

Grace had arranged for Anna, Thomas, Maryanne, Bella and Albert to come and join in and also her mother Evelyn who had been driven over in Bill's van, and because the room was too small to accommodate them, a table and chair were carried outside and everyone sat in the sunshine. Even Sadie put in an appearance and Tommy was eager to tell her about Eddie and the christening piece.

Sadie was surprised but she was pleased that her son seemed to be settling in the small community. Eliza said she had better leave early to go back to Martha but Bill and Thomas, who had drunk beer instead of tea and juice, said they would go and bring her along so she could join in the celebration.

Eliza was unsure. 'She can't walk far, Bill.'

'Then we'll carry her, won't we, Thomas? Maybe Eddie can help us.'

They set off. Martha was very disgruntled that she had been left alone but she brightened up when the men appeared. It took some manhandling but with Bill and Thomas holding on to each arm and Eddie holding her walking stick they managed to walk the few paces to the Gows' front door where she was put into a chair beside the table which held all the food. Her eyes lit up when she saw the spread and she managed to eat four or five sandwiches, four cakes and two scones with jam. Bill said with a chuckle that he was glad she was just here for an hour or two and not a fortnight and everyone laughed.

They all agreed that having a new baby in the lane was a

good sign for the future and as the sun moved from the front of the houses, it was time to break up the party. There was just the one problem. Martha was stuck in her chair and they couldn't budge her even with a lot of pushing and pulling.

Eliza was beside herself with worry but everyone else had to hide their laughter as it was like moving an elephant.

Albert joined Sadie, Grace and Anna, and with six pairs of hands they soon dislodged her and she tottered to her feet.

'Just take your time, Martha,' said Bill. 'We'll get you home okay.'

'I should bloody hope so,' she replied but she was laughing. After getting her installed in her own chair at home, Eliza joined her and she thanked the men for all their help. Sadie had watched all this and she said briskly that Eliza should invest in a wheelchair for her mother and all the women agreed.

'I must tell Eliza to ask the doctor about a wheelchair,' said Grace. 'After all, she is too heavy for her daughter to manage.'

'Especially after five sandwiches and four cakes,' replied Maryanne, who as usual had eaten very little.

Eddie stayed behind with Evie's granny, Grace, Bill and Tommy to watch the television while Sadie and her mother went home. Eddie loved Evie's house as it was always friendly and homely. He felt a bit guilty about this as it wasn't his granny's fault that her house was cold and uninviting.

Many years later he was to remember this sunny day as one of joy and laughter.

25

Sadie was up early on Monday morning as she was determined make a good impression on her first day at work. Her mother had left earlier for her job in the sweet factory and Eddie was eating a bowl of cornflakes.

'Now you will remember to go to Evie's house after school until I get home? I've spoken to Grace and she doesn't mind looking after you.'

Eddie nodded as this was the sixth time she had mentioned this routine and he would be glad when she was ready to leave as he knew she was feeling nervous. He hoped that once she had done one day at the shop she would be less jittery. As it was, she had tried on three dresses already but thankfully she had settled on an outfit and was ready to go.

'Wish me luck, Eddie,' she said and he went with her to the door where she walked to the end of the lane before turning and waving.

Eddie was torn between his love for his mother and his longing to be back home with his dad, and he hoped she would come to her senses and decide to go back to where he felt he belonged. He took the blue airmail paper from his pocket and, moving the empty bowl, he began to write his letter.

He decided to mention how unhappy he was in Dundee and how he wanted to be home. He sent news of his granny and his mother and signed off, 'Your loving son.' He would post it on his way to school but he still didn't understand why there had been no word from America and he was worried that his dad maybe didn't want him or his mother back. Evie and Tommy calling at the door made him collect his bag and he set off with them.

Meanwhile Sadie made her way towards King Street. It was another hot day and she couldn't remember such a sunny and warm summer. Normally it would be a mixture of sun, heavy rain and cold winds. When she reached the shop it was already open for business and she panicked, thinking she was late, but Bert, who was standing behind the counter, put her mind at rest.

'The shop opens at eight-thirty but the workshop starts at seven-thirty,' he said, and started to show her how to use the cash register and the cash ledger which she had to fill in every day before leaving. 'David said I can help you for today to show you the ropes so if you need to know anything just ask.'

Sadie was pleased to hear she wouldn't be expected to know how everything was run but she was confident that she was a quick learner. As it turned out, her first customer was difficult: a small woman who was unseasonally dressed in a coat with a headscarf over her hair. 'I've been looking at yon television in the window, the one with a deposit and weekly terms,' she said.

Sadie went with her to the window where the said television was displayed, along with two others. 'Which one are you interested in?'

The woman pointed to the set that resembled a piece of furniture with its screen surrounded with a polished wooden cabinet. A large placard stated that it could be purchased for ten shillings deposit and ten shillings a week.

Sadie looked around for Bert and was relieved when he came through from the back shop. 'This customer wants to buy this television on easy terms,' she said and Bert smiled at the woman.

'You'll need to fill out a hire purchase form but we'll need your husband to come and sign it.'

The woman looked annoyed. 'I'm a widow but it's my three sons who want to buy it and they'll be paying for it.'

'Can one of your sons come in and sign the form Mrs…'

'I'm Mrs Petrie and I'll get my oldest boy Robert to come in after work tonight.'

Bert said that this was ideal. 'We can deliver the set this week after one of our electricians fixes up your aeriel and he'll install it as well.'

Mrs Petrie, satisfied that everything was in place, left. Bert said that once the hire purchase form was signed and the deposit paid then the customer would get a payment book which she would bring in every week with the instalments.

As the morning wore on it became clear to Sadie that this a busy business and her next customer was a well-dressed woman wearing a summer suit and fashionable hat. She browsed around the table lamps and Sadie went to help her, finding to her amazement that she was a good saleswoman. The customer finally bought one of the dearest lamps and paid cash which Sadie rang up on the register. At midday, Bert showed her where she could eat her meal in the staff room but as she hadn't prepared anything she decided to go for a short walk in the sun.

As she was leaving she met two of the young electricians coming out of the workshop. They both stopped in their tracks and one gave a wolf whistle. 'We heard there was someone glamorous starting but we thought Bert was kidding us.'

Sadie loved having this effect so she gave them a big smile before going on her way. Then in the afternoon a young lass came in and enquired about a record player. Sadie showed her the latest Dansette model and the girl was over the moon. 'It says I can have it on easy terms,' she said.

Sadie repeated what Bert had said to Mrs Petrie. 'You'll need to get your father to come in and sign the form.'

The girl's face fell. 'Oh, he won't come in as he hates music in the house and he won't let me have it.'

Sadie wondered how she was intending to play it had she been able to buy it but instead she said, 'Maybe you should save the money up and when you have enough then come in and buy it.'

The girl was almost crying. 'That'll take ages. I wanted it now.' Sadie almost said, don't we all, and the girl went out of the shop with a disappointed face.

Then just before five o'clock a young man in overalls stained with paint came in and said he was Robert Petrie. 'I've to sign a form before we can get our television.'

Bert produced it and by five-thirty another purchase was completed. Sadie felt tired after being on her feet all day but Bert was pleased with the day's takings and it was all entered in the cash ledger. He produced a bunch of keys and said he would lock up after letting Sadie leave and she was glad to be out in the fresh air although she was pleased about her first day at work.

It had been years since she had done any outside work and the thought of earning money made her feel important. She would no longer have to rely on money from someone else. Ed wasn't a mean man but she sometimes felt beholden to him if she wanted to buy something that wasn't deemed necessary. How well she recalled old Joel muttering how his late wife never needed any money as he provided for her. Sadie had once told him he lived in the last century when women were looked upon as chattels. Ed had laughed at that but Sadie knew she had hit a raw spot with her father-in-law.

She was making her way along the street when she saw a man hurrying past her. She gasped and called out, 'Peter Ronaldson, I don't believe it.'

The man turned and it was his turn to look surprised. 'Sadie, where did you spring from?'

She pointed to the shop behind her. 'I work in that electrical shop, D. Fleming and Son.'

He seemed stunned. 'I work there as well. I'm an electrician.'

Sadie noticed they were passing a pub with a small lounge bar. 'Come and have a drink with me and we can talk over old times.'

Peter said he couldn't. 'I have to be home as we're having visitors.'

Sadie put on her wide-eyed look. 'Please, just for old times.'

Peter didn't want to go but he also didn't want to be churlish so he went in with her. The lounge was empty but there were a few tables and comfy looking chairs. Sadie sat down while Peter ordered a couple of shandies. Sadie would have loved something stronger but she smiled at him. 'You don't look a day older than when I last saw you, Peter.'

He noticed that she had brought her chair right beside his and he was uncomfortable with being so close to her. He gave a rueful smile. 'Our two young apprentices mentioned this good-looking blonde assistant but I never dreamed it was you. Are you on holiday from America?'

Sadie made a face. 'No I'm not. I've left my husband and brought my son Eddie back here. We are living with my mother at the moment but I'm hoping to get a house of my own.'

Peter blurted out, 'I'm married as well and we have two children.'

'Do you have a photo of them?' she asked innocently which was a camouflage because Sadie was never innocent or naïve.

Peter produced a small snapshot from his wallet and passed it over. 'My wife is Norma and the kids are Peter and Laura.'

Sadie was relieved to see his wife, although pretty with dark hair, wasn't a patch on her. The two children, a boy and a girl, looked primary-school age. She handed it back. 'What a lovely family. Where do you live?'

'We moved to our new house in Beechwood not long ago.' He looked at his watch. 'I better be getting along but it's been great seeing you again.'

Sadie started to cry, much to the barman's scrutiny and Peter's dismay. She wiped her eyes and looked at him. 'I should never have left you, Peter, I regret it but my head was turned by Ed who seemed so glamorous but has turned out to be an ordinary corn farmer in Nebraska.'

Peter was desperate to escape but he said, 'You broke my heart, Sadie. I asked you to marry me after I did my national service but then you sent me that letter when I was in Germany. If I remember rightly you wrote it after you had married your husband.'

Sadie looked sad. 'Yes I know and I'm so sorry.'

Peter looked angry. 'Do you know what letters like that are called in the army? "Dear John" letters, and they are so hurtful. When I came home on leave you were away as a GI bride. I took ages to get over you.'

Sadie said she was sorry again but Peter stood up. 'I have to get off home as Norma always has the meal ready and we are expecting her mum and dad to come round later.' He stopped and bent over her. 'I would be grateful if you don't make our past life known at the shop as I don't want Norma to hear any gossip.' On that final note he left.

Sadie, instead of being downhearted, was pleased. She was a great reader of faces and she knew he was still in love with her. It would be sad for his wife and family but maybe this meeting was her destiny. She walked over to the small counter and ordered a gin and tonic. She felt its warmth spread over her and she felt relaxed and languid. She was no stranger to alcohol as along with Ed and Joel she would drink rye and soda or bottles of beer on their verandah on summer nights.

When she stood up after her drink she suddenly felt unsteady. The barman was polishing glasses but she knew he was watching her. Pulling herself up she walked to the door with as much dignity as her high heels would allow.

She wasn't sure if she would manage to walk up the hill and she knew she shouldn't have ordered a proper drink. She suddenly realised she hadn't had anything to eat all day so that was the reason the drink had gone to her head. She knew she had to get home to make a meal for Eddie and herself but when she reached the house she was grateful to find that Grace had given her son his evening meal. Maryanne gave her a sharp look but said nothing as she watched her making some tea and toast with a boiled egg.

26

Peter felt a mixture of emotions as he sat on the top deck of the bus. He couldn't believe that Sadie had shown up again and also in close proximity of his workspace. She looked almost the same as the last time he had seen her. It had been at the railway station in the autumn of 1944 as he set off to do his national service.

On his first leave they had made plans to get engaged then be married when his two-year stint was over. Then he had been posted to Germany and the courtship had carried on by letters until that fateful day when she said she had married her American sailor. Seemingly his ship had docked in Dundee and she had fallen in love with him – a whirlwind affair as she described it.

That night in Bremen after getting the letter he had gone out and got drunk but thankfully his two pals had realised what had happened and they got him back to the barracks safely. Charlie had said the next morning, 'Don't worry, mate, you're not alone in getting a "Dear John" letter so just forget her as there are hundreds of girls to meet.'

But he was heartbroken as Sadie had been the most important person in his life and he spent the rest of his service feeling his life had ended. Then he met Norma at his aunt's house and he found happiness again.

'What am I going to do?' he asked himself as the bus

rumbled its way towards his destination. He was aware he still felt attracted to her and he even remembered she was wearing the same perfume as she had all those years ago. It was Coty L'Aimant and he had given her a large bottle that last Christmas. Now she had been sitting across from him with the same perfume and the same lovely face.

He almost passed his stop as he was deep in thought and he had to rush to get off. As he made his way to the house he dithered about telling Norma about Sadie but when he opened the door, Peter and Laura rushed to meet him.

'Daddy, you're late. Mummy has had to keep the tea warm in the oven.'

Norma popped her head around the kitchen door. 'Don't listen to them, Peter. They are on their way to bed. Mum and Dad can't come tonight but they'll be here tomorrow.'

A warm, happy feeling washed over him as he ushered the kids into the bedroom.

'Read us a story, Daddy.'

He looked at his wife and she nodded. 'The meal will keep another fifteen minutes.'

Later, as they sat watching television, he almost mentioned meeting Sadie but his courage failed him. He didn't want anything to hurt Norma as she and his children were his whole life. Before going to bed she asked him, 'Is everything all right at work, Peter? You've been very quiet tonight.'

He was mortified. 'Yes, the work is fine. I just feel a bit tired tonight, that's all.'

However at three o'clock in the morning he awoke from a vivid dream of Sadie. They were together again, his hands stroking her lovely long hair and her face was upturned to his in a loving look. He made his way to the kitchen and drank a glass of cold water where he made up his mind to keep out of Sadie's way as he couldn't allow another meeting in a pub or indeed anywhere. He was dreading going in to work the next morning and he almost pretended to be sick. Norma gave him a strange look.

'Are you sure you're all right, Peter? You look very pale.'

He picked up his bag and assured her he was fine but he was churned up inside and desperate for it not to show. 'I'll see you all tonight.'

The children came running through in their pyjamas. Five-year-old Laura's ones had teddy bears on hers but Peter, who felt more grown up at eight years old, wore plain blue ones.

'See you tonight, Daddy,' they said as he kissed them good-bye.

He grinned. 'Do I have a choice? Now get ready for school and be good.'

When he reached the workshop it was already open. There was no sign of Sadie but fifteen minutes later Bert came in and mentioned she had arrived late. 'I hope she's going to be a better timekeeper than this,' he muttered to David, the boss.

'If she's not then we'll have to let her go,' David replied.

The two young apprentices groaned with dismay at the thought of losing this attractive woman who was a vast improvement on the last one who had been with the firm for years but had finally retired. What a dragon she had been. Peter felt a sense of relief that Sadie might not be long with the firm but if that wasn't the case then he had decided during the night that he would look for another job. He was due to go out to fit a television aerial to a house in Fintry and he was glad to escape. As he made his way in the work's van he thought it was like escaping jail.

However the job didn't take that long so he was back in the workshop at closing time. He was dismayed when he saw Sadie waiting outside. She made it look as if their meeting was accidental but as he walked away, she stayed a couple of steps behind. When they were out of sight of the shop she caught up.

'I see you get your bus at the top of the Wellgate steps and I'm going that way as well,' she said. Peter almost made a run for it but if it meant just walking to the bus stop then that would be the end of it. Sadie, however, had other ideas.

'I thought we might go to the pictures one night.'

Peter said that wasn't possible as his wife wouldn't want that.

She sounded surprised by his abruptness. 'I wasn't asking your wife to come along, Peter. As old friends I thought we could have a night out together. We used to have such fun in the old days.'

Peter stopped and looked at her. She looked so appealing that he wanted to be kind to her but he knew if he went down that road she would make more and more demands on the pretext of being old friends. He didn't mean his words to come out as harshly as they did. 'Sadie, I'm a married man now with a wife and children I love very much. You are also married with a son and my advice is to go back to your husband and make a life for yourself with him.'

Sadie was angry at being rebuffed. 'Oh, stop being so perfectly married, it doesn't suit you.'

By now Peter was slowly getting annoyed. 'I won't deny I was madly in love with you years ago, in fact I thought you were my whole world when we planned to get married after my army service, but you changed all that when you married your husband. It took me a couple of years to get over you and that was with the help of my wife Norma. I don't like working in the same place as you but if you have any decent feelings you'll keep away from me and not bother me again.'

He marched away quickly, leaving her in tears, but he knew he had to distance himself from her as he now realised how selfish she was. This was something he had noticed during his years with her but he had put it down to her young age and by now she should have grown up and stopped wanting everything to go her way.

Sadie walked alone, wiping tears from her eyes. She could do with a drink but she didn't fancy going back into that lounge bar with the curious barman looking at her. She knew there was an off-licence shop on Strathmartine Road so she made her way there where she bought a half bottle of gin and a bottle of tonic water.

Back home she discovered there was no one in. Eddie would be with the Gows but she had no idea where her mother was, not that she was bothered. She poured a large measure of gin into a tumbler and added the tonic water. After a few sips she felt calm again but decided not to bother cooking anything. She then had a second drink before putting the two bottles in a bag under her bed.

She was lying on her bed when she heard Eddie. She called out, 'I'll get your tea ready, Eddie, just give me a minute.' She struggled to her feet and was amazed when she almost fell over onto the floor. Surely a couple of drinks wouldn't do that, she thought, until she noticed the bottle of gin now lying on the table and it was half empty.

She staggered through to the kitchen but Eddie was in his room. She called his name but he didn't open the door. 'I've had my tea at Evie's house,' he said.

Sadie was relieved she didn't have to cook but she said, 'I must see Grace and thank her and offer to pay for your food.'

Eddie didn't answer and finding the house quiet she decided to go and see Granny Duff. Bella was listening to the wireless and was surprised by the sudden appearance of Sadie. She knew she had been drinking but she didn't mention it. 'Sadie, how are you?'

Sadie was feeling sorry for herself and moaned. 'I'm totally fed up. I got a telling off at work this morning for being late and I found out that an ex-boyfriend of mine works there. I tried being friendly with him but he snubbed me and was quite nasty.'

Bella was dismayed by the dishevelled sight of the woman. She was unsure what to say, as it had been years since she left Meadow Lane. Bella didn't know what her life was like in America although she had heard rumours from Martha, but then she was a gossip who liked to dramatise every situation.

'Are you happy with your life in Nebraska?'

This simple statement opened up the floodgates and Sadie's face twisted in a scowl. 'It's been terrible and nothing like I imagined it would be. For a start we live on a farm in the middle of nowhere. All my husband and his father think about is the growing of corn or the price of corn.'

Bella said that was normal. 'You must have known his background when you married him, Sadie.'

Sadie looked at her as if she was mad. 'No I didn't. He was so dashing and different from the boys in Dundee and it was love at first sight.'

'Didn't he mention his background when you were planning to get married?'

Sadie looked down at her hands, which she noticed were shaking slightly. 'He might have mentioned living on a farm but I thought it was like the farms around here that are not far from towns. Our farm is so far from civilisation that it could be on the moon.' Sadie leant forward, a serious look on her face. 'Do you know how far we are from the nearest town, Granny?'

Bella said she didn't.

'It's over twenty miles away and that twenty miles is nothing but fields with small houses dotted about. Eddie gets the school bus every morning then Ed goes off to work and I sit in the house looking at miles of earth.' She rubbed her forehead as she felt the beginning of a headache. 'I spend every day on my own apart from Esther who is my father-in-law's housekeeper and she has the mental handicap of an idiot. All she does with her life is cooking and baking and knitting and making garish-looking quilts.'

Bella thought she sounded like a great woman with wonderful housekeeping skills that were similar to her own mother when she was alive.

Sadie was now on her soapbox. 'I managed to get a job in the town on my monthly visit for shopping. It was just an assistant in the general store but it was a busy place and I would have met lots of people to chat to but Ed put his foot down. Said he couldn't drive me there every day and pick me up. I said I could go on the school bus but he said that wasn't allowed and the bus that went there wouldn't be suitable either.' She sounded angry.

Bella could well imagine the boredom of a young woman not born into this community. 'Couldn't you learn to drive?' She stopped. 'In whatever car you've got.'

'It's a truck and Ed said it was needed for transport on the farm. Anyway, it was too big for me to drive.'

Bella felt sorry for her frustration but she had been so starry eyed with her American GI that she hadn't stopped to weigh up the consequences of her hasty marriage. Still, she wasn't alone in that respect and she could name a dozen young brides who were just as unhappy here in Dundee. 'Can I give you a bit of advice, Sadie?'

Sadie nodded. 'I always liked coming here when I was young as you were so good to me.'

Bella was pleased with the compliment. She had known Sadie from the age of four and had watched her growing up into a beautiful woman who sadly was a handful for her mother. She well remembered the tantrums of those early years that never really went away. It seemed as if Maryanne couldn't handle her and she often gave in to her daughter's demands.

'All I can say is for you and Eddie to go back to your husband.' She couldn't finish as Sadie reacted with fury.

'I've just told you I don't want to go back.'

Bella held up her hand. 'Just listen, Sadie. Please consider going back and making your husband understand your need for that job. Make him listen to your unhappiness and boredom and tell him he has to consider your feelings. Can you do that?'

Sadie said she would think about it and stood up to go. 'All

I want to do is make a life for Eddie and me here.'

Bella said she understood. 'Give it a go and if your husband is still stubborn to your wishes then at least you've tried and then you can make plans for a better life.'

After she was gone, Bella sat very still. There was no easy answer to an unhappy marriage but was she the best person to give advice? After all she had never married and who knows, maybe she would have been in the same situation had Davie survived the war.

The door opened and she half expected Sadie to walk in but it was Albert. 'I see you've had the fair Sadie keeping you company. I saw her leave and she didn't look well.' Bella had no intention of repeating her conversation but Albert continued, 'She was always a problem, even as a child. I saw lots of arguments when I used to collect the insurance money every week. I always felt sorry for Maryanne.'

Bella looked at him and shook her head. 'The one I feel sorry for is Sadie. She's at a crossroads in her life and I worry about it.'

'She should be happy, Bella. She has the looks of a film star and a lovely son, what can go wrong?'

Bella had a deep feeling of the unknown. 'Yes, you're right, Albert. What can go wrong?'

When Sadie returned home, Eddie and her mother were nowhere to be seen so she went into her room and poured out another drink.

Peter, on the other hand, was stone cold sober as he made his way home. Like Sadie, his hands were also shaking but his were with worry. Sadie could become a nuisance at work as it wouldn't take long for the staff to figure out their past relationship. This wasn't the problem: her actions were. He realised she had always been erratic and self-obsessed but he had been too much in love with her to bother about it.

He now saw what a lucky escape he had had and his wife Norma, although she didn't have the same glamorous looks, was his whole life. As he was climbing the stairs he made up his mind to leave his job although he loved working for Fleming Electrics. There were always loads of jobs for electricians and he knew he was good at his job. He would look at the newspaper after his tea and see what was available, but he was unsure how he would explain this sudden decision to Norma. He would give it another few days then he would tell her the truth. Maybe Sadie would become the best timekeeper but there again he remembered Bert being annoyed at her lateness. If she kept that up then they would give her the sack. He suddenly felt sorry for her.

27

The next morning the postman delivered four letters to Meadow Lane, two of which were for the MacCallums and turned out to be bills. Sadie awoke to the sound of Eddie talking to the man as he was getting ready for school and she was mortified to see she was late for work again. She vaguely recalled her mother trying to waken her up at seven o'clock but she must have gone back to sleep again.

She had a headache and was trying to get up when Eddie rushed into the room clutching an open blue airmail letter. He was in a rage.

'Dad has written to ask why you haven't answered his last letter.' He waved the blue piece of paper in her direction. 'When did you get this letter and why didn't you tell me about it?'

Sadie lost her temper. 'That letter wasn't meant to be opened by you, Eddie, it was written to me so give it to me.'

He snatched it out of her reach. 'No, it was addressed to me as I wrote to him, asking why he wasn't getting in touch, and he says he did write but got no answer.'

By now she was sitting on the edge of the bed, looking as if she was ready to cry. 'I was going to answer it, Eddie, but I didn't want to hurt his feelings by telling him we're not going back to America.'

'Well I'm going to write back and tell him I'm going home

even if you don't want to come, Mum.' By now he was almost in tears as well.

Then came a knock on the door; it was Evie. 'I'm not coming to school,' he said just as Tommy joined her.

'There's a row going on at home,' she said. 'We got a letter from Ireland and Dad is angry about it.'

Eddie gave his mother a warning glance and placed the letter in his pocket as Evie asked him why he wasn't going to school. Eddie gave this some thought and at that moment, as he didn't want a fight with his mother, he picked up his bag and walked out.

Sadie felt ill with shock. She had no idea that Ed would write to Eddie, and if the letter had arrived later she would have burned it. She glanced at the clock to see it was almost nine o'clock so she decided it was no use going into work, not with her head pounding like mad. A cup of coffee and an aspirin tablet would shift the headache but not the way she was feeling. Everything was going wrong with this new life she had planned for ages, saving up small sums of money in an effort to make her escape. Ed had bought the two tickets for their travel but he was under the impression it was to visit her sick mother and that they would be coming back.

She was angry and humiliated with Peter and the way he had spoken to her last night and she suddenly made up her mind about this job. She wouldn't go back and maybe her absence would make him realise how much he needed her and he would come running back to her. It had happened in the past so why not now, she thought.

She carried the cup of coffee and aspirin back to bed, satisfied she had made the right decision.

Next door at the Cassidy house, the argument was still in full flow because of the letter they had received. Anna was desperate to get off to work, as she was already late, but Thomas was still angry.

The letter had come from Anna's sister Lizzie in Belfast and it stated that she was coming over to see them. Thomas had never got on with Anna's family and he wasn't pleased about the visit. 'Why is she coming over now, Anna? Have you been in touch with her?'

Anna said she had no idea and she hadn't been in touch. 'I haven't written since sending the card at Christmas and I don't know what she wants so stop shouting at me.' She picked up her handbag and went to the door. 'I'll answer her letter tonight and ask her what she wants.'

Thomas was immediately contrite as Anna was almost in tears. 'Oh, I'm sorry, love, I shouldn't take it out on you but your family don't like me and they've never made a secret of that dislike.'

Anna walked over to him and gave him a hug. 'I know, Thomas. I don't get on with them either. That's why we live here and not in Ireland. I'll write tonight to see what's happening.'

On that note Meadow Lane returned to its placid place in the world but both Anna and Sadie knew that there were ructions looming on the horizon.

Evie had overheard a snatch of the Boyds' row as she stood at the door which had been left open when Eddie met the postman and she knew it was all about his dad in America and his mum's refusal to go back. Tommy, on the other hand, was full of her parents' letter.

'My Auntie Lizzie is coming over for a week soon and Dad can't stand her or Mum's family. It all goes back to when he lived in Ireland but I don't know what the matter is with them.' She sounded disappointed.

Eddie was still angry. He suspected his mother had destroyed his dad's first letter and as he was also worried about her, it made him confused about his feelings. He loved them both but how it was all going to end he had no idea. All he knew was the fact that he wanted to be back in his old life.

Evie felt sorry for the two of them and she was grateful for her happy home with two loving parents.

Later in the afternoon Sadie had a change of plan. She dressed carefully and made her way to her job. She would plead a sudden illness and no doubt they would be grateful for the fact that she had turned up in spite of being in pain.

One of the apprentices noticed her and he went back into the workshop to pass on the news. It was common knowledge that Bert and David were annoyed that she hadn't turned up. Peter, who was working there, stopped what he was doing for a moment then bent his head back to the radio he was repairing. It looked like he would need to search for a new job, he thought with sadness.

Bert was serving at the counter but after the customer left he told Sadie that she had to go and see the boss. She was taken aback as she thought she could just go behind the counter to see to the other customer who was looking into the glass shelves.

She went into the small back office where David Fleming was sitting behind a desk piled high with paperwork. A black telephone was on one corner and it began to ring. He motioned for her to sit down on one of the odd assortment of chairs and she sat with her ankles crossed and her hands in her lap, looking like a little girl who had been caught pinching the cakes.

After the telephone call he looked at her but before he could say a word she hurried on with her prepared speech. 'I'm really sorry, Mr Fleming, but I was ill this morning and I couldn't get in touch as I had to get my son off to school before going back to bed.'

He sat quietly until this speech came to an end. 'I'm really sorry as well, Mrs Boyd, but I'll have to let you go. We need someone who is reliable.' He gestured to the pile of paperwork on the desk. 'All these invoices have to be written up and dealt with and I can't rely on you to turn up on time or even turn up at all.'

Sadie was annoyed at him. He made her sound like she was work-shy and she wasn't like that. 'I promise I'll not be late again and I'll even stay late tonight to do all that office work.'

He wavered. He was a decent man who knew the reason for her search for work and he didn't like the thought of her son suffering. 'All right then but no more late mornings or absences. If that happens I'll have to let you go and look for someone else.'

Sadie was triumphant. She knew how to get round men and she made a start on the paperwork. 'I'll stay until I finish this and I promise I'll be in on time every morning.'

David wasn't so sure but he was willing to give her another chance. Bert however was annoyed. 'She'll let you down again, mark my words. I'm a good judge of character and she'll never change.'

David was fond of his cousin Bert, but he was displeased at the fact that he didn't think he was a good judge of character like him. 'Well let's see what happens. If she doesn't pull her weight then you can sack her.'

It was only a matter of time, Bert thought. Just a matter of time.

When Peter heard the news he felt worried and he hoped he wouldn't run into her at the end of the day. However she was nowhere to be seen when he set off for home.

In the tiny office, Sadie was getting fed up with all the work so she called through to Bert. 'I'm off home now but I'll be in early tomorrow and finish all this work.'

'Aye,' thought Bert. 'We'll see.'

Sadie emerged into the sunshine of the early evening. She half hoped to see Peter but he was nowhere in sight so she made her way along the sun-dappled pavements, stopping at the off-licence on her way home. As usual Eddie was with Evie in her house but Maryanne was sitting with Martha and

Eliza at their door. She sauntered along but only after she put her bag under the bed.

Martha said, 'Have you had a good day at work, Sadie?' knowing full well she didn't leave until the afternoon as she has seen her through the window.

Sadie said she had. 'I had a lot of the office work to do and I'll have to finish it tomorrow. They are so pleased with me in the shop.'

Martha also knew about the argument over the airmail letter as Eliza had passed the house in the morning and had heard the row with Eddie. 'How is your husband, is he well?' she asked with a wicked glint in her eyes.

Sadie said all was well in America and she asked her mother if she had made her meal. Maryanne had already eaten as had Eddie so Sadie said cheerio to the three women and made her way back along the lane.

The house was quiet with the sunlight filtering through the window which she noticed needed a good wash. It hadn't been done since Grace had cleaned the house but she wasn't going to bother with housework tonight. This room depressed her as it had done all those years ago with its ancient furniture and the worn lino on the floor.

She made up her mind there and then that she would work hard at her job and look for a place of her own. She would fill it with modern furniture like Rory and Morag's house which was bright and clean and a pleasure to be living in.

But first she would have a drink to relax and she lay on her bed with a large tumbler of gin and tonic. When she had been in the bar it had been served with a slice of lemon so she made a mental note to buy a lemon tomorrow.

She must have fallen asleep in her clothes because she didn't hear either her mother or son arrive back. And when she awoke the next morning it was ten o'clock. She hurried down to the shop but Bert was waiting for her with the news that she was no longer employed there.

'Try and get yourself together, lass,' he said as he told her the bad news.

As a reply she swore at him and marched off, which didn't surprise him. He knew all along what her nature was but she had been given the chance to redeem herself and she hadn't done that.

As she walked away in a fury she thought she would find another job easily so Bert could shove his job up his backside.

When Peter heard the news he breathed a sigh of relief but he still felt something for her and he was sorry on her behalf.

Norma noticed a difference in him that night. 'You look happier, Peter.'

He smiled at her. 'Yes, I am. I had a difficult week at work but everything is fine now.' He meant every word and maybe later he would tell her the truth but not at the moment. The peace of his house washed over him and he put his arm around her shoulders as they sat on the couch with their nightly cup of tea.

28

Grace was annoyed as she cleared up the breakfast dishes. In fact she had been quite sharp with Bill before he left for work which surprised him as she was always so calm and cheery.

Two things were to blame. Evie had been to see her granny last night and had come home with the message that Evelyn had a bad cold and she wanted Grace to come and do her shopping, which Grace didn't mind as long as her own domestic arrangements were in order. That was the second thing: they weren't. The bakery tins were all empty which meant she would have to have a baking day, but she wondered if she would have time.

She didn't begrudge looking after Eddie, giving him his meals and generally having him in the house until Maryanne came home but she had been really angry that Sadie seemed to take all this help for granted and never said thank you or contributed to the cost. It had all come to a head last night when Maryanne came in with her week's wages and offered her a ten shilling note.

'I hope it's enough to cover Eddie's food, Grace,' she had said.

Grace was furious at Sadie for allowing her mother to take money from her weekly wage when it was her job to look after her son. She had refused the money, saying Eddie was always welcome in her house. The look of relief on Maryanne's face made her more angry. She couldn't help herself when she said, 'I hope Sadie helps out with money.'

Maryanne looked embarrassed and said it wasn't easy for her to give any help when she had only started her job. 'When she gets sorted out with work then she'll help out.' Grace couldn't help noticing she didn't sound too sure about this.

After putting the dishes in the cupboard she set off for Ann Street. Evelyn was feeling sorry for herself as she sat at the fire with a blanket around her shoulders. She suddenly gave a huge sneeze and she wiped her nose with a large white hanky that looked like it had belonged to her late husband.

'I hate getting a summer cold, Grace, as it always seems to be worse than one in the winter.'

Grace just nodded and began to tidy up the kitchen. 'When I get everything tidied up I'll go and do your shopping, Mum, have you got a list?'

Evelyn picked up a scrap of paper from the table and handed it over. 'Now mind and get Anchor butter, Grace, as I don't like anything else and make sure the tomatoes are small as I hate eating a huge one, I don't like keeping a half back as it gets all soggy.'

Grace said she would bring the right butter back and the dainty tomatoes and she was almost out of the door when Evelyn called out, 'Make sure you get soft rolls and not hard fired ones.'

Grace almost threw the list at her but instead she smiled. Her mother had always been a fussy shopper which was all right when she did it herself but having to get this lecture was irritating. Then halfway down the stairs, Grace stopped to consider her anger and realised it had nothing to do with her mother or Eddie but it was aimed at Sadie. Bill kept remarking what a lovely woman she was and Grace wondered if she was jealous of her.

Later when she got back home she started her baking with a vengeance and she soon had the tins filled up again. Afterwards, sitting down with her cup of tea, she saw Sadie passing the window and she wondered what had happened to her job with the electrical shop.

Although Grace didn't know it, Sadie was also annoyed. She had just left the Potter house and Martha had been sarcastic to her. Sadie didn't like Martha although she felt sorry for Eliza having to live with this dragon of a mother who liked to stir things up.

She had been chatting to Eliza, telling her that she was looking for another job, when Martha had piped up, 'What happened to the other job you had? Did you get the sack?'

Sadie tried to look indignant. 'No I didn't. They begged me to stay on but I hated having to deal with people having to buy things on the never-never.'

'Well, hire purchase is the only way most people can buy things,' said Eliza. 'Not that we have ever bought anything without paying for it outright but not everyone can do that.'

Sadie said airily, 'Well I didn't like the job and now I'm going to an interview for another one but I don't want to say much about it as this lane is a gossip's paradise.'

Martha was outraged. 'I hope you aren't referring to me, young lady.'

Sadie didn't reply but merely stood up and said she had to be off for her interview.

After she left, Eliza had to console her mother with a couple of chocolate biscuits.

Another house at war in the lane was the Cassidys'. Thomas had asked Anna to put her sister's visit off but Anna said she couldn't. 'I haven't seen Lizzie for a couple of years and she's only coming for ten days. You'll just have to put up with her, Thomas.'

He had gone off to his job in the pub in a bad mood. His wife's family was a noisy disruptive bunch of folk who didn't like him and they didn't try to hide this dislike. He had crossed swords with Lizzie back in the early days of his marriage and he still felt bruised by the encounter.

When he opened the pub, the only customer was Albert who remarked on his unhappy face.
'Are you feeling all right, Thomas? You look really fed up.'

Thomas, who didn't want to discuss Lizzie, said he was fine but just a bit tired.

Albert took this with a satisfied nod of his head. 'Have you seen our glamour queen recently?'

Thomas said he hadn't. 'Anna tells me she got a job, she heard it from Martha.'

Albert brought him up to date with the situation. 'I don't know how Martha knows but she told Bella and I that she had got the sack because she was always late.' He added, 'One of Eliza's pals who lives in Caldrum Street has a son who worked in the same shop as Sadie so maybe he told his mother and the woman had passed on this bit of gossip. Martha seems to have her finger on all the gossip.'

Thomas said he never said a truer word.

Meanwhile, the subject of all this gossip was making her way to her interview with the owner of a pub in Logie Street. She had seen the job advertised in the paper and she had written and received an answer.

Hal's Bar was between a dry cleaning business and a chip shop in the busy and bustling street. It had a small window set in glossy brown brick and a small doorway. Sadie thought it looked a bit rundown but she was desperate for a job so she went in.

It was quite large inside with an assortment of chairs and modest tables. A plump man was behind the bar and Sadie introduced herself to him. He was about fifty years old and shabby looking but she saw he had deep brown eyes that were shrewd. She also noticed that there weren't any customers.

They went to sit down at a table. Hal shook her hand and she had to stop herself from wiping it as he left a sweaty film to her palm. He looked as if he couldn't believe his eyes that this gorgeous creature was hoping to work for him. 'I'm Harry Anderson, also known as Hal. I need someone to do my bookkeeping and also help out in the bar during the day. There won't be any evening work as you said in your letter you have a young son.'

Sadie said, 'Yes I do, his name is Eddie and he's almost eleven.'

Hal wasn't sure about employing her. He was a good judge of character, a trait that was helpful in his business, and there was something about this young woman that puzzled him.

'If you don't mind me saying this, Mrs Boyd, I'm sure you can find a better job elsewhere because of your qualifications in office work.' He pointed to her letter in which she had written down what job she had before her marriage, which had been a good position.

Sadie hadn't wanted to mention her estrangement from Ed so she just said, 'I'm married to an American man and I've come back to look after my mother who is ill but I need to earn some money as well. You did say in your advert that this might be a temporary job so I thought it would suit me.'

Hal nodded. 'Yes, my wife normally does the bookkeeping and also serves in the bar but she's had a major operation and won't be able to work for some time.'

Sadie said she was sorry to hear that and told him a temporary job was what she was looking for.

Hal made up his mind. 'Well then, I think that suits both of us so can you start work tomorrow at ten o'clock and finish at six o'clock?'

Sadie said that suited her and she would see him then. As she caught a tramcar home, the thought of this job filled her with horror but she had no intention of staying for long and this would be a stopgap until she found something more suitable. Perhaps if the pub had been more upmarket and pleasant she might have felt differently but it looked like a working man's pub and although quite clean, it still held that stale beer and smoky atmosphere. One good thing about it was that starting at ten meant she would be able to intercept any letters from Ed.

When she reached the lane she saw Martha and Eliza sitting at their door in the sun. She couldn't recall a better summer than this and she felt this was a good omen for her new life. The two women were chatting to a man and didn't notice her as she opened the door. Lying on the floor was the dreaded blue airmail letter addressed to Eddie. Without opening it she lit a match to one end and burnt it. She wasn't having this nonsense from Ed and she would write and tell him that.

Eliza knew her face was flushed when Murdo MacCallum stopped on his way to see Morag and Catriona.

'Hello, Mrs Potter and Eliza, are you enjoying the sunshine?'

Martha gave him one of her rare smiles. 'I'm Martha, that's what all my friends call me.'

Eliza couldn't think of any friends but she was so engrossed in looking at Murdo. Up close he didn't look like Michael, it was more his way of walking and his manner, but she could see her lost love in this man. She caught a whiff of his aftershave and was suddenly taken back years. My God, she thought silently, he's wearing Old Spice, just like Michael. She stood up quickly. Martha and Murdo looked at her and he asked her, 'Are you feeling all right, Eliza?'

She tried to smile but it was more of a grimace. 'I need to get a glass of water, it's this sun, we're not used to it.'

Murdo said that was true but it was good for his joinery business as he could get all the outside work done. He laughed. 'I must be getting old as I hate working outside in the rain.'

As he left, Eliza reached the coolness of the kitchen and she splashed some cold water on her face. She couldn't help thinking how her life had turned out. It was all ifs or buts. If her father hadn't died so young at fifty years old, she wouldn't have had to stay to look after her mother who couldn't accept his death and was ill with grief for a long time. But Michael became frustrated with all her apologies for postponing the wedding and one day he simply said he had decided to move away to another job he had been offered.

'I'll write to you, Eliza, and we can plan the wedding later.' Six months later he had disappeared and that was the last time she heard from him. He could be living on the moon as far as she knew but she still loved him and although she had stopped thinking about him every day, along came Murdo to rekindle all the past bittersweet moments.

Martha called out, 'While you're in the kitchen, bring me out a glass of lemonade and put the kettle on for some tea. Also bring out that tin of biscuits we got as a present from Bella on your birthday.'

Eliza sighed, she wished her mother hadn't mentioned her birthday which had been in May.

'Sixty-one years old and still living like a dried up old spinster with my mother,' she muttered.

Five minutes later she went outside carrying the tray with the lemonade, pot of tea and the birthday tin of biscuits.

29

Sadie decided she wouldn't tell anyone where her new job was. It wasn't as upmarket as she had hoped and she made up her mind as she walked back from Hal's Bar that she wouldn't be staying there for very long. She hoped to look for a better job but in the meantime it meant she would have a wage coming in until she moved on.

Eddie was getting ready for school when she came through from the bedroom. 'I've got a new job, Eddie, it's in a big office in the town and I've been taken on as a secretary.'

Eddie was busy tying his shoelaces. He looked up and nodded. 'Has Dad sent a letter to me? He said he would.'

Sadie put on an innocent face. 'No, I haven't heard anything from him either. Maybe he's forgotten all about us.'

Eddie was furious. 'Dad would never forget us.' He stopped to get a breath. 'At least he'll never forget me.'

With that statement he walked out to meet Evie and Tommy who were waiting in the lane for him.

It was Sadie's turn to feel upset. How dare her son suggest his father wanted to forget her. She glanced at the clock and made up her mind to forgo breakfast and head for the pub. Hal had said it was a ten o'clock start but she had to make her way to Lochee and she didn't want to be late on her first day.

As she made her way along the lane she met Eliza who had rushed out for Martha's paper and the *People's Friend* magazine. 'Mum likes to read her paper with her breakfast,' she said in passing.

Sadie thought that Martha should be in some home for old folk but she said brightly, 'I hope she enjoys them. I'm off to my new job in an office in town where I'm the new secretary.'

Eliza felt a pang of jealousy. Sadie seemed to have it all. Good looks, a wonderful son, and now a prestigious job. Eliza had also been in a good job as a typist in a solicitor's office before she retired. But now her life revolved around her mother. Looking after her and rushing around getting all her wants and listening to her moans and aches.

Sadie felt quite depressed as she sat on the tramcar and when she reached her stop her mood didn't improve. The pub had a downbeat look and her impression was the same as yesterday when she had her interview.

The early morning sunshine shone through the small window which made the tables and chairs look scratched and shabby. There was a smell of stale beer and she noticed the glasses that were stacked behind the bar were smeary as if they had been washed but left to dry on the wooden shelf.

Hal came through a door at the back of the bar carrying a wooden crate with bottles of beer which he proceeded to stack beside the glasses. He saw Sadie.

'There's another crate, can you bring it through?'

Sadie made her way to the back and brought the crate through. 'Where will I put these?'

He pointed to an empty shelf further along the bar. 'Put them there.'

When they were stacked up she picked up a grubby looking tea towel and gazed at it in dismay. 'Have you got any clean towels, Hal?'

He fished about behind the counter and brought forth a small pile of grayish towels and placed them on the bar. Sadie began to polish the glasses but Hal said there were invoices to sort out and could she do it?

The office was more like a cupboard but it did have a small desk and chair plus a grey metal filing cabinet. A black telephone with a badly twisted cord sat next to an ancient typewriter with a sheet of paper inserted in it.

She made her way around the desk and noticed another door in the wall. On opening it she discovered a tiny toilet with an even tinier washbasin and a rough green towel hanging from a large nail on the door.

Her mood deepened by the minute and it was made worse when the pub opened its door to admit a small clutch of elderly men with wrinkled trousers, unmatched jackets and flat caps. Hal dispensed pints of beer which the men carried over to the tables before settling down to play games of dominoes.

The customers' eyes had opened wide when faced with the newcomer but now they were engrossed in their beers and games. She was glad to escape to the office where she sorted out the bills and invoices before filing them in the cabinet.

At lunchtime, Hal asked her to serve behind the bar as he had to go home to see to his infirm wife.

'I won't be long, Sadie, and I've left the price list by the till.' Hal's house was above the pub so he didn't have far to go.

Sadie was pleased to see some young workmen come in and they were a cheery bunch.

'Lord, we've never seen you before, what's your name?'

Sadie decided to be coy and didn't answer this question. 'What do you want to drink?'

They chose their drinks and as one guy paid for his he said, 'Have a drink on me.' Hal had said if this happened she could say she would have it later while putting the money into a cup under the counter. 'That's for your tips, Sadie,' he had said. 'I would advise you to keep the money instead of taking the drink as it's a great perk to your wages.'

This had pleased her and by the time the pub closed she had a few shillings in her cup. Before leaving in the early evening she decided to use some of the money and she poured herself a drink. As usual she felt more relaxed afterwards and as she made her way home she thought this job was going to suit her which came as a big surprise to her.

If she kept her drinking down to one drink at finishing time it meant she wouldn't have to go to the off-licence shop and it would all be funded by other people's money.

30

Morag loved this time of the day. It was seven-thirty and Rory had left for work with his piece bag containing his sandwiches, a thermos flask and an apple, and she was now sitting down at the table with her tea and toast. She looked around the room at the well-polished furniture, feeling a glow of pleasure. They had been lucky to get this lovely terraced house in a quiet lane and as an added bonus the neighbours were all friendly.

Then the quiet and peace of the morning was broken by Catriona crying to get up and Morag went through to the bedroom where her lovely child was kicking her pink chubby legs in the air and making a noise that would waken the dead. Picking up her daughter stopped the noise which changed to a wide- eyed look and Morag was immediately overcome with a feeling of joy.

After feeding the baby she got the pink bath from the cupboard and they both had a great time with Catriona splashing water all over the floor and then Morag choosing which dress to put on her. They had been so lucky with baby gifts and her daughter had a wardrobe that any child would envy.

The sun was shining and Morag couldn't remember such a summer as this. By nine-thirty she was ready to push the pram for their daily outing. Coming out into the lane she met Grace, who was hurrying past but she stopped when she saw Morag.

She peered into the pram. 'Who's a lovely wee lass,' she

said to the baby who gave her a wide-eyed stare. 'She's getting bigger every day, Morag.'

They walked down the street together. 'I'm off to see my mother,' said Grace. 'She can't seem to get rid of her cold so I go to see her every morning to make sure she's okay.'

Morag said it was lucky that her mother had someone to look after her.

Grace laughed. 'Try telling her that. She's so picky and fussy that I could honestly scream at her but I don't mind getting the flak.'

Morag laughed and after they parted company at Ann Street, Morag carried on into the town. She wanted to go to Phin's hardware shop in the Nethergate to buy a new teapot as their old one had got a bit bashed when they moved into the house.

She was crossing Reform Street when she spotted Sadie hurrying up to the Lochee tram stop. Morag paused for a moment. Sadie didn't see her but Morag was puzzled. Bella had told her yesterday that Sadie was now working in the town as a secretary in an office so Morag wondered why she was going to Lochee. As she made her way to the shop she decided it was none of her business and that maybe Sadie was also going on an errand.

Meanwhile Grace was trying to keep calm as Evelyn kept changing her mind over the shopping list.

'That lettuce you got the other day was limp and I couldn't perk it up no matter how much water and vinegar I used. Tell that young lassie in the fruit shop that I want a crisp lettuce and firm tomatoes.'

Grace sighed. Her mother seemed to have firm tomatoes on her brain as no matter how many she bought for her, none of them passed the firm test. However she felt guilty about her mother as she knew she didn't manage to see her as much as wanted and the woman was lonely. Normally Evelyn would be out and about with her friend Elsie and although Elsie came up to see her most nights it wasn't the same as being out in the fresh air.

Thinking of Elsie seemed to transfer to Evelyn and she said, 'Elsie's son is coming next week to take her out for the day but I don't think I'll be well enough to go.' She sounded so sad.

Grace felt sorry for being annoyed by her mother's moans and she said, 'You'll be fine by next week, Mum, but if you can't go with Elsie then I'll come and take you out when you're feeling better.'

Evelyn immediately perked up and Grace left to go to the shop with the shopping list, determined to tackle the young assistant in the fruit shop over the lack of crispy lettuce and firm tomatoes.

Later that afternoon, as she sat down in her own house with a welcome cup of tea, she couldn't help but worry about Eddie. He seemed to spend all his time in the house and was now eating all his meals with them. She didn't begrudge feeding him or looking after him when he came home with Evie and Tommy but she was really annoyed by Sadie's indifference to her son's needs. She also knew that Maryanne was worried and Grace didn't want her to become unwell again.

Bill was an easy-going man but he was beginning to question the amount of shopping she was doing every day as it was hard work feeding an extra mouth, especially when it was a young lad with a big appetite. Eddie was always grateful and polite, saying thank you after his meal, and it wasn't his fault that he had landed in Dundee very much against his will.

As she finished her tea she suddenly thought she would like to have it out with Sadie and she made a mental note to tackle this feckless mother who swanned off every morning looking like she stepped out of *Vogue* magazine but never offered a penny towards her son's wellbeing.

She was busy setting the table later when the door opened and the three kids came in. Evie put on the television and they all sat on the settee. Evie and Tommy were chatting but Eddie sat looking at the screen before suddenly getting up and walking over to Grace.

'Can I ask you a favour, Grace?' he said quietly, glancing over his shoulder at the two girls who were still engrossed in some story from school.

Grace nodded and he continued, 'Can I have my letters sent to your house, the ones I get from my dad?'

Grace didn't know what to say but she was worried. 'Does your mum know about this, Eddie, or your granny?'

He looked miserable and said no, they didn't. 'I keep writing to him and I'm sure he answers my letters but Mum says he hasn't been in touch.'

Grace was sorry for him as he looked so helpless at this lack of communication so she said he could send his father her address but she added, 'I think you must tell your mother, Eddie, as I don't want her to think I'm interfering.'

He looked relieved and said he would, then went back to the couch where the two girls were still discussing some story about a classmate and they didn't stop talking when he rejoined them.

Later that night, after Evie was in bed and Bill was drinking his cocoa, she mentioned the subject to Bill.

'I'm not sure I've done the right thing by agreeing to this.' She sounded unhappy and Bill was annoyed.

'What will happen if his father isn't writing back, has Eddie thought of that? I'm sure Sadie would let him have a letter if it had been sent to him.'

Grace wasn't so sure. 'I think Sadie is capable of anything, Bill. I know you think she's wonderful but I have my doubts about her.'

It was Bill's turn to look amazed. 'I don't think she's wonderful. Where did you get that idea from?'

'Well, you are always saying what a beautiful woman she is. It's like you admire her.'

Bill burst out laughing. 'I might say she is a good looker but that doesn't mean I like her or think she's wonderful.' He stopped and reached for another biscuit and waited until it was finished before adding, 'In fact I don't really like her at all. I think she is selfish and she should be back with her husband. She's not a patch on you as you look after everyone and you care about people. I don't think Sadie has cared for anyone but herself all her life.'

Grace felt a warm glow of happiness flood over her at this compliment and she sat back in the chair with her cup of tea. She didn't like cocoa, not like Bill and Evie or for that matter like her mother Evelyn.

As she got ready for bed, she decided that if a letter did arrive for Eddie then she would tell Maryanne and let her deal with it, and if no letter arrived then she would also tell her. She had seen Sadie come home and she hoped that all was well in the house. Maybe a letter would come tomorrow and Eddie would get it from her and be reassured his father was in touch with him.

31

Sadie had arrived home in a bad mood. She hadn't got any tips today and it meant she had to put her own money in the till to cover the two drinks she had poured for herself. She had to be careful to drink when Hal was upstairs so she pretended she needed to go through to the back and quickly finished her gin there so the customers in the bar were also unaware of it.

Making matters worse for her was her mother's attitude when she walked in the door. Eddie had gone outside saying he wanted to see Albert, and Maryanne was also in a bad mood.

'I see you haven't brought anything back for your son's tea or anything to put in the cupboard,' said Maryanne.

Sadie snapped, 'He gets his tea at Grace's house and I'm not hungry.' She walked back out of the door and decided to go and see Bella. Bella was listening to the wireless and she didn't seem pleased when Sadie knocked once and opened the door. Sadie was oblivious to this and went and sat down.

'What a day I've had. Nothing but work, work, work.'

Bella, who was an astute person and noticed that Sadie had been drinking, said, 'If you're looking for Eddie, he's with Albert. He's promised Eddie an old fishing rod he had years ago and he's gone to get it.'

Sadie wasn't happy about this. 'I don't like him to be near

water in case he falls in.' She stood up. 'I'll go and see Albert and tell him not to give him the rod.'

Bella was annoyed. 'Oh, for heaven's sake, Sadie, sit down and let the lad have some fun. You've dragged him over here, away from his father and yet you expect him to sit and twiddle his thumbs because it suits you.'

No one had ever spoken to Sadie like this before and she didn't like it one bit. She made to stand up but she staggered. 'I can see I'm not welcomed in this lane by any of you, not even my mother.'

As she reached the door, Bella said, 'Try not to drink too much, Sadie, you've got a young boy to look after.'

Sadie gave her a venomous look and swept out of the room while Bella switched the wireless back on to listen to her play which had been rudely interrupted. She saw Eddie and Albert through her window and the lad went off with his fishing rod while Albert came in to see her. Sighing heavily she switched off the set. 'Albert, how nice to see you. Did Eddie like his rod?'

Albert said he did. 'I've told him to take it down to the esplanade and do some fishing there. Rory from next door said he would make him a small box to hold his worms and he's away making plans to catch some fish on Saturday.'

'I've just had Sadie in and she's not pleased about Eddie going fishing.'

Albert dismissed this with a laugh and changed the subject. 'Did you hear that Martha twisted her ankle when Eliza was at the shops?'

Bella said she had heard. 'She told Eliza she tripped over a chair but I've heard that she was trying to reach the box of chocolates that was on the top shelf of the cupboard. It was seemingly a present to Eliza from an old school friend and she thought she had it well hidden.'

Albert laughed again. 'Nothing is ever well hidden from Martha. She's like a bloodhound when it comes to biscuits and sweets and I hope she's learned her lesson not to go searching on top shelves. In fact I think she even looks like a bloodhound with her fat jowls and beady eyes.'

Still chuckling, he left Bella sitting in the quiet room. She decided not to try to listen to her play as she would have lost most of the plot and instead she thought about Sadie. She had always liked her even though she had been a difficult child, wayward and totally obsessed by herself, but Bella knew there was a vulnerable side to her. Maryanne had tried to bring her up in the right way and it had been a hard job but Bella knew she was relieved when Sadie was engaged to young Peter Ronaldson and equally upset when she threw him over for Ed Boyd and ended up in America.

Then there was the problem of her apparent drinking. Was it a one-off thing or was it a daily thing? A shaft of late evening sunshine shone through the window and Bella switched the wireless back on again. As she listened to music, she knew it wasn't her problem but that didn't help. She had known heartache in her life and that was why she was adept at recognising it when it reared its unhappy head again. She gave a small shiver as if the air had turned cold, and hoped her intuition was wrong.

Eddie had carried the fishing rod into his bedroom and he turned the reel with pleasure. He needed to buy some hooks and then he was ready to cast the line in the river. Maryanne had said it was good he was going to have an outdoor hobby.

There was no sign of his mother. 'She said she's got a headache and has gone for a walk,' his granny said, and he felt guilty at his pleasure that she wasn't there to make unhelpful remarks or even ban the whole idea. He placed the rod upright in the wardrobe. He couldn't wait for Saturday. Evie and Tommy could go into town with him but he wouldn't be going into any shops and he planned to spend a solitary day by the river.

He came out of the room when he heard his mother's voice. She had brought three fish suppers for the tea but she must have taken her time coming from the shop as they were lukewarm and greasy. Maryanne put the oven on to warm them up while he set the table. Sadie went into the bedroom with her coat and handbag and when she came out a few minutes later her face was a bit flushed.

Maryanne, who was bending over the oven, didn't notice this but Eddie was worried as his mother didn't look well. However she managed to finish her meal. When they were washing the dishes she suddenly remembered the fishing rod.

'I don't want you going to the river to catch fish, Eddie, so give that rod back to Albert.'

Before he could answer, Maryanne said, 'Oh for heaven's sake, Sadie, let the boy have some fun with his new hobby. You can't keep him cooped up here in this great weather.'

Sadie had a stubborn look. 'I'm not keeping him cooped up, Mum, I just don't want him to go near the river in case he falls in.'

Maryanne made a dismissive noise but she picked up the paper and began to ignore her daughter while Eddie was annoyed about his mother's displeasure at a simple fishing trip. He made up his mind he would leave the rod at Grace's house and then his mother would never know when he used it.

As if the matter was closed, Sadie said she was going to read her book in the bedroom and after she left Maryanne gave her grandson a huge wink.

'Happy fishing, Eddie. Try and catch a whopper for our tea some night.'

As it turned out, on Saturday morning, Sadie was still in bed and Maryanne had gone out for her weekly grocery shopping when Eddie went to pick up the rod. By now it was in its case and he would assemble it at the river. Albert had shown him how to do it.

Evie and Tommy were waiting for him and they said they wanted to come with him instead of going to Woolworths. Eddie wasn't too pleased about this and he said so but Tommy was adamant they should all be together so he gave in. There was a debate about the best place to go and Tommy said she had seen people fishing at the docks so that was where they made their way to, going through the Victoria Arch and crossing one of the little bridges that took them to the river.

Eddie found a suitable spot and the two girls sat down on the wooden pier while he assembled the rod and put a worm on the hook. He had dug one up from the patch of earth at the front of the house. Tommy screwed up her face at the sight of the worm while Evie stretched out her legs in the warm sun. The river was calm at this spot and there was slight film of oil on the surface but he reckoned there had to be fish in the water.

Tommy joined Evie in basking in the sun. She had overheard her parents arguing this morning and she was glad of the company of her friend.

'My Auntie Lizzie is coming for a visit at the end of next week. She's coming from Ireland and my dad isn't happy about it. He says she is a meddling besom and Mum told him to stop being nasty about her sister.'

Evie said that it was great to have an auntie coming to see her but Eddie was too intent on casting his line into the water to comment.

'Yes it is, she's Mum's oldest sister and her children are grown up now and Mum told Dad that she acted like a mother to her after my granny died and Dad mumbled something about "how noble of her".'

The sun was now getting hot and it was so peaceful to be beside the water. In the distance, people kept passing on their way to the swimming baths but apart from that everything was calm with the sound of the river lapping against the wooden pier.

Tommy called, 'Have you caught a fish yet, Eddie?'

Eddie mumbled something and Tommy called out again. He turned in annoyance. 'No, so keep quiet or you'll scare the fish away.'

An hour went by and Tommy announced she was hungry and Eddie told her to leave if she was getting bored. She looked at Evie for support but Evie said they could maybe wait a little longer. She had no sooner said this when an elderly man walked past and as he did so, he called over to Eddie.

'You won't catch anything today, laddie, as it's too sunny. You need a bit of cloud to catch fish.'

Eddie asked if this was true and the man nodded. 'Aye it is, it has to be a cloudy, grey day for fishing.'

The girls stood up and Eddie pulled the hook up to the pier where the worm was still attached and he threw it into the river. Packing the rod away he sighed and turned to the girls. 'I suppose we had better go to Woolworths then.' He walked away followed by a happy Tommy and Evie who was so sorry he hadn't caught anything.

32

Sadie was sorry she had taken this job as it seemed to be old men who were the drinkers in the pub. Every day a few of the locals would come in for their half pints and then sit playing dominoes. The young workmen who had been in earlier must have moved to another job and her tips had virtually disappeared which meant if she wanted a drink she had to pay for it herself with money she couldn't really afford to spend.

On this particular Monday, trade was so slack that she consoled herself with a gin and tonic, which she didn't pay for but she would put the money in the till on payday. Hal was upstairs with his wife who was waiting for a doctor's visit. She hadn't asked him what was wrong because it was none of her business. She had enough problems of her own and she had no sympathy with anyone.

She had heard that Tommy was telling people that her parents had had a big row over the imminent arrival of her Irish auntie. Sadie shuddered and couldn't understand why the girl had to tell everyone her family's business. She hoped Eddie wasn't telling them anything about America and his father.

The pub door had a squeaky hinge which warned her that a customer was coming in so she quickly downed her drink and washed the glass. It was Hal. He came over to the counter and laid a set of keys down on the surface.

'Gladys has to go into hospital for tests and I have to go with her, Sadie. Can you lock up the pub at closing time and then open up again at five o'clock?'

Sadie gave him a big smile and said that was no problem. 'I hope your wife is all right.'

Hal said he hoped so and he left, stopping by a small group on men who were sitting together by the side of the counter. One of them called out, 'Tell Gladys we're asking for her, Hal.'

This situation pleased Sadie because she knew there wasn't a lot of work to do in the office which meant she could maybe skive off early. She hadn't met Gladys and she briefly wondered what tests she was getting at the infirmary, before calling time on the drinkers. The men rose up and she collected their glasses and then locked the door after their retreating backs.

Filling up her glass again she carried it through to the office which was a stuffy room at the back. There was a comfy chair in the corner and she sat down with her drink. She sometimes brought a magazine in to read when business was quiet and she fished it from her bag, finishing her drink as she did so. She hadn't been sleeping very well recently, mainly because of her mother's lumpy mattress, and now she fell asleep. It was the loud knock on the door that wakened her and for a brief moment she couldn't think where she was.

Jumping up, she hurried to the door. She glanced at the clock and it was four-thirty. It was Hal.

'Gladys got her tests done early,' he said, 'so I'll open up if you want to get home.'

Sadie said she would just nip into the office to get her bag. She was thankful that she had washed the customers' glasses and wiped the tables. Spotting her own glass by the side of the typewriter, she quickly stuffed it into her bag along with the magazine and she spread out a few typewritten accounts she had done the previous day. Perhaps Hal hadn't read them so it would look like she had been busy.

As she walked along the street to the tram stop she felt

light-headed. I have to stop drinking, she told herself silently, or else I'll be falling over in the road. Later, she wished she had fallen in front of the tram.

Eddie arrived home with Evie, and Grace produced the blue airmail envelope. He took it with a look of satisfaction and said he would read it at home. He opened the flimsy letter carefully in case he tore some of the contents and he was dismayed when he read that his father had already sent two letters to him and was wondering why he hadn't answered. He said that he missed him terribly as did his grandad and Esther and he hoped that his mother would bring him home.

Eddie felt a dull ache as he read his father's words and he was so angry at his mother for hiding the letters from him. Putting the letter in his pocket he hurried down to the post office to buy an airmail letter so he could answer it right away.

He was busy at the kitchen table when his mother walked in. 'Hullo Eddie, I thought you would be at Grace's house.'

He stood up and shoved the letter under her nose. 'I got this from Dad today and he wants us to go home right away. He says he's sent two letters and I haven't seen either of them. What did you do with them, Mum?'

Taken aback, Sadie tried to bluster her way out of this. 'Your dad is lying, Eddie, he hasn't sent anything to you or me.' She stopped, suddenly wondering where this letter had come from as there had been nothing from the postie this morning. 'Where did you get that letter?'

Eddie was defiant. 'I was sure you were destroying my mail so I got Dad to send his letter to Grace's house.'

Sadie went white with rage. 'You did what?'

'Well it worked, didn't it? All these weeks and no word then when I send a letter, I get one back right away. Another thing, Mum, I'm writing to Dad to tell him to send me money for me to come back home. You can stay here if you like.'

Sadie was livid as she walked out of the door and went

along the lane to Grace's house. She was making the tea and Evie and Tommy were watching television when Sadie entered the room without knocking.

Grace looked at her and she knew what Sadie was going to say before she opened her mouth. 'I was unhappy about letting Eddie use this address and I told him he had to tell you.'

Sadie's anger exploded. 'What right have you got to poke your nose in my affairs, Grace Gow? That's what's wrong with this lane, you are all malicious, nosy parkers who think they have the moral right to interfere. I did what I thought was the proper thing in keeping those letters away from my son and you come along and tell him he can be underhand and listen to his father's lies.'

Evie and Tommy sat in silence as the television programme went on unwatched. Sadie gave it an angry glance and for one moment Grace thought she was going to throw something at the screen. Instead she said, 'You think with your fancy house and a television set that you are above the rest of us, you snooty cow.'

Grace said, 'My fancy house? What on earth are you talking about, Sadie?'

Just at that moment Bill walked in and Sadie gave him a venomous look before striding out. Bill looked bemused. 'What's wrong with her?'

Grace said she would tell him afterwards and Tommy also departed, no doubt going to pass on the row verbatim to her parents.

Sadie stalked back to her own house where her mother had arrived home from work. There was no sign of Eddie. Maryanne was busy making her tea.

'Do you want me to make anything for you and Eddie?'

Sadie picked up a cup and threw it. It shattered against the window and both broke. 'I've just come back from Grace Gow's house where I found out she has let Eddie use her address to contact his father. How dare she do this? It's none of her business.'

'Well you should have let him write and get a letter here, Sadie, so you've only yourself to blame,' said Maryanne, staring at the glass and china shards.

Sadie couldn't believe her ears, even her own mother was against her, and she picked up her handbag and walked out of the house. She walked as far as the licensed grocer where she bought a quarter bottle of gin and went straight back to her bedroom. Eddie was still out.

33

By the next morning, the entire lane had heard of the argument.

Eddie had come in at about eleven o'clock the previous night and his granny had made him a hot cup of cocoa. 'You mustn't get upset at your mum as she has your best interests at heart.' Eddie said he was going to write back to his dad and tell him about the missing letters. Maryanne said he must do what he thought best. She had covered the window with a bit of cardboard and hoped that the landlord would repair it, and she noticed Eddie looking at it but she said nothing. Sadie was now fast asleep and she hoped everything would go back to normal tomorrow.

Grace hadn't slept all night and she was sitting up drinking tea at three in the morning while Bill told her not to worry about what Sadie had said. 'Maybe you shouldn't have agreed to help Eddie. It's up to his family to sort out.'

'I was only trying to help the boy as he was sure there were letters coming and he suspected his mum was keeping them back.'

'Well it's been done so try and get some sleep and don't worry about it as it will probably be over soon.'

Grace wasn't as sure as he was and she had an awful feeling that things were about to get much worse. However, she took Bill's advice and went back to bed but she didn't sleep.

In the morning, Bill got ready to go to work and Grace was glad when the kids went off to school. Eddie hadn't come in and instead waited awkwardly at the door but she let it pass. She felt sure he would come in after school as usual.

Anna and Thomas were also full of the news of the row as Tommy had reported it almost word for word. 'I heard she called Grace a nosy parker,' said Anna, bursting into laughter, and even Thomas chuckled at the thought. He was pleased that this new row had stopped the arguments in his house over Lizzie's visit.

Martha was beside herself with glee over this latest bit of news but Eliza was annoyed at her for being so cheerful about someone's misfortune. 'Rubbish,' said her mum, 'she deserves everything she gets.'

'Grace is a lovely person so don't go on about it.' Eliza was busy making tea and toast and they planned to eat it outside as the morning was warm.

'I'm not talking about Grace. It's that Sadie who's been trouble since she got here. I think Maryanne didn't give her enough skelps on her backside when she was a child.'

Meanwhile Sadie awoke with a headache and a sick feeling in her stomach and she could barely walk to the sink to wash her face. She glanced at the bottle by the side of her bed and noticed it was almost empty. No wonder she was ill, she thought. She decided to go to work early and she made her way along to the other end of the lane as she wanted to dodge Grace's house, but she gave a groan when she noticed Martha sitting at her door.

'Good morning, Sadie, how are you after your outburst? I heard you called Grace Gow a snooty cow.' She gave a throaty laugh but Sadie was determined to ignore her so she walked past her. 'And you said she had a fancy house, are you jealous of it?'

Sadie turned round at this remark. 'I also called you a malicious old dwarf, Martha, because that's what you are.'

Martha almost choked on her toast which gave Sadie a feeling of satisfaction. She would be glad to be rid of this place when she got her own house, and then maybe Eddie would settle down instead of always fighting with her.

Albert had overheard this last remark and he shook his head sadly. He went in to see Bella who was the only person ignorant of the animosity. She was also upset when she heard. 'I hope Sadie has the sense to go back to her husband as I fear for young Eddie's health.'

Albert agreed. 'She won't go back and it's all going to end in tears I think.'

Morag had been putting the pram out prior to taking her baby for a walk to the shops and she overheard Sadie's remark to Martha and had been shocked at the venom behind it.

Evie and Tommy had tried to get Eddie to talk about yesterday but he remained tight lipped. He left them at their school gate and strode round to his playground without a word.

Grace decided to go to see her mother but when she got there she found she was out, presumably with Elsie. Her cold must have gotten better, she thought as she walked back home. To her dismay another airmail letter was lying on the mat.

She was in a quandary and wondered if she should keep it for Eddie when he came back from school or put it through Maryanne's letterbox. She sat for an hour to think of the right way to go before making up her mind and walking along the lane where she pushed it through the door.

She was busy doing some baking when she spotted Sadie coming home early and she was in a panic at what would happen when she saw Grace's address on the envelope. Fully expecting another outburst, she waited but Sadie didn't come to the door and she breathed a sigh of relief.

At quarter past four Evie and Tommy opened the door and put their schoolbags on the floor.

'Where's Eddie?' she asked, trying not to sound worried as she cut out the dough for scones.

Before Evie could answer, Tommy said, 'He's gone home but he says he'll be back soon.'

Grace thought that was good news as he would get his letter but an hour later he appeared and asked her if anything had come for him. Grace was puzzled as she explained, 'I put a letter through your letterbox, Eddie, it came this morning.'

Eddie's face fell and he turned to go out of the door when Sadie appeared. 'What have you done with my letter?' he asked.

'There wasn't any letter, Eddie.' Sadie's face was all innocence and Grace couldn't believe what she was hearing.

'Grace said she put a letter from Dad through the letterbox, Mum, so where is it?'

'Well we all know what a liar she is, Eddie. She would say anything to cause trouble between us and I can assure you there wasn't anything from your dad.'

Grace was incensed at being called a liar but she didn't want to make a fuss in front of the children, especially Tommy who was standing open-mouthed and mentally taking in every word.

'I did put an airmail through your door, Sadie, so don't deny it.'

In answer to this, Sadie turned on her heel and marched out of the door, almost colliding with Bill as he came home from work. Eddie followed his mother back to the house and saw that his granny had also arrived back. Sadie began to tell her mother all about Grace's lies, looking indignant as she did so. Eddie went over to the fireplace and raked through some burnt ashes that looked recent. He found a scrap of blue paper that had escaped the flames and he produced it in front of Maryanne.

'Mum's burnt another letter, Granny, and I'm writing to tell Dad to come and take me home.' He walked out without looking at his mother while Maryanne gave her daughter a disgusted look.

'Don't look at me like that. I'm only doing what's best for my son and he has to understand that we're here to stay and he better get used to it.'

The next morning the lane was again buzzing with the news of the latest spat. Martha couldn't believe how pleasurable she found this gossip and she made sure Eliza spoke to everyone to get their opinions on that upstart Sadie.

Only Grace, Albert, Bella and Morag felt sorry about the entire war while Evie also felt pity for Eddie. On the other hand Tommy was agog at all the trouble, as were Anna and Thomas who got a good laugh at some of the statements being bandied about.

34

It was proving to be a great summer with sunshine most days and little rain. The occupants of the lane were no exception to loving this good weather. Martha and Eliza sat out for most of the day and Morag put her Silver Cross pram holding Catriona out at her front door but made sure the baby was lying in the shade.

Albert and Bella drew the line at taking chairs out but they both kept their windows and front doors open, and at the far end Grace liked to work away in her kitchen, content that the sun was shining through the window. She hoped this good weather would last for the seven weeks of school holiday but, knowing the Scottish weather was unreliable, she suspected it would be pouring with rain when the schools closed.

She did feel a bit sorry for the Cassidys and Maryanne and Sadie for having to go to work every day and she idly wondered when Anna's sister was due. Tommy didn't seem to know except to say it was sometime soon.

She had confided to Evie that morning. 'I think my mum has stopped mentioning it as Dad gets annoyed about her visit.'

Grace wondered if this was going to be another source of friction in the lane like the argument with Sadie. Then to make matters worse the papers were saying there was a water shortage and warned people that they shouldn't waste water, making it sound like the citizens were throwing it all over the place. She was standing at the kitchen sink, debating whether to leave the breakfast dishes until teatime and just use one basin of hot water, when there was a loud knock at the door. A small, plump woman stood there with a suitcase at her feet. She was unseasonably dressed in a thick woollen coat and a felt hat above her perspiring face.

As soon as she opened her mouth, Grace realized she was Irish. 'I'm sorry to bother you but I'm looking for the Cassidy house. Sure it was some climb up that hill, I thought I would collapse with a heart attack.' She stopped and went into a spasm of coughing. 'It's all right, I'll be all right in a minute,' she said, before going into another coughing fit.

Grace said she should come in and get her breath and the woman lugged the suitcase into the house. 'I'm Lizzie, Anna's sister, and I got an earlier bus from the ferry but I've spent ages looking for this place.'

Grace made a cup of tea and put some biscuits in front of her. 'Sure and you're an angel, that's what you are,' she said, taking off her coat and hat and drinking her tea noisily while scoffing the biscuits at the same time.

Grace said Anna and Thomas were both at work but as Anna just worked in the bakery on the Hilltown it would only take a few minutes to let her know she had arrived.

Lizzie sat back with satisfaction. 'That was grand, Mrs… I'm sorry I don't know you name.'

'I'm Mrs Gow but just call me Grace.'

'Well then, Grace, I better make my way to this bakery to let my baby sister know I'm here at last. Do you mind if I leave my suitcase here till I get back?'

Grace said it was no problem and gave her directions to Burnett's and watched her walk away. Lizzie's arrival hadn't gone unnoticed by Martha and she sent Eliza along to check out the stranger with strict instructions to make sure she got all the news.

Eliza hated trying to get all the gossip so she always made

the pretence that she was just dropping in for a friendly visit, a subterfuge that fooled no one and in fact sometimes caused laughter. She had taken the sugar bowl along and when Grace answered the door, she asked if she could borrow some sugar.

'Come in, Eliza,' said Grace, trying to hide a smile. 'I'll just fill up your bowl. How is your mother today?'

'She's enjoying the sunshine, it's been a super summer so far, hasn't it?' Eliza was trying hard to bring up the mention of the stranger.

Grace decided to put her out of her misery. 'You've just missed Anna's sister from Ireland. She's gone down to the bakery to see her.'

Eliza tried to look surprised. 'We didn't see anyone, Grace, no one passed us.'

'No, she came from the Hilltown end and maybe you were both in the house when she arrived.'

'Yes,' said Eliza, 'that's what I thought.'

Eliza was hurrying out, anxious to let her mother know all the news, when Lizzie appeared.

'Anna's given me her key.' She bent down and picked up her suitcase. 'I'll get away and wash my hands and face. It's this heat that's making me all hot and sticky.' She gathered up her coat and hat and went next door.

Eliza rushed back and Martha listened open- mouthed as she passed on all the gossip. 'I'd love to see Thomas Cassidy's face when he gets back from work to see his sister-in-law sitting in his chair,' said Martha with a chuckle.

As it turned out, when Thomas arrived home in the early afternoon, Lizzie had emptied one of the cupboards and she was scrubbing the shelves, her arms almost up to her elbows in a bucket of hot soapy water. She stopped when he came into the room. 'I'm just cleaning out this press as it was all dusty.' She rose to her feet and wiped her sweaty face with a soapy hand before drying it on a towel lying on the back of a chair. 'I'll put all this stuff back when the shelves are dry.' She held up a chipped dish. 'I'll throw this out as it looks ancient.'

Thomas was so angry he could barely speak but he managed to blurt out a few words. 'I think you should let Anna do any throwing out, Lizzie.'

She looked at him as if he was an idiot. 'But it's got this huge chip in it and it's not safe to use.'

He marched over to the kitchen table that was littered with various dishes and began to put everything away.

Lizzie said angrily, 'The shelves are still wet.'

Thomas ignored her and went to put on the kettle before sitting down with the paper he had bought on his way home. Lizzie stomped around the house with a tin of polish and a duster.

'I'm just trying to help my sister as she works hard all day and doesn't have much time to do housework. Do you and Thomasina ever help her?'

He decided to lie. 'Yes we do.'

She sat down opposite him and helped herself to a cup of tea. 'How's your gammy leg?'

Thomas couldn't believe his ears. 'My gammy leg is perfectly fine, thanks for asking.' Lizzie had the type of personality that didn't register sarcasm so she nodded as if satisfied with this answer.

After his tea, Thomas headed off to see Anna at the shop which was having a quiet spell. He wasted no time in tackling her. 'Your sister is scrubbing out cupboards and going around with dusters and God knows what else.'

Anna thought this was an excellent idea and her face lit up. 'That will be a big help as I meant to spring clean sometime.'

The other assistant, Mrs Bell, was listening intently and Anna turned to her. 'My sister Lizzie is very houseproud but she's the only one amongst us who is. I'm like my other sisters, we only clean when we have to.'

Thomas turned on his heel and when he reached the lane he went in to see Albert as he couldn't bear to be in the same room as his sister-in-law. He groaned out loud when he realised he had another ten days of her.

Albert was polishing his brasses when Thomas knocked at the door and on entering he wondered if he had walked into a spring cleaning parallel universe. However Albert put the metal polish away and opened a couple of bottles of beer.

'I'm dying for a drink, Thomas, it's this hot weather to blame.'

They made themselves comfortable and Thomas moaned about Lizzie. 'I wouldn't mind but Anna's family has never liked me. It all boils down to my grandad being in the Irish constabulary years ago. It's all past history but to listen to them you would think it was only yesterday.'

Albert said it couldn't be easy and opened another two bottles of beer. When the clock struck four, Thomas rose to his feet. 'Well I better get back and face the enemy. Thank God I work in the evenings.'

Evie, Tommy and Eddie were coming home and his daughter hurried into the house to see her auntie. Lizzie was on her knees scrubbing the kitchen floor and she had laid pages of newspaper on the wet patches.

'Wait till the floor dries before you come in, Thomasina,' she called out. Thomas ignored this request and he almost exploded when he saw she had used his paper which he hadn't read.

Lizzie was unrepentant. 'For heaven's sake it's only a newspaper, Thomas, you make it sound like it's pound notes.'

Thomas muttered he wished they were and he would use the money to give her a return ticket to Belfast.

The atmosphere was tense when Anna got home but as she was so pleased with all the cleaning, he felt guilty. 'Doesn't the house look so much better?' she enthused.

Lizzie gave him a look and he said, 'Yes, it's wonderful.'

Tommy giggled but her auntie gave her another look so she decided to go next door and look at the television with Evie.

By the following morning, news of Lizzie's cleaning spree had spread to everyone in the lane and in the surrounding houses due to Mrs Bell who was a notorious gossip. Some of the younger working mothers were jealous, saying they could also do with her cleaning skills but the older generation were aghast that a visitor had to work like a Trojan while the family sat back and let her.

When Thomas passed a few of the women on the Hilltown they glared at him and after he was out of earshot they turned to one another and muttered how lazy he must be. One of the women stood up for him. 'I've heard he keeps a very good pub. The glasses are always clean and he keeps the beer pipes clean.'

When Mrs Bell heard this she retorted, 'How does she know so much about his pub?' and gave a knowing look.

It was three days into her visit that Lizzie told Anna her main reason for coming. 'Katie has to have a hysterectomy operation and she would like to see you all and so would Roseanne, Sean and Willie.' These were Anna's sisters and brothers. Anna said she didn't think they would manage a holiday this year but Lizzie said they could visit when the school broke up. 'We would all like you to come back to live in Belfast, Anna, but we know you don't want to, so just come for a holiday.'

Anna was persuaded but she knew Thomas' strong feelings against Ireland and her family. 'I'll have to talk it over with Thomas and we'll let you know.' She knew she sounded weak but that couldn't be helped.

Anna mentioned it to her husband that night as they lay in bed. Thomas was in two minds. He loved his wife and he wanted her to be happy and she would be worried about Katie, but on the other hand he dreaded meeting up with his wife's strident and mouthy family.

'The school breaks up in two weeks' time so we could maybe go then. You will be due a break during the Dundee holiday fortnight.'

Thomas said they could maybe leave it till then and Anna went off to sleep quite happy about this while he lay awake for ages. He decided to get up and have a smoke and he sat at the window in pleasurable silence.

Because he was up late he almost slept in the next morning and he wandered through to the kitchen to the sight of Lizzie swinging a wet tea towel around her head. 'The smell of cigarette smoke in here is awful,' she said. 'I don't know why Anna lets you smoke inside.'

'That's because she smokes as well, Lizzie.'

Lizzie was indignant. 'Anna doesn't smoke, she said she was glad she never started, not like her sisters and brothers who are all like you with their disgusting habits.'

He was left speechless by this blatant lie from his wife but when he tackled her before she went to work, she went bright red and said Lizzie never knew about her smoking. 'It's just for a few days. I've been getting my cigarette when I have my break at work as I don't want her to know. She was more like a mother to me because she was twenty when I was born and she looked after me when Ma became ill.'

Lizzie was outside washing the windows when Sadie walked by on her way to work. She wasn't looking forward to going as the job was getting her down. Hal's wife was seemingly getting better and he had hinted that she would be back helping in the pub and Sadie didn't relish that fact. She was behind in putting money in the till to cover all her sneaky drinks and she suspected that Hal's wife would find this out long before he did. A woman's voice broke into her thoughts and she turned.

'I said it is a fine morning but you seem to be a dozy-headed young woman,' said Lizzie, wringing out the cloth as if wringing someone's neck.

This must be Lizzie, thought Sadie, and she nodded. 'Yes, it's been a super summer.' She walked on as she didn't feel up to having a conversation this early in the morning. She had a headache and her mouth felt dry even though she had brushed her teeth with a huge dollop of Colgate toothpaste.

When she was out of sight, Lizzie looked thoughtful. If it hadn't been morning time she would swear the woman was drunk, but maybe she was just tired.

Lizzie thought about her spic and span council house with its own front garden in Belfast and her family who all had houses in the same estate, and the difference with Anna's house in this narrow lane with no hot water or a bathroom. Anna had said there were corporation houses being built in Dundee but it was just a matter of getting one and that she dreamt of the day when that happened.

Her week was going by quickly and she would be glad to be back home but first she had to persuade her baby sister to come to Ireland and then persuade her to stay. She was busy making the tea when she heard a great commotion outside.

On going out she was confronted with Grace who was trying to deal with Thomasina, Evie and the Yankee boy whose shirt was covered with blood. Both girls were talking at once so she went up and told them to calm down before turning to Grace.

'What's happened? Has he had an accident?'

Tommy spoke loudly. 'No, he had a fight with Bruce Davidson and Bruce's mum is coming to see Eddie's mum because her son has a broken nose.'

Grace managed to get them inside and she got Eddie to take his bloody shirt off before filling a basin with hot water. She bathed his face then realised he wasn't injured but had been splashed with the other boy's blood.

Tommy began to speak again and Lizzie said to let the boy speak for himself but he was reluctant to do this. Grace asked her daughter what had happened but the girls didn't really know because they were in a separate playground and hadn't witnessed the fight.

'Miss Malcolm wants to see Eddie's mum tomorrow because Mrs Davidson is saying Bruce's nose is broken.'

Eddie seemed to be in shock so the two women decided to leave the explanations till Maryanne and his mother came home, and fortunately Sadie hadn't had much work to do and had got off early. When she saw her son she was furious when it was mentioned she would have to go to the school the next day.

'What kind of school is this that lets the pupils have fights in the playground?' When Grace said the other lad's nose was broken, she denied it. 'It's Eddie who has been injured, not this Bruce boy.' She left Eddie with Grace and hurried off to the telephone box where she had to explain to Hal that she wouldn't be in to work until late the following day because of family difficulties.

Tommy was agog with this incident that night, explaining to Anna and Thomas what a big bully Bruce was. 'He's always getting into fights and he hates Eddie.'

The next morning Sadie went off to school with Eddie who didn't want to go back ever. She had reassured him that it would all blow over. 'It's just a playground tiff.'

The headmaster was waiting for both mothers, and Mrs Davidson had arrived a few minutes before Sadie. She was a small, plump woman with a fleshy face and plump white arms sticking out of a sleeveless cotton frock. She immediately launched a tirade at Sadie. 'Your Yankee son has broken Bruce's nose.'

Sadie was infuriated and answered, 'That's rubbish, your son's nose isn't broken. I saw it when I came in and it's just a bit inflamed.'

'A bit inflamed? Let me tell you I know a broken nose when I see one.'

At this point the headmaster intervened. 'Eddie, tell us what happened. I've had Bruce's version and I want to hear your side of the story.'

Eddie looked at his feet and Sadie gave him a rough nudge. 'Tell the headmaster what happened.'

He took a deep breath. 'I was waiting by the wall for the bell to ring when Bruce came up and punched me here.' He pointed to his shoulder. 'I grabbed his hand and shoved him away but he bashed his face against the wall. It was an accident, I didn't mean to hurt him but I was defending myself.'

Doris Davidson was inflamed. 'An accident, my foot. My Bruce will have to have surgery to fix his nose.'

'His nose isn't broken, I've already told you that.' Sadie was losing her patience.

The headmaster looked at both boys. 'We have a witness who backs up Eddie's story, it's David Dobson who was standing with Eddie when it happened.'

Mrs Davidson was unconvinced. 'Well, he would tell you that as Bruce says they are pals and he's sticking up for him. Bruce doesn't have any pals sticking up for him.' She stopped as she realised what she was saying. 'I mean he's got loads of pals but they never saw what happened.'

The headmaster looked at the boys. 'Well we have to take the witness's story so I hope there's no repeat of this bad behavior.' The two boys were dismissed and they went back to their class while Sadie said she had to get to work and she left Mrs Davidson still fuming.

When the girls came back from school they were full of the story. Tommy said Bruce was wild because a lot of the girls and some of the boys were laughing at his bright red nose. 'Someone said he wouldn't need a torch to go to the outside toilet,' she said.

Eddie was quiet and said nothing because he realised he had made a bad enemy.

All the neighbours heard the story and most were sympathetic to Eddie, especially Bella and Albert.

'It's a shame he's having all this trouble at school because I know Ella Malcolm and she says he's an outstanding pupil,' said Bella.

Albert agreed. 'I knew all about the Davidson family when

I was the Prudential Insurance agent. The father and his two brothers think they are great amateur boxers but they couldn't box themselves out of a cardboard carton. They were always fighting with each other and it seems to have spread to the son.'

At the end of the week Lizzie departed with a promise that the Cassidy family would pay a visit to Ireland sometime during the school holidays. She left behind a sparkling clean house and Anna was delighted with the thought that she needn't do much housework for months.

Meanwhile Thomas was glad to see the back of his sister-in-law and he wasn't looking forward to the planned visit but maybe something might happen to cancel the holiday.

Maybe the roof would fall in or something equally calamitous would happen, he thought, but then he realised he didn't want that either.

35

Tommy was excited by the thought of this holiday to Ireland and it was all she could talk about during the final two weeks at school. Evie didn't mind this enthusiasm but Eddie seemed uninterested in the constant chatter. It was as if he was living in a world of his own.

'We'll be going by a boat to Belfast and I'll be able to see my cousins and aunties and uncles. Mum sends them a Christmas card every year but we've never visited them before.'

Evie said it must be a big adventure and she gave Eddie a look which he didn't notice. She wondered if his father had been in touch but he gave no sign that he had and she felt so sorry for him. She couldn't imagine her life without her mum and dad and he must be the same. To bring him into the conversation, she asked him, 'Are you planning to go fishing again, Eddie?'

Tommy butted in, 'If you do we'll go with you.'

Eddie said no, he wasn't planning to do this and he then lapsed into silence as they made their way to school. Things seemed to have settled down with Bruce Davidson but he knew this was just an interval. Bruce's nose wasn't broken as he had alleged and the fiery redness had dulled down to a black and blue patch. The girls and boys who had laughed at him had now moved on to something else and he was no longer the butt of their jokes but that didn't stop him glaring at Eddie every time he saw him.

Eddie was annoyed at his mother as she seemed to have forgotten the incident but his granny was still sympathetic and she had told him if he was worried about anything he must tell her and she would help. This gave him some comfort but he was becoming more unhappy every day and he didn't want to worry her. She had enough to do with the daily journey to work which he suspected was still difficult after her illness.

The one thing that pleased him was the fact he was still going in to Grace's house after school each day, as she was so good to him. His initial reluctance after the letter fiasco was thankfully a past memory.

If Eddie was unhappy and miserable he wasn't the only one because Sadie was growing more downbeat about her job. She had grown so sick of the dark interior and the elderly drinkers and the pokiness of the office. The only good thing was that drink was available and she was still sneaking a few glasses every day.

She often fantasised about her ideal job in some glamorous office where she would be the personal secretary to a good-looking boss who would find her attractive and maybe wine and dine her. On reaching the pub, the smell of spilled beer on the floor almost made her sick and mopping it up didn't help as the smell of beer would be replaced with the pungent disinfectant that was used to clean the premises.

Hal came in and she noticed one of his shirt buttons was missing and a small lump of white flesh poked out as if trying to escape. She sighed and put her handbag in the office before wiping down the bar and the assorted tables and chairs.

When Hal opened the pub door, a few old men came in and she busily poured out their half pints of frothy beer which they carried over to their favourite table, the one with the box of dominoes. Hal soon disappeared to see to his wife so she quickly poured out a drink. Dear God, I need this, she thought, it helps me to cope working in this dump.

One good thing was that Ed had stopped writing and although she knew Eddie was unhappy about this she hoped he would get over it, especially when she found a good job and their own place to live. The thought of this future happy situation cheered her up and she even chatted to the next customer to come in.

He was a regular but she only knew him as Big John. He was certainly tall but very thin with a deeply wrinkled face and sinewy arms that were decorated with large tattoos of bleeding hearts dedicated to 'Mum' and 'Peggy'.

'How are you today, John?' she asked brightly.

He had a slow way of talking and she waited patiently until he said, 'I could be better, Sadie, but I mustn't grumble.' He carried his nip of whisky and half pint over to his pals and she watched as he downed the spirit quickly then emptied the dregs into his beer. This was something these old guys did regularly and she wondered if it made the beer more potent.

Hal had given her a rundown on these regulars and most of them were retired but escaped from their houses for a few hours every morning. Big Jim, however, was a widower who had lost his wife a few months ago and he was still mourning her. She had heard him tell the men that he couldn't bear to be in the house since she'd died and they all nodded in sympathy.

Sadie wondered if this was all there was to life. You were born, worked and got married then sleepwalked into old age and death. The thought depressed her and with Hal still upstairs she poured another drink for herself. She reckoned she owed the till about ten shillings which she would ring up when she got her wages.

What she didn't know at that moment, because her ears weren't burning, was that she was being discussed by Martha. 'I'm telling you, Eliza, that she's often drunk.'

Eliza said this was just a rumour and her mother should watch what she was saying.

Martha was adamant. 'I've smelled it when she comes and

visits. Oh I know she sucks mints but I can still smell it and I'm sure I saw the top of a bottle sticking out of her bag.'

Eliza still defended her. 'It might have been a bottle of cough syrup.'

Martha looked at her in amazement. 'What a naïve woman you are, Eliza. You must take after your father as I'm sharp and I notice things whereas he stumbled through life with blinkers on.'

Eliza felt sad at the mention of her late father as she had been very fond of him and she often was guilty of wondering how her life would have been if it had been Martha who had died instead of him. Charlie, her father, had always got on well with Michael and Michael in turn admired him. However it was a different matter with Martha who made it clear she didn't think he was good enough for her daughter and this had caused friction after Charlie's death. Then Michael went off to Canada to work and she had quickly lost touch with him. Martha had said if he was as much in love with her as he said he was, he wouldn't have left, and maybe there was some truth in this but now she would never know. Maybe he was happy with a wife and family and had truly forgotten her. The sound of her mother calling out brought her out of her reverie of past memories.

'Will you be making me a cup of tea or are you daydreaming again?'

Eliza sighed and went to put the kettle on.

It was the dinnertime break in the playground and Evie and Tommy were playing a game with a ball when the bell sounded and they ran to get in place before marching back to the classroom. They were all seated and the teacher told them to bring out their jotters to do arithmetic when she was suddenly stopped by some chatter amongst the boys.

'What is all the noise about?' she asked and David Dobson put his hand up.

'Eddie's not here,' he said.

All the heads turned round to see an empty space beside him. Miss Malcolm said he was probably in the toilet but as the afternoon wore on there was no sign of him. The teacher was worried and she made the class work out some fractions she had written on the board before leaving the room.

The minute she was out of sight the entire class began to talk about this latest development. Tommy whispered to Evie that she was worried but her friend said it was maybe something simple. 'Maybe he's ill and has gone home.' However she had a cold feeling in her stomach that this wasn't the reason. She had watched him over the past weeks and saw how unhappy he was.

The teacher came back in with the headmaster who asked the class, 'When did anyone last see Eddie Boyd?'

A murmur went up around the class and Bruce Davidson looked smug. 'He was in the dining hall at dinner time.' A few of the boys said they had also seen him then but after that nobody had seen him. Miss Malcolm was worried as the janitor had searched the toilet block and the playground but there was no sign of him.

After the teacher said he was probably at home, the headmaster went out and the class resumed their lessons. Tommy and Evie couldn't concentrate and they were glad when it was four o'clock and they could hurry home to hopefully see Eddie.

Grace was busy when they came in and both began to talk at once. 'Is Eddie here?'

Grace had been baking and her hands were still floury. 'Eddie's not here, what's happened?'

Before Evie could speak, Tommy blurted out, 'He's missing from school. He was there in the morning but after dinner time he wasn't there.'

Grace was as bemused as the girls. 'He must be in the house, I'll go and look.' She quickly walked along the lane with the two girls following closely behind but the door was locked. Grace knocked loudly and called out, 'Eddie, are you in there?'

There was silence. She went and tried to look through the window but Sadie had put net curtains up as she said she didn't want nosy neighbours forever peering in and Grace couldn't see anything. She knocked again but this time it was even louder and she called out his name but there was no response.

Because people had their doors open, the noise reached the other houses and Albert, Bella and Eliza came out to investigate. Albert came along and asked what the matter was. Grace tried to sound calm but she couldn't imagine where the boy was.

'Eddie left the school at dinner time, Albert, and no one knows where he is.'

Albert asked her if they had tried the house and Grace remembered she still had Maryanne's spare key from her time in hospital. She went to get it and Albert went in with her, telling the girls to stay outside. They stood at the open door with Bella and Eliza. Grace was dreading finding Eddie ill but the house was empty. Sadie hadn't cleared the breakfast table and her bed hadn't been made but there was no sign of anyone. Albert even opened the wardrobe and looked under the beds but apart from some suitcases and fluff there was nothing.

Grace locked the door and they stood outside while deciding what to do. Albert said they had to get in touch with Sadie but nobody knew where she worked.

'She said it was an office in town but she didn't say where it was.'

Bella said the best thing was to wait till she and her mother came home from work. 'He's probably playing truant because of all the trouble with the Davidson lad.'

They decided to do this and Eliza hurried back to tell her mother all about the latest drama. Martha said she could well believe it. 'With a feckless mother like Sadie no wonder he's disappeared,' she said with relish.

Eliza said Eddie would never do that to his mother or granny but Martha told her to face facts. 'He hasn't been happy since he came back from America and now he's done a runner.'

Grace quizzed the girls but they couldn't shed any light on the disappearance. 'He's in a different playground from us, Mum, so we only knew he was missing when we got back to the class,' said Evie who was near to tears although she tried not to show it.

Maryanne was back home first and Grace ran out to tell her the news and she was alarmed when the woman almost collapsed. Getting her into the house and into a chair, Grace asked where Sadie worked but her mother gave a grim laugh. 'I don't know as she never tells me anything.' Albert and Bella had come in as well and she turned to them. 'What will I do?'

Bella repeated the thought that he was playing truant. 'Do you think he's gone to see his mum at work?'

Maryanne had no idea but she didn't think he would play truant as he liked learning too much.

'Do you think he's worried about that fight with the Davidson boy?' Grace asked but Maryanne shook her head and said she didn't know. 'He keeps a lot to himself,' she admitted, 'and it's hard to tell what he's thinking.'

At six o'clock Sadie wandered along the lane; she was feeling a bit sick and she had another headache. Before she reached the door her mother hurried out along with Grace, Bella and Albert. Before she could ask why she had this welcoming committee her mother blurted out, 'Eddie's missing, Sadie, and no one's seen him since dinner time. Did he come to see you?'

Sadie was confused. 'What do you mean, Mum, where is Eddie?'

Albert took her inside and said it was time to speak to the

police and she became agitated. 'We don't want the police, he'll come home soon, I'm sure of it.'

Everyone looked at one another. Albert continued, 'He can be anywhere, Sadie, and maybe he's had an accident.' Sadie screamed.

It was decided they would call the police. Bill, who had come home to this drama said he would go to the telephone box and call them. By now Eliza had joined the company and they all sat around Sadie who was weeping loudly with everyone trying to comfort her.

Morag and Rory arrived with the baby to say how sorry they were at the news and Maryanne thanked them before they returned to put Catriona to bed. 'If we can be of any help just ask,' said Morag as she left. Sadie didn't hear her as she wept even louder.

Within an hour two policemen arrived and they began to take statements from Evie and Tommy who repeated what had happened at school. At this point everyone left to let the policemen question Maryanne and Sadie. Maryanne said she was at work and only heard of her grandson's disappearance when she got home. She told them she worked at Keiller's sweet factory.

Questioning Sadie was difficult as she couldn't stop crying but she did manage to say she was also at work and like her mother only heard the news when she came home. When asked where she worked she hesitated but when asked again she said she was employed at Hal's Bar in Lochee.

Maryanne gave her a sharp look but didn't respond to it. The policemen then began to search Eddie's room and asked her if anything was missing. Sadie looked around before saying his rucksack was gone and when she opened the wardrobe his clothes were also missing.

'Do you have a photograph of your son, Mrs Boyd?' one of them asked and she rummaged in her bag before bringing out a snapshot taken in America. She handed it over.

'I believe you came back from America with your son, was he happy about that?'

Sadie wanted to shout out that it was none of their business but she resisted the urge and said he was. Maryanne gave her another sharp look but she stayed silent.

They then left but told her that a search would begin right away, saying, 'He's probably playing truant and now he's scared to come home. Don't worry, we'll find him soon.'

Sadie burst into a frenzy of tears and her mother tried to help by saying that the policemen were right in their explanation. 'Just wait and see, Sadie, he'll be home when he's hungry.'

Sadie responded by becoming angry. 'I don't understand him. Why has he done this to me? I've tried hard to make him happy.' Maryanne stayed quiet because if she told her daughter the truth she wouldn't believe her. Eddie wasn't and had never been happy since coming here to live. He wanted to be with his father in America and Maryanne was so angry about her daughter's attitude to her son but she didn't want to make her more distraught than she was. Then just before bedtime Sadie remembered his fishing rod was also missing and she prayed he hadn't fallen in the river.

36

There wasn't much sleep that night in the lane. News had reached the surrounding streets and people had been asked to check any outdoor sheds and toilets which they did in an effort to find Eddie. Evie and Tommy were questioned again. Had he given any hint what he was planning to do or was there a favourite spot he liked to visit?

Tommy said he liked fishing from the docks and the police searched all the area but there was no sign of him. His photo appeared in the morning paper and the school was abuzz with rumours. Bruce stated that Eddie was frightened of another fight with him and his mother had said that was why he had scampered but David told him that was rubbish and Bruce didn't like being told that.

Sadie couldn't stop crying and Maryanne was at her wits' end trying to calm her down. 'I think you should go back to work and the police will keep in touch with you,' she told her daughter but Sadie had shouted at her.

'He's my son, no wonder I'm worried for he can be in all sorts of danger.' She sat down and began to wail. 'Where are you, Eddie?' Maryanne went over and tried to comfort her but she got louder. 'Where is he? I can't believe he would do this to me.'

There had been no sightings of him and the police were still checking lots of outbuildings. Maryanne said it was strange that no one had seen him after dinner time. 'You would think a young boy would have been spotted wandering about out of school. Where were all the old women who sit at their windows?'

She was referring to some of the houses she regularly passed on her way to work where elderly women sat watching the world go by and even if there was no one visible, there would be a twitch of the curtains as the householders kept an eye on their neighbours.

So it was agreed that Sadie would go to work and if there was news then the police would be in touch with her there. Maryanne had tackled Sadie about pretending to work in an office when she was working in a pub. Sadie was angry. 'What do you want me to do? Everyone is so nosy here so I pretended I had this super job as a secretary instead of working in a dingy bar.'

Sadie headed off to work with a heavy heart. She imagined the worst had happened to Eddie and that was the reason he couldn't be found. Hal had heard about this family misfortune and he was sympathetic. 'Is there any news?'

Sadie looked glum and shook her head. When the regulars came in they were also sorry for the missing boy. Big John spoke for them all. 'We hope you get good news soon, Sadie. Don't worry as he will be found soon.' Sadie nodded but she didn't think it was as simple as that. She knew Eddie was unhappy and she felt so guilty about burning his father's letters and wondered if this act has pushed him into running off.

The door opened and one of the policemen came in. Sadie hurried over. 'Have you found him?'

The policeman said no, not yet. 'Is there any place you think he would go to?'

'No I can't think of anywhere. If anyone knows it will be the two girls who go to school with him. Did he mention anything to them?'

'No, he didn't. The girls are as puzzled by his disappearance as the rest of us.'

Hal stood behind the bar. He wasn't pleased about the police coming here as the customers looked uneasy. Although he felt sorry for Sadie, he didn't want his customers to stay away. His wife had warned him about Sadie as on the one occasion she was in the pub she recognised that the woman was drinking on duty. Hal said it was probably drinks bought by the customers but now he wasn't so sure. He was glad when the police left and the customers resumed their games of dominoes and their pints of beer. He knew he had a good clientele from the overcrowded streets with their numerous tenements and he didn't want anything to harm his business.

Sadie was unaware of his dilemma but she did ask if she could leave early and he agreed. When she got home she hoped that Eddie would be back but she was disappointed to find the house empty. Her mother had returned to work as she was afraid she would lose her job as there were more rumours of possible layoffs at the factory. Grace had seen Sadie passing the window and she came in. 'Is there any news?'

She shook her head. 'I just feel helpless not knowing where he is. The police say they are searching all over but no one seems to have seen him.'

Grace said she was sorry and with the arrival of Evie and Tommy, she went home. The two girls had been subdued since Eddie vanished. Grace asked them again if there was something trivial they had maybe forgotten but they said no.

'The last time I spoke to Eddie was that morning when I dropped my library book and he picked it up,' said Evie. 'You remember that, don't you, Tommy?'

Tommy nodded. Grace said Evie had better return the book as the date was almost up.

'I haven't read it since that day as we've been so worried about him.' She picked up the book and went to take the bookmark from the pages. A piece of paper fluttered out and she picked it up. 'I don't remember putting this in the book,' she said as she opened the single sheet of paper. She gasped. 'It's from Eddie.'

Grace took it from her and read it. It was just a few lines but he said he was going to try and get back to America and thanked her and Tommy for their friendship. Grace hurried to see Sadie but wasn't home.

'Sadie has gone out but I think the police will be wanting to see this,' she said on her return. She put the letter on the sideboard. 'I'll hand this over when she comes back.'

As it turned out it was Maryanne who arrived first and Grace handed over the letter. Maryanne was dumbfounded. 'How on earth will he manage to get back to America? I wish the policeman would come back so I can hand this over.' As if in answer to her wish, the two policemen knocked at the door. Maryanne had to tell them Sadie wasn't in but before she could mention the letter, one of the men said, 'We've had information that a boy resembling your grandson boarded a Glasgow bus at the Seagate on the afternoon he disappeared.'

Maryanne handed over the letter and the man read it. 'It looks like he's trying to get on board a ship to go to America but we'll investigate this latest development.' He gave her a sympathetic look. 'Don't worry, we'll find him as he can't have got that far, not without money or a passport.'

Maryanne forgot about needing a passport and she would have to quiz Sadie when she came home about this.

Sadie returned about eight o'clock and she was carrying a bottle of whisky in a message bag. 'I feel like a stiff drink to take my mind off Eddie,' she said, pouring out a large measure. She asked her mother if she wanted one but Maryanne said no, and told her all about the letter and the bus to Glasgow in the hope of getting back to America.

Sadie was so angry that she had to sit down. 'Why didn't he leave me a letter instead of Evie? For heaven's sake I am his mother, don't I count in his life, and how on earth is he supposed to get back to America?'

Maryanne said this was something she had to deal with. 'When he's found he will still want to go back to his dad. You can't stop that, Sadie, so you have to make up your mind to go back with him.'

Sadie refilled her glass and drank almost half of it before replying, 'I'm not going back. I don't love Ed any more and I hate the life over there. No, Eddie has to stay here with me and get to like his life here.'

Maryanne was furious. 'That's a very selfish thing to say. You have to think of your son's happiness before your own, and maybe when he's grown up and self-sufficient then you can please yourself but not until then.'

Sadie laughed but it wasn't a pleasant sound. 'Do you hear yourself preaching, Mum? What about yourself, there's not one photograph of my father in this house or anything to say he was ever in our lives.' Her hand swept around the walls as if to emphasise the lack of tangible evidence of her dead father. Maryanne went pale. 'I told you years ago that your father Bernard died when you were four years old.' She went over to the sideboard and brought out a framed photo. It showed a young Maryanne and her new husband smiling at the camera. It was one of those old-fashioned studio photographs that were very stilted and posed and the young couple stood beside a huge palm plant with a painted background of misty hills behind them.

Sadie scrutinised the photo. Bernard Roberts was a bit older than her mother but he was slim with a boyish face and a lock of fairish hair falling over one eye. He wasn't handsome but there was an attractive quality about his face. Maryanne looked very young but her dress looked old fashioned and frumpish and she clutched a bunch of flowers that looked as if they had seen better days.

'Why don't you put it on the sideboard instead of hiding it away?' she asked but Maryanne said she didn't like looking at herself as she didn't feel she was pretty.

'I like to look at it every now and then,' she said as she put it back into the drawer. 'I was devastated when he died and it's been hard going financially since then. That's why I don't want you to end up like me, Sadie, as I want you to have a happy marriage and a happy life.'

37

Years later, everyone in the lane was to remember the last weekend of the school term because Eddie was found at the docks in Glasgow by a middle-aged stevedore who had noticed him lurking around for a few days before he contacted the police.

He was barely back in Maryanne's house when his father Ed appeared. It was a Saturday and Maryanne was trying to console Eddie over his aborted plans while his mother was still in bed with one of her headaches.

The tall American knocked politely at the door and when Eddie answered he was ecstatic. 'Dad,' he shouted as he threw himself into the man's arms.

Ed hugged his son as if he didn't want to let go before turning to Maryanne. 'Hi, how are you, Mary?'

She could barely speak with shock but managed to blurt out, 'Why are you here, Ed?'

Ed didn't reply but asked where his wife was.

Sadie, who had been awakened by the noise, staggered out of bed and made her way to the kitchen. She almost fainted when she saw Ed standing beside her mother and son. She made an excuse and disappeared back into the bedroom then appeared fifteen minutes later, wearing a pretty dress with her hair brushed and her face made up.

Ed seemed pleased to see her. 'Hi, honey, you look well.' He went over and gave her a kiss on her cheek.

Eddie was bubbling over with excitement. 'Did you get my letter, Dad?'

'Yes I did, Eddie, and I hope you didn't do anything stupid like you said you were going to do.'

'Well he did, didn't you, Eddie?' said Sadie. 'He stupidly ran away and caused so much worry and fuss and added years to all our lives.'

There was a stunned silence but Maryanne said she would make breakfast. 'You'll be hungry, Ed, sit down with Eddie and Sadie while I put some bacon and sausages on.'

Father and son sat close together while Sadie seemed to be an outsider who sat alone at the far end of the table. She ate hardly anything but her husband and son made up for it. 'That was great, Mary,' said Ed as he dipped his toast in the last of his egg.

Maryanne asked him how long he was planning to stay. He looked at Eddie before replying, 'I'll be here for a week then I hope we can all go back together. It's a busy time on the farm but my father and a couple of my cousins are looking after it.' He turned to Sadie. 'You'll remember Joe and Will who have the farm a few miles away. Well, they very kindly said they would help out till we got back.'

Sadie didn't look pleased but she said she remembered the two men. Later when Eddie went out with his father for a walk, she said, 'Did I remember Joe and Will? Of course I remember them because they are a couple of idiots. All they talk about is corn. The growing of it or the price of it or how to transport it, their lives revolve around their farm and it makes me so fed up.'

Maryanne said she should keep her comments to herself and try to enjoy having her husband coming all these thousands of miles just to see his wife and son.

Sadie was on her high horse and there was no appealing to her better nature. 'And another thing, why does he keep calling you Mary when your name is Maryanne?'

Her mother said he probably thought Anne was her middle name but added that she didn't care what she was called.

By now the story of Ed's trip was the talking point round the district. Martha was full of curiosity about his visit. 'You mark my words, Eliza, there's something behind him coming all this way. He could quite easily just write letters instead of turning up on the doorstep.'

Eliza said she didn't believe that and she reckoned it was one of the most romantic things she had seen in a long time.

Grace and Bill were also grateful he had come, as were Evie and Tommy who were pleased to have Eddie back with them. The police had given Eddie a good telling-off for running away but it was nothing compared to his mother's furious outburst when told of his eventual destination at the Glasgow waterfront. 'Anything could have happened to you, Eddie. I can't bear to think about that if that man hadn't found you.'

Eddie had said he was sorry for all the trouble he had caused but Sadie was still mad at him. His father, although worried at the time, was more inclined to let the matter pass but when he mentioned this to Sadie on their return from the walk, Sadie started to shout at him that he was the reason behind his son's disappearance.

Eddie ran out of the house and Maryanne told her that all this fighting wasn't doing the lad any favours so Sadie joined her son in marching out, leaving Ed looking askance at his mother-in-law. 'What a mess,' he said, which was an understatement in Maryanne's opinion. She suddenly longed for her former peace that she had before Sadie came back and caused all these traumas.

'I was going to ask Sadie and Eddie to come to a movie with me but I guess that's not an option now,' he said ruefully. 'I think I'll go and see Albert as he's asked me to visit.'

Maryanne now had a headache and she swallowed two aspirin as Ed also left the house. Albert was pleased to see him and he was soon seated in a comfy chair with a bottle of beer.

'I'm sorry the beer is warm,' he apologised but Ed said anything would taste good after the ructions in the house.

'I can't understand Sadie. I was pleased when she said she wanted to come back to see her mother and she never gave me any hint that she was planning to leave me.' He gave a mirthless laugh. 'It just goes to show I'll never understand women.'

Albert felt sorry for the young man sitting opposite him. Ed was quite a good-looking man, slim with a tanned face and rough hard-working hands. 'It can't be easy for you and Eddie as you both love the lives you've got, but I've known Sadie since she was a young girl and she's headstrong and stubborn. Maryanne did her best by her but she was hard work when she was growing up.'

'I know we live in a rural area and Sadie loves company which we don't have as we're simple farmers, Albert, but she knew that before we married as I didn't pretend I was anything else. She said as long as we were together we could live on the moon and she would be happy but now she's changed and I don't know what to do. I was in the US navy when we docked in Dundee and I was as blown over when I first met her as she was with me and we couldn't wait to get married. Then when Eddie was born I thought our lives were so happy and perfect.'

Albert went to the cupboard and brought out more beer. Ed laughed. 'That's fine, let's just get drunk.'

Albert laughed along with him but he wasn't sure how he could help. 'When Sadie came back she did tell Eliza next door that she wanted to get a job but you didn't agree to that.'

Ed seemed surprised that his wife had confided in another woman. 'It wasn't that I disagreed with her but the nearest town is over twenty miles away and as she didn't learn to drive I couldn't leave the farm to transport her back and forwards every day. I did offer to teach her to drive but she said she didn't feel comfortable with our old station wagon so we had to leave things the way they were. I did take her into town on a Saturday and she did her shopping and then went to the movie house to see a film but the movie house has closed down and she was terribly disappointed at that.'

'I'm sorry to hear that, Ed, but what's going to happen now?'

Ed didn't hesitate. 'Eddie wants to come back with me and I want Sadie to come as well. I just want to be a family again.' He put his empty glass on the small table and stood up. 'Thanks, Albert, for the beer and also for listening to my troubles.'

Albert went to the door with him. 'I wish you all the luck.'

It was after nine o'clock when he left but he had enjoyed having another man to talk to.

When he got back to the house he found Eddie and his granny sitting playing a game of snakes and ladders and his son smiled when he saw him. 'Where's your mom, Eddie?'

The boy pointed to the bedroom and Ed went over to open the door but it didn't budge. There was something blocking it but he didn't want to make a fuss so he said, 'I'll let her get her beauty sleep.'

Maryanne gave him a knowing look and shook her head slightly when Eddie whooped with joy as he landed on a ladder and went straight to ninety-nine on the board. Later Ed slept with his son as he had done since arriving but he didn't sleep. It would appear that his wife wasn't planning on having him in the marital bed and he felt so depressed.

He hoped things would work out with her before he left with his son but he didn't hold out much hope for it. He suddenly had a desire to be back at the farm with his father Joel and Esther busy in the kitchen making jams and pies. He should have known a girl like Sadie wasn't cut out to be a farmer's wife. When they met that was the last thing they considered but with hindsight it had all been horribly clear from the start.

When he awoke the next morning, Sadie and Maryanne had both left for work and he relished the thought of having a day with his son. After breakfast he asked him what he wanted to do and Eddie said he wanted to go on the ferry across the river to Fife. He also asked if Evie and Tommy could join them and although surprised by this request, Ed said that was okay. He remembered the ferry from his days during the last weeks of the war and they made their way down to Craig Pier with the three children all chatting excitedly.

Tommy said to Ed, 'We call this boat the Fifie.'

Eddie told them his dad had been a sailor in the navy and the two girls seemed impressed by this. They were also so pleased that Eddie wasn't unhappy like before. The sun shone as they stood in a large queue to get on board but soon they were sailing out on the river and the city slowly receded in the distance as the shores of Fife beckoned.

Ed bought ice creams and lemonade as they sat on the grass before having a walk around the area. Ed went to sit on a bench as the three children amused themselves by going down to the water's edge and trying to skim stones over the waves. Tommy was hopeless at this but Evie and Eddie managed to make their stones skim over the surface. No one had mentioned the incident of Eddie's disappearance as the girls both knew he had received a stern talk from the police on the dangers he could have found himself in. His parents and granny had also been annoyed and had given him a good talking to so they had remained silent.

Suddenly, he stopped throwing stones and said, 'I'll be leaving very soon as I'm going back with my dad.'

Evie knew this as she overheard her mum and dad discussing it but it came as news to Tommy who started to cry. 'Can you not stay here, Eddie, as we all like you.'

Eddie said he liked everyone in the lane but that didn't make up for being away from his home in America. 'Dad is hoping Mum will come back with us and I'm hoping the same as it won't be the same without her.' He sounded sad.

Evie said she would go back with them. 'Your mum won't

want to stay here without you.'

He stayed quiet but he didn't look too sure about this. They ran back to the bench and Ed said did they all want some fish and chips before going back on the boat. They stood in a queue then carried them to the pier and ate them on the deck with the sound of seagulls wheeling overhead. They were all tired when they got back to the lane and Grace met them with an offer of tea.

The children sat down to watch television while Grace asked if they had had a good day. Ed smiled and she was again struck by what a lovely handsome man he was. Sadie must be off her head to chuck this great man away, she thought.

'We all had a great day and there's nothing like the sea air for giving one an appetite,' he said. 'We don't have that back home as it's miles and miles of farmland. There is a river but nothing like the sea.'

Grace had never thought of that before but now she realised they were indeed lucky to have such a lovely waterfront on their doorstep.

After his tea, Ed said he better get back but Eddie was engrossed in the television so Grace said she would send him home after the programme finished. When he opened the door of Maryanne's house he was immediately struck how different it was from the Gows' place.

Maryanne had arrived home but there was no sign of Sadie. He looked at the clock and wondered where she was. Maryanne noticed this and said, 'She doesn't always come home at the same time, Ed, but she won't be long.'

As it turned out Eddie was in bed when she came home at nine o'clock, and she said as she was tired she was going straight to bed. Ed had gone along to see Albert and when he got back he was annoyed that she hadn't waited up to talk to him about the journey back to America. He walked over and knocked loudly on her bedroom door. 'Sadie, come out here as I want to talk to you about going back home.'

Her voice sounded muffled as if she was half asleep. 'Not now, Ed. I'll speak to you tomorrow.'

Maryanne looked embarrassed and buried her head in a newspaper. Ed was furious and he went into the lane and walked along the streets still busy with people enjoying the summer evening. His mood was black and he knew she wouldn't go back with him yet he had no idea why she was acting like this.

He realised it had been a culture shock for her when she first came to the farm but that was eleven years ago. Eddie was born in the local hospital and he thought she was happy. He knew she wanted to work in the town which just wasn't feasible but he now knew he would give in to this request when they got back home. His ticket for the return sea journey was just three days away and he was planning on buying two tickets for his wife and son tomorrow or the next day.

He got back and the house was quiet as Maryanne had gone to bed, so he went into Eddie's room and made himself as comfortable as possible in the large easy chair. This wasn't the welcome he thought he would get. He had imagined his wife would be overjoyed to see him and, as his mother-in-law was obviously recovered from her operation, would be ready to go back with him. He had no idea what Sadie was playing at but he was becoming increasingly perplexed by her cold attitude towards him. Before falling asleep he made up his mind to tackle her tomorrow. She was either coming back with them or she was staying. He was suddenly awake when he realised he didn't care what she did and he was immediately filled with guilt.

The next morning he was up and waiting for her before she left for her work. That was another annoyance with him as he thought her job at a pub was hardly a reason to stay in Dundee. He had heard from Martha that she had told everyone she had a high flying job as a secretary in a big office in town and it had been a source of shock when the policemen let this out in their questioning, but as far as Martha was concerned it was a great source of amusement.

When Sadie came through from her room she looked dismayed to see him. 'I don't want to discuss anything, Ed, and I don't want Eddie upset.'

Ed felt his temper rising. 'For God's sake, Sadie, it's your attitude that's upsetting our son. I've no idea what's happened between us and I don't like it.'

Sadie gave him a contemptuous look. 'Oh, you don't like it, do you? What about me stagnating on that awful corn farm with no company all day? Well I hated that.'

'I've been thinking about that, Sadie, and if you want to go to work in the town then I'll drive you in and come back for you afterwards.'

She laughed. 'As usual, Ed, it's too little too late. Do I have to spell it out for you that I don't love you any more? In fact I've been wondering if I ever loved you at all.'

Ed looked shocked. After a minute he said, 'I had no idea you felt like that, Sadie. In two days' time I'll be taking Eddie back with me and I hoped you would be with us and I still hope so.'

Sadie was mad. 'Eddie is staying here with me so you had better go back on your own.' With that she flounced out. Ed went outside to smoke a cigarette and he noticed his hands were shaking with anger. He had to make up his mind quickly if Eddie was to get away with him. He was upset at the thought of his son leaving his mother behind so he had to make sure that's what Eddie wanted. When the boy came out of his room Ed decided to ask him.

'Eddie, do you really want to go back with me?' Eddie said he did. And his father went on, 'What if your mum doesn't want to come with us, how do you feel about that?'

Eddie's face fell. 'I want her to come, Dad, but I don't want to stay here. I love Mum and Granny but I want to go home.'

'Well, it's going to be difficult but I think we should leave here earlier than I'd planned. Can you say your goodbyes to Evie and Tommy and leave a letter for your mum and granny?'

Eddie nodded and went back to his room to pack his rucksack while his father packed his suitcase. Eddie wrote his letter and placed it on the mantelpiece then went to say cheerio to his two friends.

Tommy began to cry but Evie wished him all the best on his journey. 'I'll write to you,' she said.

Bill was at work but Grace wished them well before Ed went to see Albert. He told him they were about to leave. 'Thank you for being such a good friend, Albert.' Albert nodded but he was sad.

38

Ed and his son set off to the bus station where they caught a bus to Glasgow. They would have to stay overnight in the city so Ed could book a berth for Eddie. They were due to sail early the next morning and as they sat in the bed and breakfast that evening, they were sad and upset.

Eddie couldn't understand why his mother wouldn't come with them and although he didn't want to cry, he was on the verge of tears. Ed tried to make sense of the past week as well but couldn't. Like his son, he had thought his wife would be coming with them.

'When we get back I'll write to Mum and enclose money for her to travel. I'm sure when she sees you've made up your mind to leave then she'll change her mind and we'll be reunited.' Although he said the words, he didn't believe them, but he had to do all he could to become a family again. This seemed to cheer Eddie and they went out to the small café along the road for something to eat.

While they were in Glasgow, Maryanne arrived home to see the letter. She wasn't surprised when she read it but she dreaded Sadie's reaction when she came home. Grace came in and told her about Ed having to leave a couple of days early. 'Evie and Tommy are upset about Eddie leaving but Ed had no choice. Eddie had hinted that he would run away again if he didn't get back to America.'

Maryanne said it was all in the letter and she pointed to the other one addressed to Sadie. 'I think this will make her ill, Grace, but she's her own worst enemy. Ed's passport has Eddie's name on it so there's no problem about his leaving. He is after all an American citizen as he was born there.'

Maryanne considered leaving the house and going to see her friend Dorothy as she knew there were going to be ructions and tears, but she then decided she was being a coward so she waited patiently for Sadie to come home. She was so upset she didn't even make anything to eat or drink except a cup of tea which she held in her hand until it grew cold. Throwing it away, she sat in silence.

As it turned out Sadie didn't come back till seven o'clock which made Maryanne furious so she was in a bad mood when her daughter came through the door. Maryanne noticed she had been drinking again and that was another worry. She held her temper but it was just one worry after another since Sadie had come back to Dundee. Sadie sat down with a tired sigh. 'What a day I've had. I could do with a cup of coffee.'

Maryanne ignored this request. Sadie asked where Eddie was. 'I expect he's with Evie, he seems to spend more time with them than he does with me.'

This remark was the last thing her mother wanted to hear. 'Well it's just as well he gets looking after because you're never home to make his meals or be here for him.' She handed over the letter. 'Anyway you don't have to worry about your husband and son from now on.' Sadie asked her what she was talking about but Maryanne told her to read her letter. 'That will explain it all.'

She tore the letter open and after reading it she became hysterical and screamed loudly, leaping to her feet and making for the door. Maryanne tried to calm her down but there were no words that could stop Sadie from shouting. All this noise was heard by most of the residents but they didn't want to interfere, although Grace and Anna wanted to help.

'When did Ed and Eddie go? I'm going after them to stop him, he can't take my son away from me.'

Maryanne stopped her. 'It's too late, they will have sailed by now.' This was a lie as she had no idea when they planned to leave but she couldn't have Sadie run off and try to find them.

'You should have agreed to go back with your husband and son, that's what marriage is all about, It's not all roses and feather beds but sometimes you have to make hard choices.'

Sadie rounded on her. 'What side are you on? It seems to me you've all been against me ever since I came back to this dump to stay.' She waved her arm around the house. 'I mean, look at it, everything is either old or decrepit, just like you and most of the people in the lane.'

Maryanne stood quite still at this insult then said quietly, 'If that's what you think why didn't you leave with your family?'

'Well, I'm not planning on staying here for long as I'm looking for a house of my own and then I'll make Ed's life so miserable that he'll send my son back to me.'

'Eddie wanted to go with his dad, why can't you see that? That's why he ran away and you were lucky to get him back quickly or who knows where he would have ended up.'

Sadie picked up her bag and went out and although Maryanne followed her to the door, Sadie had run to the far end of the lane. Albert and Bella saw her as she rushed past the window but Martha missed it as she was fussing with Eliza, who was trying to heave her mother towards the door so they could see what was going on.

Albert had been in Bella's kitchen and they both were shocked by the noise coming from Maryanne's house. Bella was worried. 'Do you think someone should go after her and try and calm her down?'

Albert said he didn't have the speed to run after her. 'The only ones able to do that are Rory or Thomas and I saw the

MacCallums pushing the pram out for a walk and Thomas will be at work.'

'That girl was always a handful and I feel sorry for her mother,' said Bella and although Albert agreed he still felt sorry for her.

Back in the house, Maryanne sat down and wished all this trouble would somehow go away. There was a knock on the door and Grace and Anna came in. When she saw them, she burst into tears and the two women said the best thing for her was to get out of the house.

'Come with me and I'll make you something to eat,' said Grace, but Maryanne said she was fine.

'I think I'll go and see Dorothy but thanks for the offer.' She tried to smile at them but her eyes filled with tears again. 'Why couldn't Sadie go back with her family?' she said plaintively but Grace and Anna didn't have the answer to that.

Sadie reached the Hilltown and she stopped. Where on earth could she possibly go? Then she remembered Thomas was a barman in the Windmill Bar and she also knew there was a small snug bar that often had some women in it so she made her way there.

The snug was empty when she opened the door and she was relieved when another barman served her. Thomas was busy further up the bar so she ordered her gin and tonic and sat down on the worn bench that was situated against the window.

She felt like screaming again but realised she would get thrown out. She took the letter from her pocket and read it again. How dare Ed do this to her? She planned to get the law on to him. So he was going to send her money to join them, well he could go to hell. She would fight to get her son back.

She had another drink and suddenly felt so tired. The barman who served her mentioned to Thomas about the good-looking woman in the snug. 'It's usually just those three old women from across the road who come in for their glasses of stout. I've never seen this one before.'

Thomas was curious so he had a quick look and was astonished when he saw Sadie. However he didn't speak to her. By closing time she was still there so he decided to walk her home. By now she had drunk three gins and she was swaying as she left the pub.

Thomas hurried out and said he would see her home. She squinted at him before saying, 'Oh, Thomas, that's very good of you to help a damsel in distress. Did you know my darling husband has taken my son behind my back?'

Thomas was amazed. 'No, Sadie, I didn't know that.'

She was slurring her words. 'Well he has but he's not getting away with it as I'll take him to court to get Eddie back.'

Thomas was glad when they reached home and he quickly asked Anna if she could take Sadie into Maryanne's house. Luckily Tommy was in bed asleep. Anna helped her neighbour to negotiate the step at the door.

'Get yourself to bed, Sadie, and get a good night's sleep. Things will look better in the morning.'

Sadie began to shout about her scoundrel of a husband when she saw Maryanne. Anna was glad to leave her with her mother as she didn't know how to cope with her. As she sat and had some supper with Thomas, they both said how sad it was that such a good-looking young woman was slowly disintegrating in bits.

Maryanne felt weary about the vision of another row but Sadie went into the bedroom and when her mother looked in later, she found her lying fully clothed on the bed. Her mother placed a blanket over her and retired to her own bed which, since Sadie's arrival, was the settee.

The next morning as she got ready for her work there was silence from the other room. When she looked in she heard Sadie snoring so she let her sleep off her drunken night.

It was noon when Sadie wakened up and she felt ill.

Shuffling to the sink she filled the kettle to make a cup of strong coffee. She was too late to go to work but she would explain the reason for her absence tomorrow when Hal and some of the locals would no doubt agree with her having to cope with a rotten husband.

By now all the residents had heard about the matter and although there was some sympathy for her, most people knew she was at fault for her broken marriage. Martha was one of the latter. 'A marriage is for life, not for picking and choosing the bits you like or dislike,' she told Eliza, who kept her thoughts to herself. She remembered there was a time when her father must have wished Martha would leave him. As if she knew these thoughts, Martha went on, 'Your father and I were like two peas in a pod and we always got on with one another. Not like that warring pair.' Eliza couldn't believe her ears.

39

While Sadie was recovering from her hangover, Ed and Eddie were boarding the *SS Wiltshire* on their way back to America. They weren't feeling jubilant as they both wanted Sadie to be with them but once on board Eddie's mood lightened. His father had told him it was just a matter of time before his mother joined them and he was filled with pleasure at the thought of going back to the corn farm and seeing his grandfather and Esther, not to mention his school friends from the neighbouring farms.

They were sharing a cabin and as he watched the shores of Scotland slowly recede, he was filled with a mixture of sorrow and excitement.

'Will you send Mum the money as soon as we get home?' he asked, and Ed said he would. It meant having to borrow the money from Joel and he explained that having to come over to Scotland hadn't been cheap but he meant every word he said.

Sadie knew she couldn't sit in the house all afternoon so she dressed quickly and went into the town. She did a lot of window shopping, especially at Grant's the house furnishers. She went in and looked at all the lovely new furniture and a salesman came over. 'Can I help you?' he asked and Sadie said she was interested in furnishing her house. The man showed her the selection of dining, bedroom and three-piece suites.

'This sideboard has a built-in cocktail cabinet,' he said, opening a flap to show a space for drinks and glasses. 'It makes for great entertaining at home.'

Sadie spent a lovely hour walking around the large store then said she would come back later when she got her own house and had her son back with her. She had always got what she wanted even when she was a child and she expected that this latest drama in her life would be settled in her favour.

She hoped that Thomas hadn't mentioned her being in the pub and she was kicking herself for not asking him to keep it to himself. She would find him later and give him her wide-eyed look and he would do as she asked, of that she had no doubt.

Sadie never knew that her visit had been discussed by Anna and Grace and at that moment Anna was being grilled by Mrs Bell in the baker's shop.

'I heard that she was screaming when she heard her husband had scampered with her son, did you hear that, Anna?'

Anna said it was true but she quite understood the reason for it. 'I would do the same if Thomas went off with Tommy and I would probably end up drinking in the Windmill as well.'

This was news to her colleague. 'Was she drinking in a pub?'

Anna immediately was sorry to have divulged this titbit but now it was out there was nothing to do but say it was true. Mrs Bell's ears were twitching and she couldn't wait to spread it around her close friends, telling them of course to keep it to themselves which was like trying to hold back the waves.

Grace had a visit from Bella. She was worried about both Sadie and Maryanne. 'I think there's going to be a lot more anguish in that house.'

Grace agreed but said there was nothing anyone could do. She decided to change the subject. 'Bill, Evie and I are going away for a few days. We're taking my mother to a caravan in St Andrews and we hope the good weather will last.'

Bella said a break would do them all a world of good. 'When are you going?'

Grace said it was next week and they were all looking forward to it. After Bella left, she wondered if Bill would enjoy her mother's company for three days as she always managed to rub him up the wrong way. She hoped she wouldn't mention Elsie and her big-spending son.

Evie was still upset about Eddie's departure but she at least she had the holiday coming up.

'We might be just going away for three days but the rest of our holiday will be a day here or there so I'm looking forward to it.'

Tommy was excited about her visit to Ireland and she said to Evie, 'We're going away for two weeks so it's a proper holiday.' Evie took her friend's statement with good humour.

Sadie arrived home after her trip to town and decided to have an early night as she didn't want to sleep in for work tomorrow. After all, if she didn't work then she would never realise her dream of having her own house filled with furniture from Grant's emporium.

Martha was still talking about last night's argument. 'I wonder what she'll do to get her son back. Do you have any idea, Eliza?'

Eliza was tired of her mother's fixation with Sadie and her family so she just shook her head and offered to make the cocoa.

The weather was remaining good which boded well for the Gows' holiday and Grace was busy washing, ironing and packing for their time away at the caravan. She had paid a visit to her mother and Evelyn had packed a huge suitcase. Grace was worried.

'We're only spending three days in the caravan, Mum, why do you need so many clothes and shoes?'

Evelyn was adamant that everything was essential and would be needed. 'I like to be prepared because it might be rainy and cold.'

Grace had walked down to Ann Street in her dress and cardigan as the sun was warm and she didn't think the weather forecast would be any different. However, Evelyn wasn't convinced.

'Well, I'm not taking any chances, Grace.'

As Grace went home, she wondered how Bill would view the large case and she knew he wouldn't be pleased.

On the morning of their departure he ordered a taxi to take them to the train station. This was an extra expense but he said it was too much hassle to carry cases down to the station and when he saw Evelyn's luggage he almost blew his top. It was a warning look from his wife which held his tongue but when they had a moment alone on the station platform, he erupted.

'What on earth has she brought? I bet Queen Elizabeth doesn't take as much luggage as your mother.'

Grace shushed him as her mother came towards them. She started to complain about the toilet, saying the queue was huge. 'You'd think they would make better facilities when there's crowds like this waiting on the train.'

Bill turned away and it was only Evie who heard him mutter, 'Three days of this will make me go mad.'

Evie thought, Poor Granny, it's not her fault that she's old and keeps needing to go to the toilet.

Things began to look up when they reached the caravan park that overlooked the sea. Bill had booked one with six berths although there were only the four of them. He wanted to make sure there was enough room for them all as he planned to have the bedroom as far away as possible from his mother-in-law.

Evie and Grace were entranced by the view and the fresh sea air but Evelyn complained about the distance to the shower block. 'How am I going to get there and back, Grace? Especially at night.'

Her daughter said she would accompany her every time she needed to go even if it meant getting out of bed to do so. Grace had packed food and a hamper of baked goodies and sandwiches so they sat outside and had a picnic. Evie decided to have a trip to the beach and the outdoor swimming pool so she quickly got into her swimming costume. Her parents said they would come with her but Evelyn decided to relax on the deckchair that had been supplied with the caravan. They left her half asleep in the sun and spent an enjoyable afternoon by themselves.

Because the sun was still shining at teatime they ate their meal outside and by bedtime they were all tired. Bill had allocated the beds and even Evelyn mentioned how comfortable they were.

It was three o'clock in the morning when Grace was awakened by her mother. Bill was snoring and dead to the world. Evelyn said that she needed to go to the toilet. Grace got up, feeling weary after a busy day. 'You'll have to put your shoes on, Mum, as the grass might be wet.' Evelyn said her slippers were all right so the two women went out into the darkness. There was a slight tinge of light on the eastern horizon and it would soon be sunrise. It was difficult trying to make their way through the caravans but they soon reached their destination.

Afterwards they had to make the return journey but faced by so many caravans, Grace wasn't sure which one was theirs. 'Do you remember which one is ours, Mum?' she asked, but Evelyn shook her head.

'I thought you knew where we were,' she said. 'I hope we're not lost as it's cold and my feet are wet.'

'I told you to put on your shoes.'

'Well I didn't, so don't lecture me, Grace.'

Finally after a few false starts, Grace noticed the small table and chairs outside one of the caravans. 'I think that one is ours,' she said hopefully.

'What if it's the wrong one? We can't barge into someone else's place.'

As it turned out it was the correct one and Evelyn retired to her bed, moaning about her wet feet and even wetter slippers while Grace sank gratefully into her bed beside a still-snoring husband.

The next morning they woke up to torrential rain and there was thunder and lightning as well. Grace groaned loudly and Bill said that was all they needed. 'Maybe it'll go off soon,' she said but one look at the dark clouds and the deep puddles on the grass didn't bode well for a good day. 'I saw some board games, jigsaws and playing cards in a cupboard so we can pass the time with those.'

However there was the difficulty in getting to the shower block through all the puddles. They all made a valiant try although their shoes were soaked. Evelyn moaned that she should have brought her wellies. Bill suggested going into the town and buying some from a shoe shop but Evelyn was horrified. 'I already have a pair, Bill, I don't need another pair. After all, what will I do with two pairs of wellies?'

Grace said as she took the same shoe size as her then she would buy a pair and give them to her mother. 'Then I can take them home for myself.'

'But you've got a pair of wellies at home so that means you'll have two pairs and that's a waste of money.' Evelyn sounded annoyed at this predicament. 'Let's hope the rain goes off soon so we won't need to buy anything.'

Throughout this conversation, Bill looked like he wanted to throw a brick through the window but he tried to stay calm for the sake of his wife and daughter.

The rain became heavier and it pounded off the metal roof like gunshots so Evie took out a five-hundred-piece jigsaw and began to put it together while Evelyn read one of the books she had brought with her. 'Elsie's son always takes her to a posh hotel on her holiday,' she said, putting the book aside.

'Then it doesn't matter what the weather is like.'

Bill looked ready to answer her back but once again Grace gave him a warning glance then nodded her head towards Evie who was intent on her puzzle. On hearing her granny mention Elsie, she asked her,

'What kind of hotel does she go to?'

Evelyn's face lit up. 'Oh, it's usually someplace like Edinburgh or Glasgow and it's a luxurious hotel with waiters and afternoon tea and grand meals at night and there's loads of places to visit like theatres and cinemas and art galleries.'

Grace had heard enough. 'Well, we can't afford these kinds of holidays, Mum, but if we could then we would take you on one.'

Evelyn was pleased. 'That's nice, Grace, but I'm really quite happy here even though I moan about it. I just seem to like a good moan.'

Evie burst out laughing and was soon joined by her parents. Bill said, 'Let's go into the town and I'll treat us all to a meal in one of the hotels.'

The women jumped up and soon they were walking into the town where they saw a grand looking hotel on the main street. It was quite posh inside and they were soon seated at a table with a snowy white cloth and silver cutlery. For a moment Grace was worried about the cost but then she remembered her husband had got his bonus before coming away. They had a lovely meal and the adults had alcoholic drinks while Evie had a lemonade. Afterwards they sat in the cosy lounge that had a log fire blazing in the large stone fireplace and they had tea and biscuits.

When they emerged into the street, they were pleased to see the rain had gone off and although it was still cloudy, it was at least dry. Back at the caravan, they played cards until it was bedtime and Evelyn slept through the night without a nocturnal visit.

Grace was pleased as the holiday had turned out a success.

Still, it was with a feeling of relief that the holiday was over and the following day they packed up, tidied the caravan then set off for home. Grace made sure her mother was settled in her flat before the three of them made their way to their own house. Although it was sunny there were some scattered showers that were quite heavy.

When they got home, Bill sat down with a sigh of contentment in his favourite chair. 'I'm glad that's over, Grace, as there's no place like home.' Grace looked at Evie and they both gave him an amused glance.

Tommy had seen their arrival and she came to the door. 'Did you have a good holiday?' she asked and Evie said it was super. Bill almost burst out laughing but he managed to stifle his amusement at the thought of this extravagant statement. It had been bloody awful in his estimation but he wasn't going to upset his wife and daughter.

40

Sadie woke in a bad mood as she had had a dreadful row with her mother the night before. She had said she was going to the police and a solicitor. 'I have to make Ed see that Eddie's place is with me and I think everyone will agree with me.'

Maryanne was annoyed at her. 'I think you should be going back to live with your husband, then both of you can give Eddie a good upbringing.'

Sadie was furious. 'Will you listen to yourself, Mum? Where was my father when I was growing up? Not having him around didn't do me any harm and it'll be the same with Eddie. He'll be happier with me.'

'No he won't,' Maryanne said loudly. 'He'll run away again just like before and do you want his life to be like that? Also your father died so my situation was different from yours. You have a lovely husband and son and your place is with them.'

Sadie was taken aback by her mother's tone of voice. 'Running away was just something he had to do and he won't do it again. Anyway, maybe he'll run away when he gets back to the farm, have you thought about that? As far as Ed is concerned, I don't love him any more.'

'That makes no difference, you have to stay together for Eddie's sake. He won't be a child for ever and when he's grown up then you can decide to leave.'

Sadie laughed. 'Oh, you're so old fashioned, Mum, people

don't stay together if they are no longer in love with their husband or wife.'

'Well, Ed is still in love with you but you never gave him a chance to discuss your problems. You locked yourself in the bedroom and ignored him.'

Sadie was fed up with this argument so she put on her jacket. 'I'm going for a walk.' She didn't want to pass Martha's house as she was tired of the woman's constant gossiping and she was glad there were two ways out of the lane. She liked Eliza and felt sorry for her and wondered why she hadn't escaped from her domineering mother. She made her way up the Hilltown towards the licensed grocer and bought her usual half bottle of gin.

'My mother likes her nightly drink,' she lied, but the man looked as if he didn't care who it was for as long as he got his money in the till. She popped it into her handbag and set off for the house. It was just eight-thirty but she decided to go to bed with her drink and a magazine. Then she would plan how to get Eddie back.

Now she had overslept so she decided not go to work. She reckoned Hal wouldn't mind as he had been sympathetic when she told him of her husband's sneaky journey, and even Big John had bought her a drink, just to cheer her up. She felt she had to make plans to get her son back.

She considered going into town to see if a solicitor could help her but she wasn't sure of the cost of this so she thought she would get some advice from someone. Albert and Bella were old enough to maybe have used a solicitor at some time so she made her way to Albert's house.

He seemed surprised to see her but he quickly put his housework box away, made a cup of tea and asked how she was. 'I thought you would be at work, Sadie, did you get the day off?'

'No, I didn't. I took the day off to go and see the police and a solicitor as I'm trying to get Eddie back.'

Albert looked at her with a serious expression. 'What do you want me to do?'

'I wondered if you had had any dealings with the law and if you had then maybe you can help me.'

'No, I've never had to use a solicitor or had anything to do with the law but if you want my advice then I have to tell you I think you have a great husband and son and you should be with them.'

This wasn't what she wanted to hear. 'I'm not going back, Albert, as I've no feelings left for Ed, but I love my son and want him here with me.'

He didn't speak for a minute then he said, 'I think you're wrong, Sadie, as I know you still love your husband but you don't want to admit it.'

'I don't and I also don't care what he does with his life and I shouldn't have married him in the first place. I think I was carried away with the thought of life in America but I found out too late that life is the same boring chore no matter where you live Anyway, if I change my mind then he'll be waiting for me if I do decide to go back sometime in the future.'

'Don't leave it too late, Sadie, as there is always someone waiting in the wings all ready to take your place and a lonely man will be vulnerable.'

'I know someone like that, her name is Esther and she's always goggle-eyed over Ed. She was his childhood sweetheart but he treats her like a sister and he's not interested in her. Not that I blame him as she's not pretty.'

Albert couldn't believe what he was hearing. 'Don't be so sure. Being good-looking isn't everything in a relationship.'

Sadie didn't believe this and she stood up to leave. 'Do you think Bella would have any knowledge of dealing with the problem of getting my son back?'

'You'll have to ask her but as she's never married or had any children I very much doubt it.'

Sadie was annoyed she hadn't gone to work as the day

stretched before her like a boring chasm. Making up her mind, she set off for the city centre and spent an hour looking at the brass plates of various solicitor's offices but as they all looked so old-fashioned and fussy, she made her way back home where she poured a drink and sat pondering over her choices.

She decided she would leave everything to another day.

41

The Cassidy household was getting ready for their holiday to Ireland. At least Anna and Tommy were but Thomas felt like a criminal facing the hangman's noose. He kept quiet about his feelings as he didn't want to spoil the holiday for his family.

Anna had treated the family to some new clothes from her McGills account and she was looking forward to wearing the new blue and white floral summer dress, the short blue swagger jacket and her white sandals while Tommy had a new dress and red sandals and Thomas a couple of shirts.

Thomas wondered how they could afford all these new clothes but Anna said she had been saving up from her wages every week in order to finance the whole holiday. 'It won't cost us anything to stay with Lizzie except helping with our food, and the biggest expense will be the trip over to Belfast in the ferry and anyway I want us all to look good as you know what my family are like. They like to criticise everything.'

Thomas knew this was true and his grey cloud appeared at the thought of the holiday.

Evie was going to miss her friend over the two weeks they would be away as she was already missing Eddie. She was hoping he would write when he got back home but maybe he would be busy or he might forget about his life in the lane.

The weather, although not as sunny as before, was still warm and dry and Tommy said she hoped it wouldn't rain. Her father had said it often rained in Ireland but she wasn't sure if he was telling the truth or just making his feelings known as she had heard him going on about Mum's family. Bella and Albert had called her in one day and given her two shillings each for spending and when she thanked them they said Evie had got the same when she went off to the caravan. When, along with Evie, she had gone in to see Martha and Eliza to do their shopping, Martha had said it was all right for some people to get a holiday. 'I would love to get away for two weeks but we don't have any relatives living abroad so we have to stay here and look at four walls.'

Eliza said it wasn't as bad as that but Martha said it was worse. When Tommy relayed this conversation to her dad he said that Martha and Eliza were free to take his place and she had laughed.

After days of anticipation, the departure day arrived and they walked down to the train station to catch the Glasgow train and then on to the ferry at Stranraer where the boat would take them to Belfast. Apart from the Fifie across the Tay to Fife, Tommy hadn't been on a sea journey before and she was so excited.

Thankfully the sea looked calm which was a big bonus for Anna who didn't really like boats while Thomas didn't really like Ireland. He seemed so fed up that Anna told him to look as if he was enjoying the trip.

'I hope you're not going to go about like a wet fish for the next fourteen days, Thomas,' she warned.

Later, as the ferry moved into the open sea, he began to enjoy the fresh sea air and he relaxed. Things might be fine, he thought as he walked around the deck, listening to the seagulls and watching the Irish Sea slip by under the ferry's hull.

When they reached Belfast it was a simple trip on a bus to Lizzie's house which was a semi-detached on a council estate. Katie and Roseanne lived just around the corner while Anna's two brothers were two streets away, an arrangement that filled Thomas with a feeling of depression.

Lizzie made them welcome and went to the garden gate to give Anna and Tommy a big hug. But she merely nodded to Thomas.

'Let me show you to your room,' she said, leading them up the carpeted staircase. Anna admired the carpet and Lizzie told her it was new. 'Mike got a bonus from work so we bought this carpet and the one in the living room. You know he's got a good job in a factory making parts for cars.' Anna and Thomas knew that as it had been pointed out to them on many occasions during her holiday with them in Dundee.

Their bedroom was large enough for the three of them as it held a double bed and a single divan for Tommy. Anna asked her where her own family were sleeping but Lizzie said they had plenty of room as her daughter Elizabeth had her own room while her son Billy planned to stay with a friend.

When they were in the kitchen having a cup of tea, Lizzie brought them up to date with the family news.
'Katie has had her operation but she's recovering from it. I told her we would all go and see her this afternoon.' Thomas thought his groan was silent but she gave him a baleful stare. 'You can go and see Sean and Willie as it'll be all women's talk at Katie's. Thomasina can play with Roseanne's two kids.'

After dinner, which the four of them ate at the small kitchen table, the women and Tommy set off for Katie's house while Thomas decided to catch a bus into the city. It had been many years since he was last in Belfast and he wondered if it had changed much.

Katie was sleeping in a high-backed chair with a blanket over her knees. Lizzie didn't knock but just marched in with Anna and Tommy in tow. Roseanne sat in the opposite chair while a boy and a girl played in the garden. Lizzie said, 'Thomasina, away into the garden and play with Rosie and Harry.' Tommy didn't seem too pleased but she did as she was told. Roseanne said Katie hadn't had a good sleep. 'I did tell her to go to the doctor and get some sleeping pills but she's not keen in case she gets hooked on them.'

Katie woke up and she made a grimace as she tried to get comfortable. 'Hullo Anna, I'm sorry I can't stand up to give you a hug.'

'Are you still in pain?' asked Lizzie and when Katie nodded, she went on, 'Maybe you should go back to the doctor to get something for it.'

Katie said there was no need. 'The surgeon said it would take six weeks to a couple of months to get better. I'm not allowed to do any housework or lift anything but I'm getting fed up sitting in this chair.'

Roseanne said she shouldn't worry about anything. 'Lizzie and I will help out in the house and now Anna is here she can help as well.'

Lizzie was nodding her approval at this statement but Anna wasn't happy about this at all. She thought she was coming for a holiday but it now seemed that she would have to muck in with her sisters.

Lizzie took herself off to the kitchen and they heard her washing the dishes and when she came back
into the room, her arms were covered with soapy suds. 'I'll just Hoover the carpet before we go and Roseanne can stay with you in case you need anything.'

Tommy didn't like playing with her cousins as they were noisy and liked to pull each other's jumpers as they chased each other around the garden so she was relieved when her mother appeared with her auntie.

Meanwhile, Thomas was enjoying his trip and he had found the pub he had often visited in his young days. It hadn't changed much over the years and he sat at a table by the window with his pint of Guinness, watching the world go by. He was dreading going back because the mob, as he called Anna's family, would all be together. They were such a noisy bunch, forever arguing or falling out with one or another of the gang.

The next morning they had to wait while Mike used the bathroom to shave and wash, closely followed by Elizabeth who spent so long taking a shower and slapping on make up before heading off to work.

Thomas suggested after breakfast that they should go sightseeing as he hadn't been back to the city of his youth for many years. Anna said that was a good idea so she got dressed in her new dress and jacket while Tommy also wore her new outfit. When Lizzie saw them she was amazed. 'You didn't have to get dressed up to do Katie's housework this morning,' she said as she fried bacon and eggs while popping bread in the toaster.

Anna was furious but Thomas put her right. 'We are having a day out, Lizzie, so Anna can't do Katie's housework.'

Lizzie raised her eyebrows in surprise. 'I thought that was your reason for coming to see us as we all need to help our sister out. Rosanne manages to help even though she has to leave her own housework behind to be there for Katie.'

Anna could barely talk, she was so annoyed. 'Why doesn't Roseanne's husband help out? He works on the council bin lorry and he finishes at two o'clock, surely he can wash dishes and sweep the floor.'

'Well I must say I'm disappointed in you but off you go gallivanting and leave all the hard work to me and Roseanne, who has two kids to look after unless you've forgotten, and Katie's husband can't help because he's a long-distance lorry driver and he's away just now.'

Lucky him, thought Thomas, but he was determined not to give in to Lizzie's domineering ways. Breakfast was eaten in silence then Lizzie went off in high dudgeon with her overalls in her handbag while they got ready to set off on their tour around the city. Anna said she wasn't going to enjoy herself but Tommy and her dad said that was nonsense. 'We'll have a good day out then have something to eat before coming back to Stalag Four.'

Anna said it wasn't as bad as all that but looking at the faces of her family, she realised it was much worse. Thomas was adamant. 'Tomorrow we are also going to spend the day together and that doesn't mean cleaning Katie's house.'

'But Katie's just had a major operation and she needs some help. I don't mind helping out some times but not every day.'

'Well, just a few hours this week and no more. Lizzie is forever cleaning. I was barely out of the bathroom this morning when she was tackling the bath with Vim as if we were a mucky bunch of jungle dwellers.' Tommy burst out laughing but Anna felt fed up that her family had used her in asking them over then acting like the united cleaning club.

Later as they sat having a pub lunch in a very pleasant tavern, Anna finally relaxed, especially when Thomas bought her a glass of sherry while he ordered his usual pint of Guinness. Tommy had two glasses of orangeade and her father warned her to book into the bathroom quickly when they got back or else she wouldn't get a look in as he had a suspicion that Elizabeth took up residence there.

When they got back, all tired out from walking miles on the pavements, they found Lizzie, Roseanne and her two kids in the living room. The two women still wore their overalls. Thomas couldn't resist making a remark. 'Heavens, I didn't realise Katie's house was so dirty that you would need protective clothes.'

Lizzie ignored him and turned to Tommy. 'Did you have a good day, Thomasina?'

Tommy said she had. 'We had a super day out and we had our dinner in a pub.'

Roseanne gave her sister a look that spoke a thousand words. 'We had a very busy day ourselves, scrubbing Katie's floors, changing her bed and polishing the furniture.'

Ye Gods, thought Thomas as he walked out of the room, followed by Tommy who desperately needed the bathroom.

Anna helped out the next day while Thomas and Tommy set off for another tour of the city. When they came home, Anna was sitting on the bed in their room crying. 'I can't stand this any more, I want to go home.'

Thomas headed off downstairs, ready to do battle with Lizzie, but before he could open his mouth, she said, 'There's to be a party on Saturday to welcome you. Sean and Willie and families will be here and Roseanne, Albie and their brood but not Katie as she is still convalescing.'

Thomas went back upstairs to impart this latest bit of news. 'It seems you are to be treated like the prodigal daughter with a family party. Will I tell your sister that we won't be here?'

Anna was mortified. 'No, we can't do that, not when they've gone to the bother of arranging a party.'

On the Saturday night Lizzie set out a buffet on the kitchen table and there were bottles of beer and a bottle of sherry. They sat in the living room until there was a loud knock on the door and all the family poured in. Sean introduced Florence, his wife and three burly looking sons called Sean Jr, Alex and Johnny. Willie arrived a bit worse for wear as it looked like he had been celebrating before his appearance. His wife was called Aimee; he spelled her name out in case the Cassidys were idiots. She was a thin, washed-out sort of woman who seemed to be made more insignificant by her family of three sons and two daughters. Thomas didn't catch their names but mentally called them Tom, Dick and Harry, Amy and Maime. Last of all was Roseanne with Albie, Rosie and Harry. Albie was built like a weightlifter which must have been a boon to his job as a council bin man.

Thomas noticed there was no sign of Elizabeth or Billy.

Lizzie asked Roseanne, 'How is Katie, did you go in to see her before you came here?'

Roseanne assured her she had. 'I also did a quick tidy up.'

Lizzie beamed. 'Good.' She stood up and made a little speech. 'We want to welcome Anna, Thomas and Thomasina back to the family. As you all know I am the oldest while Anna is the baby of our family.'

Thomas wondered if she was expecting a medal. He was handed a bottle of warm beer and everyone converged on the buffet. He went to sit beside Anna and Tommy, who looked miserable, but he tried to cheer them up. 'Never mind, it's not the end of the world, just one more week to get through.'

Sean and Willie came over and sat down beside them. 'Well, Thomas, how is your gammy leg?' said Willie, waving his bottle at Thomas's leg.

'As I told your rude sister Lizzie weeks ago, my gammy leg is perfect, thank you.'

'Did you just call Lizzie "rude"?'

Anna tried to diffuse the situation. 'For God's sake, he's only joking, Willie.'

'Well, I don't like jokes from someone whose grandfather was a special constable when we were fighting for independence from Britain.'

Anna had heard enough. 'Thomas and Tommy, I think we should leave this party.' The three of them went upstairs and Anna burst into tears. Thomas pulled the suitcase from under the bed and began to pack it. Anna quickly stood up. 'No, I'm not going to be hounded away by that lot.'

There was a tap on the door and Aimee came in. 'I'm sorry that Willie upset you all but please come downstairs as I've given him a good talking to and he better behave or else he'll be the one who is leaving.'

Thomas was astonished. He had labelled this woman as insignificant but she was anything but. 'Good for you, Aimee,' he said.

When they entered the room, Willie came over looking sheepish. 'Sorry about going on about your gammy leg, Thomas.'

Thomas said not to worry. 'My gammy leg likes the company of my good leg which I call Sammy.'

To his surprise, everyone roared with laughter. Lizzie came and sat beside them. 'I want you all to enjoy your holiday so don't worry about Katie as we'll manage fine.' She stood up and to his utter surprise she gave him a hug. 'Just to let you know we are all sorry for making this holiday miserable for you.'

Anna and Thomas were touched by this gesture and Anna said, 'I don't mind helping out with Katie and Tommy will also help.' She looked at her husband and he nodded.

After that the party went with a swing and at two o'clock in the morning, the families left and Lizzie, Thomas, Anna and Tommy went upstairs. There was still no sign of Elizabeth but Lizzie said she was staying with a friend. 'She hates family parties as she's quiet and shy and we are all too outspoken for her liking.'

When they were lying in bed, Thomas said, 'I suppose they're not such a bad bunch when you get to know them.'

Tommy, who was reading in her bed, piped up, 'They are all very loud, aren't they?'

Anna told her to put her book away as it was late and she needed her sleep. 'I'll go and help out with Katie tomorrow. Do you want to come with me, Tommy?' Tommy said she would.

Roseanne was late in arriving at Katie's house the next morning and the two children were quarrelsome. Rosie rushed in, complaining. 'Harry pushed me, Mum, and I've skinned my knee.'

Harry protested his innocence. 'You're lying, you fell over all by yourself.'

Roseanne told them to stop fighting. 'Why can't you be quiet like Thomasina?'

Rosie made a face at her cousin and stomped out. Lizzie was decluttering a kitchen cupboard and Anna went to sit with Katie. She was looking a bit better and Anna asked her about her operation.

'I had to get it as I didn't feel well. As you know, we've been trying to have a child for years but it just hasn't happened and now it never will. My husband Ian says not to worry but when I look at all the kids my brothers and sisters have I get really upset.'

Anna felt sorry for her and took her hand. 'Sometimes it's hard to understand what life throws at us but I know you've got the strength to see this through and come out the other end.'

Katie squeezed her hand but she looked so sad that Anna almost burst into tears. Suddenly there was an eruption of noise. Tommy rushed in. 'Rosie has pinched my hair clasp, the one I got from Evie, and she won't give it back.'

Roseanne, who was busy helping Lizzie with the cupboard, marched through and got hold of her daughter. 'Give that back to Thomasina.'

She had the clasp in her hair and she reluctantly pulled it out, handing it to Tommy who put it in her pocket. 'Well, are you not going to wear it?' Rosie said loudly.

Tommy said she wasn't, adding, 'I'm not wearing it until I clean it with Dettol as you've got nits in your hair and I don't want to get them.'

Rosie rushed in to see her mother. 'Thomasina says I've got nits, Mum. Tell her I haven't.' Roseanne was very annoyed but Anna told her daughter to apologise to her cousin, which she did. However she didn't put the clasp back in her hair until much later when she had wiped it with some of Lizzie's disinfectant which was kept in a large plastic container in a cupboard under the stairs.

Thomas had taken the bus into the city and was now sitting in the pub with his Guinness. He was sitting at a small table reading the paper when he heard a voice calling his name.

'Good Lord, it's Thomas Cassidy,' said the voice.

Thomas looked up and a tall, thickset man in a brown overcoat was standing beside him. He smiled when he recognised

Pete Murdoch who had been his boss when he worked with the Hydro Board on one of their constructions. Pete sat down with his beer. 'I haven't seen you in years, Thomas, what brings you to these parts?'

Thomas explained about visiting his wife's family. 'What about yourself, Pete, how are you?'

Pete said he was fine. 'I'm the same, I like to come over to see my parents every so often as they're getting on in years now. Are you still living in Dundee, and where are you working now?'

'I had to give up the construction work when my leg was badly broken so I'm now a barman in a pub, a bit like this one.' He waved his hand around the bar. 'What about yourself, what are you doing now?'

'I'm still in the construction business but I'm now the owner of it. We're based in Glasgow and believe me, Thomas, there's loads of work going on there as new housing schemes are being built and old slums are being cleared.'

Thomas felt wistful. 'Just like the old days then.'

Pete finished his beer and stood up. 'Let me buy you another one.' When he came back with the two glasses he said, 'How would you like to come and work for me?'

Thomas said his construction days were over because of his bad leg.

'I'm not talking about being on the building sites. I need a reliable, honest storeman and I would like you to think about it. I can get your family a house so there's no worry about accommodation.'

Thomas said he was interested but he would have to discuss it with Anna. Pete opened his wallet and took out a business card. 'This is the address of my office with the telephone number. Call me and we can arrange a meeting in Glasgow after your holiday here.' He quickly finished his beer then stood up to leave. 'I really would like you to take the job, Thomas.'

Thomas could hardly wait to get back and tell Anna about this unexpected job offer. If she was happy with it then he could arrange the meeting before heading back to Dundee.

Anna and Tommy had arrived back only a few minutes before Thomas, but as Lizzie was with them he didn't want to tell Anna his news in front of her which was just as well as his wife said, 'Lizzie has just been saying we should stay here as there is a job going at Mike's factory.'

This was the worst possible news he could think of and although he had made his peace with Anna's family, the thought of living cheek by jowl with them was unimaginable, and not only to him but judging from Tommy's expression, she also hated the idea.

Lizzie was excited by her plan. 'It's a good well-paid job, Thomas, much better than your old job back in Dundee and we can all be together as a proper family again.'

'The job sounds great, Lizzie, but where will we get a house? I'm sure it's much the same here as in Dundee as there's not a lot of houses for rent.'

Lizzie said she had thought of that. 'You can all stay with me and put your name down for a council house. I'm sure it won't take long to get one.'

Thomas looked at his wife. 'What do you think, Anna?'

His wife said it sounded like a good idea but she didn't look very happy about it. She added, 'We'll have to think about it, Lizzie.'

Lizzie, as usual, was matter of fact about the entire idea. 'Well, you better make up your mind soon as the job won't wait for you. Mike says there's been quite a bit of interest in it already.' She strode towards the door. 'I told Aimee I would go over to see her but I won't be long. Maybe you'll have made up your mind by the time I get back.'

Thomas was furious at this short timescale but he smiled. 'I doubt it but you never know.'

Lizzie gave him a baleful stare as she disappeared into the

garden. The minute she was gone, both Anna and Tommy said they didn't want him to take up the offer. Anna was especially against it. 'It's been fine having a holiday here but I couldn't bear to be over here to live. I love my family but I couldn't imagine being with them all the time, it would be like living in a zoo.'

Tommy laughed but she said the same thing. 'Having to play with Rosie and Harry every day isn't like being with Evie.'

Thomas asked them to sit down at the kitchen table as he had important news to tell them. They gave him a worried look but he said it was good news, at least for his part.

'Would you mind living somewhere else, not here but in Glasgow. It would mean maybe not seeing Evie again or any of our neighbours in the lane.'

Anna asked him to come out with whatever news he had as the suspense was making her more worried by the minute.

'I happened to be in a pub on the main street when I bumped into an old contractor I used to work with on one of the Hydro schemes and he's now got a business in Glasgow building new houses, and he's offered me a job as a storeman.'

Tommy was delighted but Anna wasn't so sure. 'Where will we live if we move there? Surely the housing shortage will be the same no matter where you live and we're lucky to have our own house.'

Thomas told her about getting accommodation from the firm. 'I thought we could go and see Pete in Glasgow and at least look at what's on offer.'

'That means telling Lizzie you don't want the job here.'

Thomas was jubilant. 'It most certainly does,' he said. 'Of course if you both want to stay here...' Anna and Tommy both laughed and said a resounding no.

Lizzie appeared an hour later. Although she didn't know it, she had a piece of a spider's web clinging to her hair. 'I've just been helping Roseanne clean out Albie's garden shed, what a load of old rubbish we've thrown out.'

Anna asked, 'Won't he be angry that you've thrown away his things? I read somewhere that men love their sheds more than they love their wives.'

Lizzie snorted. 'Don't be stupid, Anna, how can Albie love old wheels, bits of bikes and other rubbish?'

They all stayed quiet, and happy with that reaction she marched into the kitchen to make the tea. Anna and Tommy went to help while Thomas smiled to himself at the thought of the enraged Albie finding his shed had been spring cleaned. Honestly, Lizzie was a one-woman house cleaner and rubbish collector, and nobody was safe from her bright pink rubber gloves.

When Mike came home, they all sat around the table. Elizabeth wasn't there and Anna asked why they hardly ever saw her, apart from hogging the shower every morning.

'She works in a shop but she has an evening job too, she's a right hard worker and so is Billy, he has two jobs as well.'

They must take after their mother, Tommy thought, but sensibly stayed silent as they tucked into their steak pie and potatoes with Batchelors peas for the veg. This was followed by a bought apple tart from the local baker's shop served with thick yellow custard.

Anna happened to mention that her bakery job sold tarts just like this one and Lizzie pounced on this statement. 'Talking about jobs, have you made up your mind about the job here?'

Thomas tried not to grin but he felt so happy with the thought of telling them no. 'It was good of you to think of me, Mike,' he said, looking at the man. 'But although I never mentioned it, I've been offered a job in Glasgow with my old boss from the Hydro Board days and I've accepted it.'

Lizzie almost choked with annoyance. 'I think this job will be better for you and your family, Thomas.'

However, Mike said congratulations. 'I'm really glad to hear it and I hope you're happy there.' Thomas said thank you and finished the last of his apple tart.

Later, Anna asked him why he had said he had accepted the job and he said he really thought this job was the one for him. 'Still, we'll have to see what the accommodation is like, Anna, but if you and Tommy like it then I would like to take up Pete's offer as I enjoyed working with him on the dams.'

Anna said that was fine by her and they wouldn't make any plans until they got to Glasgow.

They heard Lizzie calling up the stairs, 'I'm just taking over some steak pie for Katie's tea and she has another cupboard that needs sorting out.'

Anna and Thomas laughed so much as he said, 'She's some woman, that sister of yours, Anna.'

42

Sadie had had another row with her mother over her refusal to consider going back to America. Ed had sent a letter along with a money order for her to book a passage but even an enclosed note from Eddie, saying he missed her, didn't change her mind.

'I'm going to have my son brought back here,' she said. Maryanne said it was extremely selfish of her to think Eddie should come back to a place where he was obviously unhappy but Sadie wouldn't listen to this as she was sure that once she got her own place to live, all would be well. She hurt her mother very much when she stated, 'It was living in this dump that made him run away and I can't say I blame him. I mean, look at this room, everything is either ancient or falling apart.'

Maryanne didn't say another word but she put on her coat and left to go and see her friend. She was almost in tears when she walked away and she wished she could move on from having Sadie in her house. She was then immediately filled with remorse for thinking such a thing but she realised having her daughter there was a trial.

When she reached her friend Dorothy's house she was still upset. She hadn't meant to come out with this row but when Dorothy asked her what the matter was, it all came pouring out, even the hurtful comment. Dorothy compressed her lips together and frowned. She was angry at Sadie for upsetting her mother. 'You don't deserve to be treated like that, Maryanne, you spent years and years doing without to bring her up. She had the best you could afford and with her looks she should have made a happy marriage instead of marrying in haste and repenting it later.'

Maryanne wiped her tears away. 'I shouldn't worry you with all my problems but thanks for listening to a moaning mother.'

'Have you had any tea?' asked Dot, and when Maryanne said no, she said, 'Let's go and get some fish and chips from Dellanzo's chip shop and bring them back here to eat. Then let Sadie either cook for herself or starve.'

Maryanne was grateful for this support. She was still worried about Sadie but Dorothy's insistence worked and they set off for the chip shop.

Sadie had thrown Ed's letter in the fireplace where she set fire to it. She had cashed the money order and she had no plans to use it on a ship passage. Tomorrow she would go to the police and a solicitor to get her son returned to her. She decided to go to the snug bar at the Windmill and have a relaxing drink.

She was glad Thomas was on holiday as she didn't know the young barman which meant he didn't know her so he wouldn't be able to pass on any gossip. She had heard some of the gossip that had gone around before so she was determined to be careful.

The next morning, she decided to take the day off work to see what help she could find in getting Eddie back. She went to the police desk and asked to see someone in charge but when she was sitting in the interview room, the sergeant said there was nothing they could do to help her. Sadie was astonished. 'But my husband kidnapped my son and now you're telling me there is nothing you can do?'

The policeman tried to be kind to the worried woman. 'From

what we believe, your son went willingly with his father and there is no question of kidnapping or any other offence.'

She got to her feet and said angrily, 'So I can't expect any help from the great British police force?'

The sergeant stood up and opened the door. 'I'm sorry but there is nothing we can do.'

Sadie went to Commercial Street and looked at a few brass nameplates of various solicitors. Choosing one, she entered a small, stuffy office with one woman busy at the typewriter who looked up as the door opened. Sadie said she wanted to see one of the solicitors named on the plaque outside.

'Do you have an appointment?'

Sadie, who was getting angrier by the minute, snapped, 'No I don't, but surely you have someone who can see me.'

The woman asked for her name and disappeared through a back door and Sadie stood at the counter wishing she had gone to one of the other solicitors on the street. The woman came back and said Mr Blyth would see her as soon as he finished what he was doing.

Sadie sat down on an uncomfortable chair and waited twenty minutes, growing more agitated. She was just making up her mind to leave when the door opened and an elderly man appeared. He spoke to the typist then left and a few minutes later another elderly man asked Sadie to come into his office.

'What can I help you with?' He quickly looked at her name which the woman had written down. 'Yes, how can I help, Mrs Boyd?'

Sadie went into a long story about Eddie and when she had finished the man said the same as the sergeant, that Eddie had gone off willingly with his natural father and as he wasn't a ward of the court there was nothing they could do. He added, 'I believe he's also an American citizen as he was born in the USA.'

'What difference does that make? Surely as his mother I have a right to my son.'

The solicitor said that it was a matter between her and her husband. 'You will have to come to an amicable agreement with him so you can get access. If you can, then the court will be able to allow access but as he's on the other side of the world that will be difficult.'

Sadie was becoming more downhearted by the minute. 'So that means you can't help me get him back?'

'I'm afraid so, and even if we could lodge a complaint it will cost you a great deal of money for your lawyer and any American lawyer your husband will hire, and the verdict could well be the same as it is now.'

Sadie left the office and considered going to see another one further up the street but she decided to leave it for today. She made up her mind to write to Ed and tell him she wasn't coming back but Eddie was her son and he belonged beside her. She picked up an airmail letter from the post office and wrote out her intentions before going out and posting it. That'll make him think now, she thought as she walked home.

Martha and Eliza were sitting outside and they called her over when they saw her. 'Have you got the day off again, Sadie?' asked Martha. 'You've got a great job as you seem to be more at home than at work.'

'Yes, Martha, I do have a good job and my boss recognises the importance of my fight to get my son back so he lets me have time off.' With that statement, she walked off and left Martha muttering about what a liar she was. Eliza told her to keep quiet. 'We don't know that her boss doesn't give her days off in order to get Eddie back.'

Martha gave her daughter one of her pitying looks. 'You believe everything you hear, Eliza, which makes you an idiot. I never believe a thing I hear and I don't believe a word that young woman says.'

Eliza sighed as she well knew the mischief her mother could get up to.

Sadie made herself a cup of Braithwaite's coffee and took it into her bedroom. After the coffee was finished, she brought out the bottle of gin from under her bed and poured herself a stiff drink.

When Maryanne came back from work she thought Sadie was out but as the bedroom door was open, she looked in. She was sound asleep and the bottle was sitting on the bedside cabinet. Maryanne shook her head in dismay and shut the door. No doubt that would be another day off work tomorrow and she was worried that she would lose her job. No employer wanted this amount of absences and Sadie was lucky so far that her boss hadn't sacked her.

She realised she needed help in dealing with her daughter and the first people she thought of were Bella and Albert who had known Sadie since she was a child. She made her way along to Albert's house. He was surprised to see her, especially as she seemed to be upset. She hesitated at the door but Albert ushered her in.

As he was making a cup of tea, she said, 'I'm really worried about Sadie, Albert. She won't listen to me and she's making herself ill over Eddie. To make matters worse, she's drinking alcohol and not going to her work. I don't know what to do with her.'

Albert, although concerned, didn't know how to respond to this plea. Sadie was an obstinate woman and had always been the same so he hadn't a clue how he could help.

'I wondered if you and Bella could have a word with her. She was always fond of you both and I think she'll listen to you.'

Albert felt so sorry for her and said he would see Sadie after her work tomorrow. 'I can't speak for Bella but I'm sure she will do all she can to help.'

Maryanne thanked him. 'I didn't know where to turn to as I've got this terrible feeling about her. I had hoped she would have seen sense and gone back to live with Ed. I can't understand why she seems to hate him.'

After she left, Albert went to see Bella and she was in the same frame of mind. 'Sadie never listened to anyone all of her life and I don't see how we can change her mind to go back.'

Albert said the same and Bella went over to the sideboard. 'I think we both need a glass of sherry in preparation for tomorrow.'

However, the next morning, Maryanne was surprised when she was getting ready for work to see Sadie make an appearance in the kitchen. She was dressed and she said she wanted to do some shopping before going to her job.

'I want to get my hair cut and buy some more nylons as I've got a big ladder in one of my stockings,' she said, making her coffee and putting a slice of bread under the grill.

Maryanne was pleased by this change in her and said she would see her later. She wondered if she should mention that Albert and Bella wanted to see her but thought she would leave it. Maybe she would catch them before they had a chat with her as it seemed Sadie had come to her senses.

Later, as Sadie walked along the lane, she wondered how the Cassidys were enjoying their holiday in Ireland. She hoped to have a holiday with Eddie when he came back to live with her. Grace noticed her passing as she was standing beside the sink, putting new curtains up in the kitchen window but Sadie was full of her plans for the day and the future and didn't look in her direction.

Evie was helping with the housework as there was nothing else to do. She was missing Tommy and was counting the days till she came back. She had written a letter to Eddie to let him know all the news of her holiday and Tommy's trip to Ireland and she had received an answer. He was so happy to be back on the farm with his dad and grandad. He also mentioned that Esther had made a celebration cake for his arrival and some of his school friends had met up with him again.

Tommy had also sent a postcard, saying she was liking her holiday all right but would be glad to be back. Grace said to go to see Eliza and Martha in case they needed any shopping done but when Evie saw them, they said Albert was bringing fresh bread back with him and they didn't need anything. Martha asked Eliza, 'Are you sure we don't need something? Evie can go for it if we do.' Eliza was firm with her mother; she had to be, because she suspected she would ask Evie to bring back chocolate biscuits.

Morag walked along the lane pushing her pram. Catriona was growing up so fast and her eyes were taking everything in and she waved her chubby little arm at everything she saw. Evie walked along the lane with them. Morag said she was going to the park and Evie wished she could go with her but she didn't like to invite herself. However, as she was going into the house, Morag asked her if she wanted to come with them. Grace was at the door, sweeping the step, and she was pleased Evie had something to occupy her as she knew how much she was missing Tommy.

'I'm going to Barrack Park so Catriona can play on the grass.'

That was fine by Evie who was enjoying walking along in the sunshine with the happy-looking baby and her mother.

'Have you heard from Tommy? I hope she's enjoying her holiday.'

Evie said she had received a postcard from her. 'She seems to be liking Ireland but she says she'll be glad to be back here.'

Morag said that was good. 'She'll be missing you, Evie, as you're such good friends.'

'I'm missing her as well. We've been friends for years.' She didn't mention writing to Eddie as she noticed no one seemed to want to say his name or mention his father. Perhaps, she thought, it was in sympathy with his mother. But although she didn't know it, most of the people in the lane were in agreement with Maryanne, Ed and Eddie.

When they reached the park they found a grassy spot and

Morag lifted the baby out and placed her on the checked rug she had brought with her. 'I like her to get some sun, especially at this time of the morning as the sun isn't too strong.' She had noticed the children's playground and said, 'Do you want to go and play on the swings?'

Evie said no, she would rather stay and look at Catriona as she was entranced by the baby's little legs and arms, and they both laughed when she began to blow milky bubbles from her mouth. Morag said she missed living on Skye as she loved the rural setting of her mother's house but that she was getting used to being in an industrial city. 'I love this park and when the weather's good I like to come here most days. I also love our house and all the people in the lane.'

Evie said, 'Why did you leave Skye?'

'Rory's brother Murdo has his own joinery workshop here and he asked if Rory would like to work with him, so that's why we came here. They are very busy with orders so we're lucky.'

The sun began to get a bit stronger so Morag said it was time to go. The baby was placed in the pram where she began to howl. She had enjoyed kicking her legs in the fresh air and was now annoyed at being imprisoned in the pram. Morag said she would settle down and as she began to walk along the path, Catriona decided to gaze wide-eyed at the passing trees. 'She'll get her dinner when we get home,' said Morag, and the three strolled back towards the lane.

Sadie had her hair trimmed and she bought her stockings on the way to work. She would change the one with the ladder when she got there. The pub was already open and Hal was behind the bar. Big John and two of his cronies were sitting at a small table with their dominoes. Hal said, 'Come into the office, Sadie, I'd like a word.'

Sadie was ready with her excuses for not turning up for several days. 'I wasn't feeling well, Hal, that's why I've been off work. It's all this stress over my son.'

Hal was a hard-working, decent man and he felt sorry for her but this was more serious. 'It isn't to do with your not being here, Sadie. I've done an audit on the bar stock and there's a big discrepancy. Have you been taking drinks and not putting the money in the till?'

Sadie could have kicked herself. She should have put that ten shillings in when she was paid last week but she had forgotten all about it. 'I think I owe you ten shillings, Hal, but just take it out of my wages.'

Hal looked serious. 'It's a lot more than that, Sadie.'

'It can't be. I usually take a drink when Big John offers me one and a couple of the regulars do the same.'

'Well I'm sorry but I'll have to let you go. My wife is now able to come back to work. Because of your sad circumstances I'll forget about the money you owe.' He handed over a brown paper wage packet. 'These are your wages up till last week and I haven't deducted anything.'

For a brief moment Sadie almost burst into tears but then anger took over. 'You didn't tell me when I applied for this job that it was just a temporary one until your wife got better but you know something, Hal, I'll be glad to leave this dump behind and get a decent job.'

Hal was upset. 'I did mention it was only temporary but you seem to have forgotten that, and I think you'll have to become teetotal if you want to get another job as your work record is dismal.'

Sadie turned her back and made for the door. Big John called out, 'What's the matter, Sadie?'

She looked at him. 'Ask Hal, as he's just given me the sack. I think you should all change your pub from now on.'

The men all looked over at the bar where Hal stood stony-faced. Sadie threw him a satisfied smirk then swept out into the street. As she was waiting for the tramcar, she suddenly felt deflated. Her life wasn't going in the direction she had hoped for but there would be other jobs and she was determined to succeed.

She didn't want to go back home as the nosey neighbours would all want to know why she was home early again, not that she would tell them, but she couldn't face sitting inside on a lovely day like today. She bought a *Courier* and sat on a bench in the City Square, looking for another job. All her life, she had got her own way and now she couldn't understand why her life seemed to be disintegrating. Of course, she thought, it was everyone's fault and not hers. She knew she liked a drink to relax but it wasn't an issue like Hal had implied. She thought about posting him the ten shillings she thought she owed him, then said out loud, 'Oh, stuff him.'

This amused an old woman who was sitting at the other end of the bench. She looked like she had had a tough life due to her threadbare clothes and pale, lined face. 'That's right, lass, no man's worth getting heartbroken over.' Sadie gave her a grateful smile and made her way home.

43

Thomas and Anna were both glad the holiday was almost over. He had phoned Pete from the telephone box in front of Mickey's shoe shop on the High Street and arranged to meet him on the Saturday. Pete was pleased that he was interested in the job and said he would pick them up at the station if he got in touch on arrival.

'I have a house set aside for your family, Thomas, and I hope it meets all your wife's expectations.'

He told Anna this and she said her expectations were minimal as nothing could be worse than the house in the lane. 'It's not that it's too bad but after living in Lizzie's house with a proper kitchen and bathroom, it'll be hard going back to what we have now.'

They had planned to leave early on Saturday morning so that Thomas could hopefully have the interview with Pete later in the day. However on Thursday the weather forecast was bad. After a glorious summer, a storm was approaching and strong winds were due to arrive at the weekend.

Anna was afraid the Irish Sea would be rough and she didn't want them sailing when the weather was bad. She didn't like water except if it was calm and she wasn't going to take chances. 'I think we should leave on Friday as it looks like it's to be gale force winds,' she said and Thomas agreed with her.

Lizzie seemed to be a bit put out but she also didn't want them travelling if the weather was bad. That night, they all went round the family to say their goodbyes and after lots of hugs and tears they were ready for the following morning.

Anna found it hard to say goodbye to Katie but both of them knew she was only here for a holiday. 'You'll come back and see us, Anna.'

Anna promised they would do that. 'When Thomas gets the job in Glasgow we'll be a lot nearer you all and it'll be easier to come over.'

Friday turned out cloudy but there was no sign of the gales. Lizzie was annoyed at the weather forecasters. 'They never get it right and you could have had another day with us.'

They left early to be in time for the ferry and as they went on board, the sea was rough but not too bad, but once they left the shelter of the harbour the wind strengthened and Anna and Tommy were seasick. Thankfully they hadn't eaten the huge breakfast Lizzie had prepared so it was more a feeling of nausea than actual sickness. Anna had tried to stay up on the deck to see Ireland's shoreline disappearing but she had to go into the passenger's lounge to join Thomas and Tommy.

The ferry seemed to lurch with every wave and Anna put her arm around Tommy. She thought if the ferry sank then they would go down together and she shut her eyes and said a prayer. Then as the ferry sailed nearer the west coast of Scotland the sea became calmer and soon they were disembarking at the jetty.

Anna was never so grateful to be back on dry land and when she looked at Thomas and Tommy she knew they felt the same. When the bus got to Glasgow, Thomas said that he would phone Pete to ask him if he could have his interview today but when he got through, Pete wasn't there and his assistant said to phone back later.

He decided not to bother as it looked as if Pete was busy on some building site. He told Anna, 'Do you want to catch the train back to Dundee or will we find somewhere to stay here until tomorrow?'

Anna and Tommy didn't hesitate as they had spied lots of lovely shops to visit but Anna wasn't sure of their money. 'Will we have enough to pay for bed and breakfast?'

Thomas said they did but added, 'We'll have to live off bread and cheese next week.'

They found a small guesthouse in one of the streets off Sauchiehall Street and a woman showed them a large room not unlike the one at Lizzie's house that had the double and single bed. The price was within their means so they left their luggage and went to see the sights.

Anna was amazed at the amount of shops and she spent most of the day with Tommy going in and out and looking at things they wished they could buy. At teatime, they found a fish and chip shop with a small eating area and as they were hungry after walking on the pavements they ate all their meal washed down with hot cups of tea. Anna said, 'I wish we could have packed up that super breakfast that Lizzie made and brought it with us.'

Thomas went out later and phoned Pete again and this time he got him in. He explained about coming over early but as they were staying overnight, he could see him in the morning. Pete asked the name of the guesthouse and said he would come and pick them up after breakfast.

The next morning, the wind had increased but it wasn't too bad when Pete drew up in his lovely new car. They all felt like royalty when they got in and when Thomas went to pay the bill, the owner said it had been paid by his friend.

Pete was a good driver and he negotiated the busy streets until he came to his office which was a building on a large plot of land. There were houses nearby and Pete said his firm had built them. Lying to the rear of the office was a large building which he said was the storeroom and workshop. They went inside and it was stacked with wooden planks, tools and everything for the building trade.

'This is where you'll be working, Thomas, and it's a complicated job keeping track of everything. That's why I need someone I can trust as you wouldn't believe what goes missing with some builders' yards.'

Thomas was grateful for Pete's belief in him and he said so. Anna and Tommy had stayed in the car and they were very comfortable sitting on the leather seats. Tommy said Pete must be very rich and Anna agreed.

When the two men got back in the car, Pete said, 'Well, it's time to show the two ladies where you'll be staying if Thomas takes the job.' They drove along the road, not far from the workshop, and stopped outside a new-looking bungalow. Anna thought that this couldn't be her new house but it was. They were all excited when they saw the lovely living room with a large picture window, the fitted kitchen and brand new bathroom plus the three bedrooms. Tommy said she could ask Evie to come and stay but Anna was so overcome by everything, especially the carpets and lino floors, that she was speechless.

Pete asked if everything was all right and Thomas asked when could he start work. 'I don't think I'll need to give my notice at the Windmill but if I have to, can I start after working it?'

Pete said that was fine. 'You can arrange to get your furniture sent here as soon as you like.' He handed Anna a set of keys. 'What are your plans for the weekend?'

Thomas said they hadn't made up their minds and Pete said, 'The plan was to put you all up in a hotel tonight as I thought you would be tired after your sea crossing, and that offer still holds if you want it.'

'I don't want to put you to any extra bother, Pete, as you've been good enough as it is.'

'Nonsense,' said Pete. 'I've already booked the hotel so

you're as well using it before going back tomorrow. I would have taken you out tonight but my wife's parents are coming for the weekend so I can't manage.' He handed a card to Thomas which had on it the name of the hotel and a picture of it, and it looked grand. 'Right then, I'll drop you off at the hotel.'

When they got there, Anna couldn't believe her eyes. It was situated on one of the main streets but it had five steps leading up to grand mahogany and glass doors. After they got out and stood on the pavement, Pete rolled down his window. 'I'll say cheerio for now but give me a ring when you can start, Thomas.'

The three of them stood bemused on the pavement. Anna was so pleased she had worn her new dress and jacket as well as Tommy being smartly dressed. Thomas had on one of his new shirts and as they climbed the stairs, she thought she was dreaming.

Their room was lovely and overlooked a garden at the back and it had a bathroom attached. They had never seen anything so luxurious as this. The receptionist had told them that dinner was at seven o'clock which puzzled them as dinner was usually served in the middle of the day in Dundee. Thomas said they should give this a miss as it was probably very expensive and he was about to tell the young receptionist this when she smiled. 'A table has been booked for you at seven-thirty.' Anna asked what this would cost but the girl said it had already been paid for, and they couldn't believe it.

'Just think, this has all come about because I went into that pub in Belfast and met Pete.'

Anna shuddered when she thought how strange life could turn out. Thomas might have gone somewhere else or maybe missed his old boss by minutes but by good fortune they were now in the position of having a good job and a wonderful house. She could hardly wait to get back and tell everyone in the lane.

Tommy noticed a rack of postcards that showed the picture of the hotel. 'I want to give one to Evie and get one for myself.'

They decided to go and see some more shops but the wind was very strong and litter was rolling across the pavements. 'I'm glad we came back yesterday as it will be bad at sea,' Anna said.

After a delicious meal served by a waiter in a white shirt and black trousers and waistcoat, they went into the lounge for a drink. There was a television in the corner and the news was on. There were scenes of trees blown over and the announcer said that ferries were cancelled because of the high winds. He said the gales would travel eastwards through the night and Thomas said he was glad they were all safe in this hotel. 'No doubt we'll get it tomorrow when we get back.' He was also pleased that they had left when they did as it meant they would have been stuck in Ireland if the news was right and the ferries had indeed been cancelled.

44

Sadie got home to find a letter waiting for her. She was opening it when her mother came in from her work. It was from Ed and when she read it she began to scream loudly and cry. Maryanne got the shock of her life. 'What's the matter, Sadie, don't tell me it's bad news?'

'Ed says he's filing for a divorce,' she shouted. 'He can't do this to me.'

Maryanne took the letter. Ed had written that as she hadn't considered coming back to him, the best thing was that they get divorced. He had seen a lawyer and she would hear more in due course but as she was the one who had caused the separation, the divorce would go through.

'I feel Eddie needs a mother to look after him and Esther is doing her best to make his life easier,' he wrote.

'Esther,' she shouted. 'She's the one behind all this, sucking up to him with her sly ways. No wonder I left as I couldn't stand her. She was always in the house, baking and trying to make me look a fool just because she was rejected by him when he married me.' She began to cry loudly and Maryanne was at a loss how to deal with her. She hurried out to get Albert and Bella, who came back with her. Albert tried to get Sadie to sit down and be calm.

'We'll do our best to help you, Sadie, but you have to help yourself. Shouting and screaming won't do you any good.'

She sat down but she wanted to know why they were here, poking their noses into her affairs. Maryanne told her she had confided in them as she couldn't cope with her on her own.

Sadie went totally ballistic. 'How can two old fogeys help me when my husband and son are thousands of miles away and Ed's divorcing me?'

Albert sat beside her. 'It's because we've known you since you were small and we all care for you.'

Sadie still had a mutinous look on her face, which was red and puffy-looking with all the crying and her mascara had run, making her look like a panda.

'Now the best way to deal with this shock is to write back to Ed and tell him you are coming back to him.'

Sadie began shouting again. 'I'm not in a million years going back to him, I keep telling him that and I keep telling you all the same thing. I want my son back here with me and Ed better do as I say.'

Bella said quietly, 'What can you do, Sadie? Ed holds all the cards and Eddie left of his own free will as he wasn't happy here and you know that. Please reconsider going back to your husband as you've no choice if you want to see your son again.'

'How do I manage to pay to go back, tell me that.'

Maryanne almost said Ed had sent her a money order for her passage to America but she stayed silent as she didn't want to let it become common knowledge. Bella said to write and tell him she was coming home and could he send the money.

Sadie had calmed down so Albert and Bella left. They were hoping they had talked some sense into her as Maryanne couldn't do a thing with her daughter. 'That's the problem, she's given in to her all her life and now it's gone beyond help,' Albert said while Bella agreed with every word.

'Well, we've tried our best to help so it's now up to Sadie to grow up and act like a wife and mother.'

After they left, Sadie began to argue with her mother. 'I

don't understand you sometimes, why do you bring in people to pry into my business? I lost my job today and now this.'

Maryanne was shocked. 'Why did you lose your job, what did you do?'

Sadie was exasperated by all this questioning. 'I just did. Hal says he doesn't need me now that his wife is better and she will do my job.' She didn't add anything about the drink money.

Maryanne said she was sorry to hear that but it didn't matter now that she was planning to leave.

'I'm not planning to leave as I've spent the money he sent me and I can't afford to pay for a ticket.'

Maryanne thought she couldn't take many more shocks. 'How could you have spent the money?' She stopped and glared at Sadie. 'I hope you haven't spent it on drink.'

Sadie was furious. 'It's got nothing to do with you what I spend my money on. I'll get another job and I'm writing to Ed tomorrow to tell him to send Eddie back as I'm not having that woman, Esther, looking after my son.'

Maryanne went out as she couldn't bear any more arguments. She would get her tea at Dorothy's house and Sadie could do whatever she wanted, as she was sick and tired of her.

Sadie looked at the job column in the paper but there didn't seem to be any postings that took her attention. She threw the paper down and marched out.

Martha had been sitting at the window when Albert had passed and she saw him coming back with Bella. 'Something's up along the lane. I bet it's to do with Sadie.'

Eliza said not to assume anything although she had heard the shouting as she passed earlier after picking up her mother's evening paper. For the first time in her life she was grateful she hadn't married if it brought all this strife and heartbreak.

Sadie decided to bypass the Windmill Bar and go into town, thinking she would maybe go to the pictures, but when she passed the lounge bar where she had gone with Peter, she went in and ordered a double gin and tonic. She would just have the one before going to the cinema.

Maryanne came home at ten o'clock to a silent and empty house. She peeped into the bedroom but there was no sign of Sadie. She felt drained by all the arguments so she looked out the small bottle of pills the doctor had given her after her operation. They were to make her get a good sleep so she swallowed a couple and went to bed.

45

Maryanne woke up on Saturday morning with a terrible headache and as she tried to stand up, she felt sick. She stumbled over to the sink to get a drink of water and the memory from yesterday came flooding back. She went to call out Sadie's name but there was no answer and when she opened her bedroom door the unmade bed was empty.

She sat down and looked at the clock and was amazed to see it was ten o'clock. She had never in her entire life slept this late. Then she remembered the sleeping pills. There was a knock on the door and when she answered it she saw Albert.

'I was worried about you,' he said. 'I saw your curtains were still closed and I thought something had happened.' He went to put the kettle on as she sat in the chair with her head in her hands, trying to make her brain wake up.

Albert asked where Sadie was and she told him she had gone. 'I've no idea where she is and it's just a nightmare.'

Bella and Grace appeared and Grace said she had seen Sadie go along the lane at nine o'clock. 'She looked terrible.'

Bella asked if Sadie had made up her mind to return to America. Maryanne had to say she didn't know. She knew it was a lie but maybe Sadie would change her mind and she didn't want her to know she was gossiping about her.

'She's maybe gone to ask about a passage home,' said Albert and Maryanne nodded although she knew that was the last thing Sadie would do, unless she had changed her mind and decided to follow some good advice from Bella and Albert.

Grace had overheard the shouting and screaming last night but she didn't want to say anything about it. Instead, she said, 'I've got breakfast left over, Maryanne, come along and get some food inside you.'

Maryanne knew that if she ate anything she would be sick so she said she would just have some tea and toast in her own house. 'Sadie will want her breakfast when she comes back.'

Grace said the weather forecast wasn't good. 'We're heading for strong gales later and I hope the weather doesn't affect the sea crossing for Anna and Thomas.'

Bella asked if they had had a good holiday and Grace said Evie got a postcard from Tommy that said they had, although she did say she would be glad to be home.

Maryanne listened to all this as if in a dream. She felt she could go back to sleep and wished they would all leave and let her go back to bed.

After they did leave, that was what she did. She was amazed when she awoke to see it was late evening. She checked the bedroom again but there was no sight of Sadie. By now the wind was so strong it was rattling the windows and she wondered if she should go and ask Albert what she should do about Sadie's absence. She knew Sadie was deliberately avoiding her and had probably gone to the pictures as she was a lover of the cinema, so she made up her mind to do no more worrying over her. After a cup of tea, she took one pill and hoped she would get a good sleep without the drowsy side effects like today. The wind seemed to get worse as it whistled down the narrow lane and she hoped Sadie wouldn't be too long in coming home.

As it turned out, Maryanne was correct in her assumption that Sadie was avoiding her. She had spent most of the day in the town then went to the first showing at the Plaza picture house.

Then when that was finished she made her way to the Odeon. On her way she went into the off-licence in Strathmartine Road and bought a bottle of whisky which she put in her bag.

She was glad she had put her coat on this morning as the wind was strong but once inside the cinema, she settled down to watch the film. When the film was over, everyone poured out into the street and she couldn't believe how bad the weather had turned out. The wind whipped debris across the road and she had a difficult journey getting back to the lane.

She opened the door quietly but there was no sound from her mother. Making her way to the bedroom, she gathered up a glass and a candle which was in a holder on the mantelpiece. Sometimes, if you needed to use the outside toilet during the night, it was handy to light the candle.

She lay down on her bed and filled a large glass with whisky. She was pleased to be home as it meant she could have her drink without the worry of trying to walk home. Last night had been a nightmare as she almost fell over a few times and she was still unsteady this morning when she got up. At the time she had been puzzled that there was no sign of her mother when she left as she was normally an early riser.

She was tired of all the arguments and the quicker she got another job and her own house, the happier she would be. Then she could employ a solicitor to get Ed to return her son. She was bitter about the divorce but although Esther was welcome to Ed she wasn't going to get Eddie. She couldn't understand why a mother couldn't have her son with her.

She refilled the glass and enjoyed the taste and although she didn't feel sleepy, she lay back on her pillows. What a life she had endured. She should have been a film star with her good looks, just like the ones in the films she had seen. This was going to be her last drink, she thought as she refilled her glass, and from tomorrow it was going to be all work and success in life.

She lit the candle as she liked the soft light at night but she should put it out. As she tried to get up she stumbled and the candle fell on the floor. She couldn't see it so assumed it had gone out. She poured another drink but before it was half finished she fell asleep.

Grace couldn't sleep because of the wind and she got up to make a cup of tea. The windows were rattling and she heard the gusts as they blew down the lane. As she filled the kettle she thought she smelled smoke. She hadn't put the fire on today so it wasn't coming from the fireplace. She pulled the curtains aside and saw the lane was lit up. She was puzzled by this as the lamps were at each end and not near her window so she went outside. The wind caught her nightdress and whipped it around her legs. She was appalled when she saw Maryanne's roof alight. She rushed back in and quickly woke up Bill.

'Bill, get up, Maryanne's house is on fire.' Bill had been sound asleep and he didn't take in what his wife was saying but she shouted it out again. 'Maryanne's house is on fire.'

He quickly jumped to his feet and went outside with Grace. 'Run to the telephone box and dial 999 but get Evie out of the house first and take her with you.'

Grace ran inside while he tried to get into Maryanne's house. The door was unlocked but the smoke was thick and the fire seemed to be coming from the back bedroom. He knew he needed help so he ran along the lane, banging on all the doors.

It took a few minutes before Albert came out and Bill told him to get everyone out before he ran back to the seat of the fire. The wind was whipping the flames along the backs of the houses and he tried to find Maryanne and Sadie. It was the coughing that alerted him to the front bedroom and he found Maryanne slumped on the floor. Picking her up wasn't a problem as she was so slim and he laid her out on the piece of ground in the front garden.

Albert had done a good job and Bella, Rory and Morag were hurrying out of the houses. Morag was pushing Catriona in her pram and her baby clothes were piled on the blanket. By now Grace and Evie were back. Albert said Eliza was finding it difficult to get Martha out and Morag and Grace went to help her.

Bill said that Sadie was still inside and the three men tried to get into the bedroom but it was full of thick black smoke that made them cough like their lungs were on fire so they had to retreat. Rory suggested going to the back of the houses to try and get in that way but by now the fire engine had arrived and the firemen unrolled the hoses. They had to park on the Hilltown as the lane was too narrow for the vehicle.

Bill said there was someone still in one of the houses and three firemen with masks went in. It seemed ages until they came out carrying the limp body of Sadie. Maryanne tried to sit up and when she saw her daughter she gave a loud roar of pain before dissolving into tears.

A doctor arrived as well as the police and he tried to resuscitate Sadie. An ambulance with a flashing blue light drew up on the Hilltown behind the fire engine and Sadie was given oxygen as she was carried away along with her mother.

Grace watched as the flames quickly consumed the roofs of the houses and it seemed that her house and the Cassidys were the only ones spared, but the gale quickly gusted back towards her and the roofs of all the houses were now burning.

People from around the area had heard the sirens and they stood at each end of the lane while the occupants huddled together in their nightwear and watched as their houses burnt. No one had time to get a coat or any warm clothing and Rory said he was taking Morag and the baby to his brother's house. Bill told the police that there were elderly people and was it possible to get them some shelter? He was told they were trying to get a hall on the Hilltown open to let them get under cover. 'The trouble is, we are trying to find the hall keeper to get the key but we will do our best.'

Mrs Bell had been awakened by the noise and she came to see if Bella was all right. 'You can come and stay with me until we find out what is going to happen.' Bella said she was concerned for Albert, and Mrs Bell said he could come as well. That just left Martha, Eliza and the Gows. Grace said they could go to her mother in Ann Street but there was hardly enough room for them so they couldn't take the Potters. Then old Mrs Donaldson from Caldrum Street said she had a spare room and she would take the Potters. Fortunately she lived on the ground floor so the policeman took them away to spend the night there.

Evie stood white-faced as all this carnage was going on. Grace said, 'Thank goodness Thomas, Anna and Tommy are not here.' Evie asked where they would live now but her parents had no idea so Bill said, 'Let's get you to your granny's house and we'll find out more tomorrow.'

Before they left, the chief of the fire brigade told him they could try to retrieve any belongings later that day. 'Someone will have to be with you as the houses are in a dangerous state. The fronts haven't had much damage except from water but the rears of all the properties are demolished.'

Grace's mother Evelyn hadn't heard any of the commotion so she was surprised when they knocked on her door at four o'clock.

'Who's there?' she asked in a frightened voice.

'It's us, Mum. Just open the door.'

Evelyn unlocked two locks and she almost fainted when she saw her family standing in their nightwear with black faces. Before she could speak, Grace told her the whole story and soon she was helping her mum pull the spare mattress from under the bed for them. They got washed and Evelyn provided some old-fashioned winceyette nightgowns for Grace and Evie but she couldn't help Bill who replied he was all right.

She made them hot drinks. 'Will you be able to get back in after the firemen put out the fire?'

Bill said it didn't look like it. 'The council will have to find accommodation for us all but what we'll get offered is debatable. The worst part is Sadie and Maryanne. I don't know if Sadie recovered in the ambulance.'

Evelyn asked where Tommy and her family were and was told they were thankfully away but that they would be coming home later to no house.

Finally they all went to bed. Evie was in her granny's bed and her mum and dad on the 'shaky doon', as the mattress was called.

The next morning, Grace made them all breakfast and the radio was on. Suddenly the news announcer mentioned the devastating fire in Meadow Lane, Dundee: 'There is one fatality and another person was taken to hospital where they are recovering.'

Breakfast was a subdued meal when they all realised Sadie hadn't recovered. Grace couldn't believe that such a young vibrant and beautiful woman could be dead. 'If only she had gone back with her husband, she would still be alive. Poor Eddie, I don't know how he'll take this awful news.'

'The fire chief said to meet him later at the houses to see what we can salvage and I'll have to see all the neighbours to tell them, but we've nothing to wear,' said Bill.

Evelyn said Grace could have something from her wardrobe even if they weren't the same size. Grace found a skirt with an elasticated waist and a jumper but she was glad she always wore her pants under her nightdress as she drew the line at borrowing her mother's underwear.

'I can go and meet the fire chief and try to salvage some things from the house.' She was almost crying but she knew she had to be strong to get them through this terrible time.

There was a knock on the door and Charlie Baxter, Bill's boss, was standing there with a big bag. 'I've brought round some clothes as I've heard the awful news. The woman next door told me everyone was asleep when it happened so I reckoned you wouldn't be able to get dressed.' He handed over the bag. 'I'm sorry it's just some men's clothes as my wife Beth isn't the same size as Grace.'

Bill didn't know what to say, especially when he opened the bag and found the clothes were all new. 'You're welcome to them,' said Charlie.

Bill was grateful. 'Thank you, you've saved my life as I couldn't walk about the town like this.'

After he left, Grace said what a great gesture it was. Bill didn't want to laugh because of the tragedy but he smiled. 'He's always telling me his wife buys him clothes he doesn't like so I'm sure he's grateful to have an excuse to get rid of them, which is a blessing for us.'

Grace wasn't so sure. 'I still think it was very good of him to come round.' Bill came through dressed and she had to laugh. The trousers and shirt were fine but the jumper had bold stripes down one side in shades of blue and red. 'Oh, I see what you mean,' she said.

Evie said he looked very smart but she said she was worried about everyone. Where will they get things to wear?

'People are very good in situations like this and they will all rally round. You'll have to stay with Granny as we haven't anything for you to wear but we'll try and get as much as we can from the house.'

'What about Tommy, they won't have heard about the fire so they'll get a shock when they come home.' Evie was upset but her mother said they would see them and help as much as possible.

'What we have to remember, Evie, is that Sadie is dead and her mother in hospital so what we're going through is nothing compared to Maryanne.'

Bill and Grace left and made their first call on Mrs Bell where they found Bella and Albert. Bill was surprised how well they were standing up to this catastrophe until he remembered Albert had been in the Great War and Bella had lost her fiancé in the fighting. They had both been through tough times and were made stronger by them. 'We'll be there this afternoon,' said Albert. No one mentioned Sadie but they didn't have to, their faces said everything and no words were needed.

When they got to Murdo's flat, Morag and Rory were both dressed and busy getting Catriona washed and fed. Because of Morag's quick thinking she had brought a pile of clothes out in the pram. 'I had done my ironing that night but hadn't put it away so I just picked it up,' she said. They were all shocked by the terrible news of Sadie's death but they were also very concerned about where they were going to live. 'Do you think the houses will be repaired?' asked Morag, but Bill didn't know.

'We have to see the fire chief this afternoon so we'll get a better idea of what's happening then.'

Rory went down the stairs with them. 'Murdo's flat isn't big enough for us all, in fact we could hardly get the pram up the stairs, so I do hope we can get some different accommodation.'

Grace said they all hoped that but they would just have to wait and see.

They weren't sure where Martha and Eliza were but then Grace remembered Mrs Donaldson had offered them a room at her house and they made their way there. Martha was complaining loudly about being turfed out of her house. 'I always knew that Sadie would do damage to someone or something and I'm going to give her a piece of my mind when she gets back from hospital.'

Eliza and Mrs Donaldson stood silently by and judging from the house owner's face, she looked like she was sorry to have taken Martha in.

Bill said, 'Sadie is dead, Martha, she didn't survive the fire and Maryanne is still in hospital.'

Martha had the grace to look shocked while Eliza and Mrs Donaldson burst into tears. Grace went to comfort them and Martha said, 'I didn't know that and I'm sorry for saying what I said.'

Bill took Eliza aside. 'Can you come this afternoon to try and save as much in the house as possible? I think you should leave Martha behind as it will be a terrible job.' Eliza nodded and began to cry again.

When they got back to Evelyn's flat, Grace said that left just Anna, Thomas and Tommy to see but they had no idea when they would be back.

'They can't be too late as Thomas and Anna have to start work tomorrow.'

In the afternoon they all gathered in the lane where the smell of smoke was still overpowering. They were wearing an assortment of clothes that were either too big or in styles they would never wear in normal circumstances. However this was a tragedy and everyone looked as if they had been crying but trying to put on brave faces.

There were still some firemen standing by in case the fire started up again but judging from the amount of water running down the lane that seemed impossible. The fire chief warned them that a fireman would be with them and to stay as close to the front as possible. 'Don't try and get anything from the back bedrooms.'

They were all shocked when they cautiously ventured through the front doors. Everything was soaked and what wasn't burned was unusable. Bill and Grace gave a quick glance at the furniture and the television but they weren't worth taking out. Grace went into Evie's bedroom which faced the front and managed to collect her school bag and some of her little treasures. She also picked up a pile of clothes that was on the kitchen chair. Like Morag, she had done the week's ironing but hadn't put it away. The clothes were soaking and streaked with black smoke but they could be washed. She also emptied the cupboard which held her wedding china that was never used but still sentimental to her.

Bill went to help Eliza but she was at a loss what to take so he helped her empty the big sideboard and carried everything out onto the patchy grass at the front.

Rory thought he could save the baby's cot but the wood was soaking and as most of their lovely furniture was the same, he decided to gather up any mementoes of Catriona plus dishes and glasses that had been wedding presents.

Bella and Albert were the same, they gathered together household items that could be washed and Bella took her photo album and the framed photo of Davie before taking a last look at her home.

Grace said she should go and try to salvage some items from Maryanne's house but as it had suffered the most damage, she only ventured as far as the sideboard which was near the door. There wasn't a great deal in it but she carried out what she could, and like Bella, she picked up the framed wedding photos. This was the one with Maryanne and her late husband but when Grace saw the picture of Sadie and Ed's wedding she had to turn it over as it almost made her cry. From the brief glimpse of it she saw how radiant Sadie was. She looked like a girl who had the whole world at her feet and now she was dead. Grace thought life could turn out very cruel.

Then, just as they were nearly finished, the Cassidys turned up. Grace hurried over to them as Tommy and Anna began crying. Thomas said they had heard the news of the fire.

'We were staying in a hotel in Glasgow when Tommy put on the wireless that was in our room. That's when we heard about it. They said there was one death…' He stopped as he couldn't go on.

Anna came over and Grace had to tell them that it was Sadie. 'Maryanne is in hospital but she'll probably get home soon.' She pointed to all the possessions lying on the grass. 'We've been told to try and get some things from the houses but to stay near the front as the backs of the houses are all burnt.'

Thomas went in and, like Grace, he concentrated on Tommy's bedroom, gathering as much as he could. He also took out the trunk from under her bed which was full of photographs and other sentimental items.

As they carried things back to their temporary homes, they agreed to meet up the next morning and decide what the next step would be. Before leaving, Grace asked where Anna and her family were going to stay.

Anna said, 'Thomas is away to phone Pete to see if we can move into our new house tonight.' She told her friend about the new job and the lovely house they were moving to. 'I don't know what we'll do about furnishing it but we'll get by. At least we're all still alive while poor Sadie is dead.'

Grace said she was also worried about the elderly neighbours like Martha, Bella and Albert. 'I don't know where they'll end up but wherever it is it will be a shock after living a lifetime in the lane.'

Anna asked if she could come with Tommy to say goodbye to Evie and Grace felt a wave of sadness wash over her. She tried to smile but failed. 'We're living with my mother in Ann Street, you know where it is and we'll see you later.'

It was teatime when they came. Tommy and Evie were in tears at the thought of parting. Anna said they would soon make new friends at school which made them cry even more.

Thomas said, 'We're catching the train tonight to Glasgow. I've phoned my boss at the Windmill Bar and he says not to worry about working my notice. He sends his sympathy to us all.'

As they were leaving, Grace asked if they would manage to make it through to the funeral and they said they would. Tommy said she would always be in touch with Evie. 'I'm going to wear my hair slide all the time so I don't forget you and the times we shared living here.'

46

The next few days passed in a blur of emotions. Maryanne came home to stay with Dorothy. Sadie's funeral was ten days away as there was a post-mortem to be done. Maryanne was distressed when it showed that Sadie had been very intoxicated before she died. They assured her that she wouldn't have suffered much as the smoke had killed her and not the flames.

Ed came over from America but didn't bring Eddie. He told Maryanne, 'I've just told him his mum was dead but not how she died. He keeps blaming himself but I've told him that he's only a child and that adults sometimes make their own decisions. Sadie made hers and we all have to live with the memories.' He added, 'I hope it wasn't my letter about the divorce as I only wanted her to think about her marriage and come back to me. I would never have divorced her and she knew it.'

They were sitting in Dorothy's kitchen and Maryanne said she was to blame as well. 'I should have been stricter with her when she was a child but I wasn't.

I was there when she got your letter and although she was furious, she said she had no intention of going back so don't worry about that. She wanted to fight you over Eddie but she wouldn't have won her case. I hope she is now resting in peace.'

Ed asked what was happening to everyone who lost their

homes. Maryanne said the council was trying to get them sorted out but it was going to take time. 'The Salvation Army has been a great help and they promise they'll help out with what's needed. Martha and Eliza have got a ground floor flat in Church Street and the MacCallums have moved into a new house at Fintry which I hear has been a great success for them. Morag has been telling Grace that it's great to have a kitchen with hot water and a bathroom. Thomas, Anna and Tommy have moved to a new job and house in Glasgow.'

Ed said he was pleased to hear that, as he felt responsible for all the trouble. Maryanne stopped him. 'It wasn't your fault or anybody's fault. Once Sadie made up her mind, nothing ever changed it so I think she should never have left you and that's the truth.'

Grace was out shopping when she met Albert. 'Any word on another house?' he asked. Grace said they were meeting the council tomorrow as a house had become vacant above the ice cream shop on the Hilltown. 'It's got a living room, two bedrooms, a kitchen and a bathroom so we're over the moon about that. To be honest, Albert, although we're grateful to my mother for putting us up, it's getting stressful because she hasn't the room. Thankfully she's going off with her friend Elsie and her son for a day out tomorrow. Do you have any news of a move?'

Albert said the problem was that they were both single people. 'Bella has been offered a one-bedroom house in Hepburn Street and she says she can put a settee in the living room and I can stay with her. But I'm not sure. I don't want people to talk about us living together.'

Grace said he shouldn't let that bother him. 'I'm hoping Maryanne gets something soon as well.'

The weather turned cold on the day of the funeral. The service was held in Bonnethill Church where Sadie used to go to

Sunday school. Everyone from the lane was there to support Maryanne and Ed, and quite a lot of the people from the surrounding streets came to pay their respects even though some of them hadn't known Sadie.

Ed placed a huge wreath of golden chrysanthemums on the coffin and as everyone stood up to sing the first hymn, he had to wipe tears from his eyes as did most of the congregation. Hal Anderson was there as well as David Fleming from the electrical business. They both felt guilty that they perhaps contributed to Sadie's state of mind. Peter was there with his wife Norma. He had told her of his previous relationship with Sadie and she had been so sorry to hear of her death. She held his hand during the service while he recalled the happy times he had spent with his beautiful ex-fiancée. He saw Sadie's husband wipe tears away and he felt an overwhelming feeling of wasted lives.

The burial at Balgay Cemetery was just for the family and folk from the lane. Martha was in a wheelchair, and they all gathered around. Suddenly a bright shaft of sunlight shone down on the coffin, turning the flowers into a ring of gold. There was a moment of silent amazement but Maryanne was comforted by this. Sadie was truly at peace.

After the burial, they all went for refreshments at the Royal Hotel where Ed had booked a room.

Thomas and Anna had arrived from Glasgow but had left Tommy with Pete's wife. Evie was also missing, she was at Evelyn's house. It was a subdued meeting but Anna told Grace how wonderful everything had turned out for them. 'Pete, Thomas's boss, gave us a loan to furnish the house and he'll take just a small amount back every week. Tommy has started in her new school and has made a few friends.'

Grace said she was pleased to hear such good news and mentioned they were also delighted with their new house. 'You know the building, Anna, it's the modern houses above the ice cream shop.'

Anna said she did. 'I always fancied one of those myself.'

Ed came and spoke to everyone and said how grateful he was that they had all been so good to Sadie. Martha said she was her special friend and everyone raised their eyebrows at the blatant lie. However, Ed took it as a compliment to his late wife.

'I'm trying to persuade Maryanne to come back with me to America as I don't like her living on her own. It was fine when you were together but now you are all separated,' he said.

Maryanne had been allocated a flat in Kinghorne Road and she was happy there but she was touched by Ed's concern. 'I'll maybe come and live with you when I get old,' she said. What she didn't say was she didn't want to be far from Sadie and she planned to take flowers to her grave every Sunday.

Morag and Rory went up to Ed to give their condolences and he asked them how they were doing.

'Catriona's getting bigger every day and soon she'll be crawling into every corner,' said Rory while Morag said she was delighted with her new house. 'It means Rory has to catch a bus every day but it's worth it,' she said.

While all this chatter was going on, Albert and Bella had been sitting quietly with their tea. Just as the waitress came in to clear the table, Albert stood up. He seemed hesitant and had to take a drink of water before speaking. 'I'd like to tell you that Bella and I are to be married next month.'

There was a silence in the room then everyone converged on the couple to give them their congratulations.

Albert said, 'Bella thought I should make an honest woman of her as we share a house.' Everyone laughed but he went on, 'Seriously, we have known one another since we were in our teens so it hasn't been a whirlwind courtship.'

Ed went over and said how pleased he was at their good news. 'Maryanne told me that you both tried to persuade Sadie to come back to me and I appreciate that very much.'

Bella said they had both known her since she was a child

and they had been very fond of her. 'I only wish now that she had taken our advice and we wouldn't be mourning her death.'

Ed said he felt the same. Before leaving, he made a speech. 'I just want to thank you all for the part you played in Sadie's life. You tried to help her and Eddie but it wasn't to be. Sadie was like a breath of fresh air, a free spirit and a golden girl and that's what I'll remember about her. Not the way she ended up but the way she lived.'

As they shook his hand on leaving, they all said the same thing. 'We'll remember her as she was.'

Ed was sailing back home at the end of that week. He had helped Maryanne move into her new house and had left money for her to buy whatever she needed. Friends had been so good to her, and the flat had been furnished by them and even people she had never met. She went to the train station with him, and said, 'Tell Eddie I'm here if he ever needs me.'

Ed asked her once again about joining him but she said maybe in the future. She watched as the train moved away and went and bought a bunch of flowers from the City Arcade. She caught the bus and was soon at the cemetery where she placed them on Sadie's grave which now had a small headstone. It stated: *Sadie Boyd, dear wife of Ed and mother of Eddie. A golden girl taken too soon.*

Maryanne walked away saying amen to that.

47

Bella and Albert's wedding took place in September. It was a quiet affair with only their old neighbours and a few old friends there. It was held in the registry office on the first Saturday and a crowd of Saturday shoppers stopped to look as they emerged.

Their expressions ranged from interested to amazed when they saw the elderly couple standing with big smiles. Grace threw confetti which blew away on the autumn breeze before the couple entered the wedding car.

The reception was held in the Royal Hotel which was a stone's throw from the City Square and all the guests walked there, laughing and catching up with one another. Since the fire, they hadn't been together like this en masse and it was clear they were making the most of the happy occasion.

Grace, Bill, Evie and Evelyn walked with Maryanne, Anna, Thomas and Tommy. The girls were chatting to each other, glad to be back in one another's company. Eliza was with Rory and Morag and Rory was pushing Martha in her wheelchair with Mrs Bell and a couple of Bella's old friends taking up the rear. There was a chilly breeze and they were glad to be inside the hotel where it was warm and welcoming.

Bella was wearing a long grey dress with a sequin collar and Albert looked smart in his navy blazer and grey trousers. He looked so proud and pleased standing beside his new bride that it made Grace think that love wasn't just for the young.

Albert made a speech which made the guests laugh when he said he hoped the *Courier* newspaper wouldn't print their photo on the wedding page that came out every Monday morning. 'We'll look like two ancient dinosaurs amongst the youngsters,' he said.

Thomas called out, 'Speak for yourself, Albert, Bella looks stunning.'

He looked fondly at his bride. 'I know she does and I'm a lucky man that she said yes to my proposal. As you all know, I lost my wife a couple of years ago and I was reconciled to a lonely old age but Bella has rescued me. Many years ago she lost her dearest fiancé. Davie died on the battlefields of France which was a traumatic time for her but she has lived her life with dignity and grace and I'm so glad to be called her husband.'

Everyone applauded and Thomas gave a loud, 'Hear, hear.'

The waitress brought the drinks for the toast and everyone wished the couple the best for the future. Albert raised his glass to his wife but added, 'Let us drink to absent friends.' He then added, 'We have had a lovely card from Ed, Esther and Eddie from America and I know Maryanne has also had one and we are all in their thoughts.' Everyone remembered Sadie and also Ed and Eddie. There was a moment's silence until the waitress announced the buffet was open and they gathered round the table, gossiping like they had in the old days in the lane.

Tommy was full of her new house and her new school while Evie hadn't much to say about her life. She would soon be in her final year at Rosebank and, like Tommy, they would then be starting a secondary education on the road to growing up.

'I'm hoping to be a teacher,' said Evie. 'What are you hoping to be, is it still a film star or a model?'

Tommy said she didn't know. 'I'm keeping my options open.'

Martha was complaining about one of her neighbours. 'She keeps popping in and out all day and I'm fed up with it. It's not like it used to be when we were all together.'

Eliza said the woman had only popped in once three days ago and Martha glared at her and said, 'Well, it feels like she's in and out all the time.'

Albert had overheard and he whispered to Grace, 'Nothing ever changes with Martha, does it?'

Grace laughed and said a truer word was never spoken. 'Poor Eliza, I had hoped moving to a new street would be stimulating for Martha with fresh bits of gossip and new neighbours to complain to.'

Albert made another speech. 'A lot of people might think I got married to Bella because she had a house and of course I did.' He turned to his wife. 'I'm just joking. No, I've always admired her for her strength and lovely nature and I know Effie Bell, Davie's great-niece, will second that.'

All eyes turned to the woman who looked so pleased to be singled out for a compliment and she nodded and smiled while raising her glass.

Later the happy couple left to go back to their house in Hepburn Street. Albert laughed as they went through the door to the waiting taxi. 'At our age, Hepburn Street is like going to the South of France, as it feels like the same distance for our arthritic legs.'

Grace said, 'You are both young enough yourselves and you're not arthritic.'

With the wedding couple away, the party broke up and they all made their way back to their new homes with promises to stay in touch with one another.

Meadow Lane was now a past memory except in the minds of the occupants who would always remember living beside one another, and nothing would ever take that away.

48

Dundee 1975

Evie stood where the entrance to Meadow Lane used to be, but there was no sign that it had ever been there. Even the black and white street sign was no more. So much had happened over the twenty years since Sadie died and everyone had to move out. There was a new building there with modern windows and a door with names and buttons on it.

She wondered what had happened to the grassy or often muddy bit of ground at the front of the houses but now she would never know. A young woman came out pushing a baby in a modern looking buggy and she thought of Morag and Rory's Silver Cross pram which had looked so majestic.

After a backward glance she made her way to the top of the street where the car was waiting. There was a small crowd around it and she saw Eddie talking to her parents and granny while Maryanne was chatting to Esther, Ed and Tommy's family. They had just returned from Eliza's funeral, a sad occasion where a few tears had been shed.

When she reached them, Eddie came over and put his arm around her. 'As you all know, we got married quietly a month ago and we are sorry that none of the family could come over for the wedding but Grace, Bill and Maryanne are coming over to see us soon,' he said. 'We are pleased to see Albert and Bella still hale and hearty and so sorry about Eliza.'

Tommy came over when he went to speak to his father. She looked successful. Evie knew she had married Pete's youngest son a couple of years ago and they now had a young daughter. Tommy said she couldn't believe how they had turned out. 'Do you mind when we were at school, you said you were going to be a teacher, Evie, well, you did. I never had any ambition but I've got my lovely family, and Mum and Dad are happy.'

Evie said that she never believed how the simple act of going to New York to teach in a school there would lead to her marriage to Eddie. 'I wrote to him for years after he left and we kept in touch. He has his own accountancy business in New York and we met up and now we're married. Life can turn out strange, can't it?'

Tommy said it certainly could. 'Do you remember when he was at school with us, how great he was at sums?'

Evie laughed. 'Yes, I do, and I remember Miss Malcolm blushing when he called her "ma'am" which annoyed that horrid Bruce Davidson. What is he doing now?'

Tommy said she didn't know and she cared even less.

It was time to go. Evie and Eddie had been staying at Maryanne's house while Ed and Esther had checked into a hotel, but their flights were booked for early the next morning. Evie gave Tommy a hug. 'Keep in touch, Tommy. I hope we meet again sometime.'

Tommy said she would and she pointed to her head. 'I still have that hair slide you gave me.' Evie said she had noticed.

Eddie was behind the wheel and his father and stepmother Esther got in the back while Evie slipped in beside her husband and they all waved as the car drove off.

Grace, Bill and Evelyn had declined a lift as had Maryanne because Thomas had brought his new car and he was taking them home before heading off for Glasgow.

Eddie, Evie and his parents along with Maryanne had

visited the cemetery where Eddie placed a large bunch of flowers on Sadie's grave. Ed and Eddie had stood for ages in silence before turning and walking away. Evie saw Eddie wipe tears from his eyes and Esther took his arm. 'She is still your mother, Eddie, and take comfort from the fact she desperately wanted you back with her. She didn't desert you.' Eddie nodded but was so overcome he couldn't answer.

When they drove away, Ed said he hoped Evie's parents and grandmother would fly over to see them. 'I hope they persuade Maryanne to come as well. I did ask her to come and stay with us for good but she said she would think about it.'

Evie asked how Joel was managing with the farm. 'You know how he is, Evie, a born farmer through and through, so he's managing just fine.'

Esther said she liked Eddie and Evie's new apartment in New York and they said they both loved it as well. Eddie gave his wife a loving glance. 'You saved my life back then while we were living in the lane. It was your friendship, Evie, that helped me. Both you and Tommy.' Evie gave him a smile and said it was a pleasure as he had been such a lovely boy.

They were staying in Glasgow overnight and would catch the early morning flight to America. Evie glanced out of the window to take in as much of her homeland as possible, as it would probably be a while before she would see it again. She knew she was going to miss her parents and her granny but Grace had said that the world was getting smaller now that planes were used instead of long sea journeys so they would all meet up soon. 'That's a promise.'

'It's a pity we didn't see the McCallums,' said Eddie, 'but Maryanne said they were on holiday in Skye.'

Evie sounded sad. 'I'm sorry about Eliza's death and glad it was peaceful. I heard her neighbour saying she passed away in her sleep. She also said she had never recovered from losing her mother not long after moving into their Church Street

House. She always believed it was the trauma of moving away from Meadow Lane.'

Eddie nodded, but added 'Still, I bet she caused mayhem with her gossip before departing.'

Although the funeral was sad as Eddie and Evie always liked Eliza, they all laughed at the memory of the indomitable and gossip-laughing Martha. As Evie looked out of the window at the passing streets, she also mourned the now-forgotten Meadow Lane.

Maryanne thanked Thomas for dropping her off at her door. It was lovely seeing her grandson and his dad looking so well. She was grateful to Esther for all her care during his growing up years and she thought that the tiny woman, she was just five feet one inch, didn't have a pudding face as Sadie had once stated. She was a lovely, caring woman who had tried to get her to come and live with them.

She went to the sideboard and brought out her wedding photo. Thankfully it hadn't been damaged in the fire. Bernard looked so young, even although he was sixteen years older than her. He had been a lovely husband and father to Sadie.

She remembered those far-off years when she left the orphanage at fourteen. Her father had been killed in the trenches of France and her mother had died not long after she was born. Some people said it was a broken heart.

She had gone to work with Bernard in his hardware shop in the Overgate and had got lodgings with an elderly woman in the West Port. Just before her sixteenth birthday she went off to Blackpool with a friend from the orphanage, Lily Spence. Bernard had given her an extra week's wages for her fare and the price of the caravan they were staying in and the two girls went off, laughing and full of fun at the thought of a week away from work and home.

Well of course it all turned out differently. Lily didn't like the caravan or Blackpool and she went home after a couple of days. Maryanne thought she would stay a couple more days before going back. That was when she met Alexander, or Sandy as he called himself. He was tall and good looking and was over for a holiday from Australia. He said he was visiting his grandmother but had come away for a holiday.

Maryanne fell for him like a ton of bricks and he seemed to feel the same. She couldn't understand why a golden-haired god like him was interested in her although Lily had told her she was very pretty.

The painful memories almost made her cry. Well, she fell in love and spent the rest of the week in his caravan. When it was time to come home, he gave her his address in Glasgow, promising to come and see her as soon as possible as he loved her like she loved him.

She waited on him to write but nothing ever came although she made excuses for him. Maybe he was looking after his grandmother and didn't have time to get in touch.

It was a month later when she knew she was having a baby but when she wrote to him, the letter came back, saying there was no address like this in Glasgow and she never heard from him again.

One day Bernard found her trying to swallow tablets as she dreaded becoming an unmarried mother and when he asked her why she was being so stupid, she told him the whole story. She had been crying bitterly, not only because of the baby but the fact that Sandy had told her a pack of lies. Bernard later came and said he would marry her and give the child a name.

She couldn't believe it and told him he should think about marrying someone he loved but he said there was no one in his life, so they got married right away and when Sadie was born he adored her. Because she couldn't name a girl Sandy she chose Sadie which was as near as she could get. Bernard would take her out in her pram for walks and when she was a bit older they would go to the park or the beach on a Sunday.

Maryanne thought her life had turned around until the fateful day when Bernard was taken ill.

He had been injured in the Great War and developed tuberculosis. She recalled the dreadful weeks before he died. After the funeral, she found out she had inherited the shop which she ran until Sadie was four years old. She was a wayward child with a temper and Maryanne couldn't be working and coping with her. So she sold up but unfortunately the shop was rented which meant she only got the goodwill sale on it as the new owner bought over all the stock.

Bernard had rented the house they lived in which was above the shop and when she found the rent was too dear they moved to Meadow Lane. She found Sadie very hard to bring up because of her nature but she marvelled at what a lovely child she was. Lots of people commented on it which went to Sadie's head.

Maryanne was glad when she got engaged to the Ronaldson boy but when she announced she was going to be a GI bride, her mother was worried. She didn't think it would last and she had been proved right.

For years she had suppressed the memory of her past life but, seeing Eddie today, it had all flooded back. She took the back of her wedding photo off and brought out a snapshot taken in Blackpool. It showed the tall, handsome, blond Sandy smiling at the camera. Sadie had looked so like him that she had been reminded of her folly every day until Sadie's death.

Now she saw that Eddie was also the spitting image of his natural grandfather and it worried her until she realised he was nothing like Sandy in nature. He was kind and considerate and very, very clever. He was beginning his new life with Evie, who Maryanne had always liked, and he had a good father and grandfather in Ed and Joel. Esther, after she married Ed, had also made him the man he turned out to be.

She placed her wedding photo of Bernard and herself on the table by the side of the fireplace. She couldn't remember looking so young but she was amused by her outfit and the faded-looking flowers. She had grown to love her husband over the few years they had together and she always remembered him with love.

She then put Sadie and Ed's wedding photo beside it. Bernard might not have been her natural father but he was better than that. He was a man who had looked after and loved her until he died just as she had done. She loved Sadie and she always would, in spite of all the rows and bitterness.

She glanced once more at the faded photo of the handsome Sandy who had turned that week in Blackpool into a nightmare but that had been her fault, not Sadie's. For years she had watched her daughter look more and more like him and she had despaired.

She knelt down by the fireside and put a match to it, setting it alight. The last part to burn was his face and golden hair. She knew she would take this secret to her grave and she suddenly felt better as if the burning of the photo had released all the pent up emotions she had suffered from over the years.

Ed and Esther wanted her to come and live in America and maybe she would go. Yes, perhaps one of these days.